RAISE FOR ALFRED ALCC

The Pull of the Earth

"A novel as convincing as a tightly roped load; I took pleasure in the hydraulic grip which Alcorn's writing exercises upon place and period, his collusion with what is stunted in his characters, his tenderness towards all that is needy and courageous about their lives."

Seamus Heaney

"We realize we are in the hands of a serious novelist with the enviable ability to create credible, moving human beings."

N.Y. Times Book Review

"Alfred Alcorn has composed a wonderful novel, his first, out of the stuff of ordinary life... [He] treats his characters with a rare combination of intelligence and tenderness."

Boston Globe Vestments

"...a gift for brilliant satire and outright comedy within the framework of a solid, serious novel."

The Providence Sunday Journal

The Long Run of Myles Mayberry

"Alcorn's description of Myles' single shot at immortality in the 1976 Boston Marathon was truly *'déjà vu* all over again' for me."

Jack Fultz, winner of the 1976 Boston Marathon

Murder in the Museum of Man

"An adroit, hilarious send-up"   *The New Yorker*

"Sly and spicy from start to finish, Alcorn's unexpected hybrid blends academic spoofery, cannibalism and a murder mystery, serving it up with a just-right balance of innocence, subtle malevolence and cheeky irony.

Publishers Weekly

AUTHOR SYNOPSIS:

Set in the near future, *Sugar Mountain* is a saga about the struggles of an extended family to survive a lethal avian flu pandemic. Within days, the world changes radically and forever as the infrastructure of civilized life crumbles. In short order, there exists no power grid, no internet, no media, no medical facilities, dwindling supplies of food, and, for most people, very little hope.

A committed pacifist, Cyrus Arkwright has been preparing for several years to make Sugar Mountain, his ancestral farm located in western Massachusetts, into a self-sustaining haven for his extended family. He is, in the modern parlance, a "prepper," one of the growing number of Americans (that range from the militant right to the communal left) who are getting ready for some kind of apocalypse.

As the family in-gathers during that calamitous May when a deadly form of H5N1 begins its destruction of the human world, the Arkwrights are not only besieged by pleas from friends and loved ones, but realize they are vulnerable to the violence and lawlessness that is spreading with a contagion of its own. Having laid in supplies, devised basic systems, and established a self-sustaining farm, Cyrus, his wife Grace, and their three sons and their families become prime targets in a ravening world.

As national, state, and local governments shrivel to all but non-existence, it falls to son Jack, an Army Ranger veteran, to organize the defense of Sugar Mountain. It is Jack, over the protests of his father, who earlier acquired a store of weapons and now teaches the others how to use them.

The principal threat to the refuge arises in the form of the McFerall brothers. Men in their late fifties, Duncan and Bruce live with their families in a hollow several miles from the Arkwright refuge. For more than a century there has been a festering feud between the two families as to the ownership of Sugar Mountain. Empowered by the possession of stolen antiviral medicines and as a member of the National Guard, Duncan is in a position to command weapons and men. In the guise of suppressing "terrorism," the brothers launch a systematic campaign of attacking and taking farmsteads in which they place their retainers. Sugar Mountain is high on this list.

In its situations, in its characters, *Sugar Mountain* explores the human species in extremis—that is, in those conditions that existed through most of our evolutionary history.

SUGAR MOUNTAIN

ALFRED ACORN

PLEASURE BOAT STUDIO
NEW YORK / SEATTLE

Sugar Mountain by Alfred Alcorn

ISBN 9780912887937
Library of Congress Control Number 2013950399

Cover art by Katherine Remick
Cover design by Lauren Grosskopf

Pleasure Boat Studio books are available
through your favorite bookstore and through the following:
PLEASURE BOAT STUDIO: A LITERARY PRESS
pleasureboatstudio.com | Seattle, Washington
&
SPD (Small Press Distribution) 800-869-7553
Baker & Taylor 800-775-1100
Ingram 615-793-5000
Amazon.com & Barnesandnoble.com

For Sally

1

The news comes obliquely, unvoiced, a flicker of words across the bottom of the screen: *World Health Organization raises concern about reports of deaths from avian flu outbreak in Xinjiang Province. Beijing officials deny access to WHO inspectors, calling the outbreak "a local matter."*

Moments later, the item is upgraded to a breaking news bulletin. The newscaster, an attractive young woman with practiced authority in her voice, tells her morning audience: "This just in: The World Health Organization has designated an avian flu outbreak in a remote province of western China to be at Phase 5 of the pandemic alert level. A Phase 5 designation involves human-to-human transmission, affecting larger clusters, or communities, of people. At this point, there is a much higher risk of a pandemic although not a certainty. We'll keep you updated as more information becomes available."

In his farmhouse in the hill country of western Massachusetts, Cyrus Arkwright watches the news about the outbreak and feels his own alarm level ratchet up. It is a foreboding mingled with a sense of vindication that he resists. Will this be it? There have been several flare-ups of lethal flu in China in the recent past. But in those instances, the Chinese government cooperated with international health agencies as to the specifics of the pathogen involved. Now it is clamping down. Why? What are they hiding?

In his early seventies, of medium height and slightly stooped, Cyrus has a full head of white hair and an Amish beard of darker hue, a suitable frame for his slow-smiling patrician face. He notes the name of the province. He muses. Phase 5.

He tuned in CNN this warm spring morning to follow a forest fire flaring along the Grand Canyon. That footage showed a blackened expanse east of Canyon Village where junipers, pinion and ponderosa pines once mantled the South Rim. Also news about floods along the Mississippi for the second year in a row. Signs, he thinks, that global warming is looming faster than predicted.

Or is Grace, his wife of forty years, right? Is he becoming a connoisseur of disaster? Or what their daughter-in-law Allegra smilingly called a "Malthusiast," a literary allusion no doubt. Not that Grace hesitated to join him in transforming Sugar Mountain, the old family farm, from a weekend retreat into a self-sustaining refuge for their extended family. Should the need arise.

It took some doing. It began five years before when he retired, in stages, from his architectural practice in Cambridge. They sold their roomy house on Francis Avenue with more than a few regrets and moved back. It was as much a move in time as geographically, at least where Cyrus was concerned. For he grew up on this farm in the northern Berkshires named for its grove of sugar maples where in early spring the sap rises with its sweet bounty. He knows like a farmer the three hundred or so acres, some of it good for pasture and hay, a lot of it ledgy, rising forest that extends nearly to the Vermont border.

His interest in disasters is more than academic. Cyrus is a prepper, a homesteader, a survivalist. Along with millions of others in America and overseas, he calculates the probability of catastrophe as too high to be ignored. A general awareness of possibilities came into sharp focus in 2009 when a bird flu scare made the Centers for Disease Control urge people to take precautions. That blew over, but left Cyrus wondering when avian influenza or some other highly mutagenic virus would turn into a mass killer.

He didn't have to wait for nature to take its course to make the nightmare scenario more than theoretical. In November of 2011, news broke that a virologist working in the Erasmus Medical Centre in the Netherlands had tinkered with the genome of the H5N1 virus and come up with a lethal, contagious variant. The research was part of an international effort to understand the virus so that antivirals could be developed to fight it. The new strain caused immediate concern about its possible use as a bioterrorism agent.

Little more than a year later, researchers at China's Harbin

Veterinary Research Institute combined a deadly avian flu virus with an infectious strain of human flu. Western critics pointed out that the record of containment at such labs was not reassuring. That news soon dropped from the national consciousness. But not from that of Cyrus Arkwright. He spent time studying what was happening. He concluded that, given the proclivity of people to kill people and the ingenuity involved therein, someone, somewhere would develop and deploy the pathogen as a weapon. Or it might mutate on its own into a monster of death. The human species could survive in relatively large numbers a planet parched by droughts and drowned in floods. A pandemic caused by a weaponized variant of H5N1 would be another matter altogether.

The roomy alcove in his studio in which he sits contains an array of electronic equipment. There's a citizens band radio; a wide wall-mounted screen to which Cyrus' laptop can be connected; an aging desktop tower; a mike for the intercom wired into the rooms of the house and those in the outbuildings; and two laptops to be dedicated to surveillance cameras. Jack, their oldest son, an ex-Army Ranger, had dubbed the alcove "comcen," giving it a military ring that Cyrus, a pacifist, found objectionable. They discussed it, settled on the more neutral if not exactly accurate "recon room." War and peace, fight or flight, violence, nonviolence figured in the planning from the start. Cyrus conceded, very reluctantly and after much soul searching, that Jack, now living at Sugar Mountain with wife Nicole and their two children, could acquire the means with which to defend themselves. Meaning weapons. But only to be used as a last resort.

Grace comes in and sits next to him. He unbends from his laptop and turns to her, his slow smile one of fondness. "Come and have a cup of tea in the real world," she says, touching his arm and returning his smile, their smile.

In her late sixties and womanly in slacks and cotton blouse, Grace has kept her dark-eyed blond looks. Like Cyrus, her face remains remarkably smooth and animated without the benefit of lifts or transplants. He follows her into the large farmhouse kitchen where she has tea steeping in a pot under a cozy. They add milk

3

and sugar and take their mugs onto the colonnaded side porch where Grace has the mail ready to open. It is something of a morning ritual during which they catch up with each other and any news about the rest of the family.

Settled into the comfortable wicker armchairs, she hands him a letter with an impressive looking letterhead. "The McFeralls have hired another lawyer. He wants to meet with us and our legal counsel to review the case."

Cyrus grimaces, distracted. He can't get the term "larger clusters" out of his head. He says, "There is no case. God, will they never give up?"

They are talking about a claim by the McFerall brothers, Duncan and Bruce, to the effect that Sugar Mountain belongs to their branch of the family. The brothers base their claim on a maze of documents and non-documents stretching back more than a century.

Grace shrugs. "It gives them bragging rights. We all need those."

"It runs deeper than that," Cyrus says, thinking how his distant kin have pursued the matter with a dogged and at time ugly animosity. He is also thinking, the news out of Xinjiang fretting his mind, that the brothers could be a problem if the worst happened.

"Should I send it on to Frank?"

"I suppose."

Frank is their second son and a New York attorney. He dismissed the case several years before as "utterly without merit" while providing minimal lawyerly responses on a *pro familia* basis.

"Speaking of Frank," she says, showing him an opened envelope, "he's sent us a check for five thousand dollars and a note saying he can't make the rehearsal but is with us in spirit."

Cyrus is looking south where new leafage colors the Berkshire hills with a tinge of chartreuse. A large raptor circles in a thermal. An eagle? More like a vulture. He is not unaffected by what might be omens.

The rehearsal Grace refers to is a periodic gathering of the extended family in which they inhabit the farm for a long weekend to test the feasibility of a longer stay. Cyrus, sipping tea and watching the bird, doesn't repeat what he has said before: Frank might like

4

the idea of a refuge for himself, his wife Allegra, and three-year-old Lily, but being a busy and successful lawyer, he doesn't want to spend the time the others put into it. He sends money instead.

Unlike Jack, their eldest, who moved to Sugar Mountain with Nicole and nine-year-old Mary and seven-year-old Cy at the end of a long stint in the Army. More than two years now. In that time, Jack and Cyrus, with the help of a contractor, have created living quarters for as many as twenty people. Thad, their youngest son, comes out regularly from Boston with his partner Duvall Jackson. At the farm, Thad works on wiring, the electronics, the power systems. Duvall carpenters with the skill of a cabinet maker. "You make us look good," Cyrus told Duvall more than once.

"Don't let it bother you," Grace says, referring to Frank's letter. "He really is busy..."

"It's not Frank," Cyrus says. "He'll be here when it counts."

"Then what is it?"

"There's been a flu outbreak in a remote part of China."

"Doesn't that happen all the time?"

"Right. But this time the Chinese authorities don't want any outsiders poking around. The WHO has designated it as Phase 5."

"That's serious, isn't it?"

"Could be very serious. I was wondering if Jack..."

"Jack's gone with Nicole and the kids to Greenfield. It's Cy's birthday tomorrow and he wants a Count of Monte Christo outfit. With a real sword." Little Cy might share a name with his grandfather, but not his antipathy for the appurtenances of war. "What do you need him for?"

"I was wondering if his friend in intelligence might know something."

She reaches out and takes his hand. "Dear man, you are obsessing again."

"I know, but this time... I don't know, it's at Phase 5 and there's something about it..." He trails off. They don't have to voice what is going through their minds. Are we crazy? Perhaps, but... But there has been the pleasure of building, rebuilding, remodeling, reviving. Not to mention Nicole's plans for a B&B.

5

Then the rightness, nay the righteousness, of working toward self-sustainability – what with the garden, the orchard, the goats, the chickens and the huge old sow. Even if they still buy a lot of their groceries and cheat by having the Neills, who live on the other side of the old Fallgren place, help with the chores from time to time. So that, in the end, it could be taken as a kind of hobby, a serious hobby.

Cyrus lives the conundrum of the prepper: He strives to prepare for what he dreads might happen. Dreads – at least by his better self, that upright, principled, Quaker meeting persona he presents to the world and, most of the time, to himself. But there are darker levels in the character of Cyrus Arkwright. Doesn't the teeming, ravening human world need a corrective? Would it really be a great tragedy if about half of the seven billion or so human beings ceased to exist? Well, yes, it would.

"Are Thad and Duvall going to make it?" he asks.

"They say they're on board. Which is good. Nicole needs Duvall's help with the garden."

"He does have a green thumb." It is a standing family joke of sorts, Duvall being black, at least on paper.

Cyrus puts in a call to Jack. Not available. He wants to be patient but frets inwardly as he descends the steps from the porch, goes around the rebuilt silo that now serves, with a ground-floor addition, as a bath house. Not far beyond it on the east side of the barn garden stands the horse barn. Inside the main door, he gathers up a hand sander, a tin of linseed oil and a couple of rags for finishing touches to the interior.

He stops to admire the comfortable living room and a ship's galley kitchen to one side behind cafe doors. A hallway leads off to a bedroom and common bathroom. Next to a built-in wood stove, a mail-order circular staircase rises to the second floor on polished, maple treads. Nicely done, he thinks, though the place, which has room for five, possibly six people, depending on sleeping arrangements, resonates with its emptiness, its contingency.

He gets to work, sanding, wiping, and oiling the surrounds of the only window in the first floor addition, structurally little more than a lean-to but so well insulated it will scarcely need heating.

Cyrus is wiping excess oil off the gleaming pine when he hears the main door open. Jack comes through the living room and into the small bedroom. He stops and sniffs the pleasant fumes of the oil. "Looks good," he says, admiring the window, which opens to the north. "Always loved this view. Too bad to put up curtains."

Slightly taller than his father and wiry, Jack has an intense gaze and a sharp nose that makes his face appear to point wherever he looks.

"Curtains can be opened," Cyrus says amiably. Then, "You got a minute?"

Jack's face cracks with a smile. "Got the rest of my life. For what that's worth." Even after nearly three years, Jack misses the ordered, knife-edged life of an elite soldier. As an Army Ranger, he had been at the top of a singular profession. But he doesn't miss it enough to re-enlist. That would mean riding a desk and saying "yes, sir" to regular army brass.

They go into the living room, already faintly musty from lack of use. From the small fridge in the galley Jack takes out a can of Coke and snaps it open.

Cyrus bends towards his son as they sit on the sofa, which faces the glass-fronted wood stove. "You know your friend at the NSA..."

"Matt Selig?"

"Yes, Matt Selig. I was wondering if you might call him and ask him about this flu outbreak in Xinjiang Province..."

Jack's face seems to sharpen with surprise. "How do you know about that?"

"It was on CNN. A news bulletin."

"Really? Just now?"

"An hour ago or so ago."

Jack leans closer to his father. "The fact is Matt called me..."

"In Greenfield?"

"We were pushing a cart around Fosters. He knows we're interested in this stuff."

7

"And...?" Cyrus finds his alarm level rising again. Officialdom does make things seem more real.

"Some of it's classified and I guess some of it's already out in the blogosphere... Even on CNN. The Phase 5 designation apparently was used by the WHO to put pressure on the Chinese to get them to share data on the outbreak. Then it turned real. The outbreak, according to Matt, is centered in a high-security prison east of Hotan. That's in the southwest corner of the province. It's been a hotbed of Uigher resistance..."

"Uigher?" Cyrus asks, seeing the word as "Weeger."

"They're Muslim, more Turkic than east Asian. Anyway, there's an isolation annex on the prison grounds used to hold Uigher militants, really hard cases..."

"I don't get the connection."

"Yeah, and here it gets tricky. Remember the reports of the hybrid virus developed in Harbin in 2013?"

"I remember it very well."

"According to Matt, one of the larger Chinese pharmaceutical companies got their hands on the virus and developed an antiviral for it. Or tried to."

"Good God..."

"Matt told me, and this really is secret, that, at least from what they were able to pick up from intercepts, researchers from the company tested the antiviral on some of the Uighers in the isolation unit..."

"Exposing them first?"

"That's assumed."

"And the antiviral didn't work?"

"Apparently not."

"Was this done with official sanction?"

"More than likely local officials were bribed. Matt tells me that happens all the time there."

A silence grows between them as the possibilities register. At length, Jack says, "I think we should alert the others."

Cyrus glances around the room. It and the rest of Sugar Mountain have taken on a relevance that is both comforting and disquieting. He nods slowly. "I think you're right."

2

The news out of China continues both dire and vague. Cyrus composes a short report for the extended family and a network of like-minded homesteaders in Franklin County. Using terse sentences in what he calls a "standby to standby," he describes what he and Jack have learned about the outbreak in China. The notes of thanks he gets in response confirms to himself a possibility almost too monstrous to consider.

His immediate family is very much on board. At BJ's in Greenfield, Grace and Nicole stack a flatbed with bags of rice, flour, cooking oil, canned tuna, and other staples. Not that they don't already have reserves in depth on hand. Jack drives into Buckland to load up on kerosene that he stores in an underground bunker. They go over check lists of hardware supplies, spare parts for their own infrastructure, all the nuts and bolts they will need when the world shuts down.

Nicole orders a truck-load of aged cow manure from nearby McCoomb dairy farm. The pile is dumped inside the fenced garden and covered with a tarpaulin to keep the rain from bleaching out its nutrients. By herself, Nicole wheelbarrows the stuff over the opened ground and works it into the soil.

The question arose as to whether they should plow up another acre and experiment with a high-yield wheat crop. Nicole is very much for it. She already has a counter-top mill for making flour and has just received a grain husker of the same size. She plans to make bread from scratch, from home-grown wheat. Cyrus is dubious. How will they harvest the stuff? Cut it like hay? Bundle it in sheaves? Thresh it with flays on what floor? But he said okay. He and Nicole agree on many things, if for different reasons.

Nicole, who is attractive in the way of animated, dark-haired plump women, takes great pride that their garden produced a cornucopia of food the summer before – eggplant, tomatoes, potatoes, lettuce, squash, peas, cucumbers, lima beans, onions, and

9

corn. Though raised in the suburbs of Connecticut, she finds it deeply satisfying to produce food from the garden and orchard, from the goats and the chickens, and, eventually, from the old sow with its farrow of squealing young. She remains in thrall with atavistic wonder at the way soil can be transformed into food.

"It's my gym," she likes to say, proud of her dirty hands.

The garden, just above and beyond the outbuildings on gently rising ground, has been fenced to keep out woodchucks and rabbits. Jack promises that any deer that jump the fence will end up in the freezer.

In fact, Nicole's ambitions go well beyond brute survival, should that prove unnecessary. She nurtures a dream to own and run a self-sustaining country inn. Upon arrival with Jack at Sugar Mountain, she began her quiet campaign to turn the place into a bed and breakfast, "to start with." Beyond bed and breakfast she has in mind lunch and dinner, with everything except, perhaps, olive oil, coffee, and chocolate, produced on the farm.

Her plans to turn Sugar Mountain into a hostelry appealed to Cyrus. A B&B gave the project a dual purpose and a use for the place should the worst never happen. Making it an inn meant a couple of extra bathrooms given the American penchant for that kind of privacy. It meant combining a bit more comfort with the necessities of survival. The big refectory table in the kitchen, where all guest meals would be served, at least in the bed and breakfast phase, would hearken back to the days of the boarding house.

Nicole's ambitions changed Cyrus' redesign of the horse barn. A gambrel-roofed structure of generous proportions that originally served as both a carriage house and stable, the building had remained sound through decades of neglect. The year before, he and Jack took down the inner partitions, careful to preserve the old beams and boards, some of them rubbed shiny by generations of horses. Almost finished now, it had four bedrooms, two of them quite small, and one and half baths. Nicole was in on all of the meetings. She contributed suggestions about closets, door and window placement, and the use of floor registers to heat the upstairs rooms.

Ari Fineman, Grace's nephew and a New York restaurateur, became Nicole's co-conspirator. She tapped into Ari's obsession about home-grown or locally produced food. They talked endlessly about details. When he mentioned Simon Pearce for tableware and stemware, she shook her head. "Too clunky. It's like we would be catering to upscale peasants." He had replied, smiling, "Isn't that what most of us are?" She reconsidered and then found a raft of it on craigslist. They traded recipes. "Keep it simple," he told her, "and don't try to cover all the bases. If you find something that works, keep it on the menu. You'd be amazed how many sophisticated customers order the same thing again and again."

Nicole delighted in the attention she and Jack received when they drove to New York to visit Frank and Allegra. At the Gilded Goose, Ari's restaurant, they were treated like royalty by Ari and his wife Lise Xu, a stockbroker. Both Ari and Frank had a respect for Jack bordering on awe. Not only because he has been *there* – repeatedly – but because, as Ari once admitted to Nicole, Jack was carrying the moral burden of serving whether one agreed with the wars or no.

A good listener and an acute observer, Nicole took notes on the decor of the Goose. Polished wood, pastel-tinted plaster, and lots of mirrors produced the effect of simple luxury. The table tops of inlaid marble "make it feel like you're eating off an altar," Frank remarked on one occasion. She also noted how Ari served a sour dough baguette with olive oil. She went over his formidable cellar. He told her to keep that simple as well. "There are lots of good mid-range reds now that come from all over the world."

For his part, Ari, as a member in good standing of the Sugar Mountain community, procured and brought to the farm root stock to grow grapes for wine. With help from Cyrus and Nicole, he and Lise planted them the year before on the west side of the drive leading from the town road. The vines did well – so far – on the well-drained easy slope facing south. Chateau Sugar Mountain, Nicole joked. Ari also shipped to the farm several cases of an Argentine Malbec and a California blend he particularly liked.

Nicole treasures these visits to New York, but she wants the world to come to her. That had been impossible as the wife of an active-duty special operations soldier. She lived on base whenever possible to save money, money she invested with Lise's advice to good effect. At the same time she perused real estate sites for old farms for sale in upstate New York, western Massachusetts, and Vermont.

It was all part of a larger life plan. A few years before, not long after Cy was born, Nicole began to work on Jack to give up his career in the military. He had been sympathetic, but he didn't budge. "I don't know anything else. I would be a fish out of water. It's who I am. It's what I do." And, with just the shadow of a threat, "It's what you married."

Nicole played fair but she played hard. "Every time you leave for another tour," she told him the last time he deployed to some remote, dangerous part of Afghanistan, "I think it's going to be the last time I touch you and see you." Then, "Your life is not just your own, Jack, not anymore. Not if you love us the way you say you do."

What convinced Jack to retire were his own words – amplified and played back to him by Nicole in one of their marathon sessions. "Listen to yourself, Jack," she implored, sitting in the wretched kitchen of base housing she now forgot where. "Again and again, you come home and tell me that you don't know what good we're doing there. You tell me again and again that they're too backward, too tribal, too uneducated to want anything but what they've got. You tell me that the corruption goes from top to bottom. You tell me about civilian contractors getting ten times your pay for installing phone lines behind the security that you provide. And the big American contractors who are just raking it in."

He listened to himself through her. And once misgivings began, the carapace of words like "duty," "sacrifice," "corps," "mission" began to flake off even as he remained the patriot he became the day after Nine Eleven, the day he signed up as an enlisted man.

Then a growing self-doubt. Soldiers of his caliber and purpose

12

were a species of athlete. They played a deadly serious game that required skill, intelligence, quick thinking and quicker responses, not to mention courage. In the field, every day was Super Bowl Sunday, but with consequences far more profound for yourself, your comrades, and ultimately, you wanted to believe, for your country. But he had been losing his edge. He could no longer rely on instincts finely honed by training and experience. Or on the enabling pulse of adrenaline each time he and his small, hand-picked squad went into action. He caught himself in the kinds of lapses that put him and those under him at risk. The fiasco just north of Laskar Gah still haunted him.

Then the question he had asked himself daily, hourly: Was he, when all was said and done, little more than a highly trained killer? He was certainly proficient at it, one of the best. What haunted him was a piece of seemingly irrefutable advice he got early on. *In order to kill the enemy you have to stay alive.* Which grew in time to conflate with the notion that he lived to kill.

He was good at keeping himself and his comrades alive. Until Laskar Gah. He had a knack for nosing out traps, ambushes, suspicious characters, and IEDs. Once he shot a sheep tethered to the side of the road setting off an explosive artfully disguised on the animal's back under a sheepskin.

He had been good at it, no question, one of the best. Others regarded him and he regarded himself as a consummate professional especially when it came to working with small units. Perhaps because he resisted the dark elation of killing that some of his fellow Rangers didn't try to dissemble. He kept in mind, or tried to, the admonition of his pacifist father: Whatever else you do, don't lose your humanity. Until Laskar Gah. After that, he had grown worse than callous. He had killed wantonly then, with malice aforethought and with the acrid pleasure of hate.

As he contemplated retiring, he kept asking himself the question: what am I to become? If I am not a soldier, what am I? Husband, father, brother, son... farmer? B&B handyman? Nobody? He would have to create a whole new Jack Arkwright.

Nor did they make it easy for him to give up his captain's bars and everything that went with them. They wanted him. For one more tour. For promotion. For training others. They made him feel needed. And he might have yielded because he did have a home in the military, in the order, the tradition, the consistency it gave daily life.

Then a call from Cyrus and Grace – instigated by Nicole – asking him to bring his family and come live with them at Sugar Mountain proved decisive. The spell broke and his Army career ended.

Re-inventing himself was a day-to-day struggle. As he told himself and others, he had to decompress, to change the way he thought, to watch the way he thought. Driving, his mind drifting, he would find himself looking for likely places to plant IEDs. Someone pushing a baby carriage or a shopping cart snapped him into alert about suicide bombers, making him tense, making him glance around, until he realized it was just another homeless man with his worldly goods or a mother with her child.

And if that part of the experience passed soon enough, the flashbacks persisted. He still saw faces, heard voices, tasted the consistency of MREs, meals ready to eat, and felt the warmth of unrefrigerated canned and bottled water in his mouth. Not to mention the dust, the industrial noise and chemical smell of combat. His own stink. That of his comrades. And death, sometimes rare, sometimes common as dirt.

He escaped into work on his father's prepper paradise. It, too, was a mission, one he convinced himself was about saving lives.

*

By the end of the week, the story about the flu outbreak in China has gotten lost in the welter of other news – continuing violence in the Middle East, deadlock in Congress, the tentative economy, floods and fires. Besides, there have been so many stories over the years about people getting sick and dying after being around infected poultry that one more incident, however disquieting on close inspection, doesn't signify. A follow-up release from the

14

China News Agency, which serves, under most circumstances, as little more than the mouthpiece of the Beijing regime, reports that a quarantine has been declared around Hotan and its environs. The article quotes a Chinese health official to the effect that the quarantine is strictly a precautionary measure. Again, inspectors from the World Health Organization are denied access to the area.

Cyrus and Jack find this news ominous. Their concern deepens when Matt Selig reports a clamp-down on intelligence regarding the outbreak. He tells Jack, "It's all been classified secret, top secret. I think something's up."

They turn to Grace for information about avian flu itself. Trained as a nurse practitioner, she has worked in wretched places overseas as a medical missionary and knows as much if not more than a lot of GPs. She explains that the incubation period is a critical factor in the dynamics of an epidemic. They are having dinner on the porch, the kids ensconced in front of the television arguing about what to watch.

"And as important as the incubation period is the point at which the disease becomes contagious," she says as she hands around a chicken and mushroom casserole.

"You mean a person with the disease could become contagious before symptoms appear?"

"That's what we don't know. It's more than likely that a person would be contagious well before he or she has signs of the disease."

"How does it pass from one person to another?" Nicole asks. She thinks she knows the answer but wants it affirmed.

"Sneezing, coughing, just talking. Doing what we're doing."

Cyrus says, "Then the situation could be a lot worse than what we've been led to believe?" He helps himself to the kale Nicole has chopped and sautéed in olive oil to go with the chicken. In the back of his mind he wonders where they would get olive oil should a mega disaster strike.

"How so?" Jack asks.

Cy comes in and stands beside his mother. "Mary wants to watch *The Black Stallion* again and we've seen it about a zillion times."

Nicole plays referee. "Tell Mary it's your turn to pick. But nothing too violent. And if you keep arguing, I'll just turn the thing off."

The others have waited, the elders charmed simply by the presence of their grandchildren.

"You were saying?" Nicole says.

Cyrus takes a moment to chew. He puts down his fork and touches his beard. "If the first cases were covered up, which can happen in authoritarian regimes, then the outbreak, if that's what it is, could have started a month ago."

"Which means," Jack says quietly, "there's a good chance that an infected individual or several individuals could have traveled from Hotan to Beijing or Shanghai or Hong Kong."

"And from Hong Kong to London..."

"Or New York..."

"Or," says Grace, who does not share her husband's apparent enthusiasm for catastrophe, "We are just speculating about a localized incident."

Cyrus slow smiles his agreement. But he is still apprehensive. Why would American intelligence classify as secret or top secret information about the incident? It was one thing for the Chinese to keep their heads in the sand, but it was quite another for Washington to help them do so. And why had the State Department put out a warning about traveling to western China?

Afterwards, sitting at his laptop in the communications alcove, Cyrus sends out a second report. Reiterating what he has said before, he notes, "What continues to disturb me about the situation is the refusal of the Chinese government to let any representatives from the World Health Organization inspect and report on the outbreak. Also worrying is that American intelligence services have classified information about the outbreak as secret. Finally, just minutes ago, the State Department updated a travel warning to include all of China."

The bulletin goes out to a list comprising the members of the Sugar Mountain community. In addition to Cyrus and Grace, their three sons and their families, the group includes Lance Arkwright.

16

The son of Cyrus' cousin Jeremy, Lance is just finishing his junior year at Williams College. There is Meredith, Grace's divorced and ailing sister who lives in Bernardston, a town several miles to the east. Finally, if events require it, Grace will drive to Greenfield to fetch her father, ninety-two year old Henry Carlton, resident there in a retirement home.

It also goes to the loose association of like-minded families in the western half of Franklin County. They are linked by all the usual media – telephone and e-mail – but also citizen-band radios, should it come to that.

3

The disconnect among those who are fervent about climate change and yet look down their noses at doing anything to prepare for it on an individual basis puzzles Cyrus Arkwright. If warming is going to devastate the planet sooner rather than later, surely it made sense to prepare yourself and your loved ones for that eventuality. Nor did such preparation obviate the need to espouse and practice conservation.

He ran into this attitude when he began to establish a network linked by citizens-band radio. He tried to sound a low-key note as he doffed his Red Sox cap with the bright red *B* on the front and settled into the commodious kitchens of retirees who, like himself, were spending their final decades in the beauty of western Massachusetts. A lot of them have substantial acreage and enough structures and resources to establish a refuge for an extended family. They listen politely, being well-mannered if not urbane, their professional lives having been lived in or near the big cities of the nation.

It took patience and tolerance. Typical of one kind of response were the indulgent smiles that Emma and Sam Bartlett gave him when he explained what he was doing. They served him gourmet coffee and delicate biscotti in the kitchen of their renovated farmhouse in Rowe, a place very much like Sugar Mountain in its setting. Well off, politically liberal, the Bartletts indulged Cyrus' suggestions with social if not moral condescension. "You mean all those redneck vigilante types?" said Emma. But then, she is one of those people who throw around the word "racism" while living in the palest of possible worlds.

Cyrus had smiled to himself thinking of his son Jack and the locked boxes of assault rifles and ammunition in the cellar at Sugar Mountain. Did the Arkwrights qualify as redneck vigilante types despite their debates, some of them acrimonious, about defending themselves with violence? Or that he fervently hoped it wouldn't come to that.

As he made his cordial good-byes, he wondered, being a fair-minded sort, if his perception and tolerance of the Bartletts' sense of moral superiority wasn't in itself a kind of snobbery, only more subtle.

But the Rossi family, the Roths, Learys, Becks, Phelps, Curstons, Melnikovs, Spinneys, Tallmans, and McBrides all signed up. Within six months, Cyrus had all but the Curstons connected on a CB network. Some of them began to stockpile food, medicine, fuel and even arms. All of them thought it would come in useful should another hurricane of Sandy's dimensions sweep through again.

Marshall and Marilyn Roth with two hundred and fifty acres in Shelburne have lots of room for their extended families. But they knew little about weapons or how to farm. Jack offered to help train them in the use of the former, but they politely demurred. When the time comes, they said. But they did begin to store provisions.

Pat and Pam Cummings have a few open acres on their wooded retreat. Pat, being ex-Army, is familiar with weapons and survival. Pam, a GP still practicing part-time in Greenfield, is alert to the dangers of a pandemic. Their natural constituency, as Pat put it, includes their son and daughter, both married with children and living in the Boston area. Along with the Becks of Becks Cheese, a family farm business in Buckland, the Cummings and the Roths form the nucleus of the group. In their meetings, they invariably got around to the main disadvantage – the distance between their homesteads in the event that mutual aid becomes necessary during a crisis.

From the start, they called themselves the Mutual Aid Group, or MAG and they met once a month at the home of a member for dinner and discussion. Jack and Pat Cummings spoke to them about self-defense. Grace and Pam took them through the protocols of quarantine should an in-gathering of their families require it. Cyrus urged them to create a second retreat if they were unwilling to use violence to defend themselves.

What worries him and what he communicates to the others is

the possibility of rogue National Guard units with access to heavy weapons loose in the rural areas. Though he doesn't mention them, he has in mind the McFerall brothers whom he fears would not scruple to use violence, perhaps extreme violence, should the rule of law collapse.

The group might have lapsed into nonexistence had it not been for the announcement of a deadly engineered variant in 2011. That development revived the MAG and brought in several new members. Cyrus half expected to hear from the Bartletts, but he didn't.

*

The first inkling that the outbreak in Xinjiang Province is something more than a local incident comes when the Chinese Ministry of Health reports that the Haidian District, a trendy area of Beijing, has been put on "a quarantine alert." Suspicion in the world medical community quickly ramps up and demands are made that international inspections be allowed. The issue hangs fire as diplomats and foreign businessmen send their families home. The State Department expands its travel warning to include all of the PRC. The United Nations erupts in a fog of words and blocked resolutions. China has lots of bought-and-paid-for friends, especially in Africa.

Cruelly ironic then that in the wake of reports of outbreaks in other Chinese cities, Abuja, the capital of Nigeria, a country with strong economic ties to China, petitions the World Health Organization for help in containing an outbreak of "a flu-like epidemic." For the first time, the WHO is able to investigate what is happening without hindrance.

It takes time and courage for the team of experts to fly into what is already a chaotic situation. The upscale Central District of Abuja is in virtual lock-down except for a nervous cordon of soldiers defending it from the rioting, looting, and burning in the surrounding areas. The resident physicians at the modern Primus Hospital, many of them of Indian origin, have already confirmed from blood tests and symptoms – cough, diarrhea, fever, and difficulty breathing – that it is avian flu that has the reception area littered with the sick and dying.

Researchers from the World Health Organization find that at least five substrains of HPAI – highly pathogenic avian influenza – are loose in Abuja and the surrounding areas. They can't determine if they are the same strains now wreaking devastation in China as they still do not have access to that data. Nations across the globe begin collecting the names of recent arrivals from China and information as to where they have gone.

On opinion shows in the United States, experts with academic credentials warn that this flu is highly mutagenic even by the standards of H5N1. "It's loose and mutating," one of them says. "It's very much a deadly, shape-shifting pathogen."

An epidemiologist of international stature tells his interlocutor that the world faces a monumental crisis. "The task of containing this outbreak will be complicated by what appears to be overlapping incubation and infectious periods of the various strains. In the late stages of incubation, but before symptoms appear, individuals could be infectious, unwittingly spreading the disease to those around them, including loved ones. Of course the contagion depends on the individual and the particular strain of the virus."

Crouched over his laptop in the recon room, Cyrus follows these events obsessively. He reads the on-line editions of the *New York Times* and *The Wall Street Journal*. He listens to *NPR* and the *BBC*. He watches the more intelligent talk shows and every morning checks a medical news site designed for physicians. He confers with Jack whenever he has been in touch with Matt Selig, his NSA contact. The latter reports that the threat assessments on the part of analysts in the panoply of intelligence services wax more dire by the hour even as the news about the outbreaks grows repetitive. "Washington's full of bunker talk," he tells Jack. "There are a lot of worried faces."

Still, the panic part of the looming pandemic holds fire even when a virulent form of avian flu appears among residents in Glodok, the Chinatown of Jakarta. Satellite coverage shows bodies in the street, but whether from the disease or from troops sent in to keep order no one seems to know. There are unconfirmed reports by Reuters of an outbreak in Luanda, the capital of Angola.

One after another, governments across the globe clamp down on anyone and anything coming from overseas but especially from China. Airliners from an infected area are turned around in mid-air. Those that land are refueled by personnel in biohazard suits and forced at gunpoint to takeoff. Cruise ships with passengers from China on their manifests are made to anchor offshore and undergo a two-week quarantine.

Cyrus keeps those family members who are part of the Sugar Mountain community apprised of what is happening. Yet even as the situation worsens, he encounters what to him is a curious and maddening phenomenon: No one wants to leave home, whatever the dangers of remaining in, say, Manhattan. It is perhaps understandable. People have careers, friends, family, homes, businesses, routines, comforts, and a million other strings tying them to where they are living their lives.

In their Greenwich Village co-op, Allegra begs Frank to evacuate with her and Lily. He nods and persists in his legal career and social swirl even as both begin to come apart. Allegra, like most of her colleagues, has already posted a notice on her e-mail and her office door to the effect that the last bits and pieces of the courses she teaches at Columbia will have to wait until the crisis passes.

Standing in their living room with its view of the new World Trade Center building, Allegra says, "We have to get out of here, Frank. It's not an option." She has already packed for herself and Lily. Their bags are in the corridor near the door.

Frank won't budge. "I can't just drop everything and leave."

Allegra is furious but controls herself. "Your cases can wait. We can't. If you want to stay here, fine. I'm leaving and taking Lily." But she stays and fumes. What is he thinking?

Ari Fineman's restaurant stays open even though reservations have dropped to near nothing, or been canceled, or simply ignored. His wife Lise is spending fourteen hours a day at the investment firm where she works. The market, already sagging, drops and then drops again as the news worsens. Brokers, she tells Cyrus, are running around with their hair on fire.

Then get out of there, Cyrus begs her, begs everyone. "What do they think is happening?" he complains to Grace as they sit over their morning cup of tea. She calms him and opens the mail, which has withered to the junk stuff. She finds that she must also calm herself.

Thad and Duvall, because they are close and because they feel responsible for their students, continue to work at the high school. On the second weekend in May, they drive out to Sugar Mountain from their Beacon Hill condo for a three-day stay, bringing things to store along with a large canister of dried beans, several ten-pound bags of brown rice, three gallons of olive oil, and a bottle of soy sauce. Over Cyrus' objections, they return to Boston. They, too, have careers, appointments, friends, goals. They, too, don't quite believe it can happen.

Perhaps because Americans have grown used to disasters elsewhere. Famine in Africa. Wars in the Middle East. Floods or droughts in India. Murders in Mexico. So now there are outbreaks of avian flu in China, Africa, Indonesia, and perhaps Singapore. You could get morally exhausted pitying them all, writing a check, scarcely aware that you might be next.

At the same time, a lot more people become preppers. As the month of May warms toward June, the shelves of staples in supermarkets grow thin and then bare. Where they can, people stock up their weekend houses or shift things around in the cellar to make storage space. The price of camp stove fuel goes up steeply and then becomes meaningless as supplies run out. Candles are hard to find. Bottles with closable tops get rinsed and filled with water. Just in case.

Cyrus takes calls from far and near as he has a reputation as the go-to guy when it comes to preparing for disasters. He counsels his brother George in Florida to load his forty-five-foot sloop with supplies to use as a refuge if things get dicey on shore. Emma Bartlett calls and grudgingly admits a CB radio might be of use. He tells her politely that he has no more and gives her the name of a supplier. Colleagues and old friends from the architectural firm he helped found call for advice. What can he tell them? Stock up and lay low.

Jack uses the farm's pickup to fetch the final lengths of a heavy chain-link fence with posts and footings waiting for them at a dealer in Springfield. He barely makes it. The price of gasoline has shot to ten dollars a gallon – when you can find it.

The President goes on nationwide television with the head of the CDC and announces that the worst thing would be to panic.

With the pandemic alert level at Phase 6, the Global Alert and Response office of the World Health Organization puts up a map of the globe on their site coded red, orange, and yellow on a background of white. Cyrus notes that the WHO has finally colored several places in China as red along with cities in Africa, and Indonesia. Melbourne, Singapore, and New Delhi are coded orange for suspected outbreaks, with a lot more places coded yellow for vulnerable. So far, the entire western hemisphere has remained white.

Until cases are reported in Havana, Cuba. According to Matt Selig, who calls Jack from a pay phone, the source of the infection appears to be a Cuban trade delegation that had been given the red-carpet treatment in China before returning home. The question is, how long has the flu been incubating in Havana and what has been the contact between members of the trade delegation and any friends or family visiting from the United States and elsewhere?

When Flores Chavez, a waiter at El Chico, a four-star Mexican restaurant in Washington, D.C., shows up at the emergency room at Georgetown University Hospital with flu-like symptoms, the color on the map for the nation's capital goes from white to orange. Within an hour of her admission, the color changes to red.

It turns out that her boyfriend, a low-ranking member of the trade delegation that visited China, flew to Washington shortly after arriving home. He was found in their apartment close to death.

The panic edges closer. The media adds to what someone calls "justifiable hysteria." Reporters with faces drawn with more than canned solemnity spend time describing the CDC's attempt to find out anyone who has been to the restaurant or has any contact with the infectious couple. Using credit card receipts, the CDC closes a large quarantine net around the hundreds who ate at El Chico and their families and associates.

The measures appear to work. People in quarantine become sick and a lot of them die. But the red spots on the map don't spread in the United States the way they have begun to freckle the map of the rest of the world. Americans who fled urban and suburban areas for weekend homes or resort hotels and lodging begin to return. Commentators talk about American "exceptionalism."

Then, a week later, a food worker at Princeton is brought to an emergency ward by EMTs in full biohazard gear. Cause of death a day later is attributed to HPAI, highly pathogenic avian influenza.

Cyrus, usually mild in his exhortations, turns adamant that the in-gathering begin. "Ari, what are you waiting for?" he asks his wife's nephew. "It's going to get dangerous driving once the real panic starts."

"We're packing," Ari tells him. "I'm bringing the restaurant van. It's a hybrid, the kind you can plug in."

"Don't pack. Just come."

Ari and Lise have their own contentions. Lise wants to stop in New Jersey on the way and pick up her mother Chee. Chee, who lives in a boarding house of sorts, is ambivalent at best about leaving. She does not want to be a bother.

Cyrus reiterates the same to Frank and Allegra. "When the panic hits, you won't be able to get out of New York." He speaks with resigned exasperation. "When the first case gets reported in the city, you'll be trapped."

The argument between Frank and Allegra simmers until she gathers up Lily and a few last things and heads for the door. She stops, turns, and tells him, "You're free to risk your own life, Frank, but not Lily's and not mine." She is in the parking garage under the co-op unlocking their small town car when he calls her on her cell.

Cyrus doesn't worry as much about Thad and Duvall. They

live closer, but their apartment in Boston is more than a hundred miles away.

Grace drives to Greenfield to collect her aging dad Henry Carlton. She called him that morning to tell him to pack for a long stay at the farm. Because his mind goes in and out of focus, she hopes he remembers.

There is no one at the reception desk when she arrives at Oak Grove Suites. It doesn't matter. She has been there many times, waved to the receptionist, passed through the "library," and taken the corridor to the apartment where Henry lives in roomy comfort.

Not wanting to be a burden on anyone, least of all his family, Henry moved to the Grove several years before of his own volition. It is a leafy sort of place, variously a condo association, assisted living community, country club, restaurant, and, discreetly, off behind some pines, a hospice "for those continuing their journey in another realm."

Entering the carpeted living room after a knock, Grace finds her father sitting on the sofa next to Edith Hamell. Grace has met Edith on several occasions. She is Henry's card-playing friend. A well-groomed and well-spoken woman in her eighties, she seems a good match for her father, who is tall, courtly, and silver-maned. He wears a lightweight summer suit, open shirt, loafers, and golf cap. Edith has on pressed black slacks, off-white blouse, and tan jacket. Her modest suitcase is next to Henry's two larger ones.

Henry stands and smiles. He holds out a hand for Edith who also rises. He says, his voiced measured but with a quaver, "Grace, I think you know Edith. She's decided to come with me to the farm."

Grace nods and smiles grimly at Edith. Her heart is sinking. This is not going to be easy.

"I'm afraid, Dad, we can't take Edith with us this time." Grace has, belying her words, made her voice sweetly accommodating. She is seized by a kind of moral panic. "And we have to go now."

Edith sits down. Both women know it's a death sentence. Edith, who is holding her black, zipped purse in both hands, says, "There are no staff left here to speak of." Like Henry she is dressed to travel, perhaps on the *Sea Cloud* among the Greek isles.

Henry is confused in his distress. He says, "Oh dear, oh dear..."

Edith says, "I have helped Henry live independently, the way he wanted to."

Grace cannot bring herself to respond to the woman or to comfort her. She knows if she reaches out and touches her, she might capitulate to her feelings. Edith would not be just another person at the farm, she would be a liability. Old, decorative, and useless, like Meredith, she thinks in a footnote.

She says, "Dad, we have to go now. Things are not getting any better out there." She takes one of the suitcases, tips and rolls it to the open door. Her father follows, pulling the other behind him. He stops at the doorway and looks back. His face is a mask of pain. Grace does not look back. Doors open along the corridor. The doomed peer out at her and say good-bye to Henry. He stops and shakes hands.

More residents have gathered in the library, which is mostly a television lounge with comfortable chairs, a few shelves for books, and several card tables. "Where is everybody?" one balding, red-faced man in a wheelchair asks Grace. "We had to get our own breakfast."

Grace pushes on. People have crowded into the reception area as news of her visit spreads. She fights the panic growing in her as they push through to the double glass doors.

A man in a cardigan follows them out into the late May sunshine. He comes up to them as she is heaving the suitcases into the back of the Prius. He says to her father, "You know, it doesn't matter, Henry. You won't survive either. I don't care where you're going."

Grace drives. She hates fleeing. Her instinct is to stay and organize the residents so that they can help themselves.

She gets to the rotary and takes the interstate north to Bernardston where her sister lives in a mansion-sized cottage. A twice married classic beauty and now a self-contained older woman who wears spectacles, Meredith greets Grace with complaints about having to leave her cat Boots with a neighbor. No pets are to be allowed at Sugar Mountain under any circumstances once the final in-gathering begins. And this, it is becoming clearer by the hour, is to be the final in-gathering. She has several bags, and the car is weighed down as Grace starts back to Sugar Mountain.

Cyrus watches as the Prius pulls up near the corner porch. He would go out and help with the unloading except that Jack and Nicole are already there. Henry and Meredith. They represent the past. He is concerned for the future. He returns to the recon room where he fumes and waits for the rest of his family to show up, at least on the screen that he watches like some flat crystal ball.

4

The twelve-passenger van with tinted windows had stopped on West 77th Street not far from the American Museum of Natural History. It could no longer move in the parking lot that Manhattan had become on that sunny morning in May.

What happened less than half an hour after the van pulled to a stop was caught by someone with a video camera on the third floor of a nearby residence. Two men, one with a red do-rag tied around his head and the other wearing a Yankees cap backwards, approached the van from behind, coming up between the lanes of stalled traffic. Both openly carried revolvers. When they reached the van, the one in the cap pointed his gun at the driver through the window.

The driver, a heavy-set man in a turban, got out with his hands up. Finding himself ignored, he fled into the surrounding traffic. The man in the rag walked along the side of van. He signaled its occupants to open the sliding door, which, apparently, was locked. When no one budged, he fired into the handle. Whether that broke the lock or someone released it from inside, the door slid open.

The capped man joined his accomplice and together they pulled an older, well-dressed woman roughly from the vehicle. But when they grabbed at her purse, she resisted, her face twisted in indignation. The man in the scarf lifted his revolver and struck her sharply on the side of the head with its barrel. She collapsed, releasing her purse. Just then the capped man clutched at his arm and appeared to yell.

Shakily, the camera's field of view pulled back to show a third man, perhaps an off-duty cop, automatic in hand, taking aim and firing at the robbers from behind the open door of a car several vehicles away.

The robbers ducked and ran, snaking away through the traffic, one of them holding the side of his arm, the other clinging to the purse. The man firing at them had a clear shot, but he lowered his weapon and put it into a shoulder holster.

29

Another elderly passenger, also well-dressed, emerged from the van. He called out something to the man who has fired on the robbers. He then helped the stricken woman to her feet and with the aid of a passing pedestrian got her back inside the van. The door closed and the segment ended.

Cyrus watches the incident with horror, pity, and a recurring sense of vindication mingled with chagrin. This particular crime, a minor incident in the scope of the descending cataclysm but emblematic nonetheless, has been repeated on the news several times. It draws his attention because it happened a block away from the condo where Ari Fineman and his family live. If they haven't left the city by now, they may never get out. The news switches to an aerial view of Manhattan. It shows a chaos of people moving on foot amidst motionless vehicles.

He has seen the same thing happen over the past couple of weeks in other cities, in Delhi, Rome, and London, the deadly flu sweeping like a Biblical plague across the world. Panic, looting, and worse erupted as people did everything they could to get away from other people. But this is the first time he has witnessed such graphic violence in his own country. It is part of the mass hysteria that has erupted in the United States as the pandemic moves inexorably outward from Washington. Quarantine after quarantine has collapsed. The plague is spreading with unceasing contagion.

"Any word from Ari?" Grace asks, coming to the doorway of the alcove.

Cyrus glances at her and smiles ruefully. "Nothing since early this morning. I think they left the building. They have a landline and no one's answering it. Not that it signifies. Communications are down in lots of places. I can't link to his GPS. It may not be working."

"They should have left earlier," she says, echoing a common refrain among them.

"I told them. And then I told them again."

"Come and have a cup of tea. You've been glued to that thing all night."

Cyrus gets up and follows his wife into the kitchen.

"How are the others doing?" Grace needs some good news.

"Frank and Allegra have crossed the Hudson and are headed through Old Chatham. There are a few tricky places around Pittsfield, but they should be okay."

Frank and Allegra and their precocious three-year-old daughter Lily are in their small hybrid with enough range to make it to the farm. Grace, who is wearing a white cotton blouse, amber necklace, and gray linen skirt – as though dressing for company – says, "Well, Frank didn't want to leave. I know he doesn't care much for this place, but really..." She sighs. "And what about Thad and Duvall?"

"They got out of Boston just in time to judge from the traffic. Route 2 is at a standstill inside 128. The Pike looks clogged as well. They should be here momentarily."

Though a lot of people had already evacuated the cities in the northeast, reports of an outbreak in Bayonne, just across the Hudson from Manhattan added to a general panic.

"What about Lance?" Grace asks.

"Nothing. Not a word. I tried calling."

"That's worrying. But Williams isn't that far."

Cyrus nods thoughtfully. "But he doesn't have a car."

"Well, you did tell them..." Grace begins, but is interrupted by the sound of a vehicle pulling up outside.

They come out onto the porch as Thad and his partner Duvall get out of a vintage Volvo station wagon packed solid in the back.

Hugs and handshakes and the laughter of relief. Blue eyed and shaved bald, Thad has his mother's sensual lips and easy smile, though where he got his sense of humor is anyone's guess. Duvall looks like Thad's brown brother only two sizes larger. His fine physique has begun to thicken around the waist. Duvall teaches history and a shop in wood-working in the same school where Thad teaches computer science.

Grace's dad Henry is among those who come out to greet the new arrivals. He is a combat veteran of World War II and he moves slowly, a touch of arthritis in his left hip. He wonders if they have brought Edith, whom he still thinks about. Of course not.

He catches himself. Probably gone, like most of his life.

Little Cy bounds out of the family room to be hoisted up by Uncle Thad who says, "Who are you? What do you want?"

"I'm the Count of Monte Christo and I have a real sword."

"Then we must duel to the death."

Which makes the tow-haired boy screw up his face. "Then get ready to die."

Up on the colonnaded porch that squares off the east end of the house, there are more hugs and kisses as Jack and Nicole greet the arrivals. Mary, also a favorite of Uncles Thad and Duvall, hugs them with more than her usual enthusiasm. A sense of relief, of rescue and celebration charges the air. Even the children know that something horrendous is happening, that the game of life has become deadly.

They move into the family room, a comfortable, commodious space between the kitchen and another, smaller porch, one that is screened and overlooks the sunken garden where an old barn once stood. The family room occupies a single-story structure that connected the house to the barn back in the day, making it easier to get to the livestock when the snow was five feet deep. It now has large windows, two of them with cushioned seats. Cyrus, working with Duvall, used cherry cut on the farm for the paneling, bookcases and cabinets. Couches and armchairs more or less face a fireplace of old brick. It contains a glass-fronted wood stove that gives off enough heat to keep the room warm in winter. Atop the mantel under a Navajo rug is a flat-screened television. The room makes obvious that Cyrus has indulged his architectural fancies in re-making Sugar Mountain from an old farmstead into an upscale refuge.

Meredith, dressed in a pale blue cocktail number that sets off her hair, which she keeps blond, comes in as though onto a stage. She smiles wanly and shakes hands with the newcomers. "Is it really as bad as they say?" she asks, her consternation mild as she wonders when she might get to the hairdressers.

A pot of coffee brews. Conversation focuses on Ari, Lise, and Rachael.

"I know what happened," says Thad, who is perceptive about family matters. "I'd bet they crossed over to New Jersey to pick up Lise's mother."

Jack grimaces. He says, "She's not part of the group. Remember, we invited her, and she said no."

Thad nods as though in agreement. "But Lise is not going to leave her mother behind. We'll be lucky if she doesn't show up with other relatives."

Nicole plays the placater. "We do have lots of room. And Ari helped a lot financially."

Jack sighs and looks at the ceiling, which is neatly plastered between exposed beams. That's true enough, he thinks. But he and Nicole along with his mom and dad did most of the heavy lifting that went into installing the extra living quarters, provisioning the food depots, and setting up the elaborate network of defense and fallback that comprise the family's survival strategy.

Cyrus says gloomily, "They'll be lucky to get here at all at this rate. Random killing has started, at least from what I've seen."

"And a lot of talk about group suicides." Duvall, a touch of doom in his baritone, might have been on vacation as he sports a Hawaiian shirt, white shorts, and flip-flops. "There was supposed to be one this morning on Boston Common."

Family rejoicing resumes an hour later, albeit in a lower register, with the arrival of Frank, Allegra, and Lily. In the graveled yard next to the porch in the warm May sun, they all hug and kiss on the cheeks. Mary Arkwright takes Cousin Lily in tow while Cy stands back, aloof.

Once unloaded, the car is parked with the other vehicles in a lot behind an array of south-facing solar panels to the east of the house. If they decide not to use it, Jack will siphon any gas from it to add to their stores of fuel.

It is lunch time. Grace and Duvall set out sandwiches, tea and more coffee in the kitchen. The exhilaration of calamity brightens and darkens the air. Allegra stands at one point to raise her coffee mug. "To Cyrus, Grace, Jack and Nicole. You've given us a chance to survive." There are cheers.

Thad says, "Hear, hear."

Allegra sits down, wiping away a tear.

Frank looks balefully at his wife and then away. He has his father's taciturn character. He does not try to conceal his despondency. The spreading chaos and lawlessness, the reports of mass death in the wake of the pandemic mean the end of his professional life. Lawyers will be about as useful as pet snakes in the dark ages to come. He wants to ask, why are you cheering? The human world is collapsing with a suddenness and completeness beyond the most dire of predictions, beyond the scope of any imagining.

He wonders what happened to Elsa. Is she still in New York? She hasn't answered her cell. Did she make the Lufthansa flight?

"Any word from Bella?" Grace asks. Bella Pulans is Meredith's daughter from her marriage to Victor Pulans. That followed quickly her divorce from Stan Fineman, Ari's dad. Bella had turned down offers to join the Sugar Mountain refuge. On several occasions she openly derided it. "It's a lot of redneck nonsense," she proclaimed more than once, adding with careless bravado, "Who would want to survive if everyone died, anyway?" She managed to intimate the question, who would want to survive with you people? Because Bella, by turns a performance artist, a poet, a painter, and a patron of the arts thanks to the prodigious fortune left by her late father, looked down on the others with a disdain mingled with a neediness that repelled even the children.

Grace's question hangs in the air. Bella, the possibility of Bella, is already a sore subject.

Cyrus, back in the recon room, picks up a message on the laptop. It is Ari. Thad is right: they have driven across to Paramus to pick up Lise's mother, Chee Xu. Cyrus frowns at Ari's heavy bald face, which fills the screen. "Where are you?" he asks.

"We're on the Parkway heading north. We're coming up on the interchange near Monsey."

Cyrus locates their position using Google Earth. He then searches for and finds a local station broadcasting traffic conditions. "Okay, I don't know how recent this update is, but I would take 303 over to 9 West and take it north all the way to 84. Though Newburgh may get sticky."

"Will do."

"Everyone okay?"

"Fine."

"What about fuel?"

"I filled it with gas and charged it a few days ago. It should get us out of harm's way, anyway."

"That sounds good. Let's keep this channel open as long as we can. Either I'll be here or Jack will take over until you're some place we can come get you if we have to."

"We really appreciate this," Lise says from the seat next to Ari's.

"No problem." Cyrus knows Jack will object to the last-minute inclusion of Lise's mother. He is about to add something when the screen goes blank. It doesn't particularly concern him as the coverage has gotten patchy.

Jack does object. "Dad, if we don't draw the line, this is going to be a mob scene." He reminds his father that the terms of the contract were explicit and repeated: You had to have signed on to be a member of the group. He specifically mentioned Chee several times, asking if she would like to be part of it.

Jack is conflicted. He likes and admires Ari. And Lise has helped him and Nicole with their investments. Not that investments will be of any help to them now. But Jack does wonder how much he might count on Ari when things get difficult. Bella's half-brother and, like her, the scion of more than comfortable wealth, Ari never had it rough. His restaurant is, was, more like an expensive hobby – though it made money. It was where Ari worked with the chefs and played the gracious host, drifting from table to table, dispensing charm as only one with the capacity to appreciate others can do.

In the kitchen for a glass of water, Jack glances out the window and sees a double-cab Dodge pickup come up the drive from the road at a growling speed. The pickup slows and follows the drive as it loops in front of the house at the bottom of the lawn. The men inside give the place a thorough look. Then it roars off.

Not long afterwards Jack meets with Thad and Cyrus in the studio. When they are seated around the smooth hardwood drafting table, now level and placed in the center of the room, Jack says, "I think we need to set up the surveillance system as soon as possible."

Thad nods. "I saw that truck. Checking us out. Who was it?"

Jack glances significantly at his dad, "The driver was Mark McFerall." He turns to his brother. "Mark's the older son of Dunc and Marge McFerall."

The McFeralls worry Cyrus more than they do Jack, who thinks he can handle them if it comes to that. But he wants to be ready for them.

Cyrus asks, "Perhaps we should put up the security fence first?"

Jack shakes his head. "That will take too long. If we get the surveillance up and running, we'll be able to know who, what, and where. And react appropriately."

"Duvall and I could rig it this afternoon," Thad says. "A lot of the camera mounts are already in place. Still the same plan?"

"Same plan," says Cyrus, a down note in his voice. He would rather the fence, which would make resistance to any incursions from outside less violent.

Jack reaches a hand over to his dad's shoulder. "We'll put the fence up ASAP. But right now we need surveillance and a response team if things get sticky."

His father smiles. "That's what I am afraid of."

In the horse barn, where they have a bedroom next to a small one for Lily, Frank and Allegra unpack what they managed to pile into the car before leaving New York. Clothes mostly, jewelry, favorite objets, some of Lily's toys, old photos, camera, computers, a few books, a few bottles of fine wine and good whiskey. It seems pathetic compared to what they have left behind – all the things that made a life they may never have again.

They change out of their clothes and take showers. They

rehearsed the survival mode during a trial visit the summer before and at Christmas time. They participated at first to humor Cyrus and Jack. Then Allegra began to feel that human life, including their own, had grown precarious on an over-populating planet. But they had not anticipated this – the wholesale collapse of everything they ever had or imagined they had.

Frank hangs around in a bathrobe and tries to contact friends and colleagues in New York. He manages to get through on his cell phone to Doug Charterman, one of the firm's founding partners.

"Frank, where the hell are you?" The voice is slurred.

"In the Berkshires. At the family farm. What's happening there?"

"You don't want to know. It's the end. The governor called out the National Guard. It's a joke. People are walking out of the city with nowhere to go. The gangs have taken over."

"Is there anyone in the office?"

"Not a soul. Why should they be? This is the end."

"Have you heard from anyone?"

"You mean Elsa?"

"Yes." Frank keeps his voice neutral.

"She was trying to get to Kennedy last I heard."

"What are you going to do?"

His senior colleague laughs. "Drink until I have the courage to use a little Lady Glock I keep handy." A silence grows between them. Then he says, "Good-bye, Frank. Take care of yourself and the lovely Allegra."

Frank touches the off button. He turns to the lovely Allegra. "It's over. We're not going to survive."

Allegra, changed into what look like old-fashioned army fatigues, "survival dress," sits next to him. She has poured them each a shot of Balvenie neat. Like so much else, the availability of single malt can no longer be taken for granted. "At least we're alive," she says and smiles into his profile.

He doesn't smile back. "I'm serious," he says. He holds the whiskey in both hands reverently, as though it will be his last drink.

37

"So am I." She stands up, moves about. "Look, darling Frankie, this is more like the beginning than the end." Her eyes betray a subdued excitement. "We're embarking on the oldest adventure known to mankind..."

"Which is...?"

"Survival."

Frank sips his whiskey and regards her balefully over his glass. "Be sure to keep notes."

"Oh, I definitely will. An old-fashioned pen and ink journal."

"There won't be any publishers left. Probably no readers, either."

Allegra sits at the small desk across from the bed. The window in front of her opens to the north. Over the chicken and goat shed, she can see the fenced garden, the pasture, the woods, the sky. "That's not the point..."

"There is no point."

"No. We'll do what we've always done... as a species. We'll keep a record."

Frank finishes his whiskey with a swallow. He regards his wife for a moment. In her finely wrought Italianate features framed with dark hair and in the sudden hardness of her bright eyes, he sees a stranger. But then he saw a stranger not long before as he gazed into the bathroom mirror. His thick blond hair, square jaw and regular handsome features mocked him. His pale Arkwright eyes stared back edged with fear. It occurs to him that he no longer loves his wife. That he no longer loves himself. He resists the temptation to hate her, this woman, his wife of six years. The catastrophe ravaging the world excites and challenges her. She will thrive.

A fug of futility signals a bout of depression. Even when Lily comes bounding up the circling stairs followed by Cy in his Count of Monte Christo outfit and, more decorously, by nine-year-old Mary, Frank cannot shake the feeling that something has snapped within him. Right then, the taste of good whiskey fading in his mouth, he is unable to imagine a future, certainly not the one that has narrowed to what swirls clamorously around him.

*

The mood at Sugar Mountain darkens after lunch as though reflecting the change in the weather – rain-heavy clouds have moved in from the west burying the sun. It isn't only that Ari and his family seem to have vanished; the calls for help begin to come in from far and near. Though they have kept their prepping low key, word has gotten around that the Arkwrights have been readying for just such a disaster over the last few years.

At one point on that gloomy day everyone except for the children appear to have a phone up to their ear and tears in their eyes. The calls range from the wheedling to the hysterical. Many have a distinct overtone of terror. When the callers hear the response – there is no room – they are variously incredulous, outraged, fatalistic. The difficult part is telling people you have known all your life that you can't help them, that there is no room left on your life raft. To give himself and the others a break, Cyrus turns off the satellite dish they use for television, internet and phone hook-ups. Calls still get through, but relief among those safely ensconced at Sugar Mountain is palpable, however mingled with worry, regrets, and a good dose of self-loathing. A kind of vicarious shock settles over the house. The old-fashioned word, Grace thinks to herself, is despair.

Late in the afternoon, Grace, helping Nicole to make a dinner of beer beef stew, glances up to see a lone figure on a bicycle laden with saddle bags laboring up the lane from the main road. "Oh, thank God," she cries. "It's Lance. He's made it!"

Once more the family celebrates with an edge of hysteria. Perhaps because Lance stands in for all of those friends and loved ones they have turned away. Then there is the young man himself. Tall, fresh-faced, pale-eyed and dark haired, Lance Arkwright combines a diffidence of voice and a confidence of manner that charms. People instinctively like and trust him, the more so when they discover an intelligence he is reluctant to parade.

It is Grace who suggests that they all turn off their phones and gather in the family room for what she calls "a Quaker session." It is as close to something religious the community has partaken of in building the refuge. Though optional, everyone shows up, except the children who are left in front of a small television in the studio.

When Thad and Duvall come in, taking a break from installing the surveillance system, the members stand in silence in a circle holding hands. The silence continues for a minute after they sit down.

Then Cyrus says, "I received a call from my brother George in Fort Meyers this morning. I told him we were already filled up and besides that the chances of him getting here with Annette and the three kids was next to nil. I told him earlier to stock up his sailboat, but he wishes now he had taken me more seriously."

Ten years younger than Cyrus, retired and married to a second wife with three young teenagers from an earlier arrangement, George Arkwright teased Cyrus about "camp survival."

"He says they managed to get some provisions aboard *The Bounty*. It sleeps about six. They've anchored in a cove with several like-minded families and have put up large quarantine signs in English and Spanish. George has a revolver and a hunting rifle, which he hopes they don't have to use. Ashore he says there are armed gangs. Bodies in the street. He says it's the end for a lot of people down there."

Allegra speaks next about a colleague at Barnard who was angry and then resigned when told there was no room at Sugar Mountain. "To save face, to placate her, to give her hope, even false hope, I was tempted to tell her she could come, knowing that her chances of getting here are almost non-existent. But, also, I'm in no position to invite her here unless we all agree to it."

She hesitates. Then, "I've also heard from Mom and Dad and my sister Dina that many of you know. My dad used to kid me the same way about camp survival but he called it something else. Then *Sandy* came along. And because they live on Staten Island, they were almost washed out to sea. So they started getting ready for the next one. Dina's with them and there's a neighborhood watch with lots of cops and firemen around. I think they have a

40

good chance. I mostly worry about my brother Sebastian... and his wife Mary and their two little boys. They live or lived in Bronxville. They're on their way to stay with Mom and Dad."

Lance tells them that the Williams campus had been nearly deserted when he left. He spoke about having to hide from a freshman who began to cling to him. "I felt really bad about it. He was like a little kid. Like a child almost."

"Your folks?" Duvall asks him.

Lance shakes his head. "I think they had something going in the desert near Santa Fe. No contact."

Grace waits her turn. Then, "On a positive note, I got a call just ten minutes ago from Helen Neill. She and her husband Greg and their son Alex live just down..."

"And Linda," Nicole interjects.

"Yes, and Linda," Grace continues, giving her daughter-in-law a smile. "They've helped us a lot with Sugar Mountain, especially to do chores when we wanted a break. I told her that we would be ready to help if they run low this winter. But she says they've been doing quite a bit of prepping themselves, thanks to Cyrus, and should be all right."

Jack grimaces. "What else did you tell her?"

"I told her to stay away from other people and to let us know if things get really desperate."

Cyrus explains, "We have set up some depots off the property. They are for others and perhaps, even ourselves ... You know, to use if things get bad."

Grace wonders whether to talk about a particularly painful series of calls. "Of course, we've gotten a lot of requests, to put it mildly, from friends in Cambridge, Boston, and even New York. All I could give them was advice. Which we did earlier, but none of them listened..." She breaks off. Like Cyrus, she gets little satisfaction from being right. Most of the calls were from close, life-long friends.

Meredith, who is sitting next to her, says in her careful voice, "Bella called and says she's on her way here with a friend."

Jack bridles visibly and swears under his breath. "That's not going to happen. Not on my watch."

Grace tries to smooth things over. It is, she says, a matter for the Family Council to decide.

Nicole, confessing she knows better being Jack's wife, makes a plea on behalf of an old high school friend, a woman who lives in Fitchburg with her five-year-old son. Cyrus has the same answer. When it gets really desperate, we'll let them know where the common caches are. If they're still alive.

Duvall speaks about his brother Claudius who lives in Albany with his wife and three kids. "Man, he used to rag me about this place. Now he's begging me to come here. What could I tell him? Lie low and hope for the best."

Cyrus says "What we are doing in this regard is very difficult and perhaps impossible. It's bad enough saying no over the phone. What will we do if loved ones show up on our doorstep? We were thinking of buying some adjacent property and setting up outlying survival camps just for this contingency. But there hasn't been time."

Thad, silent till then, says, "There's no one at the Fallgren place. We could send people there if no one shows up to claim it."

"It's derelict," Jack says. He knows what will happen if people start camping next to them.

"It's a roof."

Cyrus glances at both of them. "Let's take a look at it. But the real point is that what we are doing is right because it is the only thing we can do. If we start taking in others we will be overrun or infected or both. All we have worked for will come to naught. And instead of suffering and dying we might as well enact the Final Protocol right now and get it over with."

Jack nods. His voice tense, he says, "It's not just that we don't have room and enough supplies. The chances are that anyone who has not arrived within the next forty-eight hours could be infected. And we all know now what that means. I know we've all had flu shots and I know we have some antivirals. But this flu is deadly and mutating. It will kill us as surely as bullets."

He glances at his dad before he continues. "Speaking of bullets, we are prepared to defend ourselves if and when we come under attack. That means meeting violence with violence."

Going from slow frown to slow smile, Cyrus says, "The only thing I can add to that is that we will make every conceivable effort to remain nonviolent."

Jack, nodding, conciliatory, says, "If anyone disagrees with the use of violence as a last resort, they are welcome to leave and will be generously provisioned if they do."

He sits silently after that but restless. He looks at Meredith and thinks about Bella on her way to Sugar Mountain. He checks several nasty thoughts. Bella. If there was one good thing about a disaster like the one befalling the world, it was the likelihood that people like Bella Pulans wouldn't survive. He excuses himself to go out to keep an eye on the road with binoculars. He hadn't said anything about the people out there that he knew. How to explain his own demons of guilt? When you are in combat, the members of your squad became part of you. They would die for you and you would die for them. Now, pacing outside on the lawn in front of the house, cell phone to his ear, he speaks to and sympathizes with his wartime buddies, guiltily relieved that most are too far away for him to have to say no.

But not big, lumpy, one-armed ex-Corporal Denny Silva who lives in Pittsfield with his large lumpy wife Annette and their two lumpy kids. What will he say to him when he calls, inanity in his "Reporting for duty, Cap."

Jack is the one who should do the calling. Not that he doesn't wrack his brain for somewhere to provide for this man who, wounded in the leg, had volunteered to stay behind in that shattered house outside of Laskar Gah. The place that he, Jack, the commanding officer, picked for their outpost only to find it was an ambush. Unable to leave himself, Denny had volunteered to cover the retreat of the rest of the squad. He had collected all their spare clips and grenades "to show the bastards."

Jack cannot think about Denny Silva without playing that debacle over and over in his head. It didn't matter that intelligence had okayed the location. It wouldn't have happened a few months before. He would have smelled a rat the minute he saw the recon photos. The place was ruined just enough to be defensible, just enough cover to move in and set up. Even, God damn it, the ease with which they had taken it. All but a welcome mat out. The bitch was he had noted the rise of ground to the north and the surrounding buildings, not ideal for cross fire, but good enough. He had said yes when he should have said no.

They were there less than ten minutes when the mayhem began. RPGs, AKs, and some wicked heavy machine gun fire, probably a Russian KPV. The first to go down was Pfc. Connor, hit in the crotch and legs, bleeding out in minutes. Then Pfc. Harvey, a neck wound they couldn't staunch. Then Sergeant Lopez, in the stomach, but not bleeding too badly, at least not externally. Finally Denny, in the thigh, a crippling but not fatal wound. But he wouldn't be able to walk out of there.

They were too close to the enemy to call in mortars. Air cover wouldn't arrive in time. The withdrawal would be complicated if even possible. They might be expecting it. They might have set up secondary ambushes. It was something Jack would have to coordinate.

When he returned in force and with air support several hours later to recover the bodies of Denny and the others, the corporal was still there, tourniquet tightened with a stick of wood above his shattered left arm, down to a few rounds and single grenade. Reporting for duty, Cap.

It was then Jack turned to the kind of killing that verged on murder.

The session in the family room is interrupted by Mary, Cy, and Lily at the door. Mary, an Arkwright to the bone, has her chin up. "I want to say something, too." They have been just outside the door listening.

"I want to talk, too," says Cy, not to be outdone by his sister.

There is consternation mixed with admiration among the adults.

"Go ahead, Mary," her grandmother urges.

Mary lifts her head. She has Nicole's pretty features and Jack's intensity. She says, "I've been calling my friends, too. They are all scared. Two of them want to come here but I said they couldn't. I think some of them... I think they've left or they're already... dead."

"We don't know anything yet," Cyrus tells her gently.

Lily, who is sitting on her father's lap, pipes up, "Are we going to die?"

"Not if I can help it." Allegra smiles reassuringly at her daughter. Or tries to. She counts on Lily to bring Frank out of his funk.

Grace says, "No. That's the reason we're all here. We have food and supplies..."

"And guns," Cy says.

"And your sword," Thad puts in, making everyone laugh except Meredith, who misses her cat and her house in Bernardston. Her garden club friends on Long Island from the old days have called her to ask what she plans to do.

Mary persists. Close to tears, she asks, "But what about all the other people?"

After a silence, Cyrus says, "We will help all the people we can, Mary. And that's the best we can do."

When the gong sounds for dinner, Jack maintains his patrol around the perimeter. It gives him a chance to brood about Bella. A while later, Duvall comes out to relieve him. Jack thinks about bringing it up with Duvall, bitching, letting off steam. But then he checks himself. It won't make any difference.

Jack finds that most of the family has eaten frugally as though practicing for when it will no longer be a choice. There is little conversation, each in his or her own way relieved, humbled, and agonized to have been chosen for survival or at least the possibility thereof.

Afterwards, though the twilight lingers, they go off to be by themselves.

Out on the small porch overlooking the barn garden, Cyrus, his mild face twisted by worry, says to Grace, "I don't like it. It'll soon be dark. We should have heard from them by now."

Grace touches his arm. "Ari and Lise are both very resourceful."

"Yes, but that may not be enough."

In the living room they share with Thad and Duvall in the horse barn, Allegra begins her journal. She has an up-to-date tablet, but she no longer trusts technology. She opens instead a new notebook with lined pages and a black cover of simulated moleskin. "The world is coming to an end," she writes. "The world is starting all over again."

5

The second day of the in-gathering breaks cool and overcast, promising rain the land needs. The gloom that pervaded Sugar Mountain the night before persists as its residents wake from troubled sleep to the new world order, to the human disaster that has come like a thunderclap.

Chores help occupy the mind and lift the spirit. At least that's what Grace has decided as she steps with Duvall among the hum of fifty or so chirping hens in the hen house. It works for her, the doing of necessary things.

"This stuff," she tells him as she shakes high protein feed from a bucket into the hoppers, "will soon be too valuable to give to the hens."

"What will we do with it?" It dawns on him in the low-ceilinged, pungent place that this is no fantasy about farming. These large white hens and the eggs they lay are food.

"I'll seal it in ten-pound bags and have it handy for refugees. Or for ourselves if it comes to that."

"How would you cook it?"

"Grind it. Bake it. Make porridge. It's supposed to be organic."

"Do we have much of it?" They begin to collect the eggs, lifting the lids on the straw-lined nesting boxes.

"Half a ton, perhaps a little less." She stops and points to the wall. "Listen."

Through the partition that divides the shed, they can hear Nicole teaching Lance how to milk the four she-goats tethered there. "You've got to want to milk the suckers," they hear Nicole say. "Put pressure on it and pull down."

There is the sound of milk hitting the bottom of a pail in squirts. Then Nicole, "That's it, you've got it. It's humble work, but it makes good cheese and it goes well enough in coffee."

Just beyond the northwest corner of the barn garden, Cyrus gives Allegra lessons in how to muck out the pigsty. The sty leans off the north side of the ell-shaped equipment shed which has two bays on either side of a machine shop. The ill-lit place is dominated by a giant old sow named Miss Piggy who sprawls in a corner attended by a litter of month-old piglets.

"God, it stinks," says Allegra, watching as Cyrus scrapes the square shaped shovel along the concrete floor. She is grateful for the denim work clothes and a pair of rubber boots.

Cyrus dumps the shovel of sopping wood shavings and dung into a wheelbarrow. "It's overdue," he admits. "Should be done at least once a week." He wheels the barrow outside to a pile that later will be spread on the garden.

He gives Allegra the shovel. "We'll keep one or two of the piglets from the litter for breeding."

"What about the big one?"

"We'll butcher Miss Piggy this fall..."

"And put her meat in the freezer?" She starts the edge of the shovel under the muck and stops.

"Not this time. We'll smoke the hams and shoulders, salt away the bacon. Maybe make some sausages for smoking as well."

"What about the rest of them?" She hefts a shovel full. Too much. She lets half of it fall back.

"Roast suckling pig. Maybe barter a couple of them if there's anyone left to barter with."

"You mean around here?"

"Around here."

They get back to work.

"This is heavy stuff," Allegra says, getting the hang of filling, lifting, and emptying the shovel. "I'm not in shape."

"You will be." He smiles at her and takes over.

Allegra steps back. She fishes out a folded-over piece of plain paper that she uses as a walk-about notebook and scribbles down, "There's a subtle consistency between the smell of pig shit and the smell of baked ham. What we will eat when Miss Piggy is butchered will be a refined quintessence of what's here."

They finish the floor, spread wood shavings mixed with dried leaf litter around, and empty the kitchen bucket into the feed

48

trough. Shucking her litter, the old sow grunts over to it and begins to feed.

"Well done, Professor." His eyes are warm with ironic humor.

Allegra smiles back. "I can see now why we keep barn clothes out in the bath house."

Coming into the house after a brisk, lukewarm shower in the bathhouse, Allegra finds Thad has worked up a breakfast of scrambled eggs, toast, and home-canned fruit. It will be served to everyone at eight o'clock at the long table in the kitchen. It has been decided that all meals, with a few exceptions, will be taken together. Coffee and, to a lesser extent, tea, is to be rationed along with refined sugar. There will be plenty of milk – as long as they have goats.

"Anyone seen Frank?" she asks, snitching a piece of toast to go with a cup of coffee.

"He's in the family room," Thad tells her. "He's helping Meredith watch the kids."

Earlier Frank had scarcely been able to get out of bed. "For what?" he said, rolling over.

"To live," she said.

"That's not enough."

"It is if that's all there is."

But he was not mollified. Now he sits in the family room with Meredith who has dressed smartly in navy blouse, wheat-colored skirt, and espradilles. She doesn't know quite what to do with herself.

Henry comes in, the tap of his cane announcing his approach. He glances around, just a bit confused. "No paper?"

"No paper. Not much broadcast news, either." Frank stands and stares out the window. He keeps thinking that everything will be all right when Ari arrives. As though Ari will bring some of New York with him – not just the good life but a touch of tough guy optimism.

"What did it say on the broadcast news?" Allegra wants to engage him, bring him out of himself.

He shrugs. "It's going from bad to worse. The President's going to address the nation. A lot of good that will do."

The children, Mary and Cy, are squabbling over Lily and who is in charge of her.

The mood of the place does not improve with breakfast. As Lance and Allegra do the dishes, pleas for help from family and friends resume with an intensity that leave them morose and anguished. With the exception of Henry and Meredith. They set up the cribbage board on the card table in the family room and quietly attend to their cards.

It is clear from the calls and the sporadic news that the pandemic, though confined to the east coast, is spreading. From Boston it has reached north into southern Maine and west to Worcester. From New York it is moving northeast as though taking aim at Springfield in Massachusetts. New Yorkers fleeing to their weekend retreats are taking it up the Hudson.

Cyrus announces over the intercom that the President is to make a nation-wide broadcast with members of his emergency team that afternoon. Attendance in the common room to watch it is optional, of course, but he says they should all be there. "Especially if you want an extra cup of coffee."

Meredith harrumphs at that. A moment later the LEDs on the appliances in the kitchen and family room blink off and then came back on blinking zeros.

"The grid's gone down," Jack says.

"What grid?" Meredith asks, ready to be indignant.

"The power grid," Cyrus explains to her. "I thought it would last longer than this."

"What will we do?" Meredith has led a sheltered life.

"We have our own sources of power." Cyrus speaks with a certain pride. "It's already kicked in, but it means that everyone, and I mean everyone, will have to cut back. It means lights out at ten every night."

"Any word from Ari and Lise?" Allegra asks coming into the family room. She has been crying. She has just gotten off the phone with Elaine Seagal, a friend and colleague. She's stuck in an apartment on the thirty-fourth floor with her husband and baby and nowhere to go.

"Nothing," Jack says.

"Not good, is it?"

"Not good at all."

*

That same morning, Thad, the resident techie, explains and initiates the surveillance system he and Duvall have installed. With most of the adults crowding around the opening of the recon room – he switches on the two laptops set aside as monitors. Each screen is split into four segments and each segment is dedicated to a small all-weather, camera wired into the Sugar Mountain grid. These have been placed to provide wide-angle coverage of the town road from both directions, the sugar bush and mill, a vulnerable site higher on Talbot Brook, and the woodlot to the east purposely planted with brambles and vines. There are two for the close-in grounds and out-buildings of the farm. The last camera, high on the house, can be moved remotely to take in three hundred and sixty degrees.

Thad explains the controls, how to use the full screen for one of the segments if you want a more detailed view. How to manipulate the lens on top of the house. How and when to sound the alarm, which is coded yellow, orange, and red.

"Jack, you want to talk about watches?"

Jack, standing beside his brother, nods. "We'll each do a daily or twice daily two-hour watch to start with. Dad's in here a lot anyway monitoring the CB radio. We can always spell one another, switch off, that sort of thing. But I don't want to make it too loosey goosey because things are getting bad out there. People are getting desperate. Any questions?"

"Twenty-four seven?" Nicole asks.

"Twenty-four seven."

Allegra puts up her hand. "Is there an instruction manual of any kind?"

Thad takes it. "Not really. But Jack, Duvall, Lance or I will be with you for your first hour or two to help you get the hang of it. It's really not complicated, except maybe at night when the night vision program kicks in."

Jack says, "There will be a sign-up sheet on the bulletin board just outside the family room. Any volunteers for the first watch?"

Allegra puts her hand up again.

Thad nods. "Great. Lance, why don't you show Allegra the ropes."

Lance smiles. He already likes Allegra more than he should.

The power returns an hour and half later. Cyrus relieves Allegra at the screens before her watch is up. "Anything happening?" he asks taking the swivel chair next to hers.

"You're early." She's grateful for the break.

"Got to see if I can raise Ari and company."

"It is worrisome."

"Especially with time."

"Nothing much," she says, "to answer your question. There's a large hawk that perches on the roof on the mill..."

"A redtail. He keeps the squirrels in check."

Grace and Duvall make a lunch of early greens and goat cheese to go with slices of Nicole's bread. They arrange the meal on the kitchen table for people to help themselves. The kids come and go, playing, as though vacation has begun early. Munching from a small plate with a glass of cider, Cyrus sits in front of the monitors and hunches over his laptop. He is still trying to make contact with Ari when the CB transceiver on the desk crackles to life. It is Hal Beck, a member of the network.

A few moments later, Cyrus comes into the kitchen, his face grave. When he says nothing to those still at the table, Grace asks, "Cyrus, what's happened?"

"That was Hal. He's gotten reports that several masked men broke into the National Guard headquarters in Greenfield, killed three guardsmen and made off with the supply of antivirals set aside for this area."

"Dear God." Grace is appalled. "Most people don't have any of their own."

"Any suspects?" Jack asks.

"One speculation is that lower-ranked Guard members were involved. Or someone who knew where the medicine was being kept."

"Sounds like the McFeralls," Jack says.

"But murder?" Grace looks at her son, engaging his eyes. Jack points his face at her. "Mom, I hate to tell you, but murder is going to become as common as..."

Nicole asks, "Is it really that critical? I mean if it was just Tamiflu."

Grace makes a don't-know gesture. "At least it was something. And perhaps the latest version."

*

When the television screen in the family room goes blank and the Emergency Alert System tone sounds, Thad takes over from Cyrus in the recon room. "I can catch it in here," he says. "I've got some adjusting to do."

Cyrus comes into the family room just as the Presidential seal fills the screen.

Then the President himself, looking tired and subdued. "My fellow Americans," he begins, speaking apparently without any prompts, "I don't need to tell you that we have entered a perilous time in our nation's long and distinguished history. The pandemic of avian flu, which we were able to resist while the rest of the world suffered, has descended on us with diabolical speed and with a lethality that can scarcely be described. ` It is my duty to tell you what most of you have already surmised: Along with the rest of the world with the possible exceptions of New Zealand and a few other remote places, we are facing a pandemic of catastrophic proportions. We are placed in the strange position of having to pull together even while we must practice what the medical experts call social distancing.

"I want to assure you that your government is still operating effectively if not at full capacity. I have assembled my cabinet and critical advisors here at Camp David. Those members of Congress not back in their districts and the surviving members of the Supreme Court have been sequestered in emergency quarters with ample supplies for the duration of the crisis."

Jack, standing back from the screen, a cup of coffee in hand, can read the measure of the crisis in the fear showing in the President's usually confident face and in the tone of his words. Typical, he thinks. For all their personnel and programs and expert advice, the government has been caught off guard by the pandemic and the speed of its spread.

The President is saying, "To help me in this crisis, I have appointed a management team that will report directly to me. The members include Otis Carter, Director of FEMA, General Max Harmon, Chairman of the Joints Chiefs of Staff and now commandant of all National Guard units, and Dr. Helena Burns, Director of the Center for Disease Control.

"First, I would like General Harmon to say a few words. General..."

"Good choice," Jack says to no one in particular.

With close-cropped hair, a muscular face and the upright bearing of a soldier, General Harmon looks every inch the commander. He also sounds like one when he takes the podium and begins, in a voice like sandpaper, "Thank you, Mr. President. First, I am ordering, as of this moment, that all able-bodied National Guard members report in electronically to their units immediately if you haven't already done so. More detailed orders will follow subsequent to further consultations with state and local authorities regarding policy, particularly in regard to emergency medical measures. In addition, and if necessary, regular military units will be deployed in the event that National Guard units and local law enforcement are unable to maintain order.

"To keep the pandemic at bay, we are organizing the lower forty-eight states into twelve quarantine zones. These in turn will be divided into quarantine subzones. That means no travel without permission between these zones until further notice. The perimeters of these zones are being organized as I speak and checkpoints and satellite surveillance will be put in effect."

He pauses and his eyes narrow. "There have been reports of rogue units in the Guard taking matters into their own hands. I would like to make one thing clear: Any members of the National Guard or the regular military who use their power and authority to break or bend the law for their own personal advantage will be dealt with to the full extent of the law. And by that, I mean martial law. Mr. President..."

"Thank you, Max. Now, Dr. Burns will give us an update on the status of the pandemic. Dr...."

The camera angle widens to take in a blond woman in her fifties, her good looks obscured, perhaps deliberately, by an impersonal professionalism. She speaks in a precise, authoritative tone with an overlay of the upper Midwest in her accent.

"Thank you, Mr. President. Ladies and gentlemen..." She pauses, as though puzzled by the camera. "As of this morning at 10 a.m. Eastern Daylight Time, the pandemic had clearly established itself along the east coast from northern Virginia up to Boston. We now have reports of cases in Los Angeles and San Francisco. We will do everything in our power to confine the pandemic to the coastal areas."

In a voice suddenly sounding tired, Dr. Burns continues. "Our measures to date have been extraordinary, even drastic. But the time we have had to prepare has been very short..."

"Bullshit," says someone watching the screen.

"Shhhh..."

"...It is now little more than a month ago that this virulent strain of flu appeared in China. It has all the earmarks of an engineered pathogen. How and why it was developed is a matter of speculation. How it got loose among a civilian population also remains a matter of speculation. Nor can we ascertain how long it has been infecting populations as statements from the Beijing government have not proved reliable.

"Indeed, the onset has been so sudden that containment with buffer zones as recommended by WHO has not proven any more effective than they have in other parts of the world. Because of its efficient transmission and variability including substrains with long incubation and infectious times, H5N1X, as it has been designated, is proving to be a relentless and catastrophic killer.

"Fortunately, there has been time to stockpile and distribute reserves of antiviral medication. Our most compelling task right now is the distribution and administration of these available antivirals. Unfortunately, there are not enough doses for the entire population even if we get to everyone. Difficult choices will have to be made."

She turns to her left. "Mr. President."

"Thank you, Dr. Burns, for your succinct account of the situation. You are right about having to make difficult choices. To help us in that task, I now turn to Director Otis Carter of FEMA. Otis..."

Tall, gaunt, and slow speaking, Otis Carter grimaces as he looks at the cameras. He runs a brown hand through his whitening fuzz of hair. He says, "Difficult choices indeed. First, let me tell you that we have, with the cooperation with the CDC, established local emergency shelters nationwide. These will be under the supervision of specially deputized medical personnel. Enforcement of their policies will rest with the federalized National Guard units and local police and authorities."

He sighs. "As for the distribution of the remaining flu vaccine and antivirals, the team has decided on the following. First, those in the age cohorts between newborn and fifty-five will be given first priority in the following categories: Members of federal, state, and local agencies involved with essential services starting with security. Those individuals responsible for the nation's infrastructure, including its power grid, road, rail and air communications as well as all electronic communications. Farmers and farm workers. For a complete listing, please consult our website at cdc.gov.

"Exceptions in the age cohorts to receive the antivirals include the very sick, those institutionalized for whatever reasons, the morbidly obese and anyone with a criminal record. I know this sounds heartless, but our survival collectively and individually demands that such exclusions be made. Mr. President."

"Thank you, Otis. As you can see, we are truly facing a national emergency. How we act individually and collectively will determine whether we will survive as a functioning society or break into anarchic and bloody conflict. I am confident that we will find within ourselves the spiritual and moral resources not only to survive, but to continue as a great and enduring nation."

The emergency broadcast signal sounds again with the words, "This concludes this special broadcast of the Emergency Alert System. Further notices regarding the pandemic can be found on the site cdc.gov."

"I think it's very hopeful," says Grace, an optimist at heart. They certainly sound like they're still in control."

Allegra half laughs. "It's a relief to know we even have a government."

Cyrus is still thinking about the stolen antivirals. He asks Grace, "Are you going to the shelter?"

"Tomorrow. I've been trying to get in touch with Dr. Longi, but a lot of communications are down."

Jack, upstairs shaving, happens to see a vehicle he doesn't recognize come up the lane. He watches as his mother, wearing a facemask, goes out to greet the car, a late-model Porsche. Presently, Bella Pulans and a man in his twenties enter the house accompanied by Grace. Jack, clattering down the stairs, knows exactly what is afoot. After years of saying she would have nothing to do with Sugar Mountain, openly and snippily deriding it, Bella wants in. Along, no doubt, with the big supercilious guy with the loafers, expensive creased slacks, and cashmere sweater.

Jack greets both of them with a cold nod. To his mother, he says, "What's up?"

Grace says, "Bella and her friend have just driven down from north of Hanover. There's no flu reported there and they're symptom free."

"You're sure?"

"The Connecticut River valley is still considered safe. She wants to join us."

Jack says, "We don't have room. We already have one more

57

person than we planned for."

"Who?" Grace is puzzled.

"Chee."

Bella turns to him, all simpering smiles and batting eyes. She is on the heavy side with lank, dark hair pulled back in a ponytail to the disadvantage of a round, sallow face. She has on a shirt, bomber jacket, and skin-tight yoga pants that do her too much justice. "Oh, Jack, really. You won't even notice us. And how are you? This is Marko Slone. He's my special friend."

Jack ignores the man, who is blond and muscled. "I'm sorry, we don't have room."

"I'm your cousin."

He shakes his head.

"We can pay," Bella says, a little less cocky.

"Big time," says Marko, now openly appraising his surroundings.

"Money is meaningless." Jack resists a homicidal fantasy. Quick burst from an M4. "It won't buy you anything."

Meredith comes in and her daughter rushes to greet her.

"Jack says we can't stay." Bella leads her mother over to where Jack stands, his face grim.

"She can have my place," Meredith says.

Jack says, "It doesn't work that way, Meredith."

"Well, if she can't stay, then I'm leaving."

"And if Marko can't stay," I'm leaving." Bella knows when she has the upper hand.

Jack swears to himself. He says, pointing himself at Bella, "For the last couple of years you've done nothing but mock us about what we've tried to arrange. And now you come crawling and you don't even have the grace to admit you were wrong."

She shrugs. "Okay, I was wrong."

"We need to meet." Jack speaks to his father with resignation already in his voice. "You can check on Ari later."

They assemble the Family Council, an interim governing committee that comprises Jack, Thad, Cyrus, Grace, and Frank. Jack knows it will be hopeless. But he wants his say as they sit in the studio around the table. He launches right into it. "If we do not insist to the letter on what we agreed, then we won't survive. None of us. I'll bet anything that neither one has had a flu shot. And that was the unconditional condition that we agreed to. Besides all that, Bella is a walking liability and God knows what jerko is." The muscles of his face are taut with suppressed anger. "If we can't enforce the most basic rule..."

He is thinking again about Denny Silva and how he hasn't heard from him. How he should call him. How his comrade and family and not these losers should be taken care of.

"We have more than enough food and things stocked..." Grace says. "I can give them both a shot and I have some Tamiflu and Relenza on hand. But I doubt it will be necessary." She's afraid her sister is mindless enough to leave. She's still haunted by the memory of Edith left standing alone with her bag.

Jack shakes his head. "Right here and now, yes. But we may not be able to stay here. Supplies at the fallback location will be minimal. At best." But he knows he can't hold out against his mother, not with his father wavering and with Frank in something of a daze agreeing with everyone.

Thad says, "I agree with Jack. But maybe we could give them a tent and some supplies. They could set up across the stream on the Fallgren place. No one's there."

"They'll be over here all the time," says Jack.

Grace speaks again, a mother's authority in her voice. "I'll make sure they conform. Because, Jack, really, I can't make Meredith leave. You know how ill she is. She's depressed. She's very nearly suicidal. Things are bad enough."

Cyrus is clearly agitated. "It's getting worse by the minute out there. A lot of the news media are no longer broadcasting. That White House performance was not at all reassuring."

Jack insists, "Which is precisely why we have to turn them away. We are going to be on our own."

Grace says, "Oh, come on, Jack, you've never liked Bella. Admit it."

"Of course, but right now that's beside the point."

"What exactly would you do for them?" Grace is ready to challenge him.

"I would... I don't know. Give them a tent and let them set up in the Fallgren place."

Cyrus sighs audibly. "Jack, your mom's right. We can't make them leave. Bella is family... for better or worse."

"Then where are we going to put them?" Jack stands up, sits down. He wants to do something with his hands.

Cyrus says, "There are quarters just above here..."

"Those are for Ari and Lise and Rachael." Jack will insist on this. "They have actually put in time not to mention financial support. Meredith, who's far from poor, has contributed exactly nothing."

"Jack... We haven't heard from Ari and Lise in twenty-four hours."

"No. But we will..."

"Then there's the space in the equipment shed bay." Cyrus glances at Grace.

Grace makes a face. "It's not finished..."

Jack shakes his head, pulls in breath through clenched teeth. He knows when he is beaten. "It's that or nothing. They can stay out there as long as they conform. To the letter. And I do this under protest. And if they don't conform to the letter, they're out of here."

He leaves the meeting with a determined look on his sharp face. Out of earshot of the others, he takes out his cell phone and punches in the number for Denny Silva. He scarcely knows what he will say. He's thinking: a tent at the Fallgren place. A couple of tents while they rig up something adequate. He hears the noises of connection and momentarily expects a "Hey, Cap, what's up?" The line goes dead. He tries again. Nothing.

At his laptop trying to re-establish contact with Ari and his family, Cyrus knows Jack is right. He also knows there will come a point when they will have to get brutal, even with those they love. Because, for all his planning and thought, he can scarcely comprehend the surreal nightmare of reality from which they can no longer awake. That comes home to him as, between attempts to find Ari's vehicle and checking the surveillance monitors, he flips via satellite from one news program to another, to scenes of collapse, chaos, violence, and despair.

Duvall was right about suicide on Boston Common. More than one group. The bodies of affluent-looking people of all ages, some still holding hands, lay around just across from Park Street.

Over Washington, smoke plumes into the already blighted sky as crowds mill around burning and looting.

Off the Florida coast, a cruise ship has drifted onto a reef, its crew already gone in the tenders and life boats. On deck passengers are holding up signs that read "help!"

The cities of China, where corpses have lain in the streets for weeks, look like petri dishes in an experiment gone bad.

Closer to home, Humvees with National Guard insignia prowl the roads. But to enforce the law or to break it?

No one voices it as night falls but they all think it: Ari, his daughter Rachael, his wife Lise, and her mother Chee are not going to make it.

6

On the third morning of the in-gathering, Grace takes Frank's small car after charging it and drives down the town road west as it descends toward the town center and, just beyond that, the district middle school. There the cafeteria has been set up as an emergency center. She wears the equivalent of a hazmat suit – coveralls and a hat as well as a facemask.

Dr. Paul Longi and Eve Rugg, a nurse assistant, meet her at the door. People are already starting to gather, picking up masks as they arrive and sitting on the plastic chairs set up in rows facing a table near the front.

The doctor, an older, retired general practitioner, gestures Grace and the nurse into a side room. He doesn't wear a mask. His pallid face is worried. "We don't have any antivirals to administer to anyone...regardless." He keeps his voice low as he confirms reports that the consignment of Tamiflu and other anti-virals for Franklin County have been stolen. "The commandant told me a group of renegade members of the Guard broke into the building where the anti-virals were stored, killed an officer and two enlisted men and walked off with the whole stock."

Grace thinks again of the McFeralls, Duncan and Bruce. She asks, "They don't know who took them?"

The doctor shrugs. "If they do, they're not saying anything. There's not a whole lot of command and control left there. Or anywhere else for that matter. I doubt you'll find a store that's not been broken into and looted, especially drug stores and food stores."

The news startles Grace. "Even around here?"

The doctor looks wonderingly at her.

Eve Rugg, a pleasant-faced younger woman states the obvious: "We need to tell people what's happened."

Grace asks, "But there must be something else we can do..."

The doctor puts on his hat and shakes his head. "Tell them

to..." He sighs. "There is nothing to tell them. A lot of them, a lot of us, will not survive."

"What about this emergency station?"

"What's the point now? It will only act as a vector for infecting the healthy ones that show up here."

"You're leaving?" Grace is incredulous.

"I am. And it's what I would prescribe for everyone."

Eve Rugg puts on her jacket as well. "Good luck, Grace." She holds her hand up to her face and then turns and leaves abruptly.

The cafeteria has begun to fill up as Grace, alone, goes back out to face the townspeople. Among them are some she knows well, some she recognizes, and a few she has never seen before. She moves to the table in front of the counter where hot lunches are served when the school is in session. "Friends, neighbors," she begins.

"Where's our medicine?" a young woman with a babe in arms all but screams at her. A rumble of assent goes through the room.

"I can only report what the commandant of the Greenfield Armory has told Dr. Longi. The supply of antiviral medicine for Franklin County was stolen at gun point. Three men were murdered in the robbery."

"Aw come off of it," someone shouts above the ensuing din. "You medical types took it for yourselves and your families."

"As a matter of fact, we haven't," Grace says, when something resembling order has been restored. "And I am not a medical type, I am a volunteer." She ponders telling them that Tamiflu might prove useless against this particular scourge.

"We want our medicine..."

"Please let me speak."

The hubbub quiets down. "As far as I know, a renegade unit of the local Guard, three men, apparently, murdered an officer and two enlisted men. Those killers, whoever they are, have become the distributors of what antivirals there were... I suggest that if you know anyone in the Guard that you give them a call. In any case it may only be Tamiflu which has not proven all that..."

"The rich people have the stuff," one heavy, middle-aged man says. He has not bothered to put on a mask.

"I'll bet the McFeralls are in on this," someone says.

Grace holds up her hand once more. "I can only advise you to stock up on whatever you can and try to wait until this... thing blows over."

She is drowned out again. She waits to speak. "If any antivirals show up, I'll notify everyone I can and distribute them."

"How are you going to get in touch?" a worried mother asks.

"Communications are already starting to come down."

"I'll post notices around the town with the times I'll be available here if the antivirals show up. I would appreciate it if any of you would volunteer. I will do what I can, but frankly, it won't be much. I'm assuming now that you are all flu free. If you have folks or friends fleeing from near Boston or New York to stay with you, I would suggest you set up an ironclad quarantine, and that's not easy to do."

"How long's this thing going to last?" asks Parker Johnson, a local farmer who had begun to stock up a year before and was part of a loose confederation of survivalist groups that Cyrus kept contact with.

"No one really knows, Parker. A few weeks. Months? A year? I think it took the Spanish influenza a year to burn itself out. And even when it's over, there will be other pathologies... diseases."

A man Grace recognizes but whose name she can't recall says, "How come you medical people didn't let us know sooner this was going to happen?"

She sighs. "If it is an engineered flu, there is no way the CDC or anyone else could have prepared for its release whether that release was deliberate or more than likely an accident. But, you're right. I think the extent of the pandemic caught the authorities off-guard. And when they started to issue warnings, people thought they were crying wolf."

"Yeah, but this wolf's real."

"And right at our door."

Leaving a lot of disgruntled people in the cafeteria, Grace

continues west to a road that veers back to the east and then south and downhill to a sprawl of dereliction where the McFeralls live as one large extended family. Located in a gloomy looking place known as Pitts Hollow, it is borderline Dogpatch, a hillbilly setting with vehicles and implements lying around in various states of decrepitude amidst buildings both half finished and half falling down.

"Well, I expected you'd come calling," Duncan McFerall says, opening the door to the main habitation and releasing a waft of bacon frying. "All those Arkwright men afraid to come and face me. Send their mama, huh?"

"They have no idea that I'm here."

"Don't tell me. You think me and Bruce took all the medicines?"

Grace, her mask in place, says, "So you know about it?"

"Well, yeahhh..." He is a large, still handsome man, his swept-back hair starting to thin, his heavy face set in a skeptical if not dismissive expression.

To her relief, he doesn't invite her in. Grace has always found it difficult to believe that Cyrus and Duncan McFerall are kinfolk, however distant. "I thought you might know something about what happened to them?"

"And what makes you think I'd tell you if I did?"

"Duncan, people are going to start dying. A lot of people. Your friends and neighbors. If we don't start distributing them now." She is exaggerating, but it might save some lives.

"You mean to say that if we have the stuff or know where to get it then... I mean we'd be like gods."

"Dunc..." But she cannot tell if he is serious or not. His humor came with a mean streak.

He says, "Do you need some for your own people? I notice you've got quite a crowd gathered there. But of course you don't. The medicals always take care of themselves first, don't they?"

There is venomous glee in his pale eyes. "You know what it used to say on the wall in the locker room? It said, 'when the going gets tough, the tough get going.' And the times, lady, are getting tough."

65

Strange, Grace thinks, when civility goes, the worst becomes possible. She says, "You might want to know that most of the antivirals are a version of Tamiflu. They may not be very effective."

"We're just going to have to live with that, aren't we?"

"Or die with it."

For a moment he seems to realize they are in the same badly leaking boat. Then the old machismo takes over. "Yeah, die with it. There's gonna be a lot of dying and it ain't going to be me."

She turns to go.

"Oh, and by the way, you tell Cyrus that he'll be hearing from the McFeralls. You know, about that unsettled matter between us."

Grace drives home slowly. The town has already changed, with little or no traffic on the roads and with a shuttered aspect to the houses and the general store in the center of town. There is no appeal to the law. There are nothing but voice messages at the county sheriff and the state police. Without them, Duncan and Bruce McFerall will become the law, at least for the time being. What could she say, anyway? I think the McFerall brothers have the stolen antivirals?

*

For decades an ugly if somewhat farcical enmity has existed between the Arkwrights and the McFeralls. With the kind of pertinacity, perhaps typical of a Highland heritage, Duncan "Dunc" McFerall, the elder of the brothers, has openly nursed the fallacy that the Arkwrights had done their family out of the Sugar Mountain property, starting when Cyrus' great grandfather married into the McFeralls. Hardworking Seth Arkwright bought out the rest of the presumptive heirs. There was, admittedly, some sharp dealings in the transactions, but nothing overtly illegal. Seth passed the property on to successive generations of Arkwrights with the unwritten proviso that it remain intact and in the family.

Chance more than anything kept the farm in the Arkwright name. Chance, because, over the decades, most of Seth's descendants preferred the rich soil of Iowa or the fleshpots of California to the rigors of farming in the northern Berkshires of Massachusetts, where the ground grew rocks. Not so the McFeralls, who stayed put, equating their relative misery with regional loyalty as they nursed their grievance about having been done out of their birthright.

Their legal harassment of the Arkwrights about the property gave the McFeralls' claim a spurious on-again, off-again credibility, at least among the malcontents, petty criminals, part-time bikers, and swamp Yankees that constituted the brothers' circle of friends. If paid lawyers were involved, there had to be something to it. People more than once heard Dunc and Bru, well into their cups, vehemently agreeing that they should just "go up there and take what's ours."

Duncan in particular took a sour pleasure in nursing this grievance. A member of the National Guard and a ner-do-well contractor by trade, he had a reputation for bullying and, on occasion, resort to his fists. The word around the local bars: you didn't mess with Dunc McFerall.

If anything, his brother Bruce is worse. Bruce had been a deputy sheriff until he beat up a local boy so badly the kid lost sight in one eye. That landed Bruce out of a job and a year in prison. Others began to come forward with accounts of the man's brutality.

Until now, Cyrus dismissed the brothers as pathetic, the kind of people you don't take seriously except for their persistence. One night about a year before, Bruce accosted Cyrus and Grace at the Charlemont Inn, where they has gone to have a drink and watch a Red Sox game on the television at the end of the bar.

"So how's our farm doing?" Bruce began, standing right beside them, already the worse for drink. In his mid-fifties, a big man like his brother but going to fat, Bruce had a red, glabrous face that seemed enlarged by a balding pate and watery, oyster eyes.

Cyrus turned and regarded the eyes steadily. "The farm's going fine, thanks."

"Yeah, I see you've been clearing one of the upland pastures.

The one my great great granddaddy first cleared."

"Jack's working on it."

"That right? What's he planning to do there?"

"I think you should ask Jack."

He slit his eyes and made his voice ugly. "Maybe I'll do that."

Cyrus thought to himself then that this man would be dangerous if a crisis ever started. He said, "But I'd be careful around Jack if I were you."

"Is that right?"

"That is right." Cyrus leaned into the other's face. "He's not long back from the service, you know. More than ten years in special ops. Some pretty rough stuff behind the lines, I'm told. Covert operations. Counter-terrorism. He might take your bluster seriously and decide to do something about it. He knows how to mess things up. Especially people." Cyrus paused as though in thought. "And you know what I hate to admit to myself?"

"What's that?"

"I think he enjoys it."

The man tried to smile dismissively, but like most bullies he could be cowed. The swagger drained from his face. He muttered a "sheeit," and turned away.

"Good for you," Grace murmured to her husband. She sipped from her whiskey sour and turned back to the screen.

But at the time, Cyrus had cursed himself inwardly. The McFeralls were a nuisance, but a nuisance best ignored. But then, it might be wise to let them know that Jack, however determined to be a civilian, was not someone to threaten idly.

Grace leaves the squalor of Pitts Hollow and drives homeward in a state of foreboding occasioned by more than the catastrophe that is destroying the world around them. The McFeralls are a mean bunch with lots of weapons of their own, never mind what they might steal from the armory. And when food and other necessities begin to grow scarce, they will come calling with intent. More ominously, if they have acquired a supply of antivirals, and Duncan's gloating face tells her as much, then they have the means of recruiting a small army of their own.

68

All of which she reports to Cyrus and Jack back at the farm.

"It means we should get that fence in place as soon as possible," Cyrus says.

Jack's eyes take on a distant, predatory stare. He says, "I could go over there after dark and talk to them."

"You mean murder them," his father says, a frown in his voice. "I don't think that would be necessary."

Cyrus says flatly, "We don't use violence until it's absolutely necessary to protect our lives. We need to have a meeting."

*

The McFeralls have good reason to covet Sugar Mountain. Located on a town road that swings high above Route 2 to within three hundred yards of the front of the house, the farm with its maples and idyllic setting has a picture book beauty without in the least looking trite. The drive from the road comes up through an orchard, mostly apple trees spaced on the east side, and berry patches along with newly planted grape vines on the west side. The drive crosses a curiously wide and deep ditch over a metal bridge and makes a wide loop in front of the property. The house, clapboarded, white, and trimmed with green shutters, sets back behind a gently sloping lawn. A dry stonewall three feet high with irregular crenulations crosses the middle of the lawn parallel to the front of the house. That it lacks a gap for the walk from the main door makes it look like something Andy Goldsworthy might have thought of. A lane from the right side of the loop leads to a graveled yard in front of the colonnaded porch before continuing on to a parking area behind an impressive array of solar panels. A lane from the left of the loop goes by the west side of the house to the mill.

The farm, as it gets called, comprises the house and a group of outbuildings, many put up in the mid-nineteenth century and arranged to the east and north of where the old barn once stood. These include the horse barn, which perches to the east of the barn garden. It not only provides the most comfortable accommodations outside of the house, but it has two root cellars.

One of the open bays of the ell-shaped equipment shed that anchors the northwest corner of the barn cellar, now a garden, has been walled off in the front and fitted with a door and windows. It already has a functioning sink and toilet, but remains unfinished as a bedsitter. Not far to the east is another shed, this one split between the hen house and the goat barn. A ramp leads down to the barn garden just beyond the southeast corner where stands a silo that survived the fire. The silo has been strengthened to hold a large cistern half way up and, at the ground level, modified with an addition to serve as a bathhouse. In all, there is room at Sugar Mountain for upwards of twenty adults and children to live comfortably.

The house started as a cabin built in 1790 by Jeremiah McFerall, a Highland Scot who served with distinction in the local militia against the British. It stands facing south below the summit of Sugar Mountain, a high wooded hill surmounted by good pasturelands. Over the decades and then the centuries, the home grew in characteristic style. In 1804, as the farm prospered, a handsome woodframe house in the Federalist style was raised next to the cabin making the latter a west wing. Also facing south, the new house had a central stairway in the front joining the two large rooms upstairs with those downstairs.

Successive generations saw a bathroom added, central heating, modern plumbing, extensions to the rear and the cabin raised to two stories. In time, they put up a barn for a dairy herd, an equipment shed, and the other outbuildings. They continued to clear land, opening up several well-watered upland meadows.

It was here that the McFeralls, who merged with the Arkwrights when Fanny of the former married Seth of the latter shortly after he returned from the Civil War. They maintained a small dairy herd. Seth Arkwright also collected and produced maple syrup from a sugar bush of several hundred rock maples planted decades before. He enlarged the sugaring shed to include a saw mill powered by Talbot Brook. They generally prospered in their flinty, Calvinist way.

Cyrus, though strongly attached to the place, had ambitions other than farming and the year-round daily grind it entailed. He was a senior at Williams when his widowed mother decided to lease the buildings and land to the Fallgrens, who owned and worked the adjacent farm to the west. That freed Cyrus to pursue a career in architecture while at the same time keeping Sugar Mountain in the family.

With the news about the antivirals and Grace's account of her encounter with Duncan McFerall, the Sugar Mountaineers, as Thad whimsically dubbed them, hold a meeting of the adults that afternoon in the family room. Bella and Marko show up late and generally loll as they sit as though bored by the talk about work schedules, crews, security systems, and the round-the-clock surveillance. But then, Bella and Marko have so far been given only menial work to do. They have not been assigned any watches. They are not yet, as far as Jack is concerned, full members.

"But, come on, Jack, who is going to attack us?" Bella asks in a don't-be-so-tiresome voice.

"People who are hungry and desperate and well-armed," he says with deliberate civility.

"Really, Jack," Meredith puts in, "I think Bella has a point."

Jack stands and clicks on the big screen over the fireplace. He looks directly at his aunt. "Here, Meredith, are a few news items that should give you some sense of the situation." He waits until he has her attention. "Here's a YouTube snippet of the shopping center off the rotary just outside of Greenfield." The screen fills with a view of an empty parking lot. "From what we've been able to gather, Big Y has been looted along with most of the other stores in the area."

"So people have plenty of food..."

"Some people will have food for a while. Then they will need more."

He flicks on another scene. "This is the main street in Orange, just east of here." The screen shows a scene of desolation, mostly buildings gutted by fire.

The sad litany goes on. They are looking at a video of a

devastated Vassar College campus when Nicole comes in from the recon room where she has been on duty. "It's Ari! I recognize the van! They're coming up the lane!"

They all rush to the windows. And then out onto the graveled area next to the porch. Grace, pulling on her face mask, motions the others to stand back. She approaches the van and tells the occupants to wait until she has questioned them.

"We are greatly relieved to see you. And welcome to Sugar Mountain, all of you." She goes through the necessary questions. No, they haven't been in the company of anyone since they left New Jersey with Chee Xu. Yes, they have all have flu shots. None of them has any symptoms.

Grace takes off her mask to embrace the arrivals. It is a signal for the others to crowd around, the kids jumping with excitement, the adults only a little less restrained. "The prodigals," Cyrus remarks to Duvall and joins in the welcome.

Meredith embraces her son in her cool way, bends to kiss Rachael on the cheek, and shakes hands with Lise about whom her feelings are complicated. Why ever did Ari marry this little Chinese thing? But then, didn't she marry a Jew, two Jews, come to think of it. As for Chee, a stooped and wrinkled but spry older woman, well, a smile and a nod suffice.

Ari's happiness at arriving spills over to include even his half sister, Bella. Though he wonders how she managed to insinuate herself. Bella, always a bit out of sorts around Ari, especially when he is the center of attention, manages a stiff smile but stands back.

Thad and Duvall organize the unloading of the van while Nicole makes a quick snack for the new arrivals. Then they are shown to their rooms upstairs for a much needed rest. "You can tell us your adventures over dinner this evening," says Cyrus, whose smile shows immense relief and just a touch of triumph.

7

Allegra writes in her journal:

The arrival of Ari and his family did much to revive Frank's drooping spirits. A remnant of his old world has wafted in. He and Ari were up well into the night the day they arrived talking for hours about the old days. What's impossible to grasp is that the old days, which are gone, probably forever, were only days ago.

These first days have been like orientation week at a survival camp. The difference being this is a survival camp without a larger world with guys in helicopters standing by to come to the rescue if things go bad. This is not a reality show. We are alone.

I am still sore from helping to put in the footings for the perimeter fence. Theoretically, it should have been easy as Jack and Cyrus have already dug the holes for the concrete into which we insert metal sleeves for the posts while the stuff is still soft. Cyrus says we could have used the PTO from the tractor to run the cement mixer, but we need to save fuel. Once the cyclone fence goes up, I think it will feel like we've built our own prison, especially with the barbed wire curling along the top of it. It's supposed to go all the way around the buildings when it's finished with a fortified entrance gate in the front. It hadn't occurred to me before that the ditch running along the lower end of the lawn is really a dry moat. And the metal structure spanning it is a drawbridge, one they can take apart in minutes.

I get the feeling they know something that alarms them, but what I can only imagine. News broadcasts have become sketchy at best.

I haven't heard from Mom and Dad or Dina or Sebastian in days. I hope, I pray they are all right, but I doubt it. Poor dad, the way he used to scoff when Frank told him what Cyrus was up to. Until Sandy. What most people failed to grasp was that if the flu didn't get you, so many other things could once a pandemic began. I never thought it would happen. Everyone's been anguishing over missing friends and family. Grace has been besieged with calls from neighbors. She tells them to call back when things get really bad. She had the foresight – and the humanity – to provide what she calls "public caches" in various locations.

She left this morning for the emergency shelter in our car because it uses little fuel. She looked like Halloween in her bright orange hazmat outfit. She could scarcely talk about it when she came back. "I have nothing really to give them," she told me, close to tears. "Not a shred of hope. It's already like a terminal ward with sick people dying on cots in the gym and no one to tend them."

I can't bring myself to listen to the news, what there is of it. There's no longer any coverage. Everything seems to have stopped. It's like hitting a pause button when you're watching a movie. Only there's no play button. There really aren't any words for what's happening. Mass extinction, maybe. But that makes it sound painless, like something that happened in the Jurassic, something you find evidence for in buried rocks. And if not total extinction, then what? Another genetic bottleneck? Another nice pseudo-clinical phrase masking the suffering, misery, and terror of those who, as I write, are dying by the millions, the billions. Whole families. Little girls. Teenagers. Mothers.

The stories Ari and Lise told the night they arrived. Families trudging along the road carrying what they could. Thank God the weather's been okay. And not just "out there." All around the tendrils linking me and others to family and friends and dear, dear loved ones are being cut. All our little devices are but links to a void.

Allegra's eyes blur with tears of pity and self-pity. What has happened to her mom and dad in their pleasant brick house on Staten Island? Her sister Dina. Her brother Sebastian, his Mary and their two little boys, Jonathan and Peter. All dead now? They can't be. She has tried their phones, their e-mails, the local police. Nothing. Like so much else they seem to have disappeared. Allegra waits out the disabling spell of grief. Drying her tears, she puts pen to paper again:

At least Lance has gotten through to his mom and dad. A text message from them says they have been allowed to join a survivor commune in the desert north of Santa Fe when they showed up with a van full of provisions. It said they would be in touch as soon as possible but, like a lot of survival groups, they were keeping a communications silence and maintaining a very low profile until the worst of the crisis had blown over.

We live in a limbo of hope mingled with grief and incipient grief that weighs on us like a duty we can't perform. Get on with your own life is easy to say, but all those people are your life. Or had been. So now I feel the hope and grief giving way to guilt and anger. What we have is not so much a brave new world but the tattered remnants of the old one.

It breaks my heart that Frank cannot cope. Whereas Jack and Cyrus thrive in this kind of adversity – and even as Ari responds – Frank withers. He is angry and scared, but his anger has no object unless it is I, which I don't understand. Perhaps he is scared for us. He senses that he won't, can't survive and the prospect fills him with anguish. He had been a thoughtful, even passionate husband and a good, doting, if absent-minded dad to Lily. Had been until he got all caught up working on the Siemens deal. Now it's as though he's marooned on a desert island with no Friday in sight. Mere survival isn't enough for him. He feels, he told me in one of the few times he has confided in me lately, that he has become obsolete. He's not alone in thinking that. Where does a professor of English fit in this awful new world?

For that matter, where does a book titled <u>The Poem as Object</u> fit in? I might still do it. I have a draft, a very rough *draft. The research is done. My notes are all here. But to what end? Right now the world needs poetry, heroic, tragic poetry, not books about poetry.*

*

It is an orientation week in more ways than one. Within days of the arrival of Ari and his family, they hold the first official meeting of the community members. They convene in the kitchen in mid-afternoon with attendance obligatory. A special pot of coffee is brewed to go with rhubarb tarts. Rachael and Mary, the nine-year-olds, are put in charge of the two younger children in front of the television. They watch an old Disney film about dogs.

Without much discussion, the meeting begins by confirming Cyrus as "Presiding Director" of "The Sugar Mountain Community," giving him broad executive powers.

Dressed in denim shirt and jeans, Cyrus thanks the gathered members. He speaks genially but with authority, saying, "Welcome all. I think you've all got copies of the contract Frank drew up some time ago. We want everyone to sign it, not so much for legal purposes but as a gesture that you agree completely with the community's rules. These will be strictly enforced. I don't need to tell you what the world situation is. The Federal government and the Commonwealth are both operating on an emergency basis, but just. There are sporadic broadcasts from Washington and Boston. I think it safe to say that civilian rule has all but disappeared..."

Lise raises a hand, her index finger up. She is slight, her beauty in her eyes, which seem to listen, and in her smile, which takes people by surprise. Even in work clothes, she looks stylish and her voice has a New York edge to it. "On the way here, we heard about local groups starting up and taking authority into their own hands."

Cyrus turns to Jack. Jack says, "That may be happening elsewhere. Around here we've heard reports of ad hoc committees trying to come together and establish some sort of order at the town or county levels. But with the epidemic raging, very little seems to be holding."

76

Cyrus waits for other comments. He continues. "We have been in contact with the survival network to which we belong here in Franklin County. This and other groups like it may eventually form the basis of some form of democratic governance. We need it. We have also heard reports of farms not all that far from here being taken over forcibly and their owners thrown out on the road and in some cases murdered. At present, these reports are little better than rumors, but I think they signify."

He paused to let that register.

"We don't know how bad the epidemic has become in this area. Nationwide, according to the last CDC report, which apparently leaked out, the mortality rate of the flu for those without flu shots and antivirals is close to seventy-five percent."

He stops speaking because Thad, who has transferred the surveillance screens to his laptop, puts up his hand. "There's a van coming up the lane."

"Fast or slow?" Jack asks.

"Slow."

Jack gets up and peers over Thad's shoulder. "It's not one I recognize. Defense Squad stand by. Mom, get into your hazmat gear."

"We'll resume shortly," Cyrus says as everyone begins to rise and leave.

Wearing only a mask that she keeps handy, Grace goes out the front door just as the large green and white van rattles over the metal bridge and pulls to a stop at the top of the loop.

A woman in a headscarf gets out and approaches.

Grace puts up a hand and says, "Please, stand back."

The woman, young, blonde, and from wealth, judging from her clothes and accent, says in a panicky, peremptory voice, "We have seven children and we need help. Bella says we could come here."

Grace notices Arabic lettering on the side of the van. Dark-haired children peer out of the windows and a tall man of Middle-eastern appearance sits in the driver's seat.

"Bella is mistaken," Grace says. "We have no room here."

The driver gets out and comes around to stand beside the

woman. "We need place to stay," he says in broken English. "We need food."

"There is no room here," Grace repeats herself. "We can give you some food, but you must leave immediately."

"Children sick. Need beds." He begins to draw closer.

"Jack!" Grace calls.

Jack, who is watching the confrontation from just inside the front door, steps out. He cradles a double-barreled shotgun in his right arm. He approaches quickly and in a snapped off voice says, "Please get back inside the vehicle and stay there."

When the pair hesitate, he raises the gun and points it at them. "Now."

They do so reluctantly.

Grace is about to say something when the door flings open behind her and Bella comes down the front walk and over the stone wall. "Allison!" she calls to the woman in the van and starts toward it.

Grace grabs her. "The children are infected. You have to keep back."

Jack turns to Duvall who is just emerging from the house. "Get Bella to hell out of here."

Not that Bella isn't already backing off. A moment of calm ensues.

Grace says, "What are the symptoms of the children?"

Talking through an open window of the van in a sullen, defeated voice, the woman named Allison says, "Coughing, diarrhea, fever... Do you have any medication?"

Bella says, "We have medicines..."

The driver, pounding the wheel: "Please. We need help."

Grace turns to Jack. "We have to do something."

He shakes his head. "Tell her we will dig out a tent, some food and other supplies. They can pick it up down the lane. Tell them to drive east, which is left, then right after a little more than a mile. There's an old logging road there. Not far in are woods and a stream. They can use the van and the tent for shelter. It's the best we can do."

He doesn't relax his vigil with the shotgun until the supplies have been carried down the lane by Duvall and Lance. And until the van has picked them up and driven off.

Cyrus calls a recess. "Reconvene at four-thirty," he tells those still in the kitchen.

They meet again. Feelings are raw. It is Lise, practiced in eliciting unspoken doubts, who brings up the matter in the front and back of everyone's mind: "Was the gun really necessary?"

Marko puts in, "Yeah, what was that all about?"

Jack nods, giving Marko a quick hard stare. "The real question is whether or not I was prepared to use it."

"Were you?" Ari asks neutrally.

"If those children had gotten out and started to run around, we could have been infected," says Nicole. She is troubled by what has happened, but she will stand by her man.

Jack, looking down, speaks as though to the table in front of him. "We need to face the fact that there will be times when violence will be necessary to defend ourselves. If you do not agree with that as a condition for staying here, then you should in all good conscience leave. If you stay you are giving tacit consent to the use of violence to defend ourselves. As for this incident, you should know that one barrel was loaded with a blank and one with birdshot. The noise from the blank is very convincing."

Meredith sniffs, "But they were children."

Jack looks at his aunt. "As Nicole says, they were more than likely infected. If you want to go and nurse them back to health, Meredith, I'm sure Grace can equip you with supplies and drive you over to them. Of course, you won't be allowed back here."

"And would you use the gun on me?"

He smiles. "Only if I have to."

Bella stands up and sits down. "That's not funny. Not one bit." She turns to Ari. "Aren't you going to say anything?"

He shrugs. "I agree with Jack."

Jack leans forward. He points his face at Bella. "We are on a war footing whether you like it or not. If those kids had gotten out and among us, half of us would be sick and dying in a week, two at the best." Of a sudden, he is at war again, in command mode. He eyes take in everyone and his voice is like an insistent growl. "There cannot be contact with anyone outside of this group under any circumstances except for Grace. We need to wake up! God damn it!"

Ari raises his hands in the ensuing hubbub. "Let's face it, folks, Jack is right. If one tiny virus gets in here, most of us won't survive."

Duvall says, "Yeah, and what do we do when the guys with guns show up?"

Thad turns on Bella. "What the hell are you doing telling people to come here? You don't even belong here."

She tries to look arch, but succeeds only in the petulance of a spoiled heavy kid. "I told them to come because... I didn't really think they could make it."

Thad laughs into her face. "Boy, does that ever sum you up."

Bella turns to Marko. But he says nothing as he lounges back, a half smirk on his face.

Cyrus calls them to order. "I think what this episode points up most decidedly is that we will not, under any circumstances whatsoever, be taking in any more new members. I know that we all have family and friends out there who need a place of refuge. Because we are remote, it really is advisable for them to seek help where they are. It is both more merciful and easier to tell them to stay away at a distance. But even if they are close or coming close, we cannot take them in."

He pauses, looking at each of them in turn. He continues, "I know it sounds Draconian, but Sugar Mountain has neither extra food nor extra room. We already have three members that were not expected. To supplement our supplies, we will add to the acreage we plan to farm. But with random lawlessness and real violence out there, it's possible if not probable that we will not be able to stay here. If that happens, our supplies will indeed be limited."

Meredith glances around bewildered. "But if we can't stay here, where will we go?"

"Jack, why don't you speak to that," Cyrus says.

80

"We have a back-up refuge. I won't say where for now, but it will serve if necessary."

"Why the big secret?" Marko asks.

"If I told you I'd have to kill you," Jack says, the shadow of a threat behind his mirthless jibe.

"I'm really scared," Marko comes back.

"If you had any brains, you would be," Thad mutters just loud enough to be heard.

"Speaking of being scared," Cyrus starts. He reconsiders. "We'll come to that later. The situation out there is dire, but that is something Jack will speak to. Now..." He turns to his wife. "Grace, will you tell us about keeping quarantine."

She stands up. She looks careworn of a sudden. "It's very simple. If we don't keep strict quarantine and the flu gets in among us, then this whole enterprise will have been for nothing as most if not all of us will perish."

"Even with the antivirals?" Ari asks.

"Even with the antivirals. They have an untested efficacy with this strain of flu. I've listed symptoms on the bulletin board. I'll go over them now, but please be honest with yourself and with us if you develop a cough, diarrhea, fever, headache, muscle ache, runny nose or sore throat."

Frank, who has sat silently the whole time, speaks. "What if we just have a cold?"

Grace nods. "Good question. We have a test that will tell us in a few hours if you have the flu or not. If you do have it, you won't be thrown out. We have a couple of comfortable tents ready for on-ground quarantine."

"How is it spread?" Lise asks.

"Coughing, sneezing. Just talking. Just being around someone who's infected."

Jack raises his hand. "In reference to our back-up refuge, should we have to use it, we may have to collect cell phones and all similar devices if we decide to keep radio silence."

Lance asks "why?"

"Because they can be used to locate where we are."

Cyrus says, "Thank you, Jack. And, to reiterate something regarding communications. I know you all want to stay in touch with family and friends as long as possible. But, please, again, do not in any way encourage them to come here. If they do, they will be turned away. If you want to leave on that account, that will be your choice. We can direct you to caches of food that we have set up outside for others to use."

He stops and again glances around at each of them. "Is that clear to everyone?"

Into a few nods and general silence, he goes on. "It works the other way as well. Let me quote from the 'Articles of Necessity' you have all signed off on."

He waits for an agitated murmuring to subside before he begins. "Article Seven states, 'Any member who leaves the precincts of Sugar Mountain as defined below without permission or proper gear, will have to live in quarantine for two weeks if and when he or she returns. Anyone who leaves Sugar Mountain more than once without permission and proper gear will not be allowed back in.'"

Marko sounds a dismissive snort. "Oh, come on, who's going to enforce that?"

Cyrus doesn't look up. Unruffled, he says, "We will establish an internal security committee if we have to." He takes a deep breath. "Jack, Duvall, and Nicole all have training in keeping order. If coercion is necessary, they will provide it."

"What about due process?" Bella asks. "It sounds like we'll be living in a police state." She glances significantly at her boyfriend.

Cyrus nods as though agreeing. He says, "We all need to realize that we are in a life-and-death situation here. Anyone or anything that threatens the well-being of the community will not be tolerated. Having said that, I think we can count on ordinary decency to see that everyone is treated fairly."

"I second that," Duvall says.

There are ayes around the table.

Cyrus nods agreement with himself. He says, "Before we get to the situation in western Massachusetts and the world in general, I

82

would like to go over the contract that Frank helped us draft. As you can see, its preamble echoes that of the Mayflower Compact in calling for the establishment of a 'civil society carrying the force of law for the duration of the Sugar Mountain Community, hereafter referred to as the SMC.'"

He waits for questions. There are none. He reads aloud the "Bill of Necessities."

"Article One. No one else will be allowed to join the community once a crisis is under way and the in-gathering has begun..."

"To be strictly enforced hereafter," Jack interrupts.

"Right. On to Article Two. Any member who doesn't agree with the basic rules or with the decisions of the community, will be free to leave. If that member doesn't leave and his presence is deemed by the group to cause dissension sufficient to endanger the community, then that person will be forced to leave."

"Article Three. Contributions of time and labor will be according to ability and means. If any member who can work but chooses not to work, that member will not share in the community's food or other necessities." He pauses and adds, "Work schedules will be posted on the bulletin board two days in advance. Please inform the coordinator of the work team involved if you want to alter your time in any way."

"Article Four. All food will be communal." Again he pauses before continuing. "That doesn't mean you can't keep a small stash in your quarters. But there will be control over all food, especially coffee, tea, sugar, and alcohol.

"Article Five. All important decisions not involving defense will be decided by the Community Council, which includes all adults who qualify. Proposals will need a two-thirds majority to be acted on.

"Article Six. Other than extreme emergencies in which the lives of members are threatened, the use of violence must be sanctioned by a unanimous vote of the Defense Committee. The Defense Committee will comprise all members of the Defense Squad and the Family Council.

"Article Seven. We have already discussed that article. "Article Eight. Finally, any member may propose a new article. Such proposals will have to pass with a two-thirds majority to become an article in the contract." He looks up. "Any questions?"

To some surprise, it is Henry, his voice quavering, who asks, "You mentioned defense. Who is going to attack us?"

Cyrus nods as though agreeing with the sentiment of the question. He says, "I'll let Jack tell you all about that."

Jack smiles at his grandfather. A fellow combat veteran. "No one, Henry, I hope. But we'll be ready if they do." He pauses. "But to answer your question, I'll need the screen in the family room."

"Why don't we take a break," Nicole says. "We all need one."

The break lingers into an informal cocktail hour. Members show up with drinks and Chee agrees to watch the children. Jack doesn't like the informality. For him the defense of Sugar Mountain is the first priority. But then he relaxes and pops one of Nicole's dark home brews. He's more relieved than annoyed that Bella and Marko don't return. When Nicole offers to go get them, he tells her not to bother.

He stands next to the large screen with the remote in his hand. He clicks on scenes of devastation that, like those from a natural disaster, appear interchangeable. There are bodies in evidence. Tents out in fields. Building after building gutted by fire. Cars along the sides of roads with tarps rigged next to them.

He says, "As we can see already, chaos has spread well beyond the urban centers. There's looting and burning everywhere now in the northeast. What's called the rule of law has gone by the board. Thugs have taken over. Killing has become commonplace. The police have been overwhelmed. In fact some of the police have joined the mob along with members of the National Guard. Which means that some of the worst elements have sophisticated weaponry and equipment, including vectoring devices for tracing communications."

He lets that sink in. Then, "From what we've been able to gather, in this area, that is Franklin County, there may already be roving bands of armed and desperate people, including renegade

84

police and National Guardsmen."

He turns to the screen again. "Here's Boston. Here's Worcester."

"Why all the burnings?" Lise asks.

"A rumor got started that fire destroys the flu or prevents it. Some of it's probably just lawlessness."

"Where are you getting these pictures?" Allegra asks. She has been silent, taking notes.

Jack points to Thad. He says, "The net comes and goes, mostly goes, but there's a couple of sites where people are uploading their photos and video clips. Some are from police helicopter flyovers that have made it onto the net."

Marko and Bella come into the room. They look stoned and sexed. Marko flops into an armchair. Bella squats on the floor.

Jack dissembles his annoyance. He says, "I want to get back to the situation in this area. Dad, could you say a few words about that." Grace and Nicole glance at each other. They know Jack is trying to involve his dad in the defense of Sugar Mountain. Jack wants his father to face what they're up against, to voice it.

Cyrus sighs. "We do have a problem close at hand. As we may already have mentioned, a local family named McFerall claims that Sugar Mountain belongs to them. And because one of the two brothers making the claim is a member of the National Guard and another was in local law enforcement before he was kicked out, I'm afraid that, sooner rather than later, they may come up here and demand that we give up the farm to them. Should the rule of law collapse."

Grace interjects, "They and others may also come calling simply because they believe we have food and other supplies."

"We're talking about an armed attack?" Lance asks.

Jack signals to Cyrus that he'll take the question. "Exactly. To back up a bit, the McFeralls may have been behind the robbery of the antivirals from the armory. With those alone, they could recruit a following. But there's more." He again clicks on the large screen. It is a ghostly scene taken by a night vision lens. "This is the McFerall compound. Those vehicles to the left under the netting are Humvees one of which can be equipped with a fifty-caliber machine gun. Courtesy, no doubt, of Duncan, who belongs to the Guard."

"Where did you get those?" his father asks.

Jack smiles. "Thad has a new camera he wanted to test."

Cyrus doesn't smile back. "We need to talk about unauthorized excursions off the compound. Jack, that rule applies to you as well."

"Understood."

"I know Marge McFerall," Meredith says. "I can talk to her."

"We all know Marge," Grace says. "But the days of that kind of talking are gone."

"I could drop by..."

Thad bristles. "And get infected and bring it back for the rest of us? No way."

"In any event," Jack resumes, "we are going to continue manning and womanning the perimeter monitors on a round-the-clock basis. We are also going to expand and train our self-defense group." He pauses to take questions. There are none.

"Finally, we need to gather as much news and information as we can about what's happening in the area. If you come across anything while listening to the radio or surfing what's left of the internet, please let Cyrus or me know immediately."

"But how are we going to defend ourselves?" Bella asks. The scoffing tone is gone.

"We have weapons," Jack says. "And we know how to use them."

"More than a shotgun?"

"Much more."

Duvall, to elicit an answer he already knows, asks, "Yeah, but right now, like in ten minutes, what happens if we see the McFerall clan coming up the road towards the lane with their Humvees and a bunch of guys in trucks."

Jack smiles and says, "As you know, the first thing we do is dismantle the bridge over the ditch. It takes all of three minutes. That will keep the Humvees or any other vehicle from getting too close. In the meanwhile, you, Thad, Nicole, and I take up positions behind the stonewall that crosses the lawn. If it looks like we can't hold them, we evacuate out the back of the house and up to the refuge."

Cyrus, sensitive about weapons and their use, says, "As Jack will tell you, anyone who doesn't want to use deadly force to defend the community will be excused from doing so. And, as I've said before, anyone who disagrees on principle with the use of deadly force to defend ourselves will be generously provisioned if they decide to leave. In this regard, we will only use violence if attacked first." He glanced at Jack. "Isn't that right, Jack?"

His son smiles with a rueful look in his eyes. "Preemption has a long and honorable history."

Cyrus nods. "Including Pearl Harbor."

Grace says, "Given my interaction with the McFeralls recently, I think we should finish the security fence sooner than later." She explains how the fence of heavy gauge cyclone mesh would circle and enclose the buildings of the compound.

Jack's tone is accommodating in the manner of someone trying to emphasize his own points: "I agree with Grace. We should put the fence up sooner than later. Right now the Defense Squad consists of Nicole, Thad, Duvall, and myself. We'll shortly enlarge the squad and do some serious training. And, if things start to get snarky, we will go on a defense footing. That means we will not only continue round-the-clock surveillance, but we may start to ration food. And, of course, if we have to maintain radio silence, everyone will have to turn in their private communications devices."

Marko shakes his head with evident incredulity. "You gotta be kidding."

"About what?"

"Our cell phones."

Jack pauses to let his patience gather. He says in an even tone, "Let me explain what's been happening elsewhere. In brief, there have been credible reports of farms and refuges like this one being over-run by armed gangs. Reports of murder and pillaging are coming in. Cell phones and similar devices are radios. They let people know where we are. Because of that, should it become necessary, the only communications devices allowed will be our walkie-talkies and, when appropriate, the citizens band system." He looks directly Marko. There is menace in his voice. "Is that clear?"

Marko shrugs. "Sure. Whatever you say."

Thad sides with his brother. "Anyone who feels strongly about keeping their cell phone or whatever is certainly welcome to take it elsewhere."

"Amen," says Duvall. "We're with you, Jack."

Grace stands up. "I think it's time we made dinner."

8

There had been no livestock in the barn twenty years before when sparks from a frayed electrical wire ignited a clump of dusty hay. With no one around to report the fire, most of the large old structure turned into a spectacular blaze by the time the Headleyville Volunteer Fire Company sirened up the hill in its red pumping rig. They arrived in time to hose down the connecting structure, now the site of the family room, and to keep the fire from spreading to the house and the outbuildings.

"We couldn't have stopped it if there'd been wind," Russell Dunn told Cyrus and Grace several days later when they had driven out to walk around the still smoldering remains in the stone-lined cellar. Russell and his men had called in a couple of other companies and pumped water from Talbot Brook.

The Arkwrights had insurance, but no amount of money could bring back a structure made mostly of extinct American chestnut – from the eight-by-eight inch posts and beams joined by mortise and tenon with hand-hewn pegs to the inch-thick sheathing, some of it two feet wide.

Not that the family had any plans for the old barn at the time of the fire. The loft had held a mow of hay turning gray and the cellar was half full of manure dried and caked from the last winter cattle had been in the place. Before the fire Grace and Cyrus toyed with ideas of organic milk production, either with a small breed of cows like Jerseys or even with goats. They talked about starting a community for artisans and artists, but that would have changed the character of the place entirely.

Even back then, Cyrus began to plan the farm as a bastion of survival. Though serious about the prepper part of his scheme, he also knew that he wanted an excuse to create on a small scale a green, self-sustaining community in which living and working would be their own rewards.

"What about a swimming pool?" he proffered, during one brain-storming session when they were trying to decide what to do with the gaping wound left by the fire. Or a water reservoir. In either case he would have had to resurface the floor and seal with cement the cracks between the fieldstones that formed the walls of the cellar. They considered filling it in. Or building something else. But what? It was then that Grace, with her knack for landscaping, declared, "I want to keep it as a sunken garden."

Which she did, succeeding to the point where garden clubs began to include Sugar Mountain on their tours. Grace credited her success to the protected location and the soil – a rich humus of manure, wood ash, and loam. A colleague in Cyrus' firm helped her with the overall design. After cleaning out the charred rubble, restoring the drainage, and trucking in some topsoil, they started along the bottom of the north wall, espaliering a crab apple between two dwarf apple trees. They topped that with a hedge of kerria spaced with lilacs, which also served as a protective fence above the eight-foot drop. A pergola of wisteria served the same purpose along the top of the western side while a hedge of rosa rugosa lined the top of the eastern edge. Climbing roses, ivy, and clematis covered the exposed wall space below. On the southern end of the cellar, which was shallow because of the slope, Grace made terraced beds connected with flagged paths that led to the north side. There a small lawn surrounded an oval koi pond.

On the morning of their walkabout, Grace and Cyrus start at the barn garden – Grace having objected calling it Grace's Garden. It is past its full spring glory when the white lilacs spread like delicate lacing above and behind the yolk yellow kerria and when the wisteria began to open and scent the air and the apples showed pink next to the royal red of the crab apple on the south-facing wall.

Cyrus and Grace descend the flagged path and stop to chat with Henry and Chee who are putting in a kitchen garden where lilies and dahlias have been uprooted. "Looks great," Grace says, pointing to the rows of herbs and lettuce Chee has arranged. Chee nods and smiles and goes back to work. She will justify the kindness shown to her.

Henry, ruddy and young looking under an old straw hat,

90

hitches up his trousers and looks at the sky. "We could still get a frost," he says. "Thad and his friend..."

"Duvall."

"Yes, Duvall. They're going to help rig a night cover. I'd hate to lose these tomatoes." He indicates a pallet of plants already sizable and festooned with blossoms.

"And basil," Chee says. "Delicate."

Grace looks beyond the garden. "That damn fence is going to make even the flowers look imprisoned." She's referring to the security fence. A lot of the posts are already in place.

Her husband agrees. He glances at it ruefully. "And I hope we won't need it."

They circle the fish pond and go up the ramp on the east side that once provided access to the cellar. In the living room of the horse barn, they find Lance and Allegra organizing the children for classes.

"We're starting with English," Allegra tells them. "Even Lily. And then we'll do some science."

"I already know how to write," says Cy.

Rachael, a winsome combination of her father's robust face and her mother's delicate features, kids her cousin like a sister would. "He knows how to spell 'cat.'"

"I can spell lots of things. And I know lots of stuff you don't know..."

"Yeah, sure," says Mary, his real sister and tormenter. Then, "We're not going to have school all summer, are we? I want to work on the farm."

Her grandfather smiles at her. "You'll get plenty of chance for that. More than you might want."

After lingering behind the kerria and lilacs, Cyrus and Grace follow the lane that leads to Talbot Brook. Here, amid the ancient, spaced maples, the lower end of the sugar bush, is the mill, a sturdy, brown-shingled building with gable ends and a venting cupola in the peaked roof. The east side has been built out to straddle a sluice of cut stone where an undershot waterwheel once turned. Inside at one end is a large circular saw rigged to mill logs into boards and beams. Much of the space is taken up by sugaring equipment that needs updating.

After glancing around, Cyrus opens a trap door to inspect a hydro generator immersed in the water coursing through the sluice. Cables come up through the plank floor to feed storage batteries connected to an inverter. He checks to see if all is functioning properly.

Just upstream from the building, a sizable pool, half natural, half contrived, serves as both a millpond and a place to swim. The near side has sloping, smoothly-worn slabs of granite. In a shallow stretch on the west bank, great blue herons sometimes stand, still as statues until disturbed, when they lift and glide away silently.

Here Grace and Cyrus climb the path along the sugar bush side of the brook to where it is joined by Little Creek. The tributary, lined with alders and fringed with bulrushes where it feeds a couple of swampy patches, flows into the larger stream at a slant from the northeast.

They can hear jays, robins, crows, redwing blackbirds and a catbird. Grace stops her husband for a moment. From a distance comes a distinctive *seee, seeeeyeeer* call. "Meadowlark," she says. "They've come back."

"Lots of things will come back now," Cyrus says. "Not that it's much consolation."

"But significant."

They angle east, the land rising, and cross the creek on a bridge of railway ties sturdy enough to take a tractor. They are in a hayfield with grass and a profusion of wildflowers – buttercup, red clover, phlox escaped from the garden, and dandelion along the margins.

"Strange," Grace says, "that we haven't heard from Clan McFerall."

"They're around. Yesterday, there was gunfire from their direction. Jack thinks they're training a platoon of sorts."

"But they haven't made any approaches..."

"It's early yet. There's easier prey around. And still plenty of food."

"That's going to be decisive, isn't it?"

"Food. Yes." He pauses and takes her hand. "Just as we predicted, the whole thing, you know, growing, harvesting, packaging, distributing, selling, has collapsed."

They reach the end of the hayfield and start across an old pasture, part of which they have reclaimed from encroaching swaths of milkweed and golden rod along with sumac and birch saplings. Here the land and the path grow steeper. But they are in good shape, used to walking and work. Along an easy stretch they walk side by side, hand in hand.

"We'll need to bush hog the rest of this if we ever want to use it for cattle again," he says in conversational parentheses, half to himself. Then he resumes the subject that concerns both of them. "When they get hungry, they'll come here... in force."

"The McFeralls?"

"And others."

"But there must still be food around. I mean in warehouses, at the armory."

"A lot of that rotted when the power went out. Or it's already been looted. And, the brothers have a small army to feed from what we're able to gather. Not just the men. Their families and other camp followers."

At the northern end of the pasture the trail leads up through a stand of hemlock that forms an evergreen collar around Monument Rock, an outcropping of ledge that rises above the trees and provides an expansive view of the house, the outbuildings and the surrounding land.

As they have done so often before, they sit together on the sun-warmed needles that blanket much of the rock.

"This is really what the McFeralls want," Cyrus says, surveying the scene. Beyond Little Creek lay the hayfields on rich soil so level in places it needed drains. Farther down, directly above and not far from the outbuildings, they see Nicole with a farming detail getting ready to put in a large patch of potatoes. Even at a distance, it is obvious that Marko is more bother than his help is worth.

Grace says, "I'm starting to get worried about Frank."

Cyrus nods. "He'll come around. He's an Arkwright. He's one of us. It's more than you can say for that man Bella foisted on us."

"I know," says Grace. "I feel responsible. But I didn't know what else to do. And the irony is, I don't think Meredith is going to last all that long."

"I thought she was in remission."

Grace gives him a wry look. "She is, but she's self-medicating again." Then she stops and takes her husband's arm. "Is that smoke?" She points at a dense pall of blueness rising from where the Deerfield River flows between the towns of Shelburne Falls and Buckland off to the southeast.

Cyrus squints. "I don't think it's mist from the river."

"Oh God," Grace sighs. "How can people think that burning will stop this thing?"

"It only takes one or two."

"But Shelburne Falls?" She pictures the main street lined with brick and stone buildings. The drugstore where you could still sit at a counter and get a soda. The Bridge of Flowers and the bridge to Buckland, just across the river.

It is yet something else to add to the litany of loss that holds most of them at Sugar Mountain in a subdued, steady state of grief. Each of them, including the children, have friends or family who have either died or disappeared.

Cyrus' response is to act, something he has done all his life. He stands and gives a hand to help Grace up and then down off the rock. "I should get over there and help them with the planting," he says, following her back into the stricken world.

Things are not going well in the fenced confines of the garden. Nicole in her role as farm manager explained to the work crew at breakfast how to lift the sections of tarpaulin that cover the ground; how to turn them over to sweep and wipe off any soil clinging to them; and how to fold them up into four-foot squares and store them in the garden shed on the east side of the plot. She told them that the tarps, spaced with small grommets to let water through, prevented weeds and other plants from establishing a root system. That way they didn't have to spend time and fuel plowing and harrowing.

At breakfast, Marko had been in a jokey mood, grinning and grimacing to the annoyance of the others, even Bella. Now he simply gets in the way. Though given denim work clothes and a pair of sturdy boots, he wears lightweight pressed chinos, loafers, and a linen tunic vaguely Russian in design.

While the others work steadily and competently in teams – Ari with Lise, Duvall with Nicole, even Frank, though pale and downcast, by himself, – Marko goes through the motions with Bella, all the while keeping up a constant, irritating chatter.

"I can't believe there aren't any... people we could hire to do this," he says loud enough for others to hear. A moment later: "Potatoes. What are we, peasants?" Then, "This is the dumbest thing I've ever done."

Ari glances at Duvall. "I doubt that."

Twice Nicole intervenes, telling Marko they have to clean the underside of the tarp thoroughly to keep mold from growing. "You also need to fold it neatly. It has to fit with the others," she explains. But in vain. He doesn't take her seriously.

Finally, exasperated, eyes flashing, Nicole tells him, "Marko, if you don't want to work, fine. Just leave."

"Really?" He speaks sarcastically and glances at Bella. But she moves off and turns her head away.

"Really. But you won't get any lunch."

"Really? And who's going to stop me?"

"We all will," Duvall says, coming over to stand beside Nicole.

"Oh my, and what accounts for this sudden outburst of manliness?" Marko speaks in a mocking, mincing simper, the insult crude and unmistakable.

Nicole says, her voice even, "Please leave now. Everyone else, back to work."

"And what, go to my room?"

Nicole speaks into her walkie-talkie. "Jack, we've got a situation up here with Marko. Could you please come up?"

Marko makes a face. "Oh, I'm really scared."

Nicole regards him as though seeing him for the first time. "You will be," she says, and turns from him.

Work stops a moment later when Jack appears walking up the easy slope to the enclosure. He comes through the gate and goes directly to Nicole. They walk off together talking in low tones.

Jack returns presently. He goes up to Marko who has been waiting, muscular arms folded, a half smile on his handsome face. "Let's go for a walk," Jack says neutrally.

"Why should I?"

"Are you afraid to?"

Marko scoffs. "Of you? Get serious."

"Good, then let's go for that walk. It won't take long."

Marko shrugs. "Okay."

Cyrus arrives just after they leave. He asks Nicole, "What's going on?"

"Marko refuses to work. Jack's going to have a talk with him."

Cyrus shakes his head. "I wanted to avoid any of this."

Jack and Marko walk in silence down the slope toward the other side of the equipment shed. Jack considers inviting the man to the house for a heart-to-heart. But he can tell from Marko's swagger that a more palpable form of persuasion will be necessary.

When out of sight of the others, Jack stops and faces Marko, not exactly squaring off, but something close to it in the distance and tension between them. By any observable standards, they are not close to an even match. Standing six four and close to two-hundred and fifty pounds, Marko is a professional athlete who has kept himself in shape. Jack, just under six feet tall, weighs around one seventy.

Jack launches right into it. "Nicole is right. If you don't work, and I mean work effectively and willingly, you won't eat."

"This is all bullshit. We've got plenty of food."

Jack is patient. He realizes that Marko is not very bright. "This is not for now, Marko, this is for next year."

"By next year this thing will have blown over."

"I'm glad you think so. But if it hasn't then we are going to need food."

"Well, I'm going to take my chances."

"Then you're going to have to take your chances somewhere else."

"Is that right?"

"You know the rules. If you don't cooperate, if you don't work, you don't eat."

"You're going to stop me?"

"Yes."

"You like to think you could."

"I know I can."

Marko's face, handsome enough in repose, turns ugly in a sneer. "You're really getting off on this, aren't you? I mean this power thing."

Jack sighs. "I would rather not have to, if you want to know the truth." He takes out his walkie-talkie. "Grace, Marko's decided he doesn't want to work. Until further notice he gets no lunch and no dinner and no snacks. If he causes trouble, let me know and I'll make sure he leaves and doesn't come back."

Grace, starting a stint in the recon room, says "Roger that."

Marko sneers, "Wow, I'm really impressed." But an anger edged with fear shows in his pale eyes. He moves in closer, hands up in front of him. "Get out of my way," he snarls and pushes Jack.

The next moment he is on his knees, his face close to the ground contorted with pain. Jack deftly, as though gently, holds by the wrist and twists Marko's extended arm. It's basic training stuff. He says, "Don't ever do that again." He speaks quietly. "Do not threaten, or push or assault me or anyone else. If you do, I will maim you."

"Ayyy..."

Jack lowers himself beside the kneeling man and, still holding his wrist, puts his mouth close to the other's ear. He says in a low and menacing voice, "Shut up and listen. You are here only because of Meredith and Bella. You either get in line or you will leave here with your arm in a sling and with a bad limp. I doubt Bella will follow you. Understand?"

"I'll get you, God damn it..."

Jack twists just slightly more. He says, "No, you won't get me. You even think of getting me or someone else, then I will take you far enough away so that that we can't smell you rotting after I put a bullet in your tiny brain or slit your throat. Do you understand?"

"Let me go..."

Jack twists just a tad harder. "I said, do you understand?"

"Yes."

"Say 'I understand.'"

"I understand."

He releases Marko's wrist and steps back.

Marko stands up. He rubs his upper arm and glowers at Jack who stands seemingly relaxed.

Jack says, "You don't work, and I mean work, you don't eat." He pauses. He has to play good guy, bad guy, like any squad leader. He says, his tone softening, "You are going to have to get your head around a simple, critical fact, Marko. We are in a life and death situation and will be for a while to come." He points his face directly into Marko's. He is watching for any concession in the man's eyes. He says, "If you're going to stay here, we need you. We need your help, your work, your input. It's that simple."

But Marko doesn't concede, not to judge from the expression on his face where a stoniness hides a humiliation that very nearly gags him. Without a word he turns and walks up the slope to the garden.

That evening, Allegra writes in her journal:

> *With a couple of exceptions, everyone is pitching in and reasonably cheerful, outwardly, anyway. Except Frank. I don't know what's happened to him. It's as though he blames me for the mess were in, the mess the world is in. It's his silences. The way he looks at me. Several times I've walked in on him as he's staring at his cell phone, trying to reach someone or reading old messages. It's as though I'm interrupting something.*
>
> *But then, no amount of activity or work can dispel the nearly palpable gloom that descends at times on Sugar*

Mountain and, one supposes, everywhere else. We are like the survivors of a great and bloody massacre. And because all of us are shaped and sustained by those around us – the friends and family without whom we would hardly exist – all of us are utterly diminished.

It is heartbreaking to see Grace, all got up in her hazmat gear, go out and talk to the people who come begging. Most of them are shabby, hungry and on foot. She gives them what she can and sends them on their way. If they are neighbors, she tells them of a cache down the road somewhere. Sometimes a pickup truck will stop. Men, mostly, looking for work which is a disguised way of begging. Yesterday, I watched from the window when two burly men, both strangers, got out of a truck and started to threaten Grace. Jack appeared on some signal I didn't see and pointed an automatic weapon at them. They went away with the hangdog look of defeat. So now we are not only remembering and mourning our own losses and pitying those doomed vagabonds, but we also suffer a low-grade persistent fear. It's clear that we will not only have to feed and house ourselves, we will have to defend ourselves.

That same evening, Bella approaches Grace and asks to talk to her. Privately. Grace nods and braces herself to hear complaints about what Jack has done and said to Marko. The evening being warm, they go out onto the porch that overlooks the barn garden. Grace notices that Bella has dropped the patronizing tone that she had been using with most everyone.

"I'm worried," Bella starts and lets the words hang in the darkened, flower-scented air. From the fish pond comes the croak of a bullfrog. "I keep wondering what happened to Allison and those kids."

Grace muses for a moment. This is a different Bella from the one that arrived not so long ago. She says, "I think you're right. We gave them enough food for a while. But those kids... Let me talk to Cyrus and Jack."

9

Out of consideration for his father's pacifism, Jack has downplayed the acquiring of weapons – all of them legally – and the training of others in their use. An afternoon of target practice the summer before with Nicole, Duvall, and Thad resulted in a week of obdurate, silent disapproval. Gunfire, Cyrus declared more than once, is the most obscene sound in the world.

Now, with the world closing down and around them, Jack argues his case yet again. "I need more than three other people on the squad to help defend this place," he repeats in their low-voiced head-to-head talks.

"The fence is coming along."

"The fence won't keep people out by itself."

"If and when we are attacked, we retreat to the refuge."

"Then why in hell are we cutting and stacking wood, planting crops, and maintaining this place if all we're going to do is move out at the first sign of trouble? Let's just pack up and go now. And what makes you think people won't come after us there?"

Events begin to make Jack's argument for him. It isn't just the burning of Shelburne Falls, the smoke of which Cyrus and Grace saw on their walk. From what he is able to glean from the members of MAG, the mutual assistance group, it seems that people gathered at the town hall in response to a rumored shipment of medications. When there was none forthcoming, the crowd turned ugly and began a rampage of looting and burning. Some of them stole vehicles and drove out to harass outlying farms and houses.

In response, Jack tells Duvall, Nicole, and Thad to keep their AR15s within reach. Any attempt to rob or overrun the farm will be met with the threat and then the reality of well-aimed bullets. Jack tells his disapproving father, "It will at least give us time to evacuate."

Cyrus finds the members of the CB group are increasingly on edge. Marshall Roth, lamenting that a member of his extended

100

family is still missing, mentions in passing that a young man on a motor bike has watched their house through binoculars and taken pictures.

Pat and Pam Cummings also report a reconnaissance patrol. But Pat has assured Cyrus that they have weapons and know how to use them.

The Becks, who live on what had once been a busy road, tell Cyrus of two visits by a Humvee, one of them with a machine gun mounted on the back.

The Curstons' radio no longer signals, not even on stand-by. They have left the area, one report says. Committed suicide says another. Were overrun and murdered is the most persistent rumor.

Closer to home, there's an encounter with a couple of hunters who cross Talbot Brook where it narrows several hundred yards above the mill. It is early morning. Lise, on duty in the communications alcove, alerts Jack. He comes in immediately and peers over her shoulder.

"I think they're hunters," Lise says.

Jack nods. But hunting what? he wonders. He takes an AR15 for himself and one for Nicole, who knows the drill. While Jack cuts across the field in open view of the two men, Nicole goes up by the mill and keeps out of sight.

His weapon ready but pointing downwards, Jack approaches within thirty yards of the intruders, who have stopped. They hold their weapons, both hunting rifles, in front of them pointed down to the side but with their hands on the grips. Meaning they can raise and fire them in one quick motion.

"You're trespassing on private land," Jack says in a clear, challenging voice.

"Is that right?" says the older of the two, a large man and still heavy.

"That's exactly right," Jack says. "Please turn around and go back the way you came."

"Well, we got two guns against one that says we ain't trespassing," the younger man says, but without much conviction. He looks hungry.

"Wrong," says Jack. He calls, "Nicole!"

"In position," Nicole calls back. "You're covered."

Jack says, "I don't want to get hurt and I know you don't, either."

The older man is nodding. "We're just hungry."

Jack recognizes the younger man. "You're a Dunn, aren't you?"

"Yes, sir, Hank Dunn."

"Old Russell still alive?"

"Still alive."

"You live at the Travis place...?"

"Yes, sir."

"How many folks you got there?"

"Eight."

"Anyone sick?"

"Not yet."

"What do you hear for news?"

The older man, an uncle of the younger one, says, "The McFeralls have a gang. They're going around shaking people down."

"Yeah, they shot up the Morgan place over in Charlemont," Hank Dunn volunteers. "I heard the old man died right afterwards. They've got some heavy artillery."

Jack speaks into his walkie-talkie. "Grace, send someone with a couple of ten-pound sacks of the organic c-feed down the drive and tell them to leave it there. And throw in a sack of beans and a can of oil as well." He turns back to the hunters. He says, "I want you to unload your guns. The meal and beans will be waiting for you at the side of the lane. It isn't much but it will keep you for a while. You may be hearing from us. Next time, go up through Fallgrens to the ridge. You might find a deer or young bear up there. And if you get really desperate, let us know."

"We thank you," the older man says as he and his nephew unload their rifles.

Cyrus is not impressed when Jack tells him about the confrontation. But he begins to relent, especially when Ari talks to him, quietly and convincingly. Ari says, "The victims of the Holocaust did not have the privilege of defending themselves, Cyrus. They are dead. The Israelis have that privilege. They are alive."

What convinces Cyrus to let Jack arm and train a larger squad are two instances of a young man in a ski mask stopping on a motorcycle at the top of the drive. The video replay shows him surveying Sugar Mountain with binoculars on his first visit. The second time he returns with a long-lensed still camera and takes pictures. "It's plain old reconnaissance," Jack tells his father. "It's what you do before you attack. We've not only got to get ready, Dad, we've got to make it obvious that we're ready."

"How do you do that?"

"Gunfire."

*

The first training session of the augmented Defense Squad takes place in the kitchen with the doors closed. Jack sits at the head of the table facing Ari, Lance, Duvall, Nicole, Lise, Thad, and Allegra. They have all volunteered. Expectation mingles with apprehension. They will be learning how to kill and how to survive as others try to kill them.

Bella and Marko have not been invited. Frank, with little stomach for anything much less weapons, has volunteered instead to join his mother in providing medical back-up.

Using a blackboard borrowed from the studio, Jack leads them through some basic definitions. Battle area, forward edge of battle area, field of fire, fire teams, combat outpost line, flanking, infiltration, and a few hand signals.

Each member of the squad has an AR15 in front of him. Lise touches hers, finds it sinister. Lance thinks his is surprising light. Jack shows them how the weapon works. "These, being legally acquired, do not have a fully automatic capability. But that's okay for our purposes as we will need to conserve ammunition. Try to remember to make every shot count." They follow him in how to hold, aim and dummy fire the weapon. Then how to field strip, clean, and reassemble it. The small bowls of solvent give the air a waft of diesel oil. Again. And then again. Jack demonstrates how to take rounds from a box and load them into the ten-round magazines.

"The actual slugs are really small." Ari holds one up and looks at Jack.

Jack agrees. "But look at the size of the casing. It's the velocity and accuracy that does the damage."

Nicole and Thad go around the table helping the others.

While each of the squad starts with an AR15, Jack's store of weapons also includes an M24 scoped sniper rifle, a lever action 45-70 that could stop an elephant, and several cases of ammunition. He has acquired as well three Glock 19 automatics for use as sidearms, a couple of shotguns, combat knives, and a dozen military-style walkie-talkies. The weapons, along with various night-vision scopes and binoculars, are kept in a locked strong room in the cellar.

From the kitchen they move outdoors. With rifles slung over their backs and with ammo pouches heavy with clips of live bullets, they walk in orderly fashion to the upper pasture where it borders the forest. It's unseasonably hot and muggy, the black flies in attendance. But they are all in much better trim than they were when they arrived at Sugar Mountain a month before. From up here, with a slight breeze relieving the heat, they look down on their home, on what they will be defending.

Jack begins with a short lecture on safety as they squint at him in the mid-afternoon haze. His voice has an edge of command that compels assent. "Never point your weapon at anyone for any reason unless you mean to use it on that person. Never assume your weapon is unloaded. Never go around with the safety off unless we're in a combat situation. Remember, your weapon can kill you as easily as someone else."

Knowing that training people to kill involves as much psychology as skill in handling weapons, Jack has earlier set up dummies made of old clothes stuffed with straw and sawdust. He forms the squad into two-person firing teams.

He says, "Anyone attacking us will, if they succeed, end up killing us one way or another. Either they'll shoot us outright, or they'll take our food and other supplies and leave us to freeze and starve. So shoot to kill or maim. That will save lives by making those attacking us realize that we mean business and that it's best to withdraw and leave us alone."

Prone in the flower-entwined grass, the teams start twenty-five yards from the dummies, which are strung against the trunks of trees. The firing starts, the reports sharp and echoing off the surrounding hills.

Jack moves behind the teams, giving them pointers, encouragement, critiques, praise. "Breath normally. Count backwards to free your mind while you aim. Aim for the body mass. Disabling an enemy is often better than killing him."

They move back fifty, hundred, then a hundred and fifty yards.

"The dummies are losing," Thad jokes with Allegra, who's starting to get the knack.

They repeat the process using a regular target with a bullseye. Jack, checking the results through binoculars, goes up and down behind the shooters as they aim and fire one at a time.

To general surprise, Nicole and Lance prove to be the most accurate team. Both are good shots, Nicole from earlier practice, and Lance from steady hands and hawk-like vision. Jack changes them around. Nicole is teamed with Duvall, Thad with Ari, Lance with Allegra. Jack stays with Lise whose aim is getting better.

At the end of the session, he takes some shots with the big gun. "For sound effects," he tells them.

"The firing makes it very real," Lance remarks to Allegra. They are coming down from the pasture, their weapons slung casually, an esprit already among them.

"Almost too real." She can tell he has a crush on her. And, being honest with herself, she admits she is beginning to find him attractive despite or perhaps because of the difference in age. Not that there's any possibility of... But then, she never would have thought a few weeks ago that she would be in a field firing an assault rifle at the body mass of a dummy.

Wanting to be agreeable, he says, "I'm still not sure I could actually shoot somebody."

"That is the question," she says.

"Could you shoot someone?"

Allegra pauses to look at and then pick some clover and pinks blossoming in the grass along the path. "I really don't know. Perhaps in the heat of battle. I mean if they're coming right at us. I hope I don't have to find out."

"It's very noisy," Meredith complains at dinner that evening. "You can hear it all over the valley. Is it really necessary?"

They have killed, plucked, stuffed and roasted two of the older hens. There is gravy with diced mushrooms Chee found the day before, mashed potatoes, and a salad of greens. The helpings of meat are on the small side and doled out evenly.

Cyrus nods as though agreeing with Meredith. Then he tells her, "Jack has convinced me that if we are going to defend ourselves we will have to know how to use the weapons we have. And the noise should help forestall an attack because people know we have weapons and are willing to use them."

As the training progresses, Jack assigns each team a position behind the stonewall in front of the house. If it looks like a real attack, Lise and Nicole will escort the children along with Henry and Meredith to the mill. Cyrus will watch the monitors in the recon room. Grace and Frank will stand by in the clinic.

Several times Jack sounds the red alarm. By the third time, it is only minutes before the bridge over the ditch is removed, the gate secured, and everyone in place.

Bella takes Jack aside. "I want in," she says.

"What do you mean 'in'?"

"I can learn how to fire a gun."

There's a lingering note of entitlement in her voice that he doesn't like. "Let me think it over." Then, "Why don't you help Lise and Nicole with the evacuation... if it comes to that."

Bella nods and detains him, a hand on his arm. "I really would like to know what happened to Allison and those kids."

He takes her in again. She is changing. "You'll need an armed guard. I'll arrange it."

She switches gears. "What about Marko?"

"What about him?"

"What can he do?"

"Stay out of the way."

*

The training improves morale noticeably at Sugar Mountain. Not only are they ready, but they are equipped and able to defend their home against all but overwhelming force. Their home. It's more than the bucolic setting. Or that they have enough to eat and relative comfort. They have each other, each one of them – with a couple of exceptions – a treasure to keep.

The place grows on its residents – except for Frank and Marko, the odd men out. If there are no "all you can eat meals" served in the kitchen, the food is good and at times exceptional, especially when Ari puts on an apron and gets to work. There are few complaints about the accommodations, the planning of which shows Nicole's touch. If on the small side, the rooms are comfortable and well-appointed.

Thus do Henry and Meredith each have a modest room on the first floor of the wing where they share a small bathroom that has a shower. Directly above is an identical bathroom where Nicole and Jack have a large room, albeit with dormers. Cy sleeps on the top bunk in his own small domain.

In the main part of the house, Cyrus and Grace occupy the same room they have for most of their married life. And though they have a separate door to the nearly luxurious bathroom with clawfoot tub and tiled shower, they share it with Ari and Lise, who have a room down the hall and with Rachael and Mary, who use the bunkroom toward the back. A small spare room on the first floor has been furnished with a single bed for Chee. She has access to the common bathroom off the kitchen.

With their own living room and galley kitchen, the residents of the horse barn are all quite happy. Except for Frank, for whom the possibility much less the pursuit of happiness grows more remote by the day.

The only complaints come from Bella and Marko. They are not in the least happy with their quarters, the unfinished bedroom with sink and toilet in one of the bays of the equipment shed that has been closed in with wall, windows, and door. "The place smells of the pigs," Bella says, her voice now more matter-of-fact than whiny. Jack keeps himself from saying they could always leave.

Instead, while the couple stay in a tent, Duvall and Cyrus take time to transform the twelve-by-twenty foot space into something resembling living quarters. They first seal the window on the north side to keep the smell of the pigsty at bay. They also wall off the tiny bathroom and put in a door.

When it is ready, Marko asks to keep the tent "as a backup for myself." The request, easily granted by Grace, reflects a growing alienation not only between Marko and Bella, but between Marko and the rest of the community.

It hasn't helped that Jack insists that both be excluded from any positions of trust until they have proved themselves. Thus, they are not included in the Defense Squad nor are they on the roster of those standing watch over the monitor screens in the recon room.

Allegra writes in her journal:

We live in a steady state of quiet apprehension. Each day dawns like a gift to be treasured. It's as though, working the land, firing a gun, watching the monitors, there is the possibility of survival. There grows among us an intense sense of community. (Even Bella is coming around, though Marko is stuck in a sneer mode.) It springs, I think, from the realization that, unlike the rest of the world, or most of it, we have our fate in our own hands.

It's not that we don't think and worry about those on the outside. Last night at dinner, Grace says she and Bella were

going to visit Bella's friend Allison and the van full of children
— with proper precautions — to see how they were doing.

Bella, who with time has begun to lose a measure of fat and fatuity, joins Grace to go on mountain bikes in search of her friend Allison and the van full of children. They have masks to put on. They each carry twenty pounds of basic food in backpacks. Ari, an AR15 slung on his back, joins them to provide security.

They go in the early afternoon, the weather remaining in a rut of heat and haze. The road is empty. There seems no one left in the world. They find the logging road without difficulty. After a few hundred yards the track turns rough. Out of caution, they dismount and approach on foot.

Grace knows before Bella or Ari, who is bringing up the rear, that the worst has happened. It is in the air, the sweet, sick stench of rotting flesh. It is in the stillness around the van and in the way the tent sags. They pause a hundred feet away and put on masks. They don't want to see the worst.

It is Bella who approaches. Quietly, she says, "Allison... Allison..."

The children lay in and out of the tent, vague in death, gray and shriveling forms. Allison slumps in the front seat of the van, her throat slashed, her blond good looks grotesquely intact. Next to her is the driver. He has successfully slit his wrists and lies back as though relaxing in the lowered seat. The flies buzz everywhere like a mist from the nearby stream.

Grace turns away and contacts Cyrus on the walkie-talkie.

"We need a burial detail here, Cyrus my love. They're all dead."

"Dear, dear, I am so sorry. I was afraid this would happen. I'll send Thad and Duvall over with spades. I'm sorry, but Jack was right. If we had taken them in, we'd all be dead or dying now."

"At least," says Grace, ever practical, "We can fumigate the tent and even the van if someone else shows up and needs shelter."

Working from notes she jotted down during the day, Allegra writes in her journal that evening:

> *I took a mask and joined the burial party that went over to where Bella's friend and the kids had gone. You can't help thinking, I couldn't, that they were lucky to be buried when so much of the world is dying without any hope of burial. So I helped dig the shallow trenches among the roots a good ways back from the stream. We were all in a numbed state of shock as we laid out the kids and the grown-ups. It's one thing to hear about people dying like winter flies; it's quite another to deal with the actual bodies. Ari recited something remembered from a Jewish service, nicely ironic for these Muslim kids. Then a foot of soil at best and some rocks from the stream bed to keep scavengers away. It was so sad and so real I couldn't cry though I wanted to.*
>
> *Also, I couldn't stop thinking that we would be like this had they gotten in among us. So they were doomed, anyway. Only you can't let yourself think like that. Pity gets a bad rap, but without pity we become less than human.*
>
> *The fact is I have no context for any of this and for me context is everything. I reach for it and it's not there. Instead, what keeps coming over me again and again like an intermittent, deepening shock: our world is gone. Nearly everyone we ever knew or loved is dead or lost in a limbo of faint hope. I know the others here feel it in one way or another. I see it in their faces and hear it in their voices.*
>
> *Duvall broke down and wept this afternoon after we came back from burying those poor souls. There were no histrionics. He sat there in the hot shade, tears spilling slowly, one by one from his mild brown eyes. "My mom," he says finally. "I haven't been able to reach her. Or my brother Claudius. We used to kid him as a kid. We called him Clodius or just Clod. And my sisters Esme and Charlene. Their kids. I haven't heard a peep out of any of them."*
>
> *I suppose it was like this in the Holocaust and during Stalin's decimations. The world shattered beyond recognition.*

Life suddenly fragile and precious and yet so ephemeral as death rampages. So that we have to reaffirm daily, hourly, that it's worth working and fighting for.

I tried to comfort Duvall. I told him about my own lost family. I told him I wanted to take one of the emergency backpacks and set off in search of them. And no doubt die in doing so. I've often thought that the best afterlife would be searching for and finding those we love who have gone before. I'd rather do that than bask in God's love, whatever that is, in some celestial mansion.

"But you won't," Duvall said.

I smiled and said no. "Because of Lily, and myself, and Frank."

But we were getting morbid, something we try to avoid. Compared to poor Frank I am a fount of positive energy. He is fading by the minute. Though yesterday, scything the grass in the orchard, he threw off his gray lethargy and whetted the blade and cut veritable swaths through the tangled grass. But it was, I think now, the energy of rage, most of which he keeps to himself like some precious poison.

Because he has nothing for me or for Lily, not even anger. When he's not on duty, he sleeps. Or he's looking at his cell, which he keeps charged. He scarcely eats. When I suggested that he check in with Grace, he made an effort to look incredulous.

"She's my mother."

"She's helping everyone else who needs it."

"I don't want help."

"What do you want?"

"What I can't have."

I tried to cajole him. I sat next to him. I took his hand. I said, "Frank, we need you. And this is it. This is what we have."

"Yeah. I know."

*

Cyrus mentions casually at breakfast that he is going to lead a tour of Sugar Mountain so that everyone could get an idea of how the various systems work. Before he can set a time, Jack interrupts him, his index finger raised.

"Dad, I need to talk to you about this."

Cyrus regards him quizzically. "Really?"

Jack notices that few other people are paying much attention. He gives his father a meaningful stare. "It won't take long."

"Right now?"

"It can wait."

Grace says, "What about the tour?"

Cyrus smiles. "It's on hold for now." After a little thought and a touch of salt on his oatmeal, he can guess what the issue will be.

A while later, checking messages on the CB radio in the recon room, he listens patiently to his son.

Too patiently, Jack thinks, as he explains to his father why he wants Marko and Bella, but especially Marko, excluded from any opportunity to learn first hand about the Sugar Mountain infrastructure.

"Do you think he would try to sabotage us?"

Jack shakes his head. He finds Cyrus' perplexity easier to deal with than his patience. "No, but if he decides to leave and ends up at, say, the McFeralls, he would tell them everything he sees here."

"Why would he do that?"

"To ingratiate himself."

"Okay, but why would he decide to leave?"

Jack sighs, but to himself. His father is a pacifist in more ways than one. He says, "Well, he's dumb enough to leave on his own. And if he continues the way he's going, he may have to leave... under duress."

Cyrus bows his head. "You mean force him to leave?"

"Sooner or later." Jack sighs audibly this time. "Look, Dad, his attitude is lousy. He doesn't pull his weight. He doesn't have a clue of what's happening out there. Bella told Nicole that he keeps his cell phone charged because he's expecting a call any day from the Dallas Cowboys..."

Cyrus smiles slowly and thinks. "Okay, here's the deal. I'll take folks on a tour. Invitation only. To occupy Marko and Bella, we'll have them paint their quarters. But no forcible evictions unless there's due process."

"Agreed."

So it is a small group – Ari, Lise, Allegra, Lance, and Henry – that Cyrus leads on a *tour d'horizon*. He starts with the power system, walking around the solar panels, an array of which faces south on the eastern side of the house. He also points out the panels affixed to the roof of the horse barn, and explains how they feed storage batteries and an inverter in a secure part of the house cellar. In the mill, he lifts the trapdoor over the sluice to show them a micro-hydro unit and how it charges the battery that connects to an inverter and the rest of the "mini grid."

"Aside from the small windmill that runs the water pump, the panels and hydro-generator are the only power we will have access to for the foreseeable future. Which means we will all have to be extremely careful about how much we use. At night, power from the stream, as long as it flows, is used for lighting and small appliances. If there's a drought or a big freeze, we may have to institute a lights-out curfew of ten o'clock or earlier."

Cyrus describes the water supply. There are two sources. The first is an artesian well under a round metallic cover just visible in the graveled parking area. "It runs on electricity," he tells them. "There's also a spring well in the pasture not far from the horse barn." He points in the direction of the well. "The spring well operates on a siphon and feeds a holding tank in the bath house. As most of you know, the windmill on the top of the silo pumps water from the holding tank into the much larger cistern just above the bath house. When we get back to the house, you can sign up to learn any one of these systems in detail."

They walk in the direction of the silo, keeping to the tractor lane. It goes in front of the equipment shed and the shed for the goats and chickens, and finally past the horse barn. They stop at the corner of the garden at the old silo. Old, but renovated –

insulated, wired, and provided with a sturdy addition to accommodate the showers and changing room. Inside, Cyrus points up to the cistern and tells them, "From here there's a gravity feed for back-up water for the house, the apartments in the horse barn and the apartment in the equipment shed. Again, conservation is the watch word, especially if the power goes out. That mostly means frugal use of the toilets and wash basins. Each unit has a meter. Anyone who persists in using excessive amounts will have their water turned way down."

Ari, looking skeptical, asks, "But what do those who have their water shut off do for..."

"There's an outhouse next to the pigsty and there's Talbot Brook for bathing."

"You're serious?"

Cyrus regards his nephew. "Ari, I have never been more serious in my life." He continues. "All right, moving on. For the time being, we don't have to worry much about heat except for hot water and cooking. For that we will keep the stove in the kitchen going around the clock in its 'summer mode.' As you have found out by now, if you want warm water for washing up, you need to come and get it, sparingly, from the tank on the side of the kitchen range. Or, you can start up your own stoves and heat water on it. Most of you also know that you can have a hot shower in the bath house on the floor of the silo but you'll have to fire the stove there and heat the water ahead of time." He smiles. "An inconvenience, but one that makes it feel like the luxury it is."

He pauses. "Any questions? Good. That brings me to wood. We have, if managed properly, about a year and half's worth of cord wood already cut." He describes how they use a chainsaw to cut and trim trees in the hardwood glades above the pastures. How they bring the four to six inch thick logs down a "chute" by hand to the mill where they rig a small circular saw that is powered by diesel.

"What happens if we run out of diesel?" Lance asks.

Cyrus smiles. "We use hand saws."

He resumes, describing how the wood, cut into sixteen-inch lengths, is used in the kitchen range, and the stoves in the horse barn and equipment shed.

"So cleanliness is no longer next to Godliness," Allegra remarks. She has been taking notes. This is all grist for her mill.

"No, but survival is," says Grace, who has joined the group in the silo. "Besides, cold bathing never hurt anyone."

Then it's clothes and laundry. Though most of them know the drill, they stand patiently around the big wooden tub of oak staves that stands on the bath house floor on a raised platform as Grace shows them how to work its mechanical agitator and how to drain and refill it for rinsing. She instructs them in how to use a double roller ringer that swings out over the tub. "Weather permitting, we'll string a couple of lines and have a washday every week. Try to keep your laundry to a minimum. We have a stockpile of sturdy work clothes and some winter clothing. We also have bolts of cotton cloth, corduroy, and tough denim for making more work clothes. I would save your underwear and better clothes for special occasions, of which there will be some... We hope."

From clothing, they move to food. Nicole waits for them in the kitchen where they sit around the big table.

"As you all know we will have to produce, store, and process all of our food for the foreseeable future. We have supplies in depth – but we'll still have to supplement them by farming and hunting and gathering."

She goes into considerable detail. Given the subject, everyone pays attention. She tells them about the grove of maples that they will tap in March for sap which they will boil down to syrup and sugar. She tells them about the six bear-proof apiaries they hope to set up, the honey of which will be used in place of sugar once that runs out.

"What kind of crops are we going to plant?" Lance asks. "I mean besides potatoes and the usual stuff."

Nicole looks at a notebook she has to hand. She says, in a way that gets a laugh, "A lot more potatoes." She smiles a bit ruefully. "They grow easily and quickly and they store well in the root cellars. We'll also have onions, carrots, turnips, apples, pears. We'll harvest peaches and berries for canning, along with cucumbers for pickling. Corn, of course. We'll grow that mostly as a fresh vegetable. If we have a surplus, we'll dry it out and grind it into cornmeal. And we'll have an acre of wheat. We hope."

She talks generally about storage, even alluding to the real depot under the horse barn and the access to it. From the galley kitchen off the living room on the first floor, a stairway that could be made to look hidden leads down to a basement of cut stone that serves as a root cellar. It is there that a concealed door opens to second root cellar that Cyrus excavated three years before. Lined with cement blocks and sturdy shelves, it is already stocked with jars of home-canned pickles, peaches, berries, and tomato sauce as well as remnant baskets of potatoes and apples from the season before. A rat-proof nickel-lined chest awaits the smoked and salted meat of the old sow. It is the real root cellar, the place where they have decanted into quart bottles more than ten gallons of home-made apple liquor, good enough for Ari not only to dub it "Sugar Mountain calvados," but to sip it with crushed ice on occasion.

"What about coffee?" Allegra asks.

"We have quite a bit stored," Nicole says. "But once that's gone..."

Ari says, "That applies to a lot of things, doesn't it?"

Nicole nods. "But, you'd be surprised what we can do. There will be lots of herbs and spices in the kitchen garden. And once we get the greenhouse set up... I think we'll even have figs."

"Are we going to build a greenhouse?" Lise asks.

"We have all the parts stored in a bay of the equipment shed."

That sets them to fantasizing about what they might be able to produce that would no longer be available. Ari mentions the vines for wine grapes he and Frank planted the year before.

"Where's the greenhouse going to be placed?" Lance asks.

"We're thinking of putting it up on the other side of the barn garden. It'll mean fresh greens in winter."

Nicole says, "I have orange and lemon trees. Small ones." She's being mischievous.

Lance picks up on it. "Bananas, too?"

Cyrus smiles indulgently at him. "Let's not get carried away."

Sugar Mountain is not without its recreations. As the weather turns hot, more of them resort to the millpond to cool off. And while no one complains when Bella and Marko and then Thad and Duvall begin to swim and loll around in the buff on the sun-warmed granite, they decide to set aside times for what are called pelts and belts.

A special treat are the picnics at the pond that Ari arranges. He has a genius for concocting savories for the wicker baskets they bring along with napkins, glasses, and even, at times, a bottle of wine. On those occasions, Thad carries a laptop connected by wireless to the monitors in the recon room. Several AR15s lay hidden and handy in the nearby bushes.

Most nights a movie is shown in the family room. But not everyone can watch these depictions of a life no longer in existence. The evening Nicole picks *Arthur* and puts it in the CD player, Frank very nearly throws a scene. He leaves. Later he tells Allegra, "I can't stand the movies. All that's gone. All they do is remind me of a time when there were restaurants, lights, people, a million things happening. How can anyone watch them?"

Lise might have felt the same way but she had never confused movies with reality. Still, when Arthur goes to the fancy party, she can no longer sustain the suspension of credulity that most films require. She is in fact anxious about another imaginary world – her clients. She cannot stop worrying about her accounts. She has private and public pension funds, slices of endowments, trusts, and individuals. The managers and owners still hover... in her mind. All gone. She is anxious in a void. But unlike Frank, she is determined to adapt to this new, strange world.

For solace she goes to the room she shares with Ari. He is there, naked under a sheet reading, rereading, yet again, *War and Peace*. She has, Ari tells her, an ancestral capacity for minimalism. Except where he, variously her *Yiddishe* stallion, her brissed satyr, her jade stalk, is concerned. He closes the Tolstoy novel. Once again her need and her revealing laughter get him going. So they turn from their fictional worlds to themselves, to what is real and, right then, in those golden moments, infinitely richer.

The next morning before breakfast, Lise walks by herself to the upper fields to gather wildflowers for their bedroom, the common room and the kitchen table. It is something she does every few days, partly because the flowers add beauty and fragrance to the house and partly for reassurance, a reassurance she finds in the heading grass, legumes, and wild flowers that make a tangled bank of vegetation. With secateurs, she cuts a bouquet of fleabane, campion, vetch, hawkweed, yarrow and a beautifully scented white flower with umbels of tiny, five-petaled blossoms that she cannot find in the wild flower guide. Against the darkness of the woods, blooming mountain laurel shows like a bank of unseasonal snow. At the same time, bobolinks hover singing in their lark-like flights, and she can hear the meadowlarks, a rare pair that nest where the cover has stayed short.

She turns to head back and takes in the Breugalesque scene – Nicole and Lance working amidst the greening garden; Bella and Marko stacking cordwood; Henry talking to Chee who is hanging out wash. Then a troubling sight. Beyond the house, parked at the head of the drive where it reaches the road, is one of those military jeep-like things.

Lise isn't the only one who has taken note. Jack stands on the thick branch of the maple to the west side of the house and adjusts the birding scope he has rigged at eye level on a shortened tripod. The Hummer in desert camouflage is parked at the end of the drive, three hundred yards distance. He notes that it is turret-rigged but does not have a machine gun or other ordnance mounted. He also notes that the driver is Bruce McFerall and that he is talking and laughing with animation to someone else in the cab.

Mind games, Jack thinks. They're checking out the progress of the barrier fence. Should they hit us before we put up more visible defenses? And sending us a message: We're back. Because for more than a week there has been little evidence of the McFeralls or news of atrocities. That morning Cyrus learned from Pat

Cummings that there were skirmishes between the McFeralls and a well-armed gang from the Pittsfield area. As Ari remarked, "They're defending this area so that they can have it for themselves."

Right then Jack both aches to have the sniper rifle in hand and feels queasy about using it. With the M24, he could place a round right in Bruce McFerall's left ear and wipe that grin off his face. Message received. And answered. War again. But he can hear his dad saying that the man, however reprehensible, was on a public road, in his own vehicle, and breaking no laws.

The Hummer starts up, makes a three-point turn, and goes back the way it came, leaving Jack Arkwright to wrestle with a sharpening quandary: to kill or not to kill?

The new Jack, the husband, father, farmer, whatever, is loath to revive the old Jack and his particular skills. But now it seemed he would not have a choice. He knows the McFeralls will be back, will turn and come up the drive with their armed rabble. And killing isn't something you can do by halves or with the reluctance of moral qualms. He knew killing was a possible eventuality when he began to acquire the AR15s and the stocks of ammunition with which to load them. They were the tools of what had been his trade and the very handling of them affected the chemistry of his brain. Something more than a vestige of his old self lingers and hankers to kill, especially anyone who would threaten his family or their home.

Part of it, he knows, is the hubris of competence. Not long into his first tour of duty, Jack discovered that he was good at killing bad guys. The critical question then and now: just who are the bad guys? At first the category had been crystal clear. They were the jihadists who crashed the jets filled with passengers into the Twin Towers. They were the elders who would stone to death a teenage girl accused of adultery. They were the seemingly endless parade of Koran-quoting fanatics who all but sought death from the weapons he wielded with the skill of a born professional. Thus did he waste bad guys with precision bursts from his HK416. With well-aimed 40mm grenades from the same weapon. At a distance, sighting through the scope of a sniper rifle. Close in with his razor-sharp knife.

He remembered those he killed. The gaggle of young men that he and his squad surprised outside of Marjah in Helmand Province. Over in seconds. The man in the minaret he pulverized with an RPG, a rocket-propelled grenade. On a kill team in Nuristan, sniping an insurgent looking at him through binoculars. The sapper trying to get into Baghrum Air Base. Slitting the man's throat so as not to give away his squad's position should there be others. Not to mention those whose bodies he never saw.

It went deeper than some twisted pride or search for meaning. Mortal combat was the ultimate reality, beside which everything else could feel like a pleasant dream. But he knew that killing wasn't life. Nothing came of it. It was subtraction, not addition. All of which he told himself as he made the effort, successfully, he thought, to get back to life. Until the instant he had Bruce McFerall's smiling head in the birding scope and supplied the crosshairs.

But the McFeralls and their ilk are not dark-haired men in strange dress jabbering away in a foreign language. These are pale-faced Americans, neighbors, practically his kin. And still, in an elemental way, bad guys. Because, by all reports, the McFeralls were taking and would take by deadly, indiscriminate force what the Arkwrights and others had worked to make.

Once again Jack finds himself balancing on the tightrope between his father's moral imperatives and the obscene, Darwinian necessity of killing his own kind. He does not want to let loose the dogs of war, particularly the one ready to howl inside of himself.

He comes down out of his perch and makes an all-clear signal. Ari, Lance, and Duvall emerge, each carrying an AR15. They keep them discreetly handy as they go back to work on the fence.

Back to work. That simple injunction defines Sugar Mountain regardless of what is happening in the outside world. On the bulletin board next to the door leading into the studio from the kitchen is posted the work schedule for the week. After a series of meetings, the community has pretty much sorted out who coordinates and belongs to which work group. Everyone, including the children, put time in the fields.

It is closing on the summer solstice when they begin a second planting of corn, potatoes, tomatoes, carrots, green and lima beans, and leafy produce like lettuce and spinach, the latter of which can be cooked, chopped, and canned. When ripe, the lima beans will be picked, dried, shelled, and stored in burlap bags. Choice plants will be left to go to seed for next year's crop. And a section of the garden has been set aside for the production of seeds from biennial plants like carrots and beets.

Nicole works the soil and hovers over the others, showing them how to thin, carefully, the seedling for replanting. "Waste nothing," she says again and again. "It's all going to be food."

In her own way, Nicole is happy even as she shares the apprehensions that go with survival living. She has her B&B, perhaps the ultimate B&B in that her customers are her family. So much the better. Among her smaller satisfactions is the loss of weight that work and a reduced diet have accomplished. She now slides into slacks and dresses she hasn't worn in years. Not that she has any place to wear them except for Sunday morning service or those times when Ari announces, "Let's dress for cocktails."

She has her wheat field. With the John Deere rigged to a double blade plow, Cyrus opened up a one-acre patch outside the garden fence for the experiment. He cross plowed it and then worked it thoroughly with a spring-tooth harrow, all the time conscious of using scarce diesel fuel. After it has been smooth raked, he and Nicole sewed it by hand, looking like figures out of a painting by Millet as they walk ten feet apart casting the hard grains. They agreed it was a bit late in the season for seeding the patch. And, if they can't get it dry enough to mill, they can always feed it to the pigs and chickens.

In the early morning the crowing of cocks in the hen house sounds through the screened windows like heralds from a reviving past and reminds them as they wake of the chores that need doing. The cocks preside over hens that chirrup in the coop with its wired outside run. Duvall and Grace with nominal help from Meredith, feed and water the fowl, clean their roosts, putting the manure aside for the garden, and collect the eggs, a certain percentage of which go into short-term storage for the hatchery.

Lance and Thad, tutored by Nicole, take care of the goats. There is a billy goat and six she-goats, three of which have had a spring kid and give milk. The milk has to be strained and cooled. Some of it is separated for cream and cheese making. Later that summer they will mow, dry, and bring in enough hay to feed them over the winter.

When the strawberries planted the year before come in, they are picked, sorted, eaten, canned or made into jam. They grow in a plot of their own next to the berry patch, which has early and late raspberries, high bush blueberries, red currants, and thimble berries. Nicole keeps the blueberries covered with a fine light mesh. "Birds," she says when asked about it. "They'll eat every last one if you let them."

With twenty guests at the Sugar Mountain Inn – as Nicole sometimes calls it – there are sixty meals each day to prepare along with snacks and treats. There are dishes to wash, rooms and clothing to clean, fires to feed, and children to educate. And with a pandemic raging beyond the confines of the refuge, the health of everyone is taken very seriously.

As the only one with medical training, Grace holds office hours in a ground floor room of the main house. It is equipped with an examination table, blood pressure cuff, stethoscope, home-rigged autoclave, and a basic surgical kit. The case for dental emergencies includes a couple of wicked-looking tooth extractors Grace hopes she won't have to use. A closet full of medicines and potions is cleverly hidden behind what looks like a closet containing medicines and potions.

Except for Bella, Marko, and Chee, Grace has everyone's medical history on paper or in a computer file. She worries a lot about her sister. Meredith's remission isn't being helped by a pharmacopoeia of herbs and folk remedies the nature of which she is reluctant to share with her sister. Far from passing judgment,

Grace knows the placebo effect can be as powerful as any tested medication. Not that any medication, after a certain point, will cure what ails Meredith. Ari suffers from periodic bouts of Crohn's disease. It doesn't afflict his gut as much as it sometimes leaves him debilitated and tremulous. But as he tells Grace when he consults her, he suffers more from the prescription of rest while everyone else is working. Duvall has Type II diabetes for which he takes medication daily. He has a year's supply and a store of tabs for testing his blood. He tells Grace when they meet for a routine visit that he hopes hard work and limited amounts of food will all but cure him.

Most everyone else at Sugar Mountain has tanned and toughened working in the sun. They have lost weight except for those already lean. A group picture taken six weeks after the in-gathering is reminiscent, especially with the work clothes, of photographs of Midwestern farm families in the 1950s. Echoing a common sentiment, Allegra says she hasn't felt so good physically in a long time.

Frank remains the exception in this collective blooming of health. He loses weight and then loses more weight so that his face shrinks to that of a specter. A pallor shows beneath the reddening that makes the others appear healthy. He wrestles with chronic fatigue born of depression. He is depressed because he cannot extricate himself from the past. Despite his objections to movies like *Arthur*, when no one else is around, he clicks on his cell phone and punches in all the people he knew even when, holding it to his ear, he hears no dial tone or any of the little squeaks and bleats of his vast, vanished world.

He knows he should erase the endless messages he has on file on this and an older cell phone. But he can't resist revisiting them, especially the half-coded messages to and from Elsa. Elsa Sterne happened like an accident, though in retrospect he wonders if she planned it. Because, technically speaking, she was too big to be attractive despite her Nordic good looks. Or, perhaps it was her size that captivated him, provoking a sexual curiosity that waxed with time and proximity to a distinct hankering.

The mutual tutoring brought them close – he explaining American corporate law, she telling him the ins and outs of the European legal system. They were thrown together a lot. Take-out meals grabbed as evening closed down. Working lunches. Dropping by her hotel to pick up documents. Hellos and good-byes as she came and went. Until an afternoon in her suite at The Carlton hours before she was to fly out of Kennedy. It began with a good-bye kiss on the lips that turned passionate. A one off, a lark, a lollipop. Only, he couldn't get her out of his mind.

Their communications during her ensuing absence from New York were businesslike at first, as though their last-minute lovemaking had been an anomaly, a footnote to one of their long briefs. Then, from him, "I really enjoyed that last encounter," which got a restrained response from Elsa. Then flirtatious addenda, sometimes coy, reference to "a dangerous precedent."

When she returned, he had flowers waiting at her suite. An hour later they were naked and copulating vigorously on her queen-sized bed. It got intense enough for them to start planning their work around the exigencies – mostly sex – of their affair.

The intensity surprised Frank in a glancing sort of way because heretofore he had possessed what one female admirer called sexual Teflon. He had been faithful, not out of active virtue or utter devotion to Allegra, but because extra-marital affairs could, as this one did, get messy, time-consuming, distracting. And there was Allegra. Petite, tough, sexy as hell, New York smart. He loved her for herself and, he admitted to himself, because she made him look good. Professor of English. Book in progress. Entry into realms where you mingled, quite literally, with the literati. Some of the parties were like genre scenes of Bohemian cafe life right down to the black berets and art talk.

Frank never spoke of their affair to anyone else, not even Ari. He didn't believe in shrinks except as clients. Several had come to him over the years after some Wall Street sharpie took them to the cleaners. Their naiveté astounded him. One of them used the phrase "legal healing." And even when he talked to Elsa about what was happening to them, it was with a fake objectivity that mostly entangled them more in an impossible situation. Because Elsa was married to Heinrich and had a five-year-old son named Felix. She had a legal career and ambitions to be a diplomat on the European stage. Neither could conjure a future together even as they couldn't imagine not seeing one another.

All gone now. Except for memories and words and a few pictures on the tiny screen of his cell phone. Just enough to torture himself and provide grist for sessions of physical or mental masturbation that left him emptied, depressed, and angry. In this crippled state, Frank finds a strange solace in watching the monitors in the recon room. He volunteers for extra duty and takes it in place of more strenuous work. He likes it because, next to sleep, it is the most passive thing he can do.

He sits there ostensibly watching the screens but more often recharging and checking his cell phones. When not in a torpor of nostalgia, he is aware but unmoved by a deepening crisis in their part of Massachusetts. He overhears his father, another habitué of the communications alcove, documenting atrocities in the region as the pandemic rages and desperation grows.

*

Though communications have remained robust among the members of the CB network, it is difficult to confirm reports be they good, bad, or something in between. Rumors abound. The saddest involve murder-suicides in families. As well as killings, robberies, extortions, assault, and rape, there are accounts of abandoned children.

Jack and Cyrus assiduously mark the places on a large map of Franklin County affixed to the wall just outside the alcove. They use colored pushpins, red for killings, blue for robberies, yellow for threats, and orange for everything else. They also keep a journal of the violence and hold evaluation sessions. Is a pattern emerging? Who might be responsible? What could they do about it?

Defend themselves if attacked, Jack would say. Get ready to

evacuate, Cyrus would counter. What about the outside world? Grace and the others would ask hopefully. But there were only occasional flickerings on the internet or on the Emergency Alert System, most of the latter canned announcements weeks old.

The bad news and the lack of any signs of official life coupled with the appearance of vehicles at the end of the lane are enough to spur them to finish the installation of the security fence. By the Fourth of July, which passes in eerie silence, the fence encloses most of the buildings in a way that no one likes.

"It both protects and imprisons us," Allegra writes in her journal. At one of the many meetings they hold, Cyrus says they will take it down when the outside world has returned to something like normality. Or has been all but depopulated.

Allegra notes in the same entry:

> *Even in this relentlessly egalitarian society, the members of Jack's Defense Squad form an elite. We are the warrior class. Our status comes, I think, not only from the perception that we are willing to die or get maimed for the sake of everyone else, but from the conviction that we will kill and maim on behalf of everyone else. I wonder at times if it might be easier to die than to kill. Until I think of Lily and the others. And then I could use a knife or my bare hands on anyone who threatened them.*

With the exception of Marko, the elders, and the children, they take turns at the monitors in the recon room. It's twenty-four hours a day, seven days a week. Along with Cyrus, there are ten members who are on watches of one to four hours in duration, depending on the time of day and what is happening.

Jack often relieves others before their times are up. He lives in a state of vigilance. Even when someone else is there, he hovers, checking the various systems, dialing through the channels, listening and watching for news, any news.

Allegra takes night duty when she can. Like Frank, but for different reasons, she finds this time alone one of the compensations of their survivalist isolation. Alone, undisturbed, she writes her journal using notes on scraps of paper, bits and

126

pieces of recollection, remembered dialogue, and her own observations. She also indulges in erotic reveries, Lance more and more being their object. She knows he has begun to fixate on her, though he tries to hide it. Around her he is too alert, too seemingly casual, too interested in what she says or what she thinks about what he says.

Allegra for her part can scarcely keep her hands off of him. "Talk about dewy youth," she notes down for her journal. "He is a regular Adonis what with that Arkwright jaw, those steady, green-gray eyes, and the finely cut full lips. I can almost feel the tension that runs through his back and shoulders. I don't think I've ever seen him slouching. And what breaks my heart, what keeps me chaste as a nun, is that he reminds me of Frank when he had been so vital, so *there*."

Allegra is also entranced by the wildlife she sees at night – foxes, owls, deer, and more than once, a large black bear. She finally understands, she thinks, what she calls the voyeurism of nature. "These other beings, complete and perfect in their limited spheres, have lives of their own. They are the offspring of the same evolutionary process that created human kind and they are out there making a living." Thus, she watches with utter enchantment when a mother skunk and four young explore the ground around the barn garden grubbing for insects and worms. At the same time, when she sees a doe with two fauns, she writes, "I didn't see Bambi at all. I saw venison and could nearly taste the marvelous stew Ari would make of it."

*

Allegra is on duty the night of the storm. It had been gathering most of that hot afternoon, the blue black clouds building dramatically to the west, then appearing to stall. Until, with the heat going out of the air over the farm, they move in, a thunder and lightning show of brilliant, frequent flashes and ear-stunning noise. The rain suddenly pelting down seems spawned by light and sound.

The storm comes and goes and comes and goes again until its repetition achieves something like a steady state of extreme weather. Cyrus closes down their "mini-grid," and they have dinner by candlelight. Allegra quickly finishes her main course of home-made tofu, mushrooms, and rice and goes into the recon room to give Nicole a chance to eat with the others.

Dusk comes early as the storm abates, leaving behind a dense cloud cover and rising, moving mists. The reception on the laptop screens, now powered by batteries, is murky at best. As Jack has said, it's the time you have to stay especially vigilant. So Allegra is particularly watchful, even when pleasantly surprised by Mary, who brings her a dish of apple dowdy. Mary sits with her aunt and together they watch as a fat woodchuck waddles up to the horse barn and sniffs the air. Something alarms it and makes it turn and amble back up into the field.

When Mary leaves, Allegra takes out a scrap of paper on which to jot notes. She has a complex thought to record, something to do with children being the hope of the future, but wondering what future children like Mary would have.

In the midst of these musing, her eye catches movement from the camera covering the town road where it comes from the west. She clicks an icon that makes the quadrant fill the whole screen. A small figure, ghostly in the mists and uncertain light, wavers, stops, and then turns up the drive toward the house.

A child, Allegra thinks. But who? And what to do? Whoever it is doesn't pose any kind of threat unless ill with the flu. She pushes the orange button, indicating a low-level alarm.

Most everyone else is still in the kitchen, some having seconds of the apple dowdy when Jack hears the buzz from the recon room. He gets up quickly, thinking this would be a good night to attack. He checks the image with Allegra and then goes outside. He crosses the lawn and the low wall and halts just inside the heavy gate of the barrier fence. Through night-vision binoculars, he can make out the figure of a young girl as she draws closer. A trap, he wonders? But that wouldn't be the McFeralls' style. They would come at them with full bluster.

He puts on the back-up lights. Grace comes to stand beside him. "It looks like Linda Neill," she says. "I hope nothing..."

"We can't let her in," Jack says automatically as Cyrus and Nicole join them along with Nicole to look at the mist-swept scene beyond the fence.

"We can't just leave her there," Nicole says. "She'll die. Something's happened to her family."

Jack says, "This is exactly what we have to steel ourselves about. If she's infected, then she'll infect all of us. If we bring her in, we could all die." But his heart isn't in his words.

Cyrus says, "Nicole's right. Something must have happened to her folks."

The others stand back while Grace goes to the gate, without opening it, talks to the girl. She turns to the others. "Rig the quarantine tent."

"I'll get a cot and some blankets," Nicole says.

"Two cots, a towel, and clothes," Grace says. "I'll be staying with her. And tell Ari we'll need some warm soup and bread. And at least masks, though I don't think she's infected. We'll test her."

Grace unlocks the heavy gate and opens it enough for the girl to come inside.

The quarantine tent, kept in readiness to set up quickly on a platform near the bath house, is well-lit and nearly cozy as the last of the storm stirs the old maple nearby. Sitting on the cot and dressed in dry clothes, nine-year-old Linda Neill, who is slight, with black hair and blue eyes, takes soup from Grace in small spoonfuls. Her body still shakes, but color is coming back into her cheeks as she revives.

Jack sits on the other cot, the one his mother is going to use. Like her he has on a mask. "You don't have to tell us what happened now," he says gently.

But Linda wants to tell her story. "Mom died from the sickness..."

"The flu?" Jack asks.

"We don't think so. She had a condition... and her medicine ran out."

"When was that?" Grace is surprised.

"A few days ago."

"We didn't know. Someone should have said something."

The girl nods. "Dad said me and Alex would be okay. He said he had lots of things put away." She takes some bread and dips it in the soup.

With an effort, fighting tears, she goes on. "Then the men came..."

"Today?"

She nods again.

"About what time?"

"In the afternoon." She is silent. They wait.

Then Jack prompts gently, "Then what happened?"

"They broke down the door. I went and hid in the bathroom. My Dad told them he would give them anything they wanted. But they shot him anyway. And then Alex."

Very softly, Jack asks, "Do you know who the men were?"

She takes a deep breath. "One of them was Mr. McFerall and another one was his brother. They used to work with Dad. They were friends."

"But then they weren't friends?" Jack is impressed with her composure.

"They had a fight. Last winter. Dad said they owed him money."

"And the others?"

"They were just men."

"You're sure it was the McFeralls?"

"Yes. Dad used to call them Dunc and Bru."

She begins to weep, face in her hands, her sobs strangely adult.

Grace comforts her. "I and somebody will be out here with you for the next couple of days. We'll find you a place in the house. You're safe now."

The girl lifts her reddened face. "I can stay with you?"

Jack says, "You can stay with us."

11

They arrange another burial detail. Duvall, Ari, and Allegra stand watch with weapons while Lance, Marko, and Bella take the first shift digging graves next to where Helen Neill is buried in the backyard of her own house. Alex Neill, a seventeen-year-old, had been shot execution style in the back of the head. His father Greg was blasted in the chest with both barrels of a shotgun.

"It was sad beyond words," Allegra writes in her journal. "Alex wasn't that much younger than Lance. Even in death he had the fresh bloom of a boy coming into manhood. We wound both of the bodies in sheets and Jack got into the graves and arranged them, as though trying to make them comfortable."

That afternoon before a meeting of the Defense Committee, Jack pleads with his father for permission to assassinate at least one of the brothers. Or make the attempt. More specifically, he wants his dad not to oppose him when he brings up a plan at the meeting. They are alone on the porch overlooking the barn garden. Jack says, "The McFeralls are a clear and present danger. Duncan cannot control Bruce. You should have seen what they did to that boy."

Jack's quandary as to kill or not to kill is resolved, at least for the moment. Beyond preemption, he wants revenge. He remembers Alex as though he was still there. He had been a good kid, hardworking and bright with an easy, freckled smile and an honest laugh.

"It's not for us to be judge, jury, and executioner," says Cyrus who had not seen the aftermath of the killings in the Neill house. He knows he should have gone there – as a witness.

"Dad, please listen, this is warfare, not crime and punishment with due process."

Early crickets sound loud in the silence.

At length Cyrus says, as he had said before, "We are not going to give ourselves a license to kill."

131

"That means the McFeralls are going to keep murdering innocent people like the Neills because no one is willing to stand up to them."

Cyrus sighs audibly. "Even if I agreed with you, Jack, I couldn't sanction what you want to do. If anything happened to you, we would be all but defenseless. We would have to evacuate immediately. And we're not ready for that."

Jack nods as though agreeing. How to tell his father that a night raid to kill a specific target is his métier. Or had been. He would be there and gone, leaving no sign but men with broken necks or slit throats. At the same time, his father has a point: though Ari and Duvall had a good grasp of tactics, he would be essential to any defense of Sugar Mountain should it be attacked. Then, remembering the body of the teenage boy, he is angry again. Bitterness in his voice, he says, "The Neills were our people even if they didn't live here. They helped us build this place..."

"Jack..."

"The McFeralls were sending us a message... One of these days, they're going to come right up this hill and slaughter us. Bruce is a stone cold killer. He will go room to room with a shotgun or a pistol and murder us one by one..."

Cyrus doesn't rise to the bait. He looks directly at Jack. He says, "We have not been attacked. Any aggression on your part will simply provoke them to do exactly what you describe."

Jack slumps into the comfortable wicker armchair. He wants to find Ari and knock back a few shots of Sugar Mountain calvados. He says, "Then at least sanction a reconnaissance of the McFerall compound. We need to know what they're up to."

"Let's bring it up at the meeting."

Because of its importance, all of the adults, with the exception of Chee, Meredith and Marko, are members of the Defense Committee. They meet around the kitchen table, the doors closed. In a tone signaling his disapproval, Cyrus opens by saying that Jack has a proposal to make.

Jack wants to stand and talk, but he thinks better of it. He glances around at the expectant faces and starts with a description of what happened and what they found at the Neills' house. Like any atrocity, it has the staying power to shock.

He pauses. He says, "I think it would be in the interest of the whole region as well as Sugar Mountain if Bruce or Duncan McFerall or both were eliminated."

"You mean murdered?" Grace says.

"Murder is a crime. This would be self-defense. It would be justice."

Duvall smiles. "Who would administer this justice?"

"I would."

Allegra says, "Do you think you could?"

"It's what I did for ten years." He looks around at them. "I wouldn't just walk in and start firing. I would reconnoiter, even set up a surveillance camera. Once I knew their set-up, I would go at night. I could kill at least one of them."

Cyrus repeats his argument that Jack is needed to defend Sugar Mountain if it is attacked. There is general agreement on that point.

"At the very least then, we should make a reconnaissance of the McFerall place so that we know what's there."

The discussion gets sidetracked into talking about the need to drive around the area to see what's happening generally. Risky, someone proffers. Not with a couple of the Defense Squad along for the ride with weapons. What about the fuel? Charge the Prius off the mains and drive in the all-electric mode. Virtually no noise that way.

Jack listens and withdraws into himself, into plans that verge on dark fantasies. Wait for a moonless, cloudy night. Take one of the mountain bikes and pedal over. Make a recon. Find out where the brothers bed down. Return. Knife and Glock only.

*

The next morning, Grace accompanied by Allegra in the backseat and Duvall next to her in the front, eases down the drive and turns right toward the center of Headleyville and the regional middle school. Grace doesn't know what to expect. The emergency center was a scene of desolation the last time she was there. The few houses they pass look deserted, high grass on the lawns, vehicles covered with dust, windows shut, no lights.

They are alongside a field just before the town center when Duvall asks Grace to pull over. He gets out and looks at something through binoculars. Allegra joins him. About fifty yards into the field, turkey vultures, ravens, and crows cluster and flit around a dark form on the ground.

"A body," Duvall says.

Allegra nods. "Should we...?"

Duvall shakes his head. "We can't bury them all."

The town center, scarcely more than a small gas station, a Congregational church converted into a meeting hall, a decrepit general store with post office attached, is moribund. If there's anyone there at all, they are in hiding, perhaps with weapons behind curtained windows. Even the graveyard, its headstones forlorn among the uncut grass, appears deserted.

They drive through slowly and turn into the drive that arches in front of the school. Two pickup trucks are parked near the double doors, the main entrance to the place.

Allegra senses danger first. She says to Grace, who has put on a mask, unbuckled, and opened her door, "I don't think this is a good idea."

Grace says, "I'd like to know what's going on here."

Duvall gets out as well. He hesitates, then leaves his AR15 on the seat and says to Allegra. "Cover us." As they approach the doors, one of them opens. A man of about forty with shaggy hair and a rusty stubble, stands back from the opening. His shorts and tee-shirt hang off of him like someone who has lost weight. "Who are you?" he asks, his voice not as baleful as the glance he gives Duvall.

Grace says, "We live nearby. I'm just checking the center to see if it's still being used." The man is vaguely familiar but she can't recall his name.

"Yeah, well we're living here now." A four or five year old

boy comes and entwines himself around the man's legs. "Jamie, get inside."

He turns back to them. His voice conciliatory in a fake way, he says, "And just who are you folks? Where do you live?"

When Grace starts to reply, Duvall says, "We're up in Colrain. On a farm."

"Colrain, huh? Well, if you folks want to wait around a bit, I can get someone to talk to you."

That puts Grace on her guard. When she says no thanks and starts back to the car with Duvall, the man turns and yells at someone inside.

A moment later another man, tall and balding, appears in the doorway. He is trying to work a clip into an automatic weapon.

"I've got you covered," Allegra yells through the open window of the car. And she does, the sights of the AR15 right on the man's thin chest. He sees her and ducks back inside.

A moment later they are racing back towards Sugar Mountain as fast as the car will go. They are on a stretch of road after going through the center when Grace notices that one of the pickups is following them.

Duvall is on the walkie-talkie. "I think we ran into some of the McFerall gang. They're following us in a Dodge pickup. You might want to cover us as we come up the drive."

Which Jack does. He takes the sniper rifle and sets up outside the fence. Moments later, the Prius turns onto the drive with speed. As it approaches, the pickup truck slows. Jack has it in sight as it pauses at the top of the drive. Not long afterwards, a second pickup drives up from the same direction. Bruce McFerall gets out and walks toward the other pickup with a rifle in hand.

Jack has the man's left temple in the crosshairs. Maybe just a warning shot. Take off his nose. A trim on top. Or get it over with. The Jack of old wouldn't have hesitated. The day before he had been willing to assassinate the man and his brother. But killing the man now might only bring their ragtag army down on them. And, his father's words: We will not give ourselves a license to kill.

Bruce has binoculars to his face. Jack doesn't try to hide the glint of his scope. Suddenly Bruce and the others scurry to their trucks. They get in and drive back the way they came. The Prius has pulled up and parked behind the solar panels. "All clear," Jack yells to them. He is already regretting not having shot Bruce McFerall in the head.

The incident rattles the members of the Sugar Mountain refuge. It signifies that their freedom of movement, their birthright as Americans, is gone, like so much else.

In her journal, Allegra describes what happened in detail, adding what she calls commentary. "I came a hair-trigger away from shooting the bald guy in the chest. Had he raised his weapon, I know I would have done so. I make no excuses nor do I chastise myself. It's what I've become."

*

A drought begins. With the exception of a couple of thunder storms, there is no rain. The sky repeatedly promises but does not deliver. The clouds build daily to no effect beyond distant heat lightning. The garden begins to wilt. And they have planted too much for a simple bucket brigade to suffice.

So they start irrigating. Cyrus, with Duvall's help, cleans out and opens a valve that allows water from Little Creek to flow gurgling into a four-inch clay pipe. It feeds a dried-up cattle pond at the lower end of the pasture near the hayfield. Though the land is drying out, the creek, supplied by water held in vast shoals of glacial till in the surrounding hills, maintains a healthy flow.

From the cattle pond, they uncoil a stretch of one-inch PVC pipe to bring water by gravity to the garden. Soon lengths of garden hose perforated with small holes are seeping water into the soil between the rows of vegetables. The sagging leafage of the tomatoes, beans, squash, cucumbers, potatoes, eggplant and others firm up overnight.

The Sugar Mountaineers greet the revival of the garden with visceral relief. The garden is no foodie indulgence. They need it for survival. No garden means, eventually, no food.

136

But then thinking and talking about food has taken on an existential intensity. There are no grocery stores much less supermarkets, no butcher shops, roadside stands, pizza delivery, restaurants, fast food franchises. Nicole maintains a list of their provisions down to the last cup of flour. As though to practice for what is to come, they ration themselves on Wednesdays to two meals and a snack. What few scraps are left on plates goes to feed the pigs. Other leftovers are recycled into new dishes or end up in the *pot au feu* that Ari simmers periodically on the kitchen stove.

Ari is everyone's favorite cook, a job that rotates among him, Nicole, Duvall and Lise. He has a knack for conjuring seemingly gourmet meals out of basic ingredients. As a side dish to a casserole of canned salmon – not bad itself with a sauce of fresh dill – he slices several green tomatoes into half-inch slabs, dips them in flour, beaten egg, and what he calls industrial parmesan before sautéing them in spiced olive oil. He does the same with a puffball mushroom ten inches in diameter. Not so the oyster mushrooms Thad comes across while doing a routine check of one of the monitoring cameras. They bristle in cartoonish profusion along a tree trunk moldering into the ground. Ari wrings his hands in glee. He, Thad, and Allegra harvest more than a bushel. About three-quarters of these they set out on rough boards in the sun to dry. The rest, lightly salted, are also sautéed in oil to go with dinner.

Allegra notes in her journal that Ari provides them with more than tasty meals. When word spreads around that Ari is in the kitchen, even Frank perks up. He might shave and some of the encroaching gauntness would appear to abate, if only for an evening. Meredith brightens out of her perpetual funk and works on her face; even she does not want to miss the occasion of an Ari dinner.

*

Despite the dryness, or perhaps because of it, the raspberries ripen quickly and in great abundance. Nicole organizes a team including herself to do the first picking. She lists Lise, Bella, Marko and the three older girls for a nine o'clock start. The patch, about twenty by forty feet, has gotten a bit overgrown, but there are clearly demarcated rows.

They assemble just outside the security fence in front of the house, Marko arriving late as usual. Nicole leads them down the drive to the patch and preps them there. "I know it may not seem like rocket science to pick berries," she says, "but there is a knack to it." She adjusts her voice, which has begun to sound too sweetly preachy, like that of a grade school teacher. "If we're not careful, it's easy to miss some, even a lot. Also empty your basket into the pail right here before your basket gets too full. And no leaves, twigs, bugs or bubblegum..."

Mary rolls her eyes. "Mom, there is no more bubblegum."

"I know, I know. And also, keep yourselves covered. Ticks love raspberries."

They begin, each with a twenty-foot row. Nicole supervises with a light touch, checking mostly on the girls. They do well, being the right height and with nimble fingers to find and pluck the fruit that often ripens profusely under leaves. Bella keeps up a chatter with Lise, about recipes for Chinese dishes and her favorite deserts. Lise mentions the jelled raspberry juice Ari used in a trifle.

Marko Slone both dawdles and moves quickly up the row, dumping less than a pint into the pail.

Nicole sighs and checks the row. Most of the ripe berries remained. She confronts him with gentle reproof. "Marko, this needs redoing."

He shrugs and does the same again, dumping a few more raspberries into the pail.

Nicole glances up from her own row and notices him sitting on the ground, his face up to the sun. As she admits later, "I lost my cool." She goes over to him and peers down into his smug bland face. The rest stop picking and watch.

"Marko, why don't you go up to the house and see if Grace has anything for you to do."

"Why?"

"Why? Because you're useless here. Come to think of it, you're useless everywhere. So why don't you do what football players do."

"Yeah, and what's that?"

"I don't know. Find a tree and run into it."

Marko shrugs. "You're the boss." He turns and walks up the drive toward the front of the house.

Nicole is still angry that evening when she meets for a drink with Jack, Cyrus and Grace. She says, nursing the weakest of whiskeys, "The man is useless. He is deliberately useless."

"But what can we do with him?" asks Grace. She knows about his being less than uselessness. Everything he does from washing dishes to keeping the stove going to mucking out the pigs or picking up the eggs has to be redone.

"I could force him to leave." Jack is smiling his twisted smile. He might enjoy the job.

"But with violence," his dad correctly figures.

"Or the threat of violence."

Cyrus sighs. "You would think we could do better than that."

Nicole shakes her head. "I think Jack's right. That world is gone... I mean the hand-holding of misfits is over."

"I agree with Nicole." Jack looks at his father and then his mother. "And Marko is a liability in more ways than one."

"Perhaps he wants to leave," Grace offers. "Perhaps we could find a way to encourage him." She smiles at Jack. "Peacefully."

Nicole says, "I don't think Bella would object. She's getting it. She's starting to apologize for him."

"And she's starting to warm up to Duvall, of all people," Grace says.

Cyrus says, "Let's keep this discussion about Marko to ourselves. On second thought, perhaps we should bring Ari and Thad in on this. They might have some ideas."

*

With or without Marko, the raspberries pile up. Under Nicole's direction, about a quarter of the harvest goes into making jam. About half is preserved in jars in its own juice. The remainder is eaten – at breakfast and for dessert at night with ice cream made from goats milk cream and egg whites.

Picking raspberries with the others helps Linda fit in after she emerges from quarantine. They give her a bed in the room shared by Rachael and Mary. The three quickly became friends, though Linda, who is shy and accommodating, clings to Grace. "She's still in shock, the poor thing," Grace says to her husband one afternoon as they lay down for a rest in their bedroom. "She told me she dreams about her family every night. She says she feels like they are still down there waiting for her to come home."

The more aware denizens of Sugar Mountain cannot but be invidious when comparing Linda's courage to that of Frank or Marko. As Grace notes, Linda's girlhood has been wrenched from her. Though she watched her mother die and saw her brother and father murdered, Linda tempers her grief with gratitude. She moves among them, helpful and cooperative, in a state of inviolate dignity that beguiles.

Frank especially suffers in comparison, though he, too has lost his world. And he does, sporadically, try to adjust. But it is an ever-diminishing version of himself that sits at meals or hoes weakly in the garden or distractedly dandles Lily on his lap. Frank wants to be there. Or, more precisely, he wants to want to be there. But for him there is no there.

In the best of times, Frank never cared much for weekends or vacations at Sugar Mountain. What attracted everyone else – the fresh air, hill walking, nature, gardening, swimming in the millpond – bored him. So he went to the farm prepared with tickets for Tanglewood, where he and Allegra would meet friends from New York at a local bistro. Or take in an exhibition at Mass MOCA or the Sterling Clark Museum. He would even go to Saratoga for a day at the races. Anything to escape the tedium of country living.

Grace worries about him. He is both her son and her reluctant patient. His immune system is weakening. Or that's what she assumes as Frank suffers through a variety of colds, rashes, and less obvious ailments.

Marko is also fading. He is shunned by most everyone else at Sugar Mountain. It occurs gradually, spontaneously, and with such subtlety that a visiting outsider might not remark it. Or, the visitor might have thought it is Marko who is shunning the others as he moves among them like a corporeal ghost in deadpan aloofness and virtual silence except for his muttered jibes and open disdain for almost everything the group works at. Like an obedient child in class, he speaks only when spoken to and then in monosyllables.

Though he eats his meals with everyone else, he does so silently and quickly, rising wordlessly when he has finished and leaving the room. When it is his turn, he helps, sort of, with the dishes or sweeps the floor. He mucks out the pigs and shifts firewood for the bath house boiler and helps with the laundry. But he does not participate in any real sense. All the while he wears the expression of someone biding his time. Probably for the call from the Dallas Cowboys, which has become something of a running joke among the others.

Marko all but disappears during his time off, usually to the upper pasture where, just inside the woods, he has made himself a rough habitation with the old tent Grace gave him. They see him doing wind sprints on a level stretch of pasture. He does persist at that. Bare-chested, in shorts and running shoes, he gets down in a three-point stance, pauses, then rockets off, heading downfield to tackle an imaginary ball carrier. Again and again and again.

On occasion, Jack glances up to find Marko watching him with such obvious venom in his gaze that he looks like a bad actor overplaying his part. Even so, Jack is of two minds about Marko. He would have liked to have the man on the Defense Squad. Marko is big, fast, and athletic. Meaning he might be a good shot and, presumably, steady under fire. Jack considers taking him aside for a man-to-man chat. But he cannot bring himself to it. He sees Marko as smug, stupidly arrogant, oblivious to others, and suffering from an ego distended by years of witless adulation as a star high school and college athlete. But it's more than personal: he sees Marko as a threat to their security, someone who would betray them for the sake of betrayal. Among a gang like the McFeralls he would be a celebrity. A pro football player! Jack goes so far as to consider making him disappear. But that is the old Jack, and Jack keeps the old Jack not so much under restraint as in reserve.

Allegra tries late one hot afternoon to draw Marko out. They are returning from the garden with a work party. A lot of them are planning on a swim. She says, "Bella tells me you play professional football." The notion of professional football seems ludicrous under the circumstances. But then, so did the notion of being a professor of English.

He mumbles something about playing on special teams.

"So are things going any better?"

"Better than what?"

"Than when you and Bella first arrived. I mean it was pretty rough..."

"It's pretty rough now. Bella never said anything about slavery."

"You could always leave."

"Yeah, that's what I keep hearing."

She stops to watch a vee of geese go honking over.

He scarcely notices. Looking down at her, he says "So what's it to you?"

She shrugs not very convincingly. "You're one of us. Part of the family."

He looks thoughtful for a moment. He says, "You want to get it on?"

His proposition has all the charm of a rude noise. With a dismissiveness he doesn't catch, she says, "No thanks." Then, as the ensuing silence lengthens, she tries an old parry: "Why do you ask?"

He snorts. "Let's just say that Frank doesn't look like he's up to much in that department."

She winces. Is it that obvious? She fobs him off with a dismissive wave and goes up the stairs to where Frank is lying

142

down going through old messages on his cell phone. Marko's right. He isn't up to much in that department. Or in most other departments for that matter.

Later, she confides to her journal that the man's blunt proposition turned her on. "What dirty little secrets we keep even from ourselves," she writes. "I roused myself thinking of the brute astride me. But when it came to it, so to speak, it was Lance again and then again."

Indeed, as Frank fades from life and from Allegra's life, Lance begins increasingly to occupy her thoughts, fancies, and fantasies. She scarcely needs to invoke his presence in all its priapic force during moments of self-pleasuring. He is simply there, like air or sunshine. He is also there in reality, every day, several times a day, aware of her and trying not to show it. And, seemingly by happenstance, they find themselves alone more than might be usual. They are a fire team on the Defense Squad. They work side-by-side in the vegetable patch. They over-lap during stints in the recon room, often in the middle of the night.

All through this, a kind of mutual tutorial is underway. She takes him through the intricacies and ecstasies of poetry. He teaches her the endless ins and outs of evolutionary theory. In this, their disagreements have the charm of intimacy in being something apart from the others around them. Thus has Allegra claimed, in several iterations, "Evolution cannot account for art."

"Yes, but even art evolves."

"That is not the same thing. I'm saying there is no good evolutionary reason for art. There's no way it contributes to what you call..."

"Fitness."

"Fitness. Yes, reproductive success." She smiles to herself at being able to use his language.

"Then why have it?"

She shrugs. "It's both necessary and gratuitous. It's what makes us human."

He nods. "I like that."

A moment later she is smiling inwardly again but with as much pain as pleasure when he says, "I think about you a lot."

"I think about you a lot," she echoes. "But it's not something we can talk about."

"I know."

Allegra recounts the exchange in her journal:

> *The affair has begun. In prohibiting talk about our mutual attraction and what exactly we think when we think about each other, I inadvertently (or deliberately?) acknowledged the reality of it and gave it a license silence would not have.*
>
> *Truth be told, I am horny with a desire beyond sex. I want another child. I want life. I think Nicole is pregnant or trying to get there. Lise, too. And even Bella has that broody look at times. She's been working hard, losing weight, and looking much better. She's also been flirting with Duvall. Or even getting it on with him for all I know. Duvall has said more than once that he's bi. Where that leaves Thad, I don't know. Perhaps there's enough to go around.*

Not for the first time, Allegra has intuited correctly. Late that same afternoon in the time out period when people go off to their quarters to rest and get ready for dinner, Jack and Nicole relax in their room with a half bottle of wine from their private stock.

"How do you think it's going?" Nicole asks him, sitting close to him on the small couch under the window.

"So far, so good. Marko's still the joker in the pack, but Bella seems to be doing okay. I'm worried about Frank."

"Have you spoken to him?"

"I've tried. He's evasive. He always has been. It's what made him a good corporate lawyer."

Nicole says, "There are a lot of similarities between them – Frank and Marko..."

"Oh, come on..."

"No, seriously. Neither one of them can adjust. They're both in denial. Frank knows what's happened and can't accept it. Marko is too... limited...

"Stupid..."

"Okay, stupid. He doesn't realize the world has changed radically and for the foreseeable future."

They have gone over this before with variations. This time the wine helps them ease back, relax, get ready for love making. This time it is Nicole who initiates the familiar pattern sensing the timbre of his voice deepening and softening. She puts her hand on his thigh. She says in a half whisper, "I haven't been this turned on since I was twenty."

Jack returns a long, probing kiss.

She says, "I want to get pregnant."

He says, "I need to shower."

"No you don't." She begins to unzip him.

"Where's Cy?"

"He went up to the pond with a bunch of grown-ups."

Jack laughs softly. "Then let's make him a brother."

"Or a sister."

*

Cy has tagged along with Bella, Duvall, and Thad to the pond, the day being in the eighties and sunny. He is having something of a crisis. There are no other boys to play with. Lily has become everyone's pet and the older girls are beneath his dignity. He does dad-and-son things with Jack like fishing for trout in the stream. He engages Henry, getting him to talk about his memories of World War II. But if he has a special pal among the grown-ups, it is Uncle Thad or, as Cy calls him, "Taddy."

Their empathy includes a shared interest in computers and things electronic, about which Thad likes to talk at length. He has told his big-eyed nephew about the wonders of the vanished internet and how, with the click of a mouse, you could conjure almost anything you wanted onto the screen.

"Is it gone forever?" Cy asks. They are lying on the granite in the sun wearing swim suits out of deference to the three older girls, who are splashing around on the other side of the pool under the watchful eye of Lise and Chee. Lance is also there, but clothed, his AR15 at the ready.

"I hope not," Thad tells him. "But there are a lot of moving parts that have to keep moving."

"So why don't they just keep moving?"

Thad launches into a description of the net, the servers, the endless links, the redundancies that made it, in ordinary times, all but indestructible. "But it doesn't run by itself. It needs people and power." He loses Cy when he begins to compare it to a human brain, "the billions of words, ideas, pictures and all that adding up to a kind of consciousness."

Cy asks, "What is consciousness?"

Thad explains.

"So it's like the world has gone to sleep," Cy says.

12

With the virtual collapse of the internet, the world appears not only to have gone to sleep but to have lapsed into a coma. The silence, both electronic and aural, is so unremitting that there are days at a time when Sugar Mountain seems the only human reality left on the planet. It is such that the sound of a far-off vehicle makes them pause with a hope edged with fear as they wonder who could that be.

Repeatedly, they try to get through to the state police, to the regional headquarters of the National Guard, to Homeland Security. Nothing. Though, every once in a while, the radio sounds with the Emergency Broadcast warning. Those in the recon room wait, thinking, finally, here it comes. Only to have it followed by static, like some universal code for nothingness.

While a news blackout holds in the larger world, Cyrus is able with patience and persistence to glean from the airwaves some of what is happening in Franklin County. Members of the MAG are connected, however peripherally, to other networks. And if the news at times does not rise above the level of rumor, it is better than nothing. Even when the news is horrific, as in the case of the McMurrays.

The initial reports are difficult to credit. Six adults and five children murdered and buried in a common grave. Slowly, the grisly details emerge as Cyrus sits for hours over the CB set on a Sunday morning in late July. The McMurrays, Dan and his wife Ella, owners and operators of a two-hundred acre dairy and goat farm in the town of Charlemont, supplied raw milk, cream, and whey to artisanal cheese-making operations in the area. With the pandemic looming, their two grown sons along with their wives and children arrived to live with them. They kept the farm going, bartering milk and home-made cheese with friends and neighbors.

Hal Beck, grim voiced, confirms the reports. All of them, men, women, and children have been murdered in the attack and buried in a common grave. "There was an eye witness," Beck tells Cyrus. "A neighbor named Mike Landry watched through night vision binoculars. He told me he saw them use a backhoe to dig a trench and he counted the bodies as they put them into it."

"Why the killing?" Cyrus asks him.

"Apparently they resisted. You know and Bruce... He's got several like-minded thugs that helped with the dirty work. I've heard they're called Bruce's Bunch."

"But why the McMurrays?" Grace asks later. She, Jack, and Cyrus are huddled together in the studio to go over the news.

Jack says, "Food. The farm produces food and food supplies are running low. It's the new currency." He didn't have to spell out that Sugar Mountain would make a tempting target just for that reason. "They wore ski masks, but it's got the McFeralls written all over it," Jack says. "They have a couple of Humvees and one report says the attackers used two 'armored jeeps.'" He's regretting again that he didn't kill Bruce McFerall when he had him in the crosshairs. "We already know what they've been doing. How is this any different from what they did to the Neills?"

"That was a confrontation that got out of hand," Grace says. Like Cyrus, she wants to mitigate the worst.

Cyrus says, "We'll know for sure who was behind it when we find out who's been given the place to live in."

They call a meeting of the Defense Committee. It's Monday morning when they gather in the studio, doors closed. For the first time Bella is included in the group. Cyrus starts with a summary of the latest bad news.

"Do we know if the McMurrays offered any resistance?" Ari asks.

Cyrus shakes his head. The strain is starting to show in his voice. "No one seems to know. It's probable. One of the sons was ex-military."

"Are there really no authorities to turn to?" Nicole, who knew the family, especially Ella, is angry. Like Jack she wants to do something.

Cyrus, wearily, "Pat Cummings told me he got through to

voice mail at the Department of Public Security and left a message about the killing." He pauses. "Jack wants to say something about the overall situation."

Jack points to the map of the area on the wall. The red, blue, yellow, and orange pushpins now dot the western half of the county. "I'm not sure how reliable these are."

"All by the McFeralls?" Ari asks.

"Hard to say. There are other gangs out there. But right around here, a pattern appears to be forming that has Duncan and Bruce written all over it."

"But why?" Bella wants to know.

Jack acknowledges her. "Mostly for food and places to put their people. They have a considerable following. It gets to be a small army when you count wives, girl friends, children, relatives."

"You were talking about a pattern." Thad brings him back to the point he was making.

"Yes. Well, once a target has been decided on, the owners are told their property is being 'requisitioned' by the National Guard as a base of operations. The owners are given twenty-four hours to get out. If they resist, they are attacked like the McMurrays, no quarter given."

"But women and children?" says Grace, who can't quite grasp it.

"A terror tactic," Jack says. "Word gets around. And people will do almost anything other than put their kids at risk." But Jack knows it's more than a tactic. He knows the sick thrill of killing.

"And no witnesses," Duvall adds.

"But killing the children?" Grace says again.

"Bruce always had a crazy streak," Jack reminds her. "Remember the kid he beat up in Heath when he was deputy sheriff. Nearly killed him."

"And it's not the first time that ordinary people turn out to be killers," Ari puts in.

Thad, looking at the map and some of the distances involved, asks, "Where are they getting their fuel?"

Jack makes a shrugging motion. "They commandeered at least

one gas station early on. And probably hijacked a couple of tankers along the way. If we could find their depots, we could..." He smiles at the thought.

"Are we on the list?" Allegra is ready to fight.

Jack rolls the map up. "We don't really know. I don't think we're high on their list nor does Cyrus. They know we have weapons and know how to use them. But they will get around to us eventually, I'm sure of it."

"We have one advantage." To their expectant faces, Cyrus says, "They want Sugar Mountain for themselves. That's the bad news. It's also the good news because it means they won't try to burn us out, at least not at first."

"At worst," Grace adds, "That will give us time to withdraw in an orderly fashion."

"So what do we do in the meanwhile?" Ari asks. "Just wait for them to come and get us?"

Jack nods appreciatively at him. "That hits the nail on the head."

Nicole asks, "What about the state? They can't do anything? I mean about the McFeralls and people like them?"

Thad says, "Believe it or not, I was able to reach the Office of Public Safety this morning. A real person who wouldn't identify himself told me everything was under control. When I mentioned the situation here, he told me they knew all about it and that they have everything under control. Typical."

"What about the world at large?" Grace asks. "Have you been able to raise the internet?"

Thad again. "It's intermittent at best, but hollowed out. Things are not good. In places it seems that the mortality rate from the flu is eighty percent. That's probably not just the flu but all the other things that happen when the infrastructure collapses."

"So what do we do in the meanwhile? I mean before they deign to attack us?" Ari is getting impatient.

Jack turns to Cyrus. "Dad, perhaps we can start with the refuge." He is being accommodating.

Cyrus ponders for a moment. "Grace, Nicole, why don't you

150

brief us on The Ledges. Not everyone knows about it."

Nicole describes their fallback refuge in a wooded area of their property well north of the open land. She goes on, "We have the basics in place. That includes food, shelter, blankets, medicines, and fuel. But if we're going to survive, we'll need to move a lot more up there."

"So we could move up there now if we had to?" Allegra asks. She senses the tension between Jack and Cyrus over the old conundrum of fight or flight.

"We could," Nicole tells her, but only for a few months. Referring to a tablet she has open on the table, she goes through the various permutations, tallying the food supplies available and what they could expect over time from the garden, berry patches, and orchards as well as meat and eggs from the chickens, milk from the goats, and meat from the suckling pigs and the sow.

"Remember," she says, "once we leave here, we have no eggs from the hens, no milk from the goats, and nothing from the garden, berry patch, and orchard."

Cyrus says, "I'm for moving most of our provisions to The Ledges. Immediately."

Jack puts up his hand. "It's only fair to discuss other options first."

There are murmured assents.

Cyrus smiles. He plays by the rules. He says, "Okay, Jack, let's hear them."

Jack glances around. He wants everyone's attention. "We have several options. First, we pack up and head for the hills at the first sign of trouble. That begs the question: why all this work? Have we slaved all these years, months, and weeks to provide the McFerall clan with comfortable quarters, with heat, power, food, and a nice place to swim? I say no and I say there are things we can do."

They wait expectantly even though most know what Jack had in mind. Like his dad, he has done some politicking.

"Okay, the first thing we can do is hone our weapons and tactics and strengthen our fortifications. Let's call that option two, option one being evacuation to The Ledges. That may not be enough, not in the long run." He waits for comments. There aren't any.

"Option three involves two steps." He turns to the large flat screen from the recon room that has been mounted on the wall nearby. He clicks it on showing a download from Google Earth of the area around Sugar Mountain.

"How recent is this?" Ari asks.

"Within the last six months. But it should suffice." He points to a little red balloon with an A in it. "Here we are." He zooms out to show more terrain and another marker, this one with a B on it. "And here are the McFeralls. As the crow flies, it's just about three miles from here. By road, trail, and bushwacking, it's closer to four."

"The point being?" asks Grace.

"Right. First, we set up surveillance of Pitts Hollow." He hesitates, thinking back to the recent moonlit night when he stole away again to view the McFerall place through night vision binoculars. There has been bivouac tents, Humvees under cover and a couple of pickups. He had also seen what looked like foundation holes for new sheds.

"What kind of surveillance?" Cyrus already sounds dubious.

"Thad and I would mount a microphone and a camera high in a tree above their compound. With those, we'll be able to tell when they're staging and deploying for an attack. We might know how many and what kinds of weapons and vehicles they are mobilizing."

"I don't like it," Cyrus says. "If they found it, they would take it as a provocation."

Jack points himself at his father. "Dad, knowledge is power. And knowledge is nonviolent."

"It would be like watching dangerous wildlife," Thad says, only half joking.

"It would be an escalation," Cyrus persists, but there is faltering conviction in his voice.

"And the second part of this option?" Grace asks.

"We stage a raid. At night. We slip in, set some charges, and retreat. We aim only at the Humvees and any munitions they have stored."

"Exactly," Cyrus says. "That's what the surveillance is a prelude to and it's what we need to avoid at all costs."

"Dad, Mr. Presiding Director, the McFeralls are already waging war, mostly on defenseless people. They are killing men, woman, and children. And they are getting more powerful by the week. And when it's our turn, they will show no mercy." He pauses to smile. "And, really, is not the destruction of weapons an exercise in non-violence?"

Cyrus waves him away with a gentlemanly snort.

"You said four options." Nicole already knows what Jack is going to say.

"The fourth involves our network." He stops to zoom out farther, more little red balloons marking the locations of the network members. "If we learn that one of its members is threatened or under attack, we try to find some way to help them."

"How?" Ari asks.

"Ambush comes to mind. But it will have to be on a contingency basis. No point in arriving too late with too little."

Cyrus shakes his head. "I don't like this, Jack. If we make trouble for them, they'll just come up here the sooner."

"Or they'll leave us alone. Maybe even back down a bit." It is Ari speaking. He now has a bristling chin, a leonine look.

"I vote for provisioning The Ledges and retreating there at the first sign of trouble." Grace is also a pacifist.

The discussion grows heated. Fight or flight? Positions get restated. Voices are raised. It is Nicole who sounds the sensible note, tapping on the table to get everyone's attention. "Why don't we do some of both? In any event we should harvest as much as possible." So they agree that Jack and Thad will devise a way of keeping the McFeralls under surveillance while, starting the following day, weather permitting, they will increase the provisioning of The Ledges. The general understanding being that they will resist the first assault and then retreat if the attackers persist. It is a compromise with which neither Jack or Cyrus is happy.

*

Grace and Nicole plan and manage the provisioning of The Ledges for occupation. Even the youngsters shoulder small backpacks to help haul everything from foodstuffs to candles, medicines, clothing, toilet paper, towels, tools, and cans of kerosene.

The route to the retreat leads through the old pasture to Monument Rock. From there, the porters, typically a party of four or five, one of them armed, make their way up the rough, rising ground under a mix of pine, oak, hemlock, maple and cherry. Grape vines, some of them thick and ancient, climb the older trees, and rills vein the ground when it rains, in places making small, marshy areas, now dry. Well into the forest the trail winds among the eponymous ledges that rise like a series of irregular giant steps. It is an arduous hike of nearly a mile.

Unless you are looking for it, it would be easy to walk right by the refuge. Set behind a hemlock-shrouded ridge that faces southwest, the thickly wooded site has one large natural cave and several deeply cut overhangs that lend themselves to natural shelters with rudimentary modifications. Not only well hidden, the camp can be defended against all but heavy weapons. It also has an excellent water supply – a spring that flows Moses-like from a fissure in the rock face more or less year round. Its runoff contributes to a stream where bathing of the *sitzbad* kind is possible in warm weather.

The main cave varies between five and ten feet in height and provides roughly two hundred square feet of stand-up space. It is faintly redolent of hibernating bear. Its interior will serve as the common room while a niche near the entrance has been rigged out as a kitchen. They plan to cook there at night when their smoke cannot be seen or during the day using a kerosene camp stove. A table that can be taken apart and stowed occupies the center of the space with benches and a few collapsible chairs for meetings and meals.

The living quarters consist of small but comfortable tents of a breathable, waterproof canvas set under the overhanging ledges. They are fronted with sturdy lattice, some of it already plaited with evergreen boughs for extra protection. Off to one side, a short walk along a level path, there are two latrines. With time, they might erect a crude bath house with water coming from the spring above the encampment.

Though he sees the necessity of it, Jack is against preparing for retreat on the scale underway. But Cyrus does have some compelling arguments for it if push comes to a violent shove. "As much as I would be loath to give up the farm, it is not worth losing life or limb for it."

Grace supports Cyrus at every turn. She not only shares his pacifist views but, reluctant at first about the whole prepper scheme, took to it with a compassionate fervor when she changed her mind. She was a natural hoarder long before they made Sugar Mountain into a refuge. Their home in Cambridge usually had on hand twice as much as they needed of bed linen, blankets, towels, light bulbs, dish powder, aluminum foil, and plastic bags of all dimensions, not to mention aging supplies of peanut butter, preserves, condiments and the like in the pantry.

If Grace has the hoarding gene, it is one alloyed with a concern for others and a keen sense of contingency. Thus she insisted on "public" caches, most little more than five-gallon sealed pails of flour and dried beans she hid off the road leading to the farm when the crisis started. She knows, too, that it is easier to turn someone away if they have something they can go to.

The caches she establishes up in the woods near The Ledges are more substantial and based on the adage that you don't put all your eggs in one basket. For these she uses heavy duty plastic bags lined with Mylar bags that she seals and hides in natural cavities. A couple are metal garbage cans filled with tins of vegetable oil, dried beef and vegetables in foil packets, bars of "industrial" chocolate as well as flour and beans. The hiding places of these she records in a notebook known only to Jack, Cyrus, and Thad. Thad helps her establish the exact locations using a GPS navigator. As a backup, she writes down distances of each of the larger caches from prominent nearby landmarks. As backup to that, she plans to make copies for the others but never quite gets around to it.

*

A seemingly unlikely flirtation between Duvall and Bella flares into something possible on an afternoon when, taking a break from humping supplies to The Ledges, she drops by the horse barn to see if anyone has paper in which to roll some expensive weed she and Marko brought with them. Duvall digs her out some, and they sit in the small living room peaceably rolling, lighting, and passing the joint back and forth, mellowing, any residual antagonism easing into tentative attraction.

Until Bella, going into a mode Duvall knows too well, asks him, "So what do you dig?"

Another rich white soul sister talking like Mick Jagger when he still wore that diaper thing running up and down the stage. He says, "Dig? I dig the fucking garden."

"I mean, what music? I mean like rap, hiphop, Afropop...?" What had she said wrong?

"I hate that hiphop crap. You jumble enough sentences together and something comes out half-way sensible and the idiocracy of the world takes it for profundity."

In the face of her puzzlement he relents. "I'm classical jazz all the way. Duke, Jamal, Coltrane, Myles, Peterson, and Blues, of course. Ain't nobody can't like the Blues..." Sounding the black note, making her relax into smugness, which irks him anew.

"Hey, let me tell you something. I had a gene profile done, okay. Turns out I'm about sixty-five percent white. Not that I give a rat's ass about that because before I'm any of that stuff, I'm Duvall, a God damn person..."

"I know that." Bella is excited. This is real.

"No, you don't know that. You think you're some kind of soul mate, pure nigger on the inside or maybe spiritually black when you're just another rich white bitch who thinks she can buy anything she wants to be."

Bella stiffens, old doubts about herself coming up like bile. She resorts to, "Does my being a woman threaten you?"

Duvall clasps his head with both hands. "Man you are a fount of clichéd thinking. I don't even think of you as a woman." Which isn't true.

She recoils visibly. "Then what?"

"A clueless fuck."

She begins to say, now you sound like Thad, but stops herself. "That's cold."

Duvall relents again. In her hurt, he sees something he hadn't noticed before – a down-sized, more vulnerable, far more attractive version of Bella Pulans. He says, "Look, that was cold. It's just that I like to think I'm something more than, you know, a hip African American, wine-sipping, Beacon Hill fag, you know, something more than the sum of my parts."

Bella smiles as though given the upper hand. "Nice parts, I've noticed."

"You're not half bad yourself."

"Too bad you're..."

He laughs his deep knowing chuckle. "Don't be too sure of that. I am a man for all seasons..."

She draws closer. "The proof's in the pudding..."

At which point, platitudes and all, they might have reached the kind of consensus that obliterates everything but itself had not Thad walked in, his nose twitching appreciatively, followed by Cy wielding a toy AR15.

*

When they learn that the families of Arnie Brock and "Peddy" Lawlor have moved into the McMurray farm, it confirms the suspicion that the McFeralls staged the murderous attack. Brock is Marge McFerall's cousin and Lawlor is a local lowlife pedophile and drinking pal of Bruce's going way back. Even Cyrus drops his muttering opposition to keeping an eye on the McFeralls.

So it is with his blessing that Jack and Thad slip away from the farm on a night when clouds obscure the sky and makes vision difficult without infrared goggles. It is a blessing that comes with an admonition about respect for property and using their weapons only to defend themselves. Cyrus repeats that this surveillance is in no way to be construed as a "prelude to preemption."

To avoid going through the town center, they keep to a back road, much of it unpaved. After hiding the bikes, they follow a game trail through bracken and low shrub to an area wooded with saplings. They know where they are going as Jack blazed the trail with small bits of reflective tape.

They cross under a defunct power line and a track that borders it for several hundred yards. They wade a shallow brook and after another stretch of woods, reach an upland meadow clear except for sumac and other brush. The ground slants down and then farther down as they descend into the hollow. After a tumbled stonewall they come to a verge of scattered trees that overlooks the compound.

They watch through night-vision binoculars for several minutes. Jack notes that two strongly built sheds have been added to the scattering of buildings around the place. For what? Munitions. As before, two sentries patrol a rough perimeter, but in a desultory manner, stopping to chat and smoke.

The brothers choose an old maple, the remnant more than likely of a sugar bush. Then Jack points out a tall pine about twenty-five yards closer and lower down. Its upper tangle of branches will be a better site with a sweeping, comprehensive view by a wide-angle lens.

"Can you climb it?" Jack whispers to Thad.

"I'll need time," Thad whispers back.

"Let's go for it. I'll cover you."

Which they do. Thad sidles up to the base of the tree and adjusts the pack of gear on his back. He has about fifteen feet to climb to get to the first broken-off limbs. To do this he attaches tree climbing sticks, essentially footholds secured by a rope around the bole. It doesn't take him long. Within a few minutes, he is hidden in the tree, breaking off small boughs so that the camera he secures in place with duct tape will have an unobstructed view. It's not a simple operation. He positions and tapes the all-weather mike. It draws much less power than the camera and will be on continuously. When it picks up anything suspicious, like the sound of vehicles, they will activate the camera for short periods to see what's happening. Even so, the battery is bulky, heavy, and difficult both to hide and secure. He has to keep himself from falling as he ties the thing like a package and snugs it against the tree, all in the dark.

Of a sudden, there is the stab of a Maglite coming up from the compound. It is one of the guards. He may have seen the activity in the tree. Or ground sensors could have picked up movement.

"Who goes?" the guard calls, his voice uncertain, his automatic weapon following the aim of his flashlight.

Jack and Thad freeze. Jack is prone on the ground, his combat knife out. He doesn't want to use it unless he has to. A missing guard would set off an alarm. There would be armed men all over the place in minutes. And even if they escaped, a search of the area would turn up the mike and the camera. When the light comes in his direction, he slits his eyes to minimize their reflectivity.

They hear the guard answer a buzz on his walkie-talkie. "Negative. Probably a deer or coon. All clear."

They wait as the guard casts his light around one more time. He misses the tree-climbing sticks and the newly dropped pieces of pine bough. Lousy training, thinks Jack, the professional.

When the guard is back at the compound, Thad finishes securing the battery to the tree. Then the leads from the camera and the mike to the battery. Tape and more tape. Before he comes down, he has Jack test both using a laptop. A queer scene, Thad thinks, glancing down at his brother squatting on the ground with a lit screen in front of him.

"Say something," Jack whispers. Then louder, "Say something."

"Mr. Watson – Come here – I want to see you."

"Good. Visuals good, too."

Thad descends, removing the climbing sticks along the way. "Let's get to hell out of here," he whispers. "I almost pissed my pants."

Jack chuckles quietly. "And with good reason."

On the way back, Thad climbs another tree and puts in a relay station.

Before they reach the hidden bikes, they stop to rest and drink water. "I'm worried about Frank," Thad says. "I mean really worried. I don't think he's going to make it."

Jack grimaces. "I've been trying not to think about it. But you're right. I talked to him the other night. It's like the flame's gone out. I mean, to do this stuff, you've got to want to survive."

"You think it's that simple?"

"At one level. Life's a game. You play it or you don't."

"And Frank doesn't want to play?"

"This is what we have... It's not his game."

"Yeah. I think even Allegra's giving up on him."

"Really?" Jack sounds surprised and a little shocked.

"Well, she's spending a lot of time with Lance..."

"No way... You don't think...?"

"I don't think... But it wouldn't surprise me. You know that quote from Shakespeare, 'Woman, frailty is thy name...'"

Jack stands up. "Yeah, but Frank's the frail one this time. Let's get back before they start worrying."

*

When Jack learns that Marko has helped carry provisions up to the refuge, he rounds on Nicole. "I thought I made it clear that Marko was not to be trusted with anything sensitive."

Nicole shrugs at him. "Grace and Duvall organized that particular run. I'm sorry, Jack, I can't be everywhere. Is it really that critical?"

Jack checks with Duvall. "We only used him on stage one... to

160

the edge of the trees."

"Good," Jack says with a smile. "That means I won't have to kill him when we make him leave."

To his credit, Marko does make an overture. Jack is by himself reading a manual on tactics when the footballer comes onto the porch overlooking the barn garden. "You got a minute?" the big man asks, standing rather than sitting down uninvited, a concession of sorts.

"Sure." Jack puts his book aside. "What's on your mind?"

Marko sits and tries to look pensive. "I've been thinking... You and I got off to a rough start."

Jack says nothing.

"But I'd like to... I don't know... Join the security team."

"Why?"

"Because I'd be good at it. I mean Allegra and Nicole? Lance and Lise? What would they do in a knock-down fight? No offense meant..."

Jack smiles to himself. He says, "Lise could kill you easily with one shot from her assault rifle."

Marko snorts. "Yeah, but what happens when the bullets start flying?"

Jack points straight at him. "No one knows until it happens. And that includes you."

"How do you think I would do?"

"I have no idea."

"I'm in shape."

"Physically, yeah. The problem, Marko is this: You're careless with a hoe, with a broom, with the dishes. Why should I trust you with a sophisticated weapon?"

"What are you saying?"

"I'm saying that if you want to join the defense team you're going to have to earn it."

Now it is Marko who stays silent.

"I mean your whole attitude to this place and what we're trying to do and to ordinary work... It stinks."

"I'm not good at... that kind of stuff. But I do my share."

"No you don't. You do the minimum and more often than not someone has to come along and do it after you." Jack's old resentment shows. "You wedged your way in behind the skirts of a sick old lady. You don't like it here, but you don't have the balls to strike out on your own. You've got a lot to make up."

"So the answer's no."

Jack thinks for a minute. He says, "Two points: First, you show us that you're serious about contributing, and we'll reconsider it."

"And second?"

"If this doesn't work out, you leave. Voluntarily."

The man stands up. "Fair enough." He smiles, managing to look sly and stupid at the same time.

Although he still rooms intermittently with Bella, Marko spends more and more time alone. Bella doesn't care in the least. Since her brush with what she sees as the real Duvall, she has developed a serious yen for the man, be he gay, bi, or whatever. But then Bella has undergone a transformation of her own. Like Nicole she has become nearly svelte in a muscular kind of way. She makes an effort to pitch in, especially where her ailing mother is concerned. Jack has accepted her on the Defense Squad, and if she's not a natural marksman, she wields an AR15 with sufficient competence.

Bella hangs with Duvall and Thad as a matter of course, often during pelt time at the pond. But little happens among them until a scorching hot afternoon in early August when, after a swim and lie about on the granite, they dawdle back to the horse barn and the room Thad and Duvall share. There they smoke some weed Bella has brought along. Thad puts on some low-key electronic percussion.

Bella is sitting beside Duvall on the bed when she notices he's aroused, but easy with it in the languid way of a pot high. In the lightweight shorts he is wearing, he couldn't have concealed his tumescence had he wanted to. No one objects when she unbuckles his belt and unzips his fly. When she is about to bend over his admirable manhood, Thad says, "Aren't you going to kiss him first?"

That flusters her for a moment. "You cool, cousin?"

Thad nods to the music. "There's lots to go around."

"Amen," says Duvall.

But when things get started, Thad cannot abide. He has assisted in the past with Duvall's heterosexual flings, but this time, watching them for a minute, he knows there isn't enough to go around. He keeps his clothes on and silently slips from the room.

Outside, he goes down the ramp into the barn garden and sits on a lawn chair next to the oval pool. He watches the parti-colored koi moving under the water like things bejeweled. He is thinking about Frank and empathizing. Because, like Frank's, his own glittering world has all but disappeared, another victim of the scourge. He thinks parenthetically that a lot of straights never grasped that gaydom wasn't just a form of sexuality; it was a culture, one as rich and various and occasionally as brilliant as any other collective human endeavor. Gone, all gone.

But as he watches the koi beneath the dappled water, his mood lifts. His world is gone, but not altogether. More like in abeyance, like these shimmering creatures moving just beneath the surface. And with a history and persistence dating back beyond time, his world will rise again.

In the bedroom in the horse barn, where they lay around afterwards in satiated somnolence, Bella asks, "Do you think Thad will be pissed off?"

Duvall sighs. "Maybe. For a while. We're cool." He is, in fact, sorting out his feelings. He's starting to like Bella. And she does know how to treat a man. He turns on his side, facing her. He asks, "Are you on the pill or anything?"

She shakes her head and gives him a look that has him squinting back in mild surmise.

*

The provisioning of The Ledges brings to the fore the importance of basic supplies regardless of where they live. And while Jack drills his Defense Squad to a finely honed fighting force, the term "food security" comes up more often. They face, in addition to threats from the McFeralls and perhaps others, the prospect of a long winter and spring without any supply of nutrition other than what they have and what they might harvest and store.

Thus do Nicole, Ari, and Grace, the food mavens, meet more than once to decide what to do with the old sow. They can't take her with them if they have to flee up the mountain any more than they could take the goats and chickens. Nor is there a boar around to which they might breed her for another farrow. But they could butcher her, cure her meat and take some of it with them.

As though for practice, they have roast suckling pig, which they bake in a covered pit filled with heated stones. Delicious. But killing and butchering an animal as large as Miss Piggy will take some doing. And the right weather.

So, on an unseasonably cool morning and to much heart-rendering squealing, Cyrus, Jack, Duvall, Nicole, and Allegra (who writes in her journal that if she is going to eat the old pig, then she will participate in its slaughter) rope her up and tie her down to the flat bed of a trailer. Cyrus, wielding a sharpened Lamson knife, slits her throat and drains the blood into an enameled pail. Having presided over several other butcherings, he directs the others in tying the carcass by its hind legs to a nearby low branch before taking it apart to begin the processing.

They first scald the hide and shave it with a straight razor. He then places a tub of heavy duty plastic under her before making a long slit from her throat to her backend. Her innards bulge and spill dripping into the pan. Allegra, gagging, helps Nicole pull out the glistening intestines and other viscera. She thinks of Leopold Bloom and how he ate with relish the inner organs of beasts and fowls. They empty and clean the guts inside and out in warm water to serve as casements for sausage making later.

With cleaver and saw, Cyrus splits the carcass into two halves. These they hang on the stream side of the mill where the moving water and shade create a cool micro-climate. As Cyrus explains, the meat needs to chill and firm up before it can be worked.

The next day they carve the sides into bacon slabs, hams, and shoulders for brining and cold smoking. They devote one and then two pails for bits and pieces, including a lot of fat, which will go into making sausages. An old picnic table, its top replanked, serves as the butcher block. On it, Nicole and Duvall slice the extraneous meat and fat into one-inch cubes. The pails are lowered into the stream to cool the meat even further before it is ground and blended with sage and other spices preparatory to being stuffed into the casings. Grace tries and then gives up on a recipe for blood pudding, a kind of spiced, nearly black sausage.

Ari comes out early to claim a long pork roast that he rolls in flour spiced with rosemary, fennel, and basil. That will be dinner. The parts of the pig that don't preserve easily – especially the organ meat – will be served up over the next few days.

*

The next evening, after describing the pig killing, Allegra writes in her journal:

> *The work is unceasing. This morning I got naked in front of the full-length mirror in the upstairs bathroom in the house. Not only am I in shape, I'm muscular. I look like one of those Olympic swimmers. I swear my shoulders are starting to grow.*
>
> *But the work! If we're not humping supplies up to The Ledges, we're gardening. If we're not gardening, we're washing clothes or peeling potatoes or drilling with our weapons or taking care of the kids.*
>
> *This morning, four of us, Jack, Lance, Thad, and I spent hours cutting and stacking firewood for The Ledges. (Nicole explained to me* sotto voce *that it was in part an exercise in politics: Jack agreed to do it if he can have a freer hand in dealing with the McFeralls, meaning, I guess, more than a surveillance camera.) Talk about real work. By that I mean both physical exertion and a kind of dumb animal acceptance of simply doing something tedious over and over and over again. Of course there's the sociability of it. Thad and Jack took turns on the chainsaw and the trimming ax while Lance*

165

and I carried the pieces to a cleared area next to the cave. We worked in tandem, the canvas holder between us. The pieces were cut about fourteen inches long to fit the camp stove that's there, ready to be rigged.

I have to confess that working closely with Lance made it almost pleasurable. I like being near him. I like to watch his body work. He was down to shorts, socks and boots. His torso, neck, and face were polished with sweat. Ah, the smell of a man. And I could infer – I did infer – how he would move in making love.

We didn't talk much. It wasn't that kind of situation. Body language sufficed. A couple of times, going back over rough terrain, he took my hand to help me. Once he hung onto me well past the point where he needed to.

Given the heat, we broke for a drink of cold water and a quick face splash in the small stream. Then right back at it, the saw whining as Jack cut down the hardwood saplings. He preferred birch because, as he explained, the bark made a good kindling.

I was amazed at how quickly the wood accumulated. By the time we finished we had a cord and a half. "But dry stacked isn't the same," Jack reminded us. Still, there was real satisfaction in leaving a pile of wood that we can use next winter if we need it. There's also the way that kind of work makes the simplest food seem like ambrosia. We got back in time for lunch, for Ari's tomato soup with toasted cheese sandwiches – the aromas, the textures, the savor – went beyond tasting good.

In fact, I think everyone is toughening up. Except Meredith, who mostly goes through the motions, if that. Of course, she's ill and depressed. No one pays her much heed, and she withdraws into herself or watches the rest of us with baleful, judging glances. She maintains a running, low-grade disgruntlement with Grace, her son Ari and even with Bella who doesn't pander as much as she used to.

Marko appears to have undergone a conversion, but it's

like an embarrassing case of a leopard trying to change its spots. Or, pathetically, trying to be seen changing its spots. He has a fake smile that he wears like a mask. He now does the dishes with such a flourish and waste of water that Grace takes over and hands him a cloth to wipe them. The children shrink from his odd and sudden bursts of bonhomie. Nicole has to restrain his hoeing as he is as likely to chop the roots of sprouting lettuce as those of the encroaching weeds.

Still, it's an improvement on the other Marko who made disdain into an art form. He still fears and hates Jack. It's the way he looks at him when he thinks no one notices. Not that Jack doesn't read him. Though we seldom openly disparage other members, he told me the man "is a bad actor in more ways than one." It's clear that Marko confuses his size and athletic prowess with status, all the while sensing he's at the bottom of the pole. It may be a class thing. Bella told me that his father was a truck driver. So what? My dad's a plasterer and proud of it. "It's real," he used to tell me, followed by a denigration of wallboard. I hope he's okay. I hope they're all okay. But I fear the worst. I cannot think about it or I'll end up like Frank, curling up in a ball and dying.

The rest of us are more united than ever. A favorite time is the nightly movie in the common room. Last night we watched The Big Sleep. *We all got into it, even Frank stayed for a while. Perhaps because older movies are safer to watch. The world they depict has already disappeared. More recent films remind us of what we have lost. People drifted off, came back. Ari made popcorn and served hot cider. We went to bed happy.*

On Sundays Nicole rigs church, to use a nautical term. It's a service that's non-denominational in the extreme but uplifting at the same time. We arrange ourselves facing a small lectern. Grace sits to one side at the old upright. Nicole reads from various religious traditions. The twenty-third Psalm resonates with particular relevance. We don't talk about it much, but I think we all feel a need for something beyond us, something we can rely on. The word "providence" comes now with a warm glow. Maybe the old adage about no atheists in foxholes has some validity. At times, Ari puts on a kippa and reads from the Torah. *Cyrus might read from* Walden *or from something by Rachael Carson. We sing a couple of hymns. It's amazing how many of us attend – in our finer clothes.*

Even so, Thad has a laptop in front of him connected to the monitoring cameras. And several of us are assigned 'guard duty.' That means we have our AR15s and extra clips within reach. Even as Cyrus prays for peace, we are ready for war.

At the end of each service, we stand and each of us names those we remember, those who may or may not be alive. That, too, is a comfort even as it brings tears to our eyes, perhaps because it's a reminder that we will not be forgotten, not right away, anyway.

And then Sunday dinner. Ari and Chee usually come up with something special. Last week it was chicken pot pie with a salad of greens and a desert of goats milk ice cream flavored with raspberries. Even Frank brightened up. But increasingly he lies on the bed thumbing through his cell phone looking for what I cannot imagine.

13

For the first week, the mike and surveillance camera covering the McFerall compound show little activity. A small speaker perched amid the equipment on the recon room bench turned low provides a background noise of forest sounds and, more distantly, the comings and goings amid the houses and sheds at Pitts Hollow. When they hear anything unusual, they click an icon on one of the laptops to activate the camera taped next to the mike. Occasionally, a pickup or ATV shows up. Lise alerts Jack on a Sunday afternoon when several vans and pickups arrive. He counts twenty-two men in addition to the adult McFeralls having a cookout. Dunc works a double grill made from an oil drum sliced in half. There's a fist fight between two men too drunk to do much damage to each other.

It is several days later when Duvall witnesses something at the McFeralls that has him paging Jack on the intercom. "Jack to recon room. Jack to recon room."

Jack hurries in to peer over Duvall's shoulder. He has switched on the camera. The picture is blurred but shows pickups and ATVs pulling up. Men stand around, assault rifles slung over their backs. From a stairway leading underground, Duncan and Bruce emerge with five-gallon cans of gasoline to fuel the vehicles. Their fuel dump, or one of them, Jack notes to himself, fixing the location on the mental map he has of the place. If he could find the vent or the feed pipe.

"They're staging," Duvall says as they watch two other men emerge from one of the new sheds carrying a fifty-caliber machine gun. With help from a third, they mount it on the back of the turret-rigged Humvee.

"Right, but for what and where."

"Sugar Mountain?"

"I doubt it. They haven't done any reconnaissance lately. And even they aren't that dumb." He hits the red alert button and speaks into the mike, his voice coming through the public address system. "Everyone to their stations. Everyone to their stations. This is not a drill. This is not a drill."

While Jack stays at the monitors joined by Thad, Cyrus and Nicole collect the children and elders inside the mill ready to leave for The Ledges at a moment's notice. Lance and Allegra retrieve the AR15s, the M24, and the elephant gun along with ammunition clips already loaded. Duvall and Ari dismantle the metal bridge over the ditch and secure the gate. Frank, with great effort, helps Grace set up extra cots in the basement clinic.

Jack watches as Duncan stands with his brother Bruce in front of nineteen armed men. "He's briefing them. I'd give anything to know who they're going to attack."

"What would you do?"

The professional soldier in Jack sighs. "I don't know. It depends. Drop trees across the road. Pick off one of the brothers. Or both of them."

"Do you know any of those men?" Thad asks. He has let his head hair grow back in and looks more like an Arkwright than he did before.

"A few."

When the convoy of vehicles led by the two Humvees files off the screen, Jack briefs his squad in front of the house. Their appearance reassures him. Even Lise and Bella, outfitted in camouflage fatigues and holding their AR15s with professional nonchalance look more than plausible.

He says, his tone serious, the confidence in his voice unfeigned, "If they're coming, we'll have time to set up. They may feint a frontal attack and try to flank us. But I don't think they have that capability. More than likely they'll come up the lane as though we invited them to tea. We let the Humvees and trucks into the lane before we start firing. Lance and I will use the M24 and the elephant gun on the Hummers. The rest of you pick out a pickup and shoot out the windshield. And then keep shooting. Ari will coordinate targets over the walkie-talkies. If you get a good shot at anyone, take it. Go for the body mass. Any questions?"

170

Ari asked, "What if we don't stop them?"

Jack nodded. "That is always a possibility. In that case, I'll hang back to slow them up while the rest of you withdraw to The Ledges." He pauses. "And remember this: Cyrus is right in saying that we will not give ourselves a license to kill. But if the McFeralls come up that lane with men and weapons, *they* will have given us a license to kill."

The Sugar Mountaineers stay on high alert for an hour and then more. That evening they hear from Marshall Roth, who picked up a report from another network, that the McCoomb farm in Colrain had been attacked and overrun. It seem that the McCoombs, after a short and fierce resistance, retreated in the face of rocket propelled grenades and machine gun fire to a refuge up near the Vermont border.

Nicole especially is touched. She knows the family, Joe and Marian and several kids. They had talked about supplying milk and cream should the B&B ever get started.

Jack paces up and down behind Thad, who is on duty in the recon room. He says, "If only we could get a bug in one of their houses..."

Thad shakes his head. "All but impossible."

"What about outside? Where they stage."

Thad swivels around to face his brother. "They have a guard detail most of the time. You'd have to disable them."

Jack muses.

Thad says, "And then there's Dad..."

Jack points his face at him. "Yeah, Dad..." But he didn't finish the sentence.

*

Frank's malaise begins to manifest in ways beyond weight loss or the pallor showing beneath the sunburn and stubble of his ill-shaved face. Although he insists on doing his share of the physical labor, it becomes painfully evident to the others that he

171

has become incapable of anything remotely taxing despite frequent stops to rest.

Doctor Grace, as she is called when she presides in her clinic, takes Frank's temperature, measures his blood pressure, and listens to his heart and breathing. She runs some routine blood tests and checks his urine for sugar. She asks about his bowels and whether he is getting enough sleep. She knows he isn't eating nearly as much as he should.

What can he tell his mother? What can he tell any of them? That he dreams and daydreams obsessively about the work he has been doing for the pending IPO of Bay Harbor Equity Trust. About the briefcase full of thrice-vetted documents for signing and the on-line files of addenda covering every possible contingency. About the prodigious number of billable hours he has amassed. That he misses his office with its harbor view, his desk, his secretary Cerise and his fellow lawyers. Mack McDermott with his silly jokes. Abe Caan and his fetching wife Lillian. Andy Andrides, ex CIA, or so it was said. Doug Charterman, his sponsor and mentor, imbibing enough Dutch courage to pull the trigger. Where are they now? Had any of them survived?

And just when he had begun to really succeed. He was, as more than one senior partner said, a natural. He could recall case law in detail along with the footnotes and citations of precedent. His legalese flowed with a diction that was like verbal DNA. Everyone knew whose sentence or paragraph that was in the briefs and filings that landed on his desk from the corner offices with a stick-on scribbled with "Frank, take a look at this."

Now he awakes each morning to life in a survival gulag. Brown denims. Work boots. Rough bread and lousy coffee and only a cup and a half at that. He aches for a croissant with soft, unsalted butter and a dab of apricot jam to go with fresh-squeezed orange juice and a mug of that Blue Mountain special, the *Times* propped in one hand, the *WSJ* handy on the table. Then a brisk shower and shave, Brooks Brothers shirt, designer tie, any number of bespoke suits, the feel underfoot of custom-made shoes. Then the world outside, New York, waiting to be tamed by words, by the rule of law.

And, above all, Elsa. In her absence and likely death, it is she who personifies in magnified retrospect all he has lost. Even as he knows that they were an impossibility, that one day a sharp young man with blond hair would show up in her stead and their interlude would be over. Was it this impossibility, he wonders, that keeps him thumbing through the EXX file. Because it held some steamy exchanges and photographs to which he had in those days of testosterone overload masturbated while talking to her long distance. Now, like so much else, she is swallowed up in the void, rendered so ephemeral he wondered if she had ever existed.

But even when she had been there in all the luxuriance of her flesh, splayed beneath him or kneeling between his naked legs, he had doubted she was more than a figment of a need he couldn't fathom. Had he always craved an earth mother even as he wooed and married a wood nymph? Why now could he no longer turn to Allegra? She was real, as real as anything gets, but of a reality he did not want.

His mind runs in circles. All gone. What was the point? Mere existence?

Even so he tries. For Lily if no one else. For another self he has yet to find. God knows, I'm trying, he tells himself, wielding a hoe with scarcely enough strength to lift the thing much less crop back weeds that never stop sprouting. Or trying to shovel chicken shit into the wheelbarrow to trundle up to the dung heap next to the opened ground of the garden.

It only makes it worse that the others don't hide their love and concern for him. Because, to love back, he will have to live, to do his part, to affirm that their lives are worth his living for. What he can't tell them through word or deed is that he doesn't want this life, that more and more he simply wants to lie down and dream his way to easeful death.

As Frank withdraws from life and from Allegra, Lance looms for her like some inevitability of nature. She writes in her journal:

I despair of Frank and can scarcely keep myself from

173

molesting Lance, who, truth be told, has taken over my inner life like some young Adonis satyr. I was really tempted yesterday. It was hot. I stole away for a quick skinny dip in the pond. Lance was already there. He was very polite. He asked if I wanted him to cover himself. I said of course not.

How I resisted I'll never know. We were in the water together, which clothes one more provocatively than any garment. He reached out, took my hand as we stood shoulder deep facing each other. He said, 'You are beautiful.' We were inches from touching, but we didn't. I merely smiled and ducked under, making the water innocent again.

We swam. We sat on the rocks. We only talked, but I think we both were thinking of sneaking off into the bush like Adam and Eve after tasting the apple.

*

It is as much to the relief as to the surprise of the adults assembled in the kitchen on a humid morning in late August that Bella, arriving late for breakfast and looking harried, announces "Marko's gone. He took his emergency pack and a couple of thousand dollars I had stashed in my suitcase."

The news doesn't surprise Jack. At three that morning, on duty in the recon room, he saw the man emerge like a ghostly figure from the domicile he shared – on and off – with Bella and stride toward the security fence. Jack called Nicole to take over, slid one of the Glocks into his belt, and went out after the man, but leisurely. He knew Marko wouldn't be able to find a passage through the fence without assistance. He also knew he wouldn't be able to climb over the barbed wire on the top.

"Going somewhere?" he said, coming up behind him.

Marko, dressed in a bomber jacket and jeans, all but jumped in his tracks. He turned, "Yeah, I'm getting the fuck out of this place. You should be relieved."

A gibbous moon showed from behind clouds. Jack saw the edge of fear in the man's eyes. "I think we'll all be relieved,

Marko. Aren't you going to take your Porsche?"

"It's nearly out of gas."

"So where are you headed?"

Marko hesitated, then lied. "Anyplace but here."

Jack didn't believe him. He had someplace to go. Had probably made contact. He said, "This way."

With Marko walking ahead of him, his pack slung on one shoulder, they went into the mill and through a heavily barred door onto the Fallgren property. Jack picked up a spade along the way. He also took out his Glock.

"What the fuck are you doing?" Stark fear laced Marko's voice.

"Keep walking."

In the middle of the overgrown pasture on the other side of the brook, Jack stopped. He dug the spade into the ground and stood back out of range should Marko decide to go down swinging. "Dig," he ordered.

"Dig what?"

"Your God damn grave." Now it was Jack who sounded unnerved.

"No."

"Suit yourself."

Jack raised the pistol to the man's incredulous face.

"Okay, okay..." He began digging, his motions jerking. Then he was sobbing. "Don't do this, man. I don't deserve this..."

"Shut up and dig."

To make it real, Jack let himself consider shooting Marko and having done with it. It went beyond any personal animus. The guy knew too much. He knew what they had for provisions. He knew generally where the back-up refuge was located. He knew things about the surveillance system. And he was bad luck, the kind that turns up again.

It took a while, a while so strange it was like a different species of time. Marko blubbered through it, alternating between digging with the energy of anger and holding the spade like a weapons and glaring at Jack. He stopped.

"Deeper," Jack said. "Unless you want the raccoons and coyotes to eat you."

In the meanwhile Jack rootled through the bag, found the wad of cash and a small bag of weed, but nothing incriminating like notes or sketches. He put back the weed and some of the money.

When the grave hole was about two feet deep, Jack said, "That's enough. Get in and kneel down."

In that stupefied way of the hopeless, Marko relinquished the spade and knelt in the trench he had opened up. He was saying bits and pieces of *The Lord's Prayer*. He jumped when Jack placed the barrel against the back of his head. Right up to that instant, Jack was undecided, going back and forth between the old Jack and the one that listened to his father's admonition about losing his humanity. But even the old Jack had never executed anyone in cold blood. And, finally, he didn't want to kill Marko; he wanted to scare him so badly he would keep his mouth shut about Sugar Mountain.

He said to the miserable, shaking man in front of him, "Take a good look at this hole in the ground. If you come back here in any form, if you tell anyone about what you've seen at Sugar Mountain, anything, God damn it, I will bring you here, blow the back of your head off, and stick you in this miserable hole. You got that?"

"Yes."

"Now get your bag and get to hell out of here."

Half stumbling, pulling his pack after him, Marko scrambled down the pasture toward the road and then was gone.

At breakfast Jack says to Bella, "Here's most of your money. It's all but useless. His leaving is a blessing, but I don't think we should hold hands and celebrate."

14

After a few showers, another drying heat wave descends. They resort again to irrigation to keep the ripening garden from parching. The first apples come in. There follows a week of apple pies, turnovers, strudels and crisps. Ari uses a Correll cider press to dice and press the apples for juice. As well as cider, he sets aside the mash and some of the juice to distill apple liquor as he did the year before. He does the same with the bruised or half rotten peaches along with the peels and most anything else sweet enough to make grappa.

All who are able now work in the garden or in the kitchen canning and preserving. The potatoes are the easiest and most satisfying crop to harvest. It gratifies some atavistic impulse to pull up the withered stalks and find the tubers still clinging to the roots or just under the soil nearby. Most of them are cleaned and set aside for curing before being boxed for the root cellar. Once the tomatoes start to ripen, the work of canning them in jars begins. The kitchen smells deliciously of dill and vinegar as small cukes, along with onions and broccoli, are pickled and canned. Beets are washed, their greens put aside for meals or for the goats, then boiled and jarred in their own red juice.

Much of what they harvest is stored in the concealed root cellar. Given that access to the new cellar is via the old one, they debate whether to try to conceal them both. Then Thad hits on a neat solution: make it look like they tried to hide the old one. Stock it with a few things. And if anyone finds it, they will think it's the real deal.

The root cellar they will stock in earnest is accessed through an apparent section of the shelving that covers the wall of the old one. The shelving moves to reveal an oaken door that opens into a fifteen by fifteen space. This space, recently constructed, has cinderblock walls enclosing two sections: a large one for vegetables such as potatoes, carrots, turnips, cabbage, and beets; and a smaller one for apples and anything else that gives off ethylene. The larger space also contains sealed tubs of flour, rice, and several kinds of dried beans. Other containers have freeze-dried meat, fish meal, and what was once called portable soup in the Royal Navy. Commercially canned and jarred foods include hams, tuna fish, mayonnaise, various kinds of edible oils, and spices. Shelves along one side carry jars of home-canned pickles, tomatoes, fruits, and berries. And finally, there is a metal-lined floor locker in which they place the bacon, hams, and other smoked parts of the butchered pig.

What the denizens of Sugar Mountain have to decide is how much food to keep in the apparent cellar to make it look real. Nicole and Lise work on this, storing there second and third choice vegetables, dated dry foods, and canned goods near their use-by date.

Despite everything, it seems an almost idyllic time at Sugar Mountain. And perhaps it is given the conditions prevailing elsewhere. Even as the work of harvesting continues apace, the children attend classes three days a week in the family room for a couple of hours. Lance teaches them what he calls "nature," a combination of biology, geology, botany, and evolution. He keeps it reasonably simple, but is surprised by how much they pick up, including Lily who insists on being in all the classes. Allegra teaches them reading, writing, and literature, leading them through poems that she loves. Thad teaches math and elementary physics. Rachael being his star pupil makes Cy compete with her fiercely. All the while Duvall continues his picaresque romp through world history.

Ari spends time with Rachael and Mary, teaching them what he knows of the piano. At odd times, they can be heard practicing their scales and simple tunes. It is an antique, reassuring sound.

One morning after classes, Grace, with Thad and Duvall carrying weapons, take Linda down to her family's house. Linda has asked to go there more than once and, after conferring with some of the other adults, Grace agrees to take her.

It is a sad, forsaken scene. Squirrels and other creatures now inhabit the place, their skittering sounds adding to the forlorn feeling of abandonment.

The visitors go first to the graves. Linda stands at the foot of each one, head bowed, tears in her eyes, but a look of determination shaping her face. In the house she goes to her room and comes back with some clothes, her MP3 player, a journal, and "Betty Bear," who wears an old-fashioned pinafore.

"Any relation to Teddy?" Thad asks her. And gets a smile.

Later, when she thanks Grace in her abashed way, Linda also tells her, "When I'm grown up, I'm going to live there and take care of them."

"Your mom and dad and Alex?" Grace asks, trying to conceal how touched and charmed she is.

Linda nods. "I don't want them to be lonely."

*

Nostalgia, Allegra decides, can kill you.

At least to judge from the amount of time Frank lies on their bed in the paneled room of the horse barn and thumbs through his cell phones. Because there can be nothing new on them, certainly not the old one he's resurrected. The internet has collapsed as servers all over the world went down. So he can only be going through his archives reliving through spectral words what is no longer.

She confronts him about it, but only once. Coming in after two hours of weeding the garden in the sun, she strips off in front of him to get ready to go swimming. She does it purposefully. If somewhat grimy, she has toned up and her conical breasts show to advantage on a body that has grown sinuous. "That world is gone, Frank," she says with anger in check. He has scarcely noticed her naked presence. "It's dead and gone. This is our world and we're lucky to have it."

He looks at her coldly, keeping his eyes on her face. He says in a voice she has not heard before, "Go away."

Which she does, hurt, angry, despairing. Hate begets hate, but she resists that, settling for a sour pity that blurs into contempt. To the point several days later that she does not scruple to pick up one

179

of his cell phones which he left charging on the shelf along the head of the bed. Go away. She had gone away. Because this is a different Allegra, at least where Frank Arkwright is concerned, one that casually, with malice, invades his privacy.

The usual routine stuff about meetings, points of law, affidavits, a couple of bad jokes. A separate archive labeled EXX. She thumbs it to life. And then, incredulous, she sits on the bed as her knees wobble.

> *Mein Liebchen,*
> *I am in a torment waiting to see*
> *you. At six. I'll bring take-out*
> *from Wa Jeal's. I can't stay long. But*
> *long enough.*
> *Ich liebe ditch*

The message is to Elsa Sterne. It is dated April 3. Elsa Sterne? The attorney from Munich working with Frank on a Siemens acquisition. Impossible.

She wants to drop the thing on the floor and stomp on it. But morbid curiosity seizes her. She picks through the archived texts. Not just more of the same, but a Frank she scarcely recognizes. He had courted her, Allegra, with luxury, not words. Emerald earrings like a second pair of eyes. A pearl choker that made her feel regal. A long weekend in Paris. Seats at symphony that put them practically in the orchestra. And dinners at all the old and new chi chi places. And take-out from Wa Jeal's, which he liked better than she did. Damn him.

> *E, my love,*
> *I can't wait to undo your magnificence.*
> *F*

Because Elsa had the kind of breasts, udders, the cow, that makes small-breasted Allegra grind her teeth.

Then more. Elsa doesn't respond often with words but with photos of them together. And of herself, all creamy haunches and coy smiles. Taken by ... Frank? Who else?

I want to lick you...
I want to watch your eyes as you ...
I want you wet and bending in the shower...

Even as she seethes with the excited pain of jealousy, Allegra wonders why Frank had never effused to her that way. Was he too intimidated by her own facility with language? Or her knowledge of love poetry next to which he would be found wanting? Shyness comes in many forms.

She doesn't stomp on the innocent device. She restores it to its charging mode and places it back where she found it. She lies on the bed in a fetal position and weeps.

Later, recovered, some tough Sicilian ancestor coming to the fore, she decides she needs to think things through. Not that she isn't tempted to find Lance and drag him into the woods and rape him. But she will not desecrate love or even sex by making it an instrument of revenge. In the larger picture, Frank's misery is revenge enough. At the same time, lining her anger and grief is a heady sense of license.

*

When the motion-activated camera covering the boundary upstream on Talbot Brook needs a fresh battery, Jack decides it is time for a perimeter patrol. Taking weapons, walkie-talkies, and a light lunch of sandwiches and water, he, Thad, and Ari leave the compound late on a sunny morning to walk the perimeter of the property and check on The Ledges. Duvall is left in charge of security during Jack's absence.

The farm's vulnerability to attack from behind and from the sides has concerned Jack and others almost as much as any assault from the road. On the other hand, it would take a force of well-led and well-trained soldiers to make it through the trees and brush that covers the rough sloping terrain.

Jack worries that they are vulnerable to attack from an overgrown logging road that angles up through the woods of the now derelict Fallgren farm and loops within a few feet of Talbot

181

Brook. It is theoretically possible to bring Humvees up that way, but it would be easier using ATVs or snowmobiles. More critically, to get any vehicles across the brook at that point would mean bridging a boulder-strewn ravine about thirty feet across. When they reach the ravine, the three men make their way down through the rocks, but carefully and slowly as the footing is treacherous. They cross the stream, running low in the dry spell, and go up the other side. They push through brush to the old road. They follow it south for several hundred yards. Jack kneels in a mossy area. He shows the others the wide tire tracks still clear in the soft greenness.

"ATV's," he says. "Probably two of them. And fairly recent."

"McFeralls?" asks Ari.

"More than likely. I think they're getting ready."

They return to the stream and cross back. Jack glances around. He looks at and then points to a nearby hemlock. "Thad, if we move the camera up there, it would give us better coverage of that road and more time to respond."

"True. But if they come in force, will it make any difference?"

Jack smiles. "We let them get down into the ravine and then open up."

Thad remounts the camera in the hemlock and changes the battery. They continue their recce, stopping at The Ledges for lunch. They do a thorough inspection of the refuge, checking for signs of both human and non-human visitors since the reprovisioning was halted during the harvest. They check on the new caches. Jack is perturbed that there are a few he can't locate. Too well hidden, Thad says. Ari comes across what looks like raccoon scat, but that's about it. They divvy up the goat cheese sandwiches, pickles, and maple candy in the shade of a pine, the day having grown hot.

In chatting generally about how things are going – the harvest, news from outside, and the like, Frank's worsening state comes up as it inevitably did.

"We need to talk to him," Ari says. "He's losing it."

Jack and Thad agree. But what can brothers say to a brother in times like this? What, beyond the usual bromides. Thad is fatalistic. "If he's given up, there's nothing we can say that will change his mind. Or his lack of mind."

Jack doesn't agree and it shows in his sudden, pointed glance at his brother. "We can at least try."

Ari senses they've had this discussion before. He says, "Jack, why don't you and I talk to him. Tell him what's what."

Jack nods. He feels the anger of helplessness, which he dissembles. He suspects Thad is right.

They push north and cross the boundary into state park land. Grace has asked them to look at a site for a second refuge she and Cyrus came across on one of their woodland rambles. Jack is reluctant but soldiers on. He scarcely approves of The Ledges. His skepticism deepens when they arrive at the place. If it is more difficult to find, it has a paltry supply of water – a very small stream fed by a natural spring. It looks as though it might freeze over in winter or flood them out after heavy rains.

On the south side of a huge erratic is a level area large enough to pitch an all-weather communal tent. Nearby is a stand of massive old pines underlain with a thick mat of brown needles. It would make a good place for tents, Grace noted after she and Cyrus camped there the year before.

"Camp Desolation," Ari groans. "I hope to Christ we never have to use this place."

Thad is more positive. "Hey, I'd rather survive here uncomfortably than die down there comfortably."

"The McFeralls are not going to let us die comfortably," Jack says grimly.

Ari shakes his head. "You're right. Still, there are times when I know exactly how Frank feels. Let's get out of here."

*

In a therapeutic age, it would have been called an intervention. Now, it's just a talking to as Jack and Ari bring out a bottle of decent Merlot and sit around the table in the studio with Frank, doors closed.

Surprisingly, in the good cop, bad cop encounter, it is Jack who plays the former and Ari the latter. After the wine is poured and appreciatively sipped, Ari says abruptly and brusquely, "Why are you doing this, Frank?"

Frank sighs. He looks at the wine, one other thing that no longer appeals to him. He says, "What am I doing?"

"Nothing. That's the point. You're not lifting a finger to help. Mostly to help yourself. Do you think it's easy for any of us?"

Jack leans in, his voice low. "Ari's right. We need your help."

They haven't connected. Frank looks from one to the other with a lawyer's lack of embarrassment. He says, "I don't want to be here."

Ari puts the flat of his hand against his forehead. The fat of his face has shrunk and hardened and his eyes are no longer mild and accommodating. He doesn't recognize his friend and cousin. He says, "Frank, there is no other place. This is it."

"I know that, Ari. That doesn't change anything... Except to make it worse."

Jack says, "It won't always be like this... Once the flu has burned itself out, the world will revive. It always has. It won't be the same but..."

Frank is not listening. The very thing that Jack describes, the new, depopulated primitive world, is what he dreads.

"What about Allegra and Lily?" Ari is still boring in, love and fear behind his anger.

Frank does flinch, but that passes. He says, "You'll take care of them."

The other two sit in shocked silence as the implications of Frank's words register. It might have been less terrible had he said, "I'm letting myself die."

Ari subsides. He has no words for this stranger he used to know so well. He has no way of dealing with helplessness. He quaffs his wine though it tastes like gall, stands, and leaves the room.

Jack is more practiced in helplessness having been with any

number of soldiers and civilians when they died. Now all that tragedy seems to gather in Frank's withered face. Jack takes his brother's hand and holds it, letting tears blur his vision.

*

Allegra doesn't confront Frank with what she has learned about his affair with Elsa Sterne. She knows she should, at least according to the received wisdom of the world that is no more. Or because they pledged always to be honest with each other. She alternates between loathing and the twisted love that comes with heartbreak. She writes in her journal:

Was it all a sham? Right from the start? No, it couldn't have been. What did they talk about? Debt acquisition margins? Bonded derivative positions? What did he see in her? Big and blonde and those very standard good looks. A Valkyrie. My opposite. No wonder I didn't suspect. All the time I thought he was worried about Inez our baby-sitter and what Lily would think because we couldn't bring her with us. What didn't I have? Maybe I loved him too much. We had it all. Friends, art, Lily, money, a future. Maybe we had too much. But Elsa? I felt sorry for her. Before I found out she was married, I wondered where she might find a man, a normal man, not some NFL lineman. Of course I should have seen it. The way at parties they were too circumspect, which I took to be some kind of Germanic reserve. And she did have a nice smile. Can you fall in love with a smile, even that of a giantess? I am exaggerating. She did have a nice figure, shoulders and all. And she knew how to dress. What was she like in bed? It is driving me crazy.

I need to talk to someone. But who? Lance? Take him by the... Tit for tat. Tit for tit. In ten minutes we'll be together, a fire team, training in full combat kit, Jack telling us how to cover each other. How to retreat. How to kill.

15

According to everything Cyrus is able to glean from his network of Cbers, the pandemic appears to be abating, at least in some areas. But another, concurrent crisis gathers force: now it is famine that grows ubiquitous as the intricate, multilayered food production, processing, and distribution systems in the United States and other developed parts of the world have all but vanished. There is no back-up, no trucks bringing around bags of meal to be thrown to starving families. No military transports landing in ravaged areas to unload tents, medical supplies, and essential personnel. What crops get planted rot in the fields. There's no fuel to power the machines that heretofore prowled the endless acres of wheat, corn, oats, and soybeans. It's not only urbanites and suburbanites who don't know how to harvest and process what crops there are; without their technology, most farmers don't know either.

The result, as Jack terms it, is "armed anarchy." Increasingly, there are reports from around the county and beyond of homes and farms attacked and overrun. The word "cannibalism" starts to crop up.

By comparison, life at Sugar Mountain, despite everything, achieves an eerie, tenuous normality. Clothes, for instance. Like everything else, clothes and clothing have to be reconsidered, reconfigured, nearly reinvented. Simple enough the day-to-day garb, the industrial weight blue or brown denim that Grace and Nicole taught themselves to cut and sew on the machine into usable trousers and shirts. They also have bolts of oxford weave for the latter along with more delicate fabrics for the women and girls. But no one had thought to stock up on simple socks and underwear. Nicole had bought several dozen cotton turtlenecks of various sizes at a going-out-of-business sale. She had also bought any number of windbreakers and hooded down jackets thinking they would come in handy for prospective B&B guests.

Fashion, the very idea of fashion, has grown quaint, one of those receding realities of a disappearing world. Still, most of the members hoard what finery they have, the men their suits and sports coats, good shirts, even ties; the women their dresses, skirts, stylish shoes, sheer panty hose, blouses, sweaters, bras and, especially, panties, the more diaphanous, the better.

Chee emerges as the champion of fashion. Along with several bags of spices and herbs, she persuaded Ari to let her bring a couple of duffels packed with silk. A seamstress accomplished in embroidery, she is seldom without her frame, cheerfully and painstakingly bringing a traditional Chinese figure to life. She makes a shirt for Cy – with fabulous monsters on both front panels – that his mother can scarcely get him to take off. For the older girls Chee makes blouses, skirts, and dresses, all just a bit larger. "You grow into," she smiles.

*

It is a sunny but coolish afternoon during break when Allegra and Lance meet as though by happenstance at the pool. They are wearing swim suits, though Allegra's bikini suggests more than it covers. They have towels for lying on the sun-struck granite. And Allegra has brought along a part of her book on poetry to see if she can get herself going on it again.

"So tell me about it," Lance says, lying back and shielding his face from the sun. "I'm not totally illiterate."

She is pleased even as she wonders if his motives are entirely literary. She says, "First, there are many kinds of literacy, so you are not in the least illiterate. Second..." She pauses. "Second, I don't want to bore you."

He pulls himself up so that, like her, he is sitting hunched forward, knees up. When he says, "You could never bore me," it sounds like the declaration of love that it is.

She wonders if her blush shows through her tan. He has pulled away so that he can turn and look at her. She takes in his muscling

187

torso, hair getting long, eyes intent and serious. "Okay, here goes..." She stops to collect her thoughts scattered by impulses somewhat less elevated than her subject matter. "Okay, unlike fiction, all great poetry is about itself whatever its ostensible topic..." She pauses again and then recites from her preface. "In novels and short stories, words are a means to an end. In poetry, the words are an end in themselves."

He nods. "I get that."

"Fiction uses words to enter the life or lives of its characters. The words tell a story. They are about what they refer to. In great poetry, and I use that phrase because there's a lot of dreck out there, the poem takes over the meaning of its words. Their referents, that is, what they refer to, make a scaffolding that falls away once the poem is consummated."

He's nodding a little dubiously. "I could use an example."

Allegra is more pleased than she usually is with an undergraduate willing to be tutored. She says, "Okay, take the 'The Song of the Wandering Aengus' by Yeats. It's one of the poems I use in my book. It's not about a hazelwood or fishing for trout or apples although all those things are mentioned."

"So what is it about?"

"Actually, it's not about anything. That's my point. It is something in and of itself. It both provokes and satisfies a yearning for beauty. It *is* yearning and beauty."

"I like that."

Her pleasure spills over into something more than being appreciated. She says, "I could recite it for you."

"You know it by heart?" He's impressed.

She smiles at him with yes in her eyes. She has been seduced into being the seducer. She takes his hand and holds it as though to steady herself. She recites, her voice modulating to let the words speak for themselves the way a dancer disappears into the dance:

"I went out to the hazelwood,
Because a fire was in my head,
And cut and peeled a hazel wand,
And hooked a berry to a thread;

And when white moths were on the wing,
And moth-like stars were flickering out,
I dropped the berry in a stream
And caught a little silver trout."

"Beautiful," he says and keeps her hand.

"Oh, there's more."

"Then, please."

Allegra continues, looking at him directly with the words "glimmering girl" and "Who called me by my name and ran." Her smile becomes unmistakable with "And kiss her lips and take her hands;/And walk among long-dappled grass..."

"God, that is beautiful." Then, still keeping her hand, "I know a place we could go."

"Now?"

"Now."

They gather their things. He takes her hand and leads her up the path that winds through the sugar bush.

Allegra writes in her journal that night:

Well, finally it happened. To use that absurd euphemism, I slept with Lance. There, I've done it and I've said it. After that first naked encounter at the pond, it was inevitable. Perhaps even if I hadn't come across Frank's infidelity. Not that I mean to exculpate in any way what we did by invoking inevitability or justice. Right or wrong, there was a sensual poetry about it. He was never forward much less gross. And I was a lady right to the end. What I loved is that there were no words. We didn't haggle or make excuses. He took my hand and I took his hand and we led each other away from the pool where I had been Yeatsing with him. We went up through the woods, reaching Monument Rock from the back. There we lay down on the sun-warmed pine needles, kissed, fondled, undressed, and rutted like mating lions. Once and again and again until it was I, my cup running over, who said, "Enough, dear man, enough," which made him smile.

Then, awkwardly, his words portentous, wrought from some part of him untouched, he said, "I love you, Allegra."

His intensity cowed me just a bit; I feared I was suddenly responsible for an emotional orphan. Nor was I, older, wife, mother, college professor, in as much control of myself as I had imagined. Sex is not just the great equalizer, it can leave you exposed and vulnerable beyond its immediate effects. I said with an equivocation I loathed, "I'm very attracted to you."

"It's a first time for me," he murmured, his hand going down my back to rest just where my ass begins to cleave.

"Sex?" I asked, astonished.

"No." He stopped, abashed. "Maybe love. This kind of love."

"You never loved another girl?" It was the kind of virginity I didn't believe in.

"No. Not like this."

"Why not?" I was perplexed. After his evident passion and words, I didn't need reassurances where I was concerned. Quite to the contrary.

He turned those long lashed eyes on me. His words belied a look of almost comic tenderness. "I'm not sure. I think maybe selfishness. I wanted to be free. I didn't want to be responsible for someone's happiness." He frowned. "And maybe I didn't want anyone else to be responsible for mine."

"Is that what love is?"

All the while he was gently and provocatively touching me. "It's part of it. Maybe the tough part. You know, when stuff starts to happen."

At first, his words felt like a rebuke. I thought of Frank. But then it was more like he understood what had happened, what was happening. I felt humbled, liberated, grateful. An easy kiss turned passionate and once again I thought I had landed in cock heaven.

We returned by way of the stream. I couldn't tell whether we were entering or leaving the Garden of Eden. We bathed and, more or less dry, put on our clothes.

190

Before we returned to what we had for society, we sorted out the niceties of conduct. Nothing overt. We would get together when we could.

"What if Frank...?"

"Revives?" I saw no point in mincing words.

"I suppose."

I looked at his marvelous lips and eyes. I told him, 'It won't make any difference. It's already day-to-day around here. The question is will any of us survive."

What gnaws at me is not that I've made love to Lance, it's whether to tell Frank about it. Or keep it to myself. I don't owe him anything. I don't want to rub his face in it. I am empty of anything like revenge. But we were so determined, so confident of our love when we first knew each other, that total honesty seemed an easy, obvious vow. And, at first, we held nothing back and in fact have been remarkably candid about everything with each other. But that's all gone. Maybe he senses it already. Probably doesn't care one way or another. Or would telling him shake him out of his fatal lethargy? Is he too far gone to care?

There is no one to talk to about it, not that I have much confidence in verbal therapy unless it's done with a close friend over a drink. Grace is Frank's mother. Ari is like his brother. Nicole, the mother superior where the kids are concerned, has enough on her hands. I don't know Lise that well. Actually I do, but I'm subject to the prejudice that Asians have scant interest in nor suffer very much from emotional problems.

The damn thing is that, having hooked up with Lance, I shouldn't care anymore about what Frank was doing with Elsa Sterne. But I do.

*

Security matters stay routine until the afternoon Thad hears the noise of a truck engine coming from the mike covering the

McFerall compound. It's the sound of an engine he's not heard before. He switches on the camera and calls to Jack who is in the kitchen. "I think you should see this." Ari and Nicole come in as well. They cluster around and watch.

In bright sunshine, a large truck with National Guard markings and with a canvas-covered bed has lumbered into the yard of the compound. Two men get down from the vehicle. Bruce and Duncan McFerall emerge out of their respective dwellings. There are handshakes and some talk. The McFeralls point to the two newly constructed sheds with corrugated roofs and strong, padlocked doors. The driver gets back into the truck and positions it so the tailgate is about ten feet from the doors that have been unlocked and opened.

Jack sits next to his brother. Ari and Nicole also pull up chairs. They watch as the four men unload what even to a casual observer appears to be arms. Jack is no casual observer. He is earmarking the video and listing in a notebook; RPGs still in their crates, reinforced boxes containing grenades, ammunition, and even a couple of flame throwers. These are loaded in no particular order into both sheds. One of the guardsmen, if that's what they are, hands down a clutch of assault rifles to Bruce. He puts them on the ground and inspects them one by one.

"AK47s," Jack says. "Christ knows where they got those." There are also five-gallon cans, perhaps of diesel. These go into the concrete bunker Jack noted before.

The driver gets back into the truck to pull it up next to a third, larger shed. Duncan unlocks it. He and Bruce bring out familiar looking canisters and sacks.

"Food," Thad says. "Flour. Cooking oil. Beans, probably. That's a crate of what...?"

"Spam," says Nicole, who has good eyesight.

The loading continues. "Food for arms." Ari states the obvious.

"The new economy," says Thad, who doesn't expect anyone to laugh.

After the truck leaves, Jack pushes back. "We have to hit them. With those kinds of weapons, they'll run amuck all over the county."

"How do we do that?" Ari is dubious.

"A night raid. We use kerosene to make Molotov cocktails. We fire the sheds."

*

Lance and Allegra make love in the woods. They make quiet love in his small bedroom when no one else is around. They make standing up love in the root cellar, wet love early one morning taking a shower in the bath house, and blind love, groping in the darkness of the quarantine tent, which has been left in place.

Theirs is a fraught, wartime love-making, each coupling intense and poignant, a groping for meaning beyond the sheer sensation of it. It's as though each time will be their last time. Partly it's guilt, which afflicts Lance more than Allegra.

They quickly grow intimate in the way of a long-established couple, reading each other's moods without the need for words. It doesn't take long before Allegra realizes that Lance's inward-turning silence after one of their romps has more to do with remorse than any post-coital satiation.

She doesn't say anything until he does. One morning, alone together in the garden picking tomatoes, he says, not quite out of the blue, "It's just that this family has taken me in. They have saved my life. And I feel like I'm betraying them."

"Because of Frank?"

"Of course."

She put down her basket. She glances around and then takes him by the hand to the grassy verge next to the fence. It isn't the first time they have spoken about Frank, but it's the first time he's admitted feeling guilt. He might also confess that he remained silent about Frank because he didn't want to jeopardize what he and Allegra had going.

As had Allegra, but for other reasons. She doesn't want to leave the impression that he had gotten her on the rebound. She doesn't want him to think that he was her instrument of revenge. She wants their love, for that's what it has become, to be between them and only between them. Now, she thinks, looking down at the brilliant fruit in their baskets, it was time for full disclosure.

She begins conventionally enough saying, "You have to trust me. This has nothing to do with Frank and me. Frank and Allegra are no longer Frank and Allegra." Then, betraying herself with tears that verged on sobbing, she tells him the whole sad story starting with finding the file on Frank's cell phone and how that illuminated what had been happening between them well before the pandemic began.

Anyone watching from below would have seen Lance put out a hand to comfort her. With a perception she doesn't expect, he asks, "Is that why he's so miserable?"

She looks away, rendered mute by his empathy, a lover who could feel her heartbreak. She collects herself. She dries her tears. She says, "So it's over. Even if he recovers..."

He stands up with her. "I won't hold you to it," he says. He's turned, facing her, close. He wants to hug her, to deny his words.

She nods. "I know. That's why I love you." Then, with a sardonic laugh, "You'd better not give me up."

Allegra tries to separate her anger and disappointment with Frank from her blossoming passion for Lance. Frank over there, Lance over here. Frank dying, Lance living. Frank the past, Lance the future. It doesn't quite work. For all her words and resolve, she cannot keep her own guilt at bay in the after-spell of love with Lance. She knows in her heart of hearts that she is abandoning her sick and dying husband for another man. She doesn't try to justify her betrayal, to acknowledge it's part of her own psychic and physical survival.

Nor does she try in moments of doubt, to convince herself that it's just a fling. Happens all the time. That when Frank recovers... Because Lance grows on her, grows in her, the feel and weight of his body of a piece with the sound of his voice and the way he looks at her. Sex, she writes, is, among other things, the outward sign of an inner grace called love. But then she always did think Catholicism was a kind of vocabulary.

As her concern for Frank grows perfunctory and then simply ceases, she worries when Lance goes hunting or on some mission with Jack. In a remarkably short time, he is there, in front of her, in her dreams, in her mind. He may have been a student and she a professor, but he knows things with a confidence and authority that has her rethinking and retooling her own ideas about literature and life.

Once, in passing, she half wonders aloud if theirs is not an oedipal situation. The remark rattles Lance out of his usually calm intensity.

"You've got to be kidding. You're a beautiful young woman. And you're not that much older than I am. And, besides, Freud has no standing in real science..."

"I was making a joke..."

But Lance is not listening, he is talking, the glint of authority in his eyes making her the student and he the teacher. "Evolutionary biologists and sociobiologists consider him little better than a phrenologist, if they consider him at all. The only place he's taken seriously anymore is in English departments." He pauses as though catching himself. "No offense..."

She shrugs. "None taken. I never thought much of psychoanalysis."

On an afternoon when one of the goats goes missing, Allegra and Lance volunteer to look for her. Allegra carries an AR15. The animal hasn't strayed far into the woods above the upper pasture. Lance catches it easily enough and ties it to a tree with a length of rope. Behind a bower of laurel, he takes off his work shirt and lays it on the ground. "A quickie," she says. And then another one, slower even though the overhead sun appears to race through the moving clouds.

They return and she goes upstairs to find Frank in bed, propped up on a pillow staring at the ceiling, a copy of *Bleak House* open beside him. She leans the AR15 in a corner and takes out her combat fatigues. "Where did you ever find this?" she asks with a laugh, picking up the book.

"In the bookshelf in the family room."

Then he knows. He knows from the false note of hilarity in her voice, almost a mild hysteria, and the color of her cheeks and the languor of her movements. He never imagined he would bring his trained skepticism and lawyer's nose for mendacity to bear on Allegra.

He says, "You're having an affair, aren't you?"

The moment she dreaded and wanted has arrived. The counter question, "What makes you say that?" sticks in her throat. Might not her infidelity bring him lower, perhaps kill him? But if she can lie with her mouth, she cannot with her eyes, which begin to brim as she nods her head.

"With Lance?"

"Yes." She sits with a sigh on the bed next to him. "How did you know?"

"I've seen the way he looks at you."

She says, "We've kept it very discreet. No one else knows."

Sitting up, Frank has energy enough for one of his rare outbursts. "I don't care a God damn about that." It's almost as though he has come back to life.

"What do you care about, Frank. Certainly not me."

He doesn't deny it, which shocks her anew. Enough for her to say, "I mean ever since you started sleeping with Elsa Sterne."

It's his turn for shock. "How...? You looked at my cell phone?"

"Yes."

"My private..." He's snarling now.

His indignation amazes her. She stands up and back. "Private? Frank we were married." She hears the past tense and shrugs inwardly. If words joined them, words can separate them.

"You have no right..."

"Stop being a fucking lawyer for once in your life." She's angry and confused. What does he want? Some kind of capitulation?

She looks at her watch. Defense Squad assembly in ten minutes. She starts to undress and stops.

"The fact remains..." he begins and falters. They have entered a realm where the law doesn't reach. "You don't care. You have no feelings," he blurts, knowing he has lost the argument, knowing there is no argument.

"Feelings are all I have," she retorts. She's in Lily's alcove stripping off her denims and pulling on her fatigues. Then boots. Jack will inspect.

She emerges and picks up the weapon. She says, "None of this would have happened if you had been here. But you're not. You're mooning after some German bitch who's probably dead while the rest of us work our tails off to stay alive." She holds up the AR15. "And risk our lives. And you're all worked up about an invasion of your precious privacy."

"It's all I have left," he says weakly. That and a few tatters of dignity.

"All you've got left?" She thinks of Lily. She thinks of herself and all the others. "You're a fool..."

Then her anger dies. It is her last gasp of anything like love for Frank Arkwright. Her expression goes dead. This man, sitting up on the bed, his face in his hands, is no longer her husband. She is at the door checking her gear when he says into his covering hands, "I'm sorry." It sounds like a voice from the grave. It doesn't reach her. She is clattering down the stairs, reporting for duty.

An hour and a half later, hot and sweaty from an exercise in ambush tactics in the woods, Allegra returns to find Grace bent over Frank holding his wrist.

"What's happened?" she asks, alarmed. Despite everything, Frank is her husband.

"Some kind of attack," Grace tells her in a near whisper. Her expression is that of a worried mother and an attending physician. She moves aside to let Allegra see.

Frank is deathly pale, cold to the touch, and barely conscious. Allegra wonders if he took something. "How did you find out?" she asks.

"The girls brought Lily back. They knew something was wrong when he didn't answer them." She pauses, then, decisively, as though Allegra might object, "We should move him to the clinic. He needs real care."

Allegra doesn't bridle at what could have been an implied criticism. This is no mother, daughter-in-law tussle. Frank has become a problem, an embarrassment. Grace has to restrain herself from apology.

As Ari and Duvall are carrying Frank bodily down the circular stairway to an improvised litter, a call comes in from the Melnikovs up in the hills of Colrain. Captain Duncan McFerall of the Massachusetts National Guard had visited their farm with an order, signed by himself on official stationery, requisitioning a long list of supplies, including a lot of food the Melnikovs cannot spare. Was there anything the Mutual Aid Group could do?

Most everyone likes the Melnikovs. If nothing else, they know how to throw a wedding – Russian Orthodox priest up from Springfield in full regalia, vodka flowing like water, food like a Romanov feast, Lyudmila the ancient crone from the old country, not a word of English, cackling around like a Halloween witch, carrying on like someone who has won a bet with life. Her son Ivan, called John, the widower patriarch, presiding over the usual jumble of an extended American family. It includes two sons with wives and one ex-wife, their children, and a daughter married to an Argentine woman, their two adopted kids from Haiti.

Jack leaves Frank to the others and sits in the recon room next to Cyrus. They contact the Melnikovs and talk to George. He is the older son, the one chiefly responsible for the market garden the family works on and lives off.

"How much time did they give you?" Cyrus asks him. They have dispensed with the usual tags.

"A couple of hours."

"Do you have any weapons?" Jack asks.

"A couple of shotguns, an old thirty odd six."

"This is Cyrus. Any fallback place?"

"Not really."

"Then try to hide what you can. Try to bargain."

George Washington Melnikov sounds defeated and belligerent by turns. "Can you send any help? I mean, Jesus, what's the point?"

Jack, realizing the danger, says, "Have as many of your family as possible go into hiding. Get away from the farm..."

"Because of Bruce?"

"Exactly."

"Babush, she can't travel. And Dad's not all that well..."

Off mike, Jack says to his dad, "I could use the van to get a squad over there..."

Cyrus shakes his head. He can hear them bringing Frank into the clinic where a bed has been set up. It's getting complicated. "It's no use," he says. "Even if we decided to help and we haven't and won't, it's too far, too dangerous."

The problem of what to tell the Melnikovs, the words amounting to nothing but words, is solved when the connection goes dead. Cyrus tries to raise them again, but there's no response.

Imagining all too vividly what is happening at the Melnikov farm, Jack is morose and angry at himself. He should have put a bullet in Bruce McFerall's head when he had the chance.

16

In lobbying for an attack to destroy the munitions sheds at Pitts Hollow, Jack takes his father's objections seriously. Quite aside from a love and respect for Cyrus beyond any paternity, Jack knows that most of them would probably be dead if Sugar Mountain had not been established as a refuge. No stranger to violent death up close, he also has a hankering for peace that might surprise his dad. The phrase "the idiocy of war" has of late become part of his inner vocabulary. At the same time, he understands the logic of necessary war. If Great Britain had not stood alone against the Nazi onslaught for nearly two years, the world might well have become a different place.

It is in this spirit and in the aftermath of the attack on the Melnikovs – about which there has been no news for two days – that Jack convenes a meeting of the Defense Committee. He wants to explain in detail how he and a small squad would fire bomb the munitions sheds. They meet in the studio where Jack has set up a grease-pencil sheet with a diagram of the buildings – the two habitations, a rambling garage, and a scattering of sheds, including the new ones which are loaded with weapons and ammunition. There's a dotted line around the place showing where the guards mount a perimeter patrol. The plan of attack is simple: Four of them come in at night, disable the guards, and light the fuses on kerosene bombs they place in or on the sheds. Retreat.

"How close are the houses to the sheds?" Grace asks.

Jack uses a pointer. "The McFeralls knew enough to keep them at a distance. It's over a hundred and fifty feet and the garage is directly between the living quarters and the sheds. The risk to civilians will be minimal."

He points at the dotted line, "The sentries from what we've seen are careless and unprofessional. They both have walkie-talkies, but they sometimes go long periods without checking in. Also, they meet and talk, usually here. That's where I would render both of them immobile and unable to give the alarm."

"How?" Grace asks.

"Tie their hands and legs and tape their mouths."

"What if they resist?"

"I'll disable them."

Cyrus frowns and Jack thinks, here it comes.

"So attacking someone may be unavoidable?"

"I'm afraid so."

Cyrus shakes his head. "This is an offensive operation. We can only use violence to defend ourselves."

Ari says, "I would say that destroying weapons is an act of peace."

Cyrus doesn't budge. He says, "To go armed down there, subdue, perhaps maim or kill the guards, and destroy their property, is an act of war. It is not only against our principles, it will bring the McFeralls down on us with all their force."

"Amen," says Grace.

Just then, the CB transceiver buzzes. Thad gets up and tunes it in. He listens while the others wait.

Returning, he tells them, "That was Marshall Roth. He says he's heard from a source in Colrain that there was a real bloodletting at the Melnikov farm."

"Casualties?" Jack asks.

"Five dead, at least. The rest... No one seems to know."

"What happened?"

"Apparently one of the kids got his hands on a hunting rifle and took a shot at Bruce."

"Jesus Christ..."

They hold a moment of silence.

Jack resumes the meeting, gently pushing the advantage the news about the Melnikovs gives him. "I think, given what's happening, a preemptive strike at their war-making capability of the McFeralls is the prudent thing to do."

Ari ponders aloud. "Is it possible the McFeralls are bent on establishing themselves as a regional power based on warlord principles? I mean... There has to be some kind of... rationale."

"Don't count on it," Jack says. "It's murder for its own sake."

"And the authorities can't do anything?" Grace asks.

They look to Thad. He shakes his head. "Same old, same old. The Governor's office barely exists. I think the janitor's in charge at the head office of the Guard. It's very sporadic. I got a form reply the last time I was able to get in touch through the short-wave net. 'The situation is in hand,' it stated."

Nicole sums it up. "There are no authorities."

Silence followed her statement as its significance, once again, sinks in.

"We still have the network," Cyrus says.

Thad states the obvious. "It didn't do the Melnikovs any good."

Jack shakes his head. "They're going to pick us off one at a time. Within a few months, there will be no network."

Which brings them to the awkward question: what do the Sugar Mountaineers do if one of the members of the network is threatened in a way that they can render help?

Jack tries again. "Attacking and destroying the weapons supply will help everyone. It will greatly reduce the threat to us and the network."

Cyrus is adamant. The meeting slowly fizzles out. According to the founding document, there has to be unanimity for the use of violence unless they are attacked directly.

Allegra writes in her journal:

> *The sky is deepening and the night air brittles with intimations of autumn. The meadows and pastures are rank with heading grasses and wild flowers. The golden rod is particularly profuse this year according to Grace. (And, I guess it's hay fever be damned or ignored. Amazing how allergies have cleared up.) At night the crickets and cicadas set up a halo of sound that has begun to fade. I keep coming back to Keats, "Season of mists and mellow fruitfulness." Or Hopkins, "The deep down freshness of things."*
>
> *But I cannot escape into poetry or wildflowers or beauty. A darkening pall hangs over Sugar Mountain. It's not just Frank, who has grown too helpless to be embarrassed. He is dying. No one openly acknowledges it, least of all me. We think of death as a discrete event, an instant of time, the beginning of the final absence.*

But it can happen gradually. Grace can do nothing for him, though God knows she tries. He is receding as though into that disappeared New York life that now seems like a distant dream.

All around the outside threat grows. It's not just the Melnikovs. Jack predicted the predations of the McFerall clan would start up after the delivery of arms to their compound. So far he has proved right. At one level it's straight out extortion. Their M.O. is as simple as it's terrifying: They show up at a house or farm in the armed Hummer and fire off a burst of machine gun fire. Then they load up on food, medicines, fuel, or whatever's available. Like other brutal tyrannies, the McFeralls use covering rhetoric, informing their victims that they are "requisitioning supplies on behalf of a special anti-terrorism National Guard unit."

Any sign of resistance is met with an all-out assault. Less than a week after they over-ran the Melnikovs, they installed the Hoyt brothers from Hawley.

If it wasn't for Lily and the others, I might nearly welcome the danger. It distracts me from thinking about what's happening to Frank. I came across his cell phone yesterday just after they moved him. I couldn't resist going deeper into his exchanges with the Sterne woman. It's more than prurience. I need the outrage to counter the maddening guilt that periodically assails me. Their mutual lust is one thing. It's the small endearments that get to me. And it makes everything in retrospect seem so obvious – his evasiveness, his lack of passion, the way he used to plead exhaustion, absences, showing up late at parties at our friends. I can't bring myself to hate him, perhaps because it's the same coinage as love. The best I can do now is pity him. I visit him. I hold his limp hand. I am going through the motions. I turn from him with relief to the living, to Lily, to Lance, to danger, to survival.

None of this is happening in a vacuum. Murmurings about Lance and me have started. I can see it in the way the others look at me and look away. Sugar Mountain is a small village after all. Nothing stays private for very long.

17

Francis Charles Arkwright does not commit suicide so much as let his life slip away. The proximate cause appears to have been a bout of pneumonia that Grace tried to alleviate with broad-spectrum antibiotics. She got him through several days of fevers and chills when his body's thermal regulation system went awry. She tried every stratagem she had at her command, but the body that was her son Frank had begun its final unraveling.

The actual cause of death in the early hours of the day cannot be determined as there are limited diagnostic tools in the armamentarium of the clinic. Not that it signifies. The stethoscope confirmed that his breathing was growing shallow and that his heart beat was erratic. In his final hour, the up-to-date cuff with its digital readout showed his blood pressure dropping. And the under-arm thermometer measured in Fahrenheit and centigrade his slow cooling.

Those who nursed him around the clock during the four days he lay in the clinic were with him when he died. Grace, Cyrus, Jack, Ari, Nicole, and Thad each said their good-byes as he went in and out of consciousness. Allegra also held his hand, but without tears. She would not be a hypocrite. What sadness she felt was both at a remove and diffused, part of her grief for a vanished world.

In the notes she takes on scraps of paper, she writes, "It is Lily I want to shield from this. But I wonder if I'm not propping her between me and the others, who have a solicitude that I neither deserve nor need."

Later, contradicting what she has felt and wants to feel, she writes, "I have so many feelings about Frank that I can scarcely keep track of them. I am angry one moment, wanting to berate him for his betrayal and cowardice. Then I am pitying and self-pitying. I want to be free. I want him back. I want it all back. I want to drive to New York and go shopping. I want to buy some books. I want to write my own book and have it read. I want life."

She is concerned about Lance. They are in abeyance, which he understands or seems to, even as he fears any kind of rupture. Words and glances don't quite suffice, but Frank is, was, after all, her husband and a certain decorum is expected.

The only person who openly challenges her about Lance is Ari. It is close to midnight the day before Frank dies. Ari comes down the stairs in the main house with a bottle of vodka. "We need to talk," he declares to Allegra as wind and rain rattle the windows. She's been expecting it. They go into the empty kitchen and sit at the table.

Allegra sips at the small glass he pours for her. He knocks back his own, refilling it.

"You could have waited," he says with the abruptness of a long-smothered accusation. His eyes bore in on hers, his anger the more withering and righteous for being restrained.

She holds her silence for a long moment. "I could say it's none of your business, Ari, but I won't. The fact is Frank knows. And if he didn't assent, he didn't care. Didn't care about anything but...

"What choice did you give him?" The anger shows in his shortness of breath and the upturned vodka glass.

"More than once during the past couple of weeks I told him that, despite everything, I would break it off with Lance if he decided he wanted to live." Which she had, but with scant sincerity.

"Decide! He was in no position to decide anything. He's sick, very sick."

She waits again until her own sudden anger subsides. She wants to ask him if he ever met Elsa. She says, "Frank knew what he was doing... Or not doing."

"He told you as much?"

"He didn't say, 'Screw it, I'm going to let myself get sick and die.' But he said right from the first day here that his life, this life, had become his worst nightmare. He tried to rally a couple of times, but his heart wasn't in it."

"You said 'despite everything.' What are you talking about?" Now she bore back into his eyes. "If you don't know, Ari, I'm not going to tell you. And if you haven't guessed..." She trails of. "You could have..."

She's incredulous. He doesn't believe her. She snaps, "No I couldn't, Ari. I tried. I did everything I could. I wasn't enough for him *before* we left New York. And here nobody has been enough for him. Lily isn't enough. You're not enough for him. He nearly said as much."

She empties her glass and pours another one. The alcohol has no charm for her. Certainly not this expensive, artisanal vodka so emblematic of all that is gone. She says, easing back, "Frank was your friend. You loved him. I loved him. Lily loved him. This whole family loved him. But he didn't want this life. He was amazed that any of us did."

Ari relents, breathes easier. He reaches for the bottle but doesn't pour any. He puts his large face in his hands and nods, conceding, as though what she's told him has registered.

Allegra reaches out and puts a hand on his shoulder.

*

Out of a delicacy touched with superstition the family does not gather to discuss the location of a cemetery until Frank has breathed his last. Cyrus calls a meeting after the breakfast things have been cleared away and the older children have taken Cy and Lily outside to play.

Though grieved by the death of his brother, Thad manages some wry humor. "We should choose carefully. I suspect, given what's happening, most of us here will be spending a lot of time there."

Jack nods. "If we're lucky."

The only possible location is the west side of the barn garden, which has an old tractor lane threading through it from the equipment shed. On the other side of the lane, between it and the maples of the sugar bush is a grassy area of wild flowers large enough for any number of graves and the planned greenhouse. In the spring it is loud with bird life. The only alternative is up in the one of the pastures where they could make some kind of enclosure.

They talk it over. Interest is high. After some discussion, they go outside to look at the site.

"You don't think it's too close to the house?" Bella asks. She isn't being fussy, just practical. She and Frank had always gotten along.

"I'd worry more about the stream flooding," Thad says.

Jack turns to Cyrus, who says, "I've never seen it flood. Maybe once in a hundred years. We'll be safe enough here."

When no one else raises any questions, they assemble again in the kitchen and vote unanimously to put the graveyard there. It's reassuring. It's a place to go.

They plan. Duvall, with help from Cyrus, will make the coffin. Thad, Nicole, and Jack will cut back the grass and other vegetation in a corner of the plot preparatory to digging the grave. Bella, Lance, and Allegra will gather wild flowers for Lise to arrange. Ari and Chee will prepare a special dinner for the next day following an eleven o'clock service and burial.

Grace, subdued but remarkably composed, says, "I think we should all wear our best clothes tomorrow. Anyone who wants to contribute to the service, talk to me this afternoon."

The weather breaks sunny and temperate the next morning. After breakfast and chores, the adults disperse to their various tasks. In the workshop of the equipment shed, Duvall shapes a coffin of seasoned pine, which he planes and sands to a smooth finish before hand-rubbing it with wax. The rope handles on the sides give it a nautical look, as though they are launching Frank on a voyage.

When it is ready, they take the coffin into the clinic where Frank, his face washed and eyes closed, but still wearing pajamas, lies with his hands joined together in front of him. They lift his body from the bed and lower it into the bare coffin. Everyone withdraws a distance as Allegra, with Lily in her arms, say good-bye. Lily cries and lowers one of her teddy bears into the coffin. Grace and then Cyrus take a last leave. But Grace's tears don't come until Duvall positions the lid and begins screwing it shut. Cyrus, his own eyes bleared, leads her away.

Not long after, Jack, Ari, Nicole, and Thad carry the coffin in and set it on a table brought into the family room and placed sidelong at one end. Allegra puts tall white candles in pewter holders at each corner of the coffin and lights them.

The flowers are the only extravagant note. Vases have been found for pink, globular milk weed, chicory-like blue daisies, cow vetch like elongated clover still entwined with meadow grass, black-eyed susans, wild hosta, and golden rod. Nicole picks out the yellow and purple nightshade to discard.

Grace, recovered, says, "It's just after ten-thirty. We'll all meet back here in half an hour."

For the service, Allegra wears a simple dark dress and the string of pearls Frank gave her just after Lily was born. They have all worn their Sunday best, which adds a note of dignity most of them find reassuring.

Dressed in a dark suit with a white shirt and striped tie, Cyrus stands at one side of the coffin and reads from the *Book of Common Prayer*:

> "For none of us liveth to himself,
> And no man dieth to himself.
> For if we live, we live unto the Lord,
> And if we die, we die unto the Lord.
> Whether we live, therefore, or die,
> we are the Lord's."

He pauses, then recites from memory *Psalm 23*. His voice is steady until the ancient words touch close on their predicament:

> "Yea though I walk through the valley
> of the shadow of death,
> I will fear no evil;
> for thou art with me;
> thy rod and thy staff, they comfort me..."

208

Reverting to his Quaker leanings, Cyrus then asks those who want to speak about Frank to come forward.

Ari, in shirt and sports jacket but no tie, speaks first. He recalls their glory days in New York and how it combined sophistication with an intense and nurturing sense of family. "But Frank was not made for this life we have on Sugar Mountain. Not long ago he told me that an important tenet of Christianity had been reversed for him: Frank, as he saw it and as he knew it, came from a better place. If I have any hope at all as opposed to expectation, it is that he has now gone to an even better place and that he will be at peace."

Thad and Jack speak together, like a comedy team as they reminisce. The time they got lost in the White Mountains with a cold night coming on. It was Frank who thought it through and led them to a trail. The time he talked a state trooper out of giving Jack a speeding ticket. His response when Thad came out of the closet. "So what?" The times he would go hungry rather than eat in a fast food joint. "We'll miss him," Thad says, his voice breaking. "He was the glue that held Jack and me together." Jack, his voice also wavering, declares, "Frank is still with us, one of us, and always will be."

Grace speaks for herself and Cyrus. She has prepared notes but doesn't use them. "Of our three wonderful boys, Frank was the strongest and the weakest. At the age of two, he was already a lawyer, arguing with precocious logic for things he wanted but shouldn't have, like a second helping of ice cream. Unlike Jack and Thad, he had no interest in fixing old trucks or using power tools. He read books, almost any books. I once found him going page by page through an old Sears catalogue. He had a steel-trap mind. He could forgive, but he could not forget. While some people looked at the world and saw chaos, Frank saw an underlying order. And nowhere did he find that order more evident than in the law."

She pauses to compose herself. "If he inhabited a different realm than the rest of the Arkwrights, he never failed in love, love for Cyrus and me, love for Hank, love for his brothers, for Ari, and, especially love for Allegra and Lily. Above all, he did not want to be a burden to anyone. And in some ways, I have to believe that his very leaving of us the way he did was an act of love."

The silence that follows when Grace finishes is like silent applause. They look to Allegra but she doesn't stand to speak. She doesn't speak because she has nothing to say. She is not afraid of appearing as a hypocrite. Nor will she figuratively don the *A* of Hester Prynne. Nor will she affirm or impugn Grace's idealization of her dead son. She knows it is natural for the family to rally around their best memory of him. She feels judged if only by default. But she will tell none of them except Lance about Elsa Sterne. That morning she took Frank's cell phones to the workbench in the equipment shed and smashed them to bits with a hammer.

Ari sits at the old upright and runs through a medley that includes *Let it Be, Danny Boy, Coming through the Rye, I've Got the World on a String, Puttin' on the Ritz, Blue Moon, and Autumn in New York*. He ends with *Amazing Grace*, that everyone joins in singing.

Nicole, Duvall, Jack, and Ari each take a rope handle and carry the coffin out onto the porch overlooking the sunken garden. Then down the steps and out through a path cut in the high grass to the burial site. Lise and Bella bring out some of the flowers and arranged them at the head of the grave.

All the while Thad carries a laptop, surreptitiously checking the quadrants from the surveillance cameras. There are assault rifles and ammunition pouches discreetly handy.

Ari, reading from a notebook, kippa perched on the back of his head, recites an excerpt from *Kaddish*, the Jewish prayer for the dead:

"To Israel, to the Rabbis and their disciples to the disciples of their disciples and to all those who engage in the study of the *Torah* in this holy place or in any other place, may there come abundant peace, grace, loving kindness and compassion, long life, ample sustenance and salvation from the Father who is in heaven and earth and say, Amen."

Ari, Jack, Duvall, and Thad lower the coffin into the grave. Each in turn, including the children, throw a flower and a small scoop of soil onto the coffin. As this happens, Cyrus, holding up, but beginning to show the strain, reads from the committal service. They listen but mostly hear the refrain, "earth to earth, ashes to ashes, dust to dust."

Then Jack, giving a shovel each to Nicole, Duvall, and Thad, says, "We have no clergy here to bless this ground. But the way I see it, it will be sanctified enough by Frank's presence. Sugar Mountain has always been a refuge. Now, with Frank here, it has become hallowed ground. It has become home."

Quickly, but with due dignity, the grave is filled with the rocky soil mounded beside it. They don't use all of it, saving enough depth on the top to replace the rough-cut sod. Lise and Bella then arrange the flowers around the edge. There are hugs and tears. Then all but Allegra and Lily, who remain hand-in-hand at the new grave, file back into the kitchen for a dinner Frank would have loved.

18

It is not long before Sugar Mountain gets an opportunity to answer Jack's question: what do we do if a member of our network is attacked and we're in a position to help? The call from Hal Beck comes less than a week after Frank's funeral in the middle of a sunny September afternoon. His words are terse and to the point, almost a form of telegraphese.

"This is Hal Beck, Sugar Mountain. Do you read me? Over."

"Reading you loud and clear. This is Cyrus. Over."

"About a half hour ago, an armed Humvee pulled up in front. A man in a ski mask got out and pinned a note to one of the maples in front. Then someone on top of the Humvee opened up with a machine gun and shredded the pump house next to the barn..."

"Anyone hurt? Over."

"No, thank God. But the message read, 'These premises have been requisitioned by the National Guard. Vacate by tomorrow at this time. If you resist, you will be designated as terrorists and no quarter will be shown.' Over."

"Are you going to comply? Over."

"Don't think so. We have nowhere else to go. Over."

In one of those static-filled silences that come with short-wave communications, Cyrus wonders if he hears a plea to provide a refuge. "How many people there now? Over."

"Twelve. Six adults and six children. Is there any assistance you can render? Over."

Another noisy silence ensues. At length, Cyrus says, "We could take some of the children." He speaks without much conviction in his voice. He does not have the sanction of the others to make that offer.

"I was thinking about defensive help. Over."

"I'll take it up with Jack and the others. I think we could provide you with intelligence. Over."

"Talk to Jack and the others about it. And get back to me

ASAP. We are desperate. Over."

"Will do. Over and out."

A now familiar depression settles over Cyrus. He has been a pacifist since protesting the Vietnam War as a young man. Now it seems that principles are not enough. They have come down to brute survival. So that again his mind wanders off into thoughts about the Final Protocol. Isn't killing oneself preferable to killing others? At the same time he knows he cannot decide for others. Deep down he is a Calvinist: he believes the individual stands alone before God, before history, and before moral choice. We are all free and alone in that freedom.

Free, but also part of a larger entity. Not just his extended family, either. He thinks about Beck, a crusty old patriarch whose family has farmed the same land for nearly two hundred years. They would be overrun and murdered. Not just Hal, but his wife Doris who has MS. Their son Ralph Waldo, daughter Harriet and their spouses and children. A couple of nephews. They are decent, literate, hard-working people.

His heart is a dead weight as he summons an emergency meeting of the Defense Committee.

Jack notices that his father is unusually subdued as the members of the committee come in to sit around the table in the studio. They have left work in the garden, the kitchen, the woodpile. They have glasses of water and there is a basket of apples on a filing cabinet.

Cyrus relates the essence of the interchange with Hal Beck.

Ever alert, Jack asks, "What time was his call?"

Cyrus considers, then checks an informal log he keeps next to the CB. It was two forty-five, he says, returning to the table.

"Making the Humvee visit about two or two fifteen."

Cyrus nods. He sighs. He asks, "Does anyone have any suggestions for helping them that don't involve violence?"

Nicole asks, "We could bring them here. Put them up in the Fallgren place."

Cyrus nods. "I don't know. Doris is in a wheelchair, off and on, anyway. One of the grandchildren is sickly. I doubt they will want to move. And we don't have enough provisions for twelve more people. But I'll ask. He goes into the alcove and they hear him connecting to the Becks.

As they wait Jack works. In a notebook he brings to meeting, he writes in all caps "OPTIONS." It is, he was told early in his training, the most important word in the lexicon of combat operations.

Cyrus returns shaking his head. "They voted among themselves to stand and fight."

"How well are they armed?" Thad asks.

"Hunting rifles. Maybe a couple of shotguns."

After a silence, the faces at the table turn to Jack. He takes them in one by one. They are ready to listen, even his father.

He starts talking, his voice lifted into a command mode, "I want to preface my suggestions with a couple of observations. First, without the foresight of Cyrus Arkwright, most of us wouldn't be here today. Most of us would either be dead or barely alive. Also, without the instigation of my father, there wouldn't be any CB network."

He pauses and taps his pencil on the table. "But I ask, what's the point of having a network? To let people know we won't do anything to help them when they most need it? To send them condolences ahead of time? We couldn't do much for the Melnikovs, but this is different." He turns to Cyrus. "I'm sorry, Dad, pacifism isn't going to work with the McFeralls. They will decimate everyone in the network and then come up here and wipe us out."

"We have a retreat..."

"Right. And that will be next."

After a silence, Jack continues. "As I see it, we have two choices. Three, actually. First, we can attack and try to destroy their munitions dump. We would have to do it tonight. Second, we can set up an ambush right at the Beck's place."

"And the third?" Ari asks.

"Do nothing. Let them all be killed."

214

Thad says, "I checked the camera covering Pitts Hollow. There's a lot of activity. They may be starting to stage already."

Cyrus asks Jack, "If there is conflict, is there any way of keeping the fatalities down? Not just ours, but the McFeralls...?"

Jack doesn't smile when he says, "Trust me, Dad, we won't aim to kill, only to maim."

"You're not trying to be funny?"

"Not in the least."

They vote finally. There are ayes around the table to help the Becks with force to resist the attack. Except Cyrus and Grace. After a long pause, Grace says, "I abstain." Cyrus looks to her and nods. "I abstain."

Allegra asks, "Does that make it unanimous? Technically?"

Cyrus stands. "With a heavy heart, I will officially absent myself from this meeting."

Grace rises also and together they leave the room.

Duvall shakes his head. "Man, they are some people."

They vote again.

*

The first thing Jack does is choose a combat squad. "I want Thad, Allegra, Lance, and Duvall to come with me. Ari, Nicole, Lise, and Bella will remain here on alert to defend Sugar Mountain, evacuate if necessary, or come to our help should we need it."

Ari makes a face. "I want in."

Jack nods. "I understand, Ari. But they have enough manpower to attack both places. We need you here."

In the middle of the table, Jack unrolls a Geological Survey map showing the Beck farm and the lay of the land around it.

Pointing with a pencil to where the town road comes within fifty feet of the front of the house and barn, Thad says, "It looks like a frontal assault might be the best way for the McFeralls to attack."

Jack isn't so sure. "They could deploy in the fields on either or both sides and come at them that way."

"But there's no cover in the fields if they're cleared," puts in Lance. He is nervous, both fearing what is to come and wanting it to happen. He looks at Allegra, whose face is also apprehensive and eager.

Jack muses for a moment. "The fields are pastures. They're clear."

Ari asks, "What's in front of the house besides the road?"

"A line of old maples if memory serves." Jack is pondering. "I think they'll come up the road and use the maples for cover." He turns to Thad, "Let's check out the Google Earth coverage we cached. It may not be very recent but it should do."

Thad goes into the recon room and comes out with a laptop. They position it near the top of the Geological Survey map and bring up the same area, easing down until they are the equivalent of eleven hundred feet in elevation. Thad is using his pencil again. "Here, across the road, is Nichols Brook and rising land..."

"Barely rising," says Lance.

"Yes, and wooded." Jack nods around the table. "That's where we deploy and wait."

"What about an escape route?" Allegra asks.

Jack is bent over the map and the computer screen. He says, "We hit them, hard and fast. Then we go back up the hill to Ellery Road, right here. We'll have mountain bikes. If necessary, we stash them and go back through the woods."

"How far altogether?"

"Five and a half, six miles."

"That's a long walk," Duvall says.

Jack agrees. "But I don't think that will be necessary."

"Why?"

"The McFeralls and their followers are bullies and bullies are cowards. That means once we start firing, they won't turn and come at us. They'll panic and scatter. By the time they regroup, we'll be long gone but they won't know it."

Nicole says, "But if we ambush them on this attack, doesn't it mean they will strike without warning in the future?"

Jack nods. "It's a consideration. But remember, they risk much less if they can get what they want by threat. I think the benefits far outweigh the downside."

After a lot of discussion, they decide not to communicate anything to the Becks other than a terse "message received." Jack also turns up the volume on the speaker connected to the microphone covering the McFerall compound. "Any indication that they are staging, we move, Jack tells them. "We can't expect them to keep their word about giving the Becks twenty-four hours to clear out."

*

No one sleeps much that night. About ten in the morning, Thad picks up the noise of one and then two vehicles driving up to the McFeralls. The camera confirms the arrival of pickups followed by an ATV.

Jack assembles his squad. He tells them, "They've begun to stage and we can't wait until we're sure. We need to be there to greet them."

Already dressed in camouflage combat fatigues, they smear their faces with a washable compound of grease and charcoal. "We all brothers now," Duvall laughs.

Nicole, newly pregnant, is to stand by to help Grace in the clinic in the event medical aid is necessary. Lise will help Cyrus in the recon room. Ari will stand guard with Bella, ready to evacuate everyone to The Ledges should it be necessary.

The squad sets out on bikes spaced well apart. They carry assault rifles slung over their backs along with pouches containing extra clips. Jack has a scope for his AR15. As planned, the tactic is to deploy among the trees on the gently rising ground across the road and above the brook. And wait.

Jack was not being facetious in assuring his father they would try to keep fatalities to a minimum. Jack has instructed the squad more than once: "Do not shoot to kill. Shoot at the legs and butts. If that's not a good shot, go for the body mass." He was not, he explained, being humane. "A dead body is easily buried. A wounded body needs to be carried off and taken care of."

"But won't they live to fight another day?" Lance asks.

Jack smiles. "Not very effectively. Getting shot in the ass does wonders to lower mobility and morale."

There are muted, quick good-byes. Cyrus shakes Jack's hand and then puts his arms around him. "God speed and come back to us."

It doesn't go easily. The front tire on Lance's bike springs a leak a couple of miles out from Sugar Mountain. They hide it by the side of the road and then peddle on, the other men taking turns carrying Lance. It gets cumbersome. They dismount and conceal the bikes well before they intended to. At a military jog, they continue along the road.

Presently they are crossing a field. They might have felt exposed, but there are no signs of human life anywhere around them.

Duvall steps in a hole and wrenches his leg. Thad gives him a pain-killer and rubs the calf muscle. In a few minutes, he is able to keep up with the others.

Jack, a proficient map reader and navigator, guides them with confidence. They enter a wood and come out into a pasture reverting to trees, raising a doe and her two fawns, which bound away noiselessly. Jays call and then a sound like a woman screaming.

"Fisher cat," Jack murmurs.

In time they are moving amid trees covering the upper part of the slope in front of the Beck farm. They descend quietly and with a professionalism that makes Jack feel a touch of pride. About sixty yards from the road, he stops and takes in the scene through binoculars. The riddled pump house shows what the mounted machine gun can do to a wooden structure. He positions the squad in two fire teams, each at the end of a shallow arc bending away from the house with himself at its apex. Thad and Duvall are to the right and Lance and Allegra to the left. "We're pretty close, aren't we?" Thad asks in a whisper.

"Trust me," Jack says, patting his shoulder.

They settle in to wait. No talking, not even murmurs. A trap? Jack muses to himself. Have the McFeralls found out that Sugar Mountain will help the Becks? Are they moving men in behind us, trapping us when the action starts? He doubts it. At the very least, they might send someone to scout the rise to make sure it's clear. Agitated, he whispers into his walkie-talkie that he is going to look around. Which he does, silently, stopping and listening. No one. Nothing. Then he hears the sound of vehicles off in the distance. He resumes his post. They wait. The sound becomes noise as the convoy draws closer.

The McFeralls and their followers arrive early and, to Jack's assessing eye, in relative disarray. The two Humvees, one mounted with the fifty caliber machine gun, pull up in front of the farmhouse. Jack counts eight men emerging from the Hummers and taking up positions. Moments later, several pickup trucks carrying another ten men, some of them either half drunk or very nervous to judge by their loud voices and general demeanor.

"Hold your fire," Jack whispers into the closed-circuit WTs. "Let them deploy."

Deploy they do, but haphazardly, as though this would be more like a party than a murderous attack on a family and its property. Spread out behind their vehicles and the maples, weapons ready, the attackers wait in an eerie silence cut suddenly by Bruce McFerall's voice coming through a loudspeaker.

Jack finds him standing in the back of the unarmed Humvee. He is next to a man with an RPG fixed into his weapon. Jack puts Bruce McFerall's head in the cross-hairs of the scope.

Bruce is booming, "Come out now and we'll let you go. Any resistance and we'll kill all of you."

Another silence.

"I'm going to count to ten. One, two..."

This is broken by a crackle of small arms and rifle fire from the house. Bruce calls, "All right, you asked for it."

"Fire," Jack says. As he aims at the back of Bruce McFarell's head, the man moves and Jack manages only to clip off his left ear.

219

He switches to the man with the grenade and hits his left shoulder. He moves to another target.

The sound of gunfire is more intense than loud, a deadly, purposeful racket that has the attackers confused, milling about, trying to find cover. Panic sets in. Lance, his blood high but his hands steady, takes down an older, slower man with a shot to his lower back. Then, sighting another attacker running up the road to cover, he fires and misses. Thad and Duvall account for at least one each. Thad has to restrain Duvall who has an impulse to get up and charge at them. Allegra at first fires wildly. It is not in her nature to hurt people. Lance says to her, take your time. She does and blows the rear tire off a pickup trying to get away. Then, with a shock to herself that passes quickly, she wounds the driver as he emerges from its cab.

Duncan McFarell takes over the loudspeaker. "Ambush! Ambush! Redeploy. Pull back."

Ominously, the machine gun begins to swing around to point up the hillside. Into the walkie-talkie, Jack says, "Stay down and behind cover."

The gun makes an awful racket as it kicks up leaves and the ground all around the positions of the Sugar Mountain squad. Jack's adrenaline is pumping now and he doesn't resist it. He takes careful aim at the machine gunner who, unwisely, is standing instead of crouching. The man takes a round in the neck and drops off the Humvee. It turns violently and joins the other vehicles that are driving away, swerving around the stalled truck. They leave their wounded behind.

"Let's go," Jack says. "Good job."

"We ain't finished," yells Duvall, his blood up.

"We've done our job. Let's go. That's an order."

It is a struggle to get back to Sugar Mountain. Clouds have gathered and a dampness in the air has turned to a drizzle and then into a steady rain. Duvall's calf and knee are swollen and he hobbles painfully despite another painkiller. When they reach the road, Jack tells them to stay under cover. He jogs to where the bikes have been hidden, takes one, and races home. He quiets the initial apprehension that greets his arrival. Where are the others? All is well, he tells them and relates quickly what they have done. Then, he and Ari take the Gilded Goose van and using only battery power, drift to where the others lay waiting. They pick up the remaining bikes, tie them on top and make it home without incident.

Cyrus congratulates them as they sit around debriefing and having hot toddies of lemon extract, grain alcohol, and water. But he also says, "You know, they will suspect that we had a hand in what happened."

Jack agrees. "But they are going to be a good deal more cautious in the future."

*

Allegra writes in her journal:

It is after midnight. Lance is sleeping where Frank used to lie. He is restless, muttering as though in a dream. Or a nightmare. We're together for the first time since Frank died. When I write "together," I mean sex, intimacy, and especially talk. I suppose I ought to feel worse than I do about it, being a recent widow and all that. But the fact is, as I can see now, Frank started dying the moment we left New York.

Lance, who seldom drinks, had two glasses of toddy when we got back and debriefed with the rest of the defense group. It was all understated and to the point. We were essentially a team tallying up the score. I got one confirmed hit and a disabled vehicle. Thad got one as did Lance. Duvall got one, perhaps two, but he wasn't sure. Jack got three... at least. We accomplished our mission: we saved the Becks. We bested the McFeralls, at least for now. For now. Perhaps that's why we were reluctant to celebrate, never mind gloat.

Lily has a night with the girls so I was free to have Lance in. We kept it discreet. He came up the winding stairs. We could hear Duvall, Thad and Bella talking down the hall. We talked, of course. Lance was very intense about the whole thing. He said, and I am quoting from uncertain memory, "It was like being alive in a whole different way, especially when that machine gun trained on us and started firing. I thought, okay, this is it. But then Jack took out the gunner. Man, he is something else. I'd follow him into hell."

Then, as though remembering I was there, he said, "What about you. Were you scared?"

"Because I'm a girl?" I could tell from his silence that he took it for a cheap shot when I was trying to be funny.

"Because you're human," he said back to me.

I told him I didn't think about the man whose ass I was aiming at. I thought about the child inside the house who would have been murdered.

I could feel Lance's big eyes on me in the dark. He said, "Yeah, I thought about that, too. But, you know, I have to admit..."

"What?"

"I kind of got off on it."

It showed in his lovemaking. He was distracted but he soldiered on. I could tell he wasn't all there. But then, neither was I. I couldn't shake the premonition that this was just the start. That things might get a whole lot worse.

222

19

They hear from Hal Beck that the McFeralls negotiated later that day for the return of their casualties, eight in all along with two dead, one from an apparent heart attack. The Becks in the meanwhile set up a tent and did what they could for the wounded, most of whom could not walk. The McFeralls in return agreed to leave them alone.

"Don't know who to thanks for that help," he tells Cyrus on the CB, "but whoever it was certainly saved our bacon. Over."

Two days later Hal shows up at Sugar Mountain driving a Prius. His son Ralph Waldo is riding shotgun, quite literally, with an AK47. In the back is a wheel of cheddar, a carton of Hershey bars, and several bottles of red wine. No thanks, they won't come in for a cup of coffee. It's not safe driving around.

They do talk a bit about the assault. Names are mentioned. The Becks know a lot of folks. "Where's the real Guard?" he asks more than once.

Jack asks him, "Do you think Duncan will keep his word... not to attack you again?"

Hal, on the small side, full head of white hair, glinty eyed, smiles. "Well, to judge from the number of weapons pointed out our windows when they came up to get their wounded, I think he thinks we've got an army in there."

"You took the weapons they left behind?"

"Damn right we did. And I'll tell you one other thing... They're hurting. I mean we're all hurting, but they're downright hungry."

"Which makes them dangerous."

Hal snorts. "Listen, they'd be dangerous anyway. Bruce is a psychopath. Now he's walking around with his head bandaged and minus one ear, a regular Van Gogh. I think they've got him chained in the yard like a mad dog."

"I'm sorry I missed him," Jack says.

"Yeah. You'll probably get another shot. Let's stay in touch."

Jack is satisfied that the ambush has thrown the McFerall camp into considerable confusion to go by the reports being picked up by the network and by the images coming in from the camera monitoring the compound. Still photos from the camera show an armored bulldozer being used to clear junk from an area close to the dwellings. They are followed by pictures of army tents being erected. The time-lapse sequence renders the scenes seemingly old fashioned, like something Mathew Brady might have shot.

"It's a field hospital for their wounded," Jack says, going over the images with Duvall and Thad.

"Yeah, but why there?" Duvall asks. "I mean there's got to be medical facilities around no one's using." They were in the recon room in the morning, each with a cup of rationed coffee.

"Control and appearances," Jack says. He glances up from the screen. "The McFeralls not only have to take care of their wounded, they need to be seen doing it. They're essentially warlords. Their power ultimately rests on loyalty. But, you know, you're right. It doesn't make sense."

"Loyalty and that stock of weapons and ammunition." Thad has joined Jack in trying to convince Cyrus to okay a preemptive strike on the munitions sheds. "We should hit them now."

"They'll only get more," Duvall says.

"True," Thad allows. "But it will cause more chaos, buy us time."

Duvall, leg thumping with pain, looks down into his empty mug. He's had his quota for the day. Jack pushes his own nearly full mug over to him. "I've got to sleep or I'll keel over."

Duvall takes it and pours half into Thad's mug. He and Thad are having one of their good days. "Thanks. But that assumes things will improve in the big world with time. And so far..."

"Yeah, and it don't look good." Jack is peering intently at the screen again. "You know, I swear I see Marko there."

Thad looks over his shoulder, manipulates the image. "Could be." Then, "But time also makes room for things to happen. And I don't think time is on their side."

Jack stifles a yawn and says, "I've got to sleep. What's on for today?"

Duvall smiles. "Apples, apples, and more apples."

"How's the leg?"

"Throbbing. But all right."

Later, after a nap, Jack is on the porch overlooking the barn garden and writing a report on the action at the Becks. He doesn't write reports so much for the record as to jog his memory about details that could be important to any future encounters with the McFeralls. He lists strengths and weaknesses, especially the latter, looking for vulnerabilities. Like the pickup trucks. Had he taken the big gun along, he could have crippled a bunch of them the way Allegra took out one with a shot to the tire. He could go after the engines, fuel tanks, windows.

He looks up to find Linda standing there waiting to be acknowledged. He smiles at her and reaches out a hand. "How are you?"

"I'm okay."

When she doesn't say anything else, he decides against small talk and asks, "Did you want to see me about something?"

She nods, abashed and then bolder. She says, "I know how to fire a gun. Alex showed me. He had a twenty-two. He let me fire it at a target."

Jack looks back into the blue eyes, which are steady and serious. His heart rises and sinks at her words. He is moved by the girl's casual courage and even by her implicit approval of what they are doing. It saddens him to think she may have to defend herself when she comes of age.

"You're still too young to join the squad," he tells her directly. "But I can tell you would make a good soldier."

"I just want to help."

"But you are already helping. I've seen you. You do more than your share."

She nods and gives him a rare smile. They have become special friends. She says, "Thank you," turns, and leaves.

*

Duvall has two bedmates and there is little comment much less any overt disapproval of what is a more or less equilateral triangle. Duvall rooms with Thad, but he often spends nights with Bella in her bedsitter in the equipment shed bay. Far from feeling privileged, he begins to cast around for a place of his own.

Both he and Thad confide in Allegra who had any number of gay friends in New York. "He wants to move out," Thad tells her in a voice stiff with misery. "He says he wants a place of his own."

"And what do you say?" Allegra keeps a sigh to herself. The histrionics of gay love could make Italian opera seem tepid.

"I said, 'Why don't you just be honest with me. You want to move in with *her*. It's not like he hasn't done it before. He can't tell the difference between his cock and his ego when it comes to getting stroked.'"

"You think Bella strokes his ego?"

"Like only a woman can. She is always pretending to need help from a big strong man."

Then it would be Duvall's turn, his size making the living room in the horse barn seem small. "I don't have a place of my own. It's that simple. If I'm at Bella's, I'm her guest. When I come back here, it feels more and more like I'm Thad's guest." His large face has plenty of room for chagrin.

A day later, everything would be sweetness and light, Duvall and Thad all but holding hands, Bella easy with the contentment of the well loved.

None of the others say anything openly. They speak about it one-on-one, Grace concerned about their happiness as she ponders a place suitable for Duvall. Jack worries about dissension in the ranks. However unvoiced, they all agree there is little margin at Sugar Mountain for this kind of angst.

Nonetheless, with the McFeralls in disarray, a sense of normality, however strained, settles over Sugar Mountain. The children, after a two-week break, go back to school. A second attempt to hold separate classes for the three age groups again goes by the board. As before, the classes in English and writing are taught by Allegra, natural history by Lance, and arithmetic and physics by Thad. Duvall's version of world history is the last of the morning and the favorite of the children. With his knack for dramatizing, he goes into detail about what the Greeks and Trojans used for weapons. He asks them to imagine what it must have been like to be inside the famous hollow horse as it was trundled into Troy.

They meet in the studio, ranged around the drafting table from nine in the morning till noon with breaks in between. Everyone at Sugar Mountain, even Meredith, who has grown sickly, is happy that school is in session. Learning is not only valuable in itself, but it provides a needed sense of the future, a future that, like the past, has grown tenuous.

The teachers keep it flexible out of necessity. Cy will not admit that he doesn't know as much as the nine-year-olds. Lily, nearly four, is something of a prodigy. But not in all cases. Though Lily can read and spell beyond her years, she isn't up to the level of the other girls. It is something Allegra easily compensates for. In French, Lily more than holds her own as they start with basic words, phrases, grammar, and pronunciation.

Nor is Lily up to the others in arithmetic. While they start in on fractions and percentages, she is still learning multiplication. "It's like this," says Rachael, who sits next to her at the smooth, hardwood table, "times just means..." And can't find an explanation that doesn't use the word she was trying to explain. Then she takes a piece of paper and folds it in half. Then stops again. "No, that's more like fractions."

Lance is also popular with the class. Evolution gets rapt attention and giggles. "We once were monkeys?" asks Linda, who has had a Sunday school upbringing.

"My sister's still a monkey," Cy says.

Then the Neanderthals, which no amount of PC reconstruction can rescue from looking decidedly primitive.

Duvall's forays into world history overlap with Lance's teaching on evolution. Handing around pictures of the hairy mammoths, bears, rhinos, and large cats painted in the caves of

France and Spain thirty thousand years ago, he asks Lance to talk about them.

It's his cue to talk about extinction. "Extinction," he says, "happens when every last member of a species dies. And you remember what a species is."

There are nods. "Are we going to go extinct?" Mary asks.

Lance shakes his head. "Not by a long shot." He wonders if he should talk to them about selection pressure and genetic bottlenecks, about how the human race right then is going through an evolutionary event of enormous proportions. Instead he talks about how these kinds of animals ranged over Europe thirty thousand years ago and may have been hunted to extinction by early man.

"By Neanderthals?" asks Mary, using her new word.

"Perhaps, but also by people called Cro-Magnums," Lance explains. "They came into Europe and the Middle East from Africa at least a hundred thousand years ago."

"Where's Europe?" Linda asks.

"Good question," Duvall says. He pins up a map of the world and locates Massachusetts for them, then Europe, then Africa. To make things clearer, he takes out an old globe and shows them how the world works.

School time, lunch time, nap time, and work time. Their heads covered against the strong sun, the kids help in the fields while one of the nine-year-olds looks after Lily. Cy talks his way into helping with the apple harvest from a lower part of one of the trees, adding his bit to what seemed more fruit than they could use in several years.

With no boys his age, with no boys period, Cy rattles around on his own, everybody's favorite. He can't get enough of Henry's war stories. Henry, who still thinks about Edith and wonders what happened to her, signed up for the Yankee Division the day after Pearl Harbor. Unlike Jack, he will talk about his war, the memories of which seem more vivid with time. He speaks in a nearly extinct Boston Brahmin honk, lapsing into a narrative close to free association when prompted by his great grandson. "We captured

Linz, an ordinary sort of place. That's where Hitler was from..."
He drifts off into recollections. "Yes..."
"Hitler was really bad..."
"As bad as they get."
"Why didn't they kill him before?"
"He had a lot of bodyguards. And a lot of people liked him."
"Dad would have taken him out. The Germans had really good
tanks, didn't they?"
"Better than ours. But we had more. We had more of
everything."
"But we had the best fighter. The Mustang couldn't be beaten."
"Ah, but it could. They had the first jet fighter, the ME 262..."
"A Messerschmitt..."
"Yes, a Messerschmitt."
"Did you ever see one?"
"Not in the air. We saw a few on the ground and a lot of spare
parts when we liberated Malthausen. It was a concentration camp."
"Where they killed people...?"
"Not on purpose. It's where they made the jet fighter in
underground factories..."
"The Germans were very smart..."
"Yes, very smart."
"But not as smart as us."
"There are many ways to be smart."

*

Meredith weakens and dies. Like Frank, she spends her final
days in the clinic tended by Bella and Grace. Ari hovers, anguished
because he cannot feel anguish. Meredith goes quietly and with
dignity, awake and mostly alert until about an hour before she
drifts off never to return. She says good-bye to everyone, even the
children.

Other than Bella and Grace, no one mourns openly, though
everyone maintains a somber mien. Duvall and Cyrus make
another coffin. It is more rudimentary than the one fashioned for

Frank. Lance and Allegra clear grass and other vegetation for a grave next to Frank's. They take turns with Duvall and Jack in digging the hole. About three feet down, they hit on a large boulder that has to be worked around and pulled out. But they finally have a neat enough grave six and a half feet by two and half feet wide and about five feet down. Allegra fetches a small tarp to put over the pile of dirt. Lise picks bouquets of wildflowers including a lot of asters and golden rod.

Bella, Ari and Grace speak at the service. The dinner afterwards ends with hermits, cookies made with molasses and raisins, which had been a favorite of Meredith's.

That night Allegra writes in her journal:

> We now have three less adults than what we started with. There's more room. And there will be more food. But it feels lonelier here. Meredith was family and as much as I never really connected with her, I miss her. Strange to think that she and Frank are still with us, planted like roots in this place that is home like no other place I have ever lived. It is home in the radical sense that for the foreseeable future, Lily and I could not survive anywhere else.
>
> I have to confess I miss Frank. That is, I miss the old Frank, the pre-Elsa Frank. Perhaps because I miss those times. They recede like a fairy story you heard as a child. Is Barnard Hall still there? Is anyone in the offices? And the deli just off Broadway? They were magical times. And now gone, gone forever.

She adds later:

> We're all one big family now. The bonds of closeness are real. We talk a lot, perhaps because we have so little else to do in our free time. The other day Bella said, "I'm liberated from liberation." Then, "What a dork I was, always pandering to the almighty me."
>
> Nicole said she thought there was an upside to the

pandemic. "How much better food tastes when you're hungry. How much more you appreciate people because you can't take their lives or your own life for granted."

We talk a lot about family and what it means. I said I have come to think the conservative family-values people have it backwards, especially about gay marriage. In this I am much influenced by Lance. He says correctly that the only thing that matters is that you care for the children you beget regardless of who you are. In this I am, like Lance, far more of a Darwinian than a Christian. By Darwin's standards – mutatis mutandis where Homo sapiens is concerned – the only real perversion is not caring for your children. As Lance sees it, the Lotharios of the world looking to "score" with no regard to the consequences are not only the perverts of natural selection, they are the real losers considering what usually happens to their offspring.

But all that's gone. Now, if you don't take care of your children, they will die. What we have par excellence are priorities. Survival comes first, second and last. Survival means work and then more work – harvesting, preserving, storing. It means maintenance, cleaning, fixing, building. It means security, round the clock in the recon room, defense drills, informal roll calls. Everybody present and accounted for. It means, above all, caring for one another.

*

The relative normality does not last long. With the advent of October, with the days noticeably shortening and the nights cooler, the ever-vigilant Jack begins to pick up signs of renewed activity at the McFerall camp. He notices a van he hadn't seen on the spy camera when he and Thad slipped out at night to replace the batteries. Later, tipped off by sounds from the mike, he takes pictures that show pickup trucks coming and going, at least one of them backed up to the sheds used for munitions.

More images show the wounded men from the Beck farm

attack hobbling around the place. They won't stay much longer given the weather. Jack knows they won't be fully mobile for months. Not that it signifies. They watch, the camera in full motion, as pickups and ATVs bring new recruits that Duncan and Bruce, the latter's head still bandaged, lead off to a nearby field for training. At least to judge from the faint sounds of gunfire that the mike picks up.

When the sounds and picture from the McFeralls show unmistakable signs that they are staging for a raid, Sugar Mountain goes on full alert. Cyrus immediately warns members of the network. The monitoring cameras all around the perimeter are checked and double checked. Everyone, including the children, have evacuation backpacks ready to put on for the trek to The Ledges should that become necessary. Weapons and ammunition are kept handy for the members of the Defense Squad. Thad installs a special effects defensive weapon that will help hold up any attack however temporarily.

Sugar Mountain is not attacked. But the next morning they hear over the network from a source in Charlemont that an isolated farmstead in Hawley has been attacked without warning and its inhabitants, ten in all, either killed or fled.

20

As a special ops soldier Jack learned that you don't sit around waiting for the bad guys to bring it to you. Unless you have set up an ambush. But what, when, and how to attack? His plan is simple: a team of three or four would slip in under cover of darkness, plant incendiaries on the sheds with munitions, light the fuses and leave. Instead of confronting his father at a meeting, he sits down with him privately in the studio. It is evening and each has a cup of herbal tea.

"We're not even sure it was the McFerall group that attacked the farmstead in Hawley," Cyrus says after Jack broaches the subject.

"Dad, we have footage of them staging for a raid. They left their compound in force about three in the afternoon. The family in Hawley was attacked, murdered and driven off about an hour later. If it wasn't the McFeralls, who was it?"

Cyrus lowers his head. "They're not the only gang around. I've heard reports of a bunch in Savoy..."

Jack sighs. "Dad, it has to be the McFeralls. There's a finite amount of gasoline and diesel left out there. Duncan McFerall is not going to top up a bunch of pickups and his Humvees to take a joy ride."

"Okay, so what do you do about civilian casualties if you fire bomb the McFeralls? There are women and children in those ... houses. And those tents with the wounded."

Jack unrolls for his father an updated diagram on which he has outlined the whole compound – habitations, various sheds, the garage, and the tents. Standing, he points out the distances between the buildings. "If the family members stay put, they'll be okay even in a worst case scenario... for them."

"Which is?"

"We set off all of their munitions and fuel supplies."

Cyrus remains dubious. "This is still an attack. It's aggression. And if it doesn't work..."

Jack sits and sips the honey-sweetened brew going cold in the cup. He says, "They are going to come up here and attack us whether we try to murder all of them or send them peace offerings of food and medicines." He bores in, repeating a theme, his smile twisting. "Even a Quaker has to agree that destroying arms is more an act of peace than of war."

"You're a regular Jesuit, Jack," Cyrus says, conceding the point and, eventually, to Jack's surprise, the rationale of the attack. "But no violence against the people there. Other than subduing them so that you can get rid of the arms."

The Defense Committee meets. Jack goes over the same points, this time with the diagram pinned up to the cork board that is the flip side of the blackboard used in the school. There are questions but no challenges. With Cyrus neutral, it is a foregone conclusion.

"What do we have for... the things to blow them up with?" Allegra asks.

Jack nods at Thad.

He says, "We've devised and tested a kerosene incendiary that works pretty well with the fuses we have. We have some dynamite and caps, but they're dangerous to use and not always reliable."

"Why kerosene?" Lise asks.

"It burns slower than gasoline and with enough heat for the purpose. Gets things started..."

"I vote we use dynamite," Duvall says.

Jack starts to reply when Ari says, "We could practice with a couple of sticks."

Jack considers. "The dynamite is old, the caps older. It will be dangerous enough firing the sheds with kerosene. But I'll think about it."

"How do we keep our identities concealed?" asks Nicole.

"We blacken our faces like before," Jack replies. "The question, really, is whether we might deliberately let them know who is hitting them."

"Why?"

"Respect. Fear. Second thoughts about coming up here and trying to take Sugar Mountain."

From the surveillance monitor and from a final foray the night before to reconnoiter the site, Jack confirms that, as before, two guards armed with assault rifles keep up a desultory perimeter patrol, checking with each other every five minutes or so. Using a large sheet of graph paper from the studio, he replots the locations of the shed where the generator, running on diesel fuel, keeps the lights on, and the two munitions sheds and what he thinks might be the fuel bunker.

For the team, Jack picks Thad, Lance, and Ari. They are in good shape mentally and physically. Thad is adept at solving technical problems if it comes to that. Duvall and Nicole are to stand by with Ari's van should the team need picking up. The squad gathers in the studio to go over the plan.

"What if they have monitors?" Thad asks.

"We probe," Jack answers. "But I don't think they do."

"Why?"

Jack smiles. "I've been poking around the place. Their security is fourth rate. But if there's any kind of coordinated response before we set the incendiaries, we withdraw."

"And no dynamite?"

"No dynamite."

*

The following evening, an hour after sunset and with cloud cover making for relative darkness, the four slip away on mountain bikes. They are armed with AR15s, Glocks, and combat knives. Their backpacks contain tightly corked quart bottles of kerosene with varying lengths of fuse. They wear night vision goggles and keep about twenty feet apart as they peddle silently through the darkening night.

Again they take back roads to avoid the town center. At a designated spot above Pitts Hollow, they pull over. They hide the bikes off-road in a clump of bushes seemingly designed for the purpose. Then, single file, following Jack along a new trail he has blazed with small bits of reflective tape, they wind their way through woods and then a pasture reverting to bush and finally open land with the lights of the compound clearly showing.

Their primary targets remain the two munitions sheds and the fuel bunker. If they have time and opportunity they will try to fire the two Humvees and the generator, which chugs along in a small Quonset hut.

But first the two guards have to be disabled. Jack takes that job as it involves a level of training and experience the others lack. "When I give the all clear, we set the bombs and light the fuses." Bombs? he thinks. Paltry little incendiaries more like it.

"Check," the others respond.

Jack moves off and from a vantage point closer in watches as the two guards make a desultory perimeter sweep. They time it so they are roughly opposite each other on their semi-circular routes that take them up to the road, around the now mostly abandoned tents, the munitions sheds, and not far from the edge of the woods where the attackers lay in wait. One of the guards looks familiar, but Jack doesn't think it's possible. Every few minutes, they check in on their walkie-talkies. He hears their voices clearly. "All clear, Jack. All clear, Marko."

Marko! Jack's pulse quickens. The dumb son of a bitch. He feels a keen anticipation, but takes a moment to control his feelings.

Because he is closest, Jack first subdues his namesake. An older, slack kind of guy going through the motions, he faints when Jack puts a hammer-lock on his neck. Jack ties his hands behind his back and covers his mouth with duct tape. As he gasps and gurgles on the ground, Jack leans over and whispers, "You move and you're dead. Understand?" The man, eyes wide with fear, nods.

Jack takes the man's assault rifle and moves with a practiced gliding stealth to stalk Marko. He decides he won't kill the man unless he has to despite his promise to do just that. Because he promised his father that there would be no unnecessary violence. And Jack keeps his better promises. He will just disable him. Badly.

236

He doesn't get the opportunity. Marko, walking sloppily with his unconscious swagger, is thumbing his walkie-talkie. "Jack? Report." He turns and in a patch of light sees a different Jack coming toward him.

He bolts, dropping his walkie-talkie. And if he has one advantage over Jack, it's that he can run faster, even in the dark. Jack pauses and watches the form moving up the drive and out onto the road.

"Clear," Jack whispers into his walkie-talkie.

The plan, though simple, has its elaborations. Their homemade fire bombs are designed to ignite more or less simultaneously, if only to create enough chaos to cover their escape. At the same time they don't want to get hit by exploding munitions. Thus, the fuses for the munitions sheds are longer than they are for the other targets and would be lit just before Jack destroys the generator. They are working at it when the door to Duncan McFerall's place opens. A woman appears and calls out, "Jack, Marko, you guys want some pie?"

Into the walkie-talkie, Jack says, "Just keep going on the sheds. Skip the vehicles. We're almost there."

"Marko? Jack?" Then she turns back into the house, "Dunc, I think there's something going on out there."

"Shed One lit," Thad reports.

A moment later, Ari says, "Shed Two lit."

Jack rips the leads from the generator to the transformer and circuit breaker. The lights go out all across the compound. He then cuts the line to the fuel tank and the smell of diesel fills the enclosed space. He backs out uncoiling a length of fuse. Just as he lights it, a kerosene bomb goes off with a whoosh on one of the sheds.

"Let's get out of here," Jack says into the walkie-talkie.

In the light of the flames from the first munitions shed, they see several men with assault rifles take up positions and start firing in their direction. Jack orders everyone to pull back into the trees. He covers them, slowly withdrawing himself. A moment later the generator and its fuel tank blow and then the second munitions shed starts to burn.

A stray bullet catches Thad in the upper arm and tears away a chunk of flesh. They stop briefly in the relative cover of the trees for Ari to wrap a compression bandage around it. Jack watches the compound. He is waiting for the bullets, grenades, mortar shells, RPGs to start exploding. But there are no fireworks. Something he feared has happened: The upper parts of the sheds are decoys. The munitions are in bunkers under the sheds and are bomb proof or at least fire proof.

Up in the pasture reverting to brush they stop. Ari checks Thad's wound. Jack goes back far enough to scan the compound with binoculars. He sees women, and children huddling on the road well back from the burning buildings. There are no explosions. Then, something that alarms him: the two Hummers start up and their lights come on.

"We need to move," Jack says. "They're sending out patrols."

"Did we do any damage?" Lance asks.

"The ammo dumps didn't go," Jack says. "They're underground. I should have known."

"Can you ride a bike?" Ari asks Thad.

"I don't think so. I can walk, at least for a while."

They press on, Jack leading, his AR15 ready. They stop several times for Thad, who is starting to feel faint. Because of his arm, he's difficult to support on both sides even when the trail allows it.

When they get to the road and the bikes, Thad says, "Leave me here. I'll be all right. Come and get me when the coast is clear."

Jack says, "Not an option."

Ari says, "The coast may never be clear."

Jack stops, thinks. Options. He says, his voice low, "We'll rig up a two-bike litter. Ari, you and I will wheel it along on either side. Lance will scout ahead, but not too far."

While Ari tends to Thad, Jack and Lance rig the litter. Jack cuts a couple of six-foot long saplings about an inch and a half thick. With duct tape, he secures each one loosely but securely to the top tubes of the bikes. He takes off his shirt and ties the sleeves and the tails to the poles. He uses Ari's shirt the same way. With him and Ari bracing each of the bikes, Lance helps Thad to lie face up on

238

the stretched shirts.

Slowly at first, they walk along the road, wheeling the bikes, getting used to it. Lance is up ahead, stopping to use the binoculars on the longer stretches. At the sharper curves, he dismounts and checks ahead on foot.

They pick up the pace. Jack, one hand on the bike, uses the other to take out his walkie-talkie. He tells Nicole, "Thad's been wounded, not too bad, but he's lost blood. Go into evacuation mode. They're out scouting for us, but I don't think they'll attack the house."

"Roger."

About halfway home, they hear a vehicle approaching from behind at speed. They make it to cover off the road just in time. Even so, the vehicle, the Humvee with the machine gun on its mount, slows as though they have been spotted. It drives on, stops, turns around and comes back, a rack of spots on top lighting up the road and roadside. It stops again.

By then the squad are lying down in covering bracken. Jack notices they have no one manning the M2 Browning mounted on the turret. Their stupidity, our luck he thinks, not for the first time. He has his weapon up sighting in the driver. Take him out and they would capture the Humvee and the machine gun. But the angle isn't good, however short the distance. The driver has the window up. Even at point-blank range, the 5.56 mm round from the AR15 might not penetrate the ballistic glass.

They wait. A swivel light on the Humvee sweeps wide, into the trees. Too wide. It can't angle down where they are. More luck. Finally, noisily, the vehicle moves off.

When it's clear, Jack nudges Thad. "Ready?"

But Thad has passed out. His bandages are soaked with blood.

Jack calls home on the walkie-talkie. "We need the van. Grace and Nicole. Bring Allegra with you armed. Duvall stays behind to escort the others if..."

The van arrives within minutes. They lift Thad into the back and lie him on a mat. Grace gets a bag of plasma going into his good arm while she dresses the wound. Nicole, wearing night-vision goggles keeps the headlights off as they drive silently back to the house. Just as they clear the metal bridge, a second Humvee turns into the drive and stops. A moment later, it reverses and goes back the way it came.

Grace and Nicole minister to Thad while the others meet to debrief. Cyrus listens with intense interest. "So none of them got hurt?" he asks.

Jack returns his father's gaze. He's irked. "Yes. Your son."

But he takes it back with a gesture. He's more angry with himself than with anyone else. He says, "None of them as far as I know. One of the guards was Marko. But he ran off the minute he saw me."

"Did he recognize you?"

"I think so."

"We've bought some time," Ari says. "We did a lot of damage."

Jack doesn't agree. He says, after some hesitation, "I'm afraid we didn't destroy that much of their arms supplies. We burned the sheds, but I would guess there are bunkers of some sort under them."

"You blew up their generator," Lance puts in.

"They'll still need to regroup," says Ari, bent on optimism.

Cyrus looks troubled. "Or we've just poked the hornets nest with a stick. And they know whose stick it was."

"The wrong kind of stick," Jack says. "We should have used the dynamite."

21

Within the space of several days, first Lise and then Bella meet with Grace in the clinic, take a simple test, and find they are pregnant. With Nicole already underway, that means three new lives at Sugar Mountain within the year. It is happy and sobering news. It means new life at a time of mass death. And more responsibility. Before and after they arrive, they will need nurturing and protecting.

The news magnifies for Jack their failure to destroy the arms build-up of the McFeralls. He blames himself. He made the oldest mistake in the long history of warfare: he underestimated the enemy. He had let his contempt for the McFerall brothers cloud his judgment. He should have listened to Duvall and Thad and risked using dynamite. Dynamite would have worked – unless the bunkers were bomb proof, which he doubted.

"Perhaps it's a class thing," Ari says. He, Jack, and Nicole are gathered around the invalid bed in the clinic where Thad, under protest, lies with his arm bandaged in a sling.

Jack concedes as much. He is sipping from a small glass of apple liquor. "They are lowlifes. Always have been. Always wanted to be."

Thad, sneaking a glass of the liquor against Grace's orders, smiles at his brother. "Actually, Jack, they're much more like aristocrats..."

"Give me a break..."

"No, seriously, they're too proud of what they are to ever consider improving themselves."

Ari laughs. "That's good, very good. Sir Bruce de Pitts Hollow... But I don't know. Aristocrats? More like a new predator class..."

"Which is what most aristocracies spring from," says Nicole, the history major.

Thad, pacing his sips, says, "So if they're the predator class, what does that make us, the producer class?"

Ari laughs again. "Nice. You're right on. We're the hard working, endlessly self-improving middle class."

Thad again, "So what was the predator class before... what will we call this thing, the Great Death?"

Ari snorts. "The bankers and their politicians."

"The new robber barons?" Thad proposes. He's wondering if he might beg just another touch of the apple stuff.

Nicole says, "At least the robber barons built things, started industries..."

Ari looks appreciatively at Nicole. "You're right. By comparison Wall Street is little more than a big casino with the government covering the losses."

Jack says, "They're still low lifes..."

Thad again demurs. "It's not just a class thing. I've seen Teddy Wilkins in those surveillance shots..."

"Who's Teddy Wilkins?" Ari asks.

Nicole smiles at Thad. She says, "Teddy Wilkins is a CPA with a fancy house in Shelburne. His wife has her own BMW. Or used to."

But Jack is only half listening. He's restless. The failure to destroy the McFeralls' weapon cache still rankles. He wants to take a backpack full of dynamite and try again. Alone. "Low lifes," he mutters. "Criminals."

Nicole takes a taste of her husband's drink. "At another level, they're only trying to feed their families. Same as us."

"Hardly the same as us." Jack doesn't exactly round on her, but he can't rise to the banter. "Bruce and his bunch are executing people in cold blood. They've gone beyond criminality."

Thad agrees. "They could have planted crops. They have land and access to machines. They could have saved and worked and gleaned like everyone else."

"All of the above," says Jack, getting up to take his restlessness elsewhere. "They want power. They want to be like the chieftains of old. Power over life and death. All of that. In the mountains of Afghanistan they'd have fit right in."

242

At a general meeting presided over by Cyrus, who looks worried even when he smiles, they speak briefly about the good news. "With any luck, we should have three new souls among us come late spring and summer," the patriarch says, glancing warmly at the prospective mothers in turn. And, to quote Gloucester in *Lear*, I trust there was good sport in the making of our future newcomers..."

"Cyrus... Really!" But Grace does not conceal her delight.

He continues. "Also, I want to report that Thad is well enough to join us today. Your arm...?"

"It's healing fine," says Thad, his arm still in a sling.

"That is all to the good..." Cyrus pauses. "And, so far, the harvest has been beyond expectations. We have a good stock of potatoes and other root vegetables. We have apples, applesauce and apple brandy. Also tomatoes nicely canned in jars along with pickles of all sorts and other staples like rice, flour, sugar, coffee. That also is a blessing. However..."

They wait quietly for the heavier shoe to drop. "What most of you know by now is that the attempt to destroy the arms supply of the McFerall brothers failed. Or so Jack tells me. Worse, they know that we made the attack. Marko saw Jack and fled. As I told the team, who carried out the mission with bravery and intelligence, we have stuck a stick into a nest of well-armed hornets. In light of this, I feel we should move more supplies to The Ledges in preparation either to withdraw there now or to do so at the first sign of an attack. Any comments?"

After a silence, Lance says, "Why did we build the fence and do all the other things to defend ourselves if we're just going to cut and run?"

There are murmurs of assent around the table.

Cyrus acknowledges them. "When we decided to defend ourselves, I did not think any of us thought we would be facing machine guns, much less rocket-propelled grenades and even flame throwers. All wielded by men who place no value on human life, except, perhaps, their own."

Jack says, "You've said yourself, Dad, that the McFeralls may be restrained in any attack on Sugar Mountain as they want the place intact for themselves."

"Yes, and that may still apply. But do we really want to take that chance?"

After a silence, Ari states succinctly the realization that is dawning on many of them around the table. "I think it makes eminent sense to do what Cyrus suggests. But my heart rebels. We've all worked in our own ways to make Sugar Mountain our home. And now, that's what it is. We are raising our children here. We have buried our dead here. I don't want to leave until it's absolutely necessary."

Allegra feels her neck stiffen. She says, "I agree with Ari. We should stand and fight."

"Amen," says Thad.

"Count me in," Duvall adds.

They look to Jack. He nods, stands and leans forward, hands resting on the table. "I agree with Ari, Allegra, Thad, Duvall. I also agree with Dad... and with Mom. Our purpose is not to kill or maim the McFeralls and their followers. Our purpose is to survive. But I fear that if we simply abandon Sugar Mountain, they will keep coming. They won't be here long before they discover we've left them very little in the way of food other than livestock that must be taken care of. Once they realize that, they'll keep coming. Out of pride but also out of necessity. Winter is coming. There is going to be famine."

He pauses for a moment to look at each in turn. "To give them second thoughts, to sew doubts, especially in the minds of their followers, we make them pay a price. If they come up the lane, we bloody them with everything we've got..."

"But we would pay a price as well," Grace says.

"Perhaps, but given how we're situated, I think the risk is low."

"What exactly are you suggesting?" Ari asks.

"I think our best strategy is to continue to prepare The Ledges

244

for an indefinite stay. I would recommend that we remain here on an emergency footing, that is, ready to resist or withdraw within minutes. Having said that, I think we have the capability to repulse an initial assault. Thad has a trick up his sleeve that will quite stun anyone who attacks us. Look, I'm not suicidal. If they come up the lane with mortars and flame throwers and God knows what else, ready to burn us out, then we leave."

Duvall says, "But it's more than just making them pay a price, isn't it. I mean we've got our pride as well."

"Yeah, that too," Thad says.

They vote with two abstentions to make a stand, but also agree to reconsider if conditions changed.

*

Conditions change. The next morning, on duty in the recon room, Nicole hears distinct voices on the mike covering Pitts Hollow. She turns on the camera and watches as two figures, armed and in combat fatigues, approach from the direction of the compound. They disappear under the range of the lens. A little while later, a gloved hand shows for a second on the screen before it blanks out along with the microphone.

Two days later, the Bartletts in Rowe, who had disdained membership in the network, are over-run in a matter of minutes. Both are murdered. The ex-policeman hired for security fled after a few shots.

The Defense Committee meets to go over the news. Aside from the brutality of the attack, what the members find chilling, once Jack points it, out is the similarity of the Bartlett farm to Sugar Mountain, at least in its setting.

"You mean it was a rehearsal?" Allegra asks.

"A rehearsal and perhaps also a warning," Jack tells them. "They're back in business and they're taking no prisoners."

They still vote to stand and fight. In discussing tactics, Jack ponders aloud whether they should let it get out that they will offer only token resistance before fleeing to their retreat up in the woods.

"Why?" asks Thad.

"That might keep them off guard as they come driving up to take the place."

With the sanction of the Defense Committee, Jack and Lance make a night reconnaissance of Pitts Hollow. Thad equips them with an improvised scanner to detect remotely monitored surveillance gear.

Arriving there without incident, Jack sweeps the area. But he judges it unwise to go up the same tree where the surveillance camera had been fixed. So they move laterally about fifty feet. Here Jack climbs another mature pine, using the broken off lower branches to reach a perch high enough for him to see the compound.

Using a night-vision camera, he records the same two Humvees, several pickup trucks, a bunch of ATVs and, ominously, the armored bulldozer they had seen before, this time secured with come-alongs to the flat bed of an eighteen wheeler. They'll use that on us, Jack thinks, and takes time to photograph it carefully. A new, larger generator is up and running. He notes as well that there are now four perimeter guards, two stationary, two moving, their drill far more professional than before.

As he watches, he sees one of the guards listen to his walkie-talkie. He glances up in Jack's direction. Then the door opens and Bruce McFerall comes out. The place where his ear had been is minimally bandaged. He confers briefly with the man who has the walkie-talkie. Two of the guards, guns ready, start up toward Jack and Lance.

It is decision time for Jack. He and Lance can disappear back toward Sugar Mountain. Or, they can wait in ambush and either kill or disable the two men climbing towards them. The thought comes with a rush of adrenaline that Jack uses to think clearly. He climbs quickly down the tree and decides on retreat. He has good reasons: The guards might be halfway competent. And gunshots would bring a virtual army down on them. His feet touch the ground as the beams of powerful flashlights begin stabbing the darkness around them.

They make the road without incident and bike home on back roads, stopping periodically, to listen for patrols that the McFeralls might have sent out.

"We won't be able to stay here long," Jack tells Nicole that night as he settled in beside her. "I think they've already started to stage."

*

The following day everyone pitches in to transport more provisions up to The Ledges. Cyrus and Grace want to take supplies up to the second refuge as well, but no one else considers that a priority. Grace and Nicole prepare for evacuation as though getting the house and the other dwelling places ready for renters. They are scrupulous in their instructions for the care of the chickens, goats, and half-grown pigs.

Thad suggests rigging little jinxes into the systems, from the power supply to the water to the heating. When those fail, it would appear to be through the incompetence of the new occupiers. That means Sugar Mountain would grow cold as a meat locker except in those places that had stoves. The power and eventually the water supply would fail.

They decide against it, Jack saying the McFeralls will probably screw things up on their own.

As for the larders, they all appear to be well stocked. Jars of assorted canned tomatoes, pickles, and berries line the shelves of the apparent rootcellar, its door poorly concealed. Deliberately. It also contains a quart of maple syrup, a wooden box of potatoes and another of carrots – a seeming abundance when in fact there is scarcely a week's supply for ten people. The rest of the provisions have been placed in the real rootcellar or so cleverly hidden that even the hiders might find them with difficulty.

The storage pantry in the basement of the main house presents the same appearance of abundance. Grace has artfully stacked a few canisters of flour and plastic containers of vegetable oil along with packets of freeze-dried meat and vegetables to make it look like a bonanza. But there is no sugar, coffee, tea, or alcohol anywhere in sight.

"It will be like Moscow left open and empty in the face of Napoleon's advance," says Nicole, the mastermind of the strategy. "Only we won't burn down our home. We'll wait them out."

Cyrus agrees with Nicole. "Intelligence and a little courage always beats brutality in the end," he says to Grace as they pillow talk. "I'm glad that we're not sabotaging the place. It wouldn't be the most Christian thing we've ever done."

The McFeralls stage again, but not for Sugar Mountain, not this time. Without warning and with sudden and remarkable brutality, a gang of thirty men armed with rocket-propelled grenades and machine guns overrun a well-stocked and well-defended survival community in Buckland. Though a lot of the defenders managed to escape, apparently to a fallback refuge, seven, all men or boys, are either killed in the fighting or murdered execution style afterwards.

Jack meets with his dad to go over the news. They sit in Cyrus' studio.

"You know what it means," Jack says, squinting into the light of the settling sun.

Cyrus Arkwright nods wearily. "We're next."

Jack gets up, paces, sits down, and sips from a glass of water. "Like the Bartlett place, they used the old Marvin place as a practice run. I think the group was from New York or New Jersey. They were trying to dig in."

"But why all the killing?" Cyrus asks with an anguish that makes Jack put out a hand to touch him.

"Same old, same old, Dad. Terror. To intimidate us and anyone else who will oppose them. And what would they do with prisoners if they did take them alive? Besides, it's a time of mass death. It's a time when the Bruce McFeralls of the world come out of their rat holes. Life is cheap."

"Except their own." Cyrus sighs. "Perhaps we shouldn't have..."

"No, we bought time. We have a lot of the harvest in. We've got The Ledges well provisioned."

Cyrus drinks some of the rough calvados he has distilled with Ari's help. Desolation looms. It all seems so futile.

"So why don't we just withdraw?"

Jack leans into his father. "You may be right. But if we don't make them pay, they'll just keep coming. Maybe they'll keep coming anyway. I wouldn't be comfortable here knowing there was a well-armed group holed up within attacking distance. And The Ledges, frankly, may not be easy to defend. And then where do we go?"

Cyrus nods reluctantly. "Keep coming. Especially when they realize how thin the supplies are."

"And we make them pay again if they do. We outlast them. This thing isn't going to go on forever. Eventually, the government in Washington or Boston will revive. The real Guard will show up. The rule of law..." He trails off. All that now seems like a pipe dream. "And I have a few tricks up my sleeve. And who knows, they might just give up."

But neither of them believes that.

22

The denizens of Sugar Mountain hunker down and wait for a time when time seems to slow to the pace of conscious dread. No one sleeps easy. No one sleeps without an emergency pack handy. Or without their weapons handy if they are on the Defense Squad. No one is quite sure that they will have time to wake, dress, collect their things, assemble and flee to their refuge. Thad, his flesh wound healing, has positioned monitors farther down each side of the town road leading to the top of the drive. He has placed a camera to the east behind the house, though no one really expects the McFeralls to break their way through that brushy country, certainly not with heavy weapons.

Allegra writes in her journal:

Being on alert might sound exciting, but it quickly wears to tedium. Life is on hold. We live minute-to-minute, existence reduced to maintaining existence. The fear is palpable, contagious. Lily cries out in her sleep. Cyrus seems to age by the day.

Most of us secretly want to pack up and leave. But Jack, Ari, Duvall, Nicole, and Thad argue that if we retreated now, the McFeralls would simply keep coming. They say we need to bloody them, let them know they'll pay a price. It's the Hatfields and McCoys all over again. Lance didn't know what those names referred to. But then he has scant knowledge of literature, legends, the classics, and scarcely anything of the Old Testament. *But I love him. I lust him as well if that can be a verb. But it remains a fugitive love/lust, especially as the public address may sound for a drill at any time. Or the real thing. The real thing. It makes everything else unreal. Except for the AR15 and the extra clips of ammunition I keep close to hand. It doesn't get much more real than that. I think of my gun as an elaborate penis of metal and plastic, but one that spews death rather than life. I've been assigned with Lance to Post Four. It's a fortified, two-man shallow foxhole behind the stonewall in front of and to the west side of the house. Lance and I are supposed to direct our fire at anyone trying to come through or over the fence. This time Jack didn't talk about wounding them. "I don't care if you maim or kill your target. The only objective is to stop him."*

Lance has moved in with me, more or less officially. Under the circumstances, no one seems to have noticed much less said anything. We are accepted as a couple. In fact, Duvall has taken Lance's lean-to. He finally has a place of his own, but he still spends most nights with either Thad or Bella. And Bella. She is mighty proud of being pregnant. You would think she's the first woman in history to conceive. But in a good way, when I think of it. In fact, I'm just a bit envious. And, with Lance's consent, I'm trying myself. More than consent. The boy/man is unstoppable.

At times like this, nature mocks us with its splendor. "The trees are in their autumn beauty/The woodland paths are dry..." But Yeats never saw a New England fall. It's more like an autumnal flaming, a "death bloom" someone called it. Not just the trees, but the bushes have turned yellows, backlit scarlets, bronzed purples in the exquisitely chilled air, which is like some kind of inhalable wine. But we scarcely have time to look, to stop and take it in. We take beauty as a given, but there are times when I fear that our capacity to see it and feel it might also disappear, like so much else.

Another reason Jack urges that they stand their ground is the simple fact that they don't know for sure that they will be attacked. Their continued presence and obvious state of readiness might of itself deter an assault. There are certainly easier targets around. And the Sugar Mountaineers, as they increasingly refer to themselves with grim pride, have shown their considerable prowess with arms. Like any warlords, the power of the McFeralls is far from absolute. Thus argue Jack, Ari, Nicole, and the rest of the "hawk" faction in the meetings that seemed to erupt with increasing frequency.

Even so, the continuing state of fear tells on morale. No one likes the constraints, in particular the requirement that someone has to know where you are at all times. Or the makeshift necessity of meals cooked or eaten without care and pleasure. Each of them has to choose among prize possessions. Take it or leave it? Hide it? Forget it?

Precisely as they are on a knife-edge of alert with everyone assiduously accounting for everyone else, Cy goes missing. The irony is lost on the dwellers of Sugar Mountain as fear and incipient panic does not allow for much subtle musing. Mary, in charge of her brother, is nearly incoherent with sobbing as she tries to tell Nicole and Jack where she last saw him. Chee had been tending the three older girls in the barn garden where they had gone to pick herbs for stringing into little bunches for drying. Mary was supposed to keep an eye on Cy, who had a habit of wandering off.

Thad and Ari sit in the recon room going over the camera coverage from the past half hour while the other adults fan out looking and calling. Jack fears that Cy's has been abducted and will be held in ransom by the McFeralls in exchange for Sugar Mountain. His worst fear is that Cy has wandered off into the woods or down the road and gotten lost.

He is checking the millpond, his heart like a stone that is sinking, when he remembers the mornings he and Cy had gone fishing farther down Talbot Brook for trout. He sits down, calms himself, and does what he was trained to do in a crisis: think. On those excursions they talked about a lot of things. Jack might explain how nature works – how deer and rabbits ate grass and plants and how coyotes and mountain lions ate deer and rabbits. Which got them going on mountain lions, a favorite topic of Cy's, and whether any of them prowled the wooded hills and lush valleys of Franklin County.

Honest with his son to a fault, though he would not talk to him about his own soldiering experiences, Jack explained there was controversy about the existence of mountain lions in western

Massachusetts. Then explaining the word "controversy." Then saying, "If there haven't been many lions in these parts, there will be now."

"Why?"

They were in the kitchen cleaning trout after a successful spell at the brook. Without thinking, Jack said, "Because there are a lot less people than there used to be."

"Because of the flu?"

A tentative "yes."

"A lot of kids in my class probably died,"

"Who told you that?"

"Mary. She said most of the kids in her class are probably dead by now."

Jack says, "But Mary doesn't really know, does she?"

"No. Sometimes I think she tells me things just to scare me."

"But you're not scared."

"Only some of the time."

Jack nodded and was about to bring the subject back to mountain lions when Cy said, "The McFeralls are trying to kill us, aren't they?"

Jack remembers saying, "The McFeralls want to live here, but we will try to keep them out."

"With guns?"

"If necessary."

"I'm ready for them. I've got my own gun. And I've got stuff."

"And where do you have your stuff?"

"It's in a secret place."

Now Jack thinks, where? He is about to contact Nicole on his walkie-talkie, when he remembers several times seeing Cy go into and come out of the mill in the preoccupied way of a young boy doing something.

In the mill, at the bottom of a nailed-on ladder leading to a low loft too small and shaky for storing anything but junk, Jack says loudly, "Cy, permission to come up. Don't shoot."

He waits. Then he hears, "Permission granted."

Giddy with relief, Jack says into his walkie-talkie, "Missing found. On duty at the mill."

What Jack finds after he hugs his son and then lectures him about staying in touch at all times with his "unit," is a parody in miniature of Sugar Mountain. In the dim light coming through a small window on the other gable end, he finds several plastic bottles of water, a can of beans, a box of rice, and an old first aid kit. His chief weapons include an antiquated, lever action air gun Jack had used as a kid, a Swiss Army knife, and several bullets.

The general relief is mixed with an awful realization of what such a loss might be like. The vigilance notches up. They get ready for the worst.

*

As though on schedule, reconnaissance patrols, sometimes two men, other times in force, begin to be picked up by the various sensing devices and cameras Thad has placed and maintained around their bastion. One of the McFerall Humvees parks at the end of the lane with a man in the gunner position on top wielding a long-lensed camera. Jack uses the sniper rifle to aim right at the glinting glass. The camera explodes and the man drops out of sight. Whether he wounded or killed the photographer, Jack doesn't know. And he doesn't care. On another occasion, sensors pick up a group of armed men coming through the reforested pasture land on the Fallgren's property close to Talbot Brook. Jack, Ari, and Duvall send them running with a couple of well-aimed shots, perhaps hitting one of them in the leg.

The increasing vigilance takes its toll. With anxiety, lack of sleep, and at times stark fear, people grow short with one another. Scarred over old wounds opened up. Grace spends a deal of time counseling and soothing. Sentiment builds for retreat. A war of nerves, Jack calls it. Intelligence is scarce. The members of the network are on edge as well, but report little activity. Other than the patrols probing Sugar Mountain, no one knows what the McFeralls have planned.

Then it happens.

23

The McFeralls do not resort to subtlety when they attack. Just before dark with the light fading and a distinct coolness settling over the land, a convoy consisting of the two Humvees, one of them still mounted with a machine gun, five pickup trucks and a bunch of ATVs, all with their lights low, come noisily along the town road and turn onto the lane leading to the farm.

"Stations! Stations!" Jack's voice comes with urgency over the loudspeakers. "This is not a drill. Repeat. Stations. This is not a drill." Moments before, the gong sounded in the recon room where Lance was on duty. He watched with incredulity for a few seconds as the procession of vehicles and men came up the road and lumbered into view on the screen in front of him.

Slowly, purposefully, the convoy fans out on either side of the drive among the trees of the orchard and the grape vines, flattening a lot of the latter. With the Humvees flanking the drive, which is left open, the trucks and ATVs line up as in a battle formation about a hundred and fifty yards back from the fence.

As a matter of routine, the heavy grating over the ditch has already been pulled back and the gate secured.

The Defense Squad take their positions in the fortified posts in front of and to either side of the house.

They watch as the line of vehicles douse their lights. Men with assault rifles take up positions behind the pickups. The defenders act mechanically and without enthusiasm. Second thoughts abound. Maybe Cyrus was right. Withdraw while there's still time.

But the fear in their eyes and in the dryness of their throats is alloyed with determination. Mostly, though the odds seem overwhelming, they trust Jack to know what they're doing.

"No one fire until ordered," Jack says over the walkie-talkies. Let's see what they're going to do."

An eerie silence settles over the scene. Silence until, in the distance, they hear the approach of a truck. At the bottom of the drive, it stops and a massive old bulldozer, the cab of which has been crudely armored with steel sheeting, labors down the ramp off the flatbed truck and turns toward the farm.

"Evacuate everyone except the Defense Squad," Jack says into his walkie-talkie. "Lise and Nicole will escort the first group up to the mill and remain with them until further notice. Dad, you stay in the recon room and keep checking the other cameras. They might try sending a force in from the side. Grace, stand by in the clinic. The rest of us will remain in readiness to resist and then, if necessary, to retreat."

In silence and relative darkness, Lise and Nicole, both armed with AR15s, lead the children along with Henry and Chee around the garden and into the mill.

The Sugar Mountaineers wait and watch as the monstrous thing clanks its way up the drive. The dozer is, as much as anything else, an exercise in psychological warfare.

Thad says softly into his walkie-talkie, "You know, Jack..."

In reply, Jack says, "Let me take a couple of shots and then..."

The strategy of the McFeralls is obvious: The dozer will push enough fill into the ditch so that it can cross over and knock down the main gate followed by the Humvees and armed men on foot.

"Standby," Jack says as he sets up a bipod for the 45-70 elephant gun that he has equipped with a nightscope.

The bulldozer lumbers closer.

"Patience," Jack says quietly into his walkie-talkie talking as much to himself as the other. The dozer arrives and, without pausing, lowers its blade and with no hesitation scrapes a slow wave of dirt and gravel into the ditch. Just as it is reversing, Jack aims at the fuel lines to the machine's big engine. He fires. There is a wicked sparking ricochet but little else.

"Keep going," megaphones Duncan McFerall, who is standing through the roof hatch of one of the Hummers behind an improvised shield. "He can't hurt you with that thing."

The dozer again begins to advance, tearing out a sizable rock that tumbles along the ground in front of the blade with another wave of dirt.

Jack, a second round in the chamber, waits. Cyrus, watching the laptop screen in the recon room, says, "We should get out of here. One or two more loads and he'll be able to get across and knock down the gate."

Jack says nothing. He waits until the bulldozer is about to reverse. He fires. This time he ruptures the fuel line. The diesel sprays out but doesn't hit the hot engine and ignite.

The dozer engine dies and the driver jumps down from behind the improvised armor and scuttles for cover.

Duncan McFerall, still standing through the roof of the Humvee to the left, blares out, "This changes nothing. You can stop the dozer, Arkwrights, but you won't stop us. I've got more than thirty heavily armed men here. Give up now and we'll let you live. Resist, and the blood will be on your hands."

When there is no response, he clicks on again. "Plan B. Move out. Move out."

Jack watches through night-vision glasses as several attackers deploy with rocket propelled grenades fixed to their rifles. He half wonders why they didn't use them first instead of the clumsy bulldozer that now effectively blocks access to the gate.

The line of vehicles starts a slow advance. The attacking men use them for cover, firing sporadically and without much aim.

Ari mutters over the walkie-talkie, "Those are my vines, God damn it."

"Hold your fire," Jack tells his squad. The vehicles draw closer and closer still, slowing as they come and keeping in line. Duncan McFerall bellows "Now!"

A flood of lights go on – high beams, cab top arrays, spots on the Humvees. More forms drop off the vehicles and the firing becomes intense.

Jack thinks, great minds. But he has a dilemma: Take out their lights or leave them on to illuminate the men who, backlit, can be seen dodging or crawling toward the ditch and the fence.

"Aim carefully and knock out the lights," he says into the walkie-talkie. He switches to the AR15, which also has a night scope. To the crackle of rifle around him and the successive blanking of the high beams and spots on the Humvees, he shoots and brings down one of the men setting up to launch an RPG. But another man succeeds in firing a grenade into the ground to the west side of the gate. It goes off with a terrific bang, sending dirt and a section of fence into the air.

Allegra give an involuntary cry as dirt and stones shower down on them.

"You all right?" Lance asks.

"Fine. Scared shitless."

"Me, too."

Then something like terror as Duncan McFerall's voice booms out with a "Stand by," and the Browning machine gun on the Humvee pivots directly at them. It opens up with a wicked clattering along with a hail of rifle fire from the men on the ground. Another grenade lands on the east side. Even though short of the fence it blows another hole in it. Then another. The machine gun stops. McFerall orders, "Move out! Move out!"

Crouching, dodging, wiggling forms resume moving toward the ditch. More grenades land and explode.

Jack, his voice calm, says, "Hold your fire. Thad, you ready?"

"Ready."

Jack watches for five, ten, fifteen seconds. Then, "Let there be light."

At that, several powerful strobes attached to the outer branches of the maples on the lawn begin a manic, ghostly flashing in and out of sync, so bright that even the defenders below find them painful to be around.

"Fire at will," Jack orders.

The strobing lights don't make aiming easy for the defenders. In some cases they are firing at the after-images on their retinas.

But it unnerves the attackers by blinding them. Their firing sputters out and dies altogether. The men on the ground begin to get up and run for the cover of their vehicles.

"'Shoot them in the legs and butt,' Jack says over the walkie-talkie. "Take them down."

The only reason Jack doesn't use the elephant gun on the pick-up trucks is that he doesn't want to deprive the attackers of a means of retreat. But he does wreck any number of windshields and ATVs.

Moments later, the strobes flicker out. But they have done their job.

"Power's gone," Thad says tersely. "Some kind of short."

"Cease firing," Jack orders. Then, 'Any casualties?"

"Duvall has a splinter wound in the neck," Grace reports. "He's still mobile and should be all right."

They can hear men moaning and calling out for help from beyond the fence. Jack uses a bullhorn. "You can retrieve your dead and wounded. We won't fire again unless fired upon."

There is no answering acknowledgment. Down the lane trucks are backing up, one so hastily it bangs into an ATV and knocks it over. Both Humvees are in reverse and moving.

After a while, some of the pickups return. Jack watches through night glasses they load their wounded and perhaps two or three dead bodies onto the beds of the trucks.

It takes a while. The last vehicle to leave is the armed Humvee. It pauses and its loudspeaker clicks on. "This is Duncan McFerall. You have forty-eight hours to vacate. We will return with RPGs, mortars and flame throwers and burn you out if we have to."

As the vehicle turns to leave, Jack dings its cab with a shot from the heavy rifle.

Not long afterwards, Allegra, Lance, and Thad still in camouflage and with their hands and faces blackened, move quickly and quietly down the lane after them. They are checking to make sure the gang isn't regrouping to try an assault on foot. They find no one. Just a gorgeous October night, the air brisk and clear, the constellations flickering over them.

*

Allegra writes in her journal:

I've never been so scared in my life. I wet my pants when I saw the parade of vehicles turn and come up the lane. I think they had taken their mufflers off because they made such a huge racket. I wanted to get up and run. But if Lance, who was right beside me, could abide it, so could I. It was bad enough, the Humvees with their machine gun and the men spilling out of trucks and off of those all-terrain things. But then the bulldozer, clanking with sheets of armor plate hanging like skirts around its treads and the tank-like box with the slit protecting the driver came up the lane like a bad horror movie gone real.

What I savor in retrospect was not running when every particle of me wanted to. I became conscious of my own courage. If I died, I died. There would be enough adults left to escape and take Lily with them. I know part of that courage was anger. What and who gave these people the right to come up here and attack us? I wanted to start picking them off. Because, as they moved about, they didn't have much cover except darkness.

But on the walkie-talkie tabbed to my protective vest, Jack was calmness itself. "Hold your fire, hold your fire." Hold your water was more like it. Then he stopped the dozer with two shots. The rest happened so quickly I couldn't believe it was over until it was over. When they turned on the high beams of the trucks and the spotlights on the Humvees, I felt naked and exposed. I thought we were done for when the grenade went off just in front of us. Without the sandbags, I think Lance and I would have been killed or badly wounded. And then the glint of light off the barrel of the machine gun turning towards us.

They all started firing then, the big bullets from the machine gun whinging off the fences, shredding it in places. But they were firing blind. Then another grenade hit. Then Jack was on the walkie-talkie again to Thad. "Let there be light."

24

With their guard up and with particular attention paid to the camera covering the approach near Talbot Brook, the community gathers for a quick meeting in the immediate wake of the attack. Cyrus, his demeanor grave, opens by saying, "I want to thank everyone for their courage and actions. Though I abhor bloodshed in any form, I think you did the right thing in resisting this first attempt to drive us out. But now I think they will come back with heavy weapons and blast or burn us out if they have to. I think it is time we retreat to The Ledges. Tomorrow, starting early in the morning."

Jack says, "I want to echo Dad's appreciation of what we have all just done. If nothing else, the McFeralls will think twice about attacking us whether we stay here or pack up and go into the woods. And while we could stay and fight again, I reluctantly agree with Dad that we will gain nothing if we have to retreat in the face of heavy weapons which they possess and know how to use."

"Are you talking about mortars?" Lance asks.

"Exactly. They can stand back a mile and lob them in.'

"Those strobes," Allegra says, turning to Thad, "that was brilliant."

He nods. "But it will only work once."

Ari says, "We're lucky they didn't get a chance to really use that machine gun. In retrospect it seems stupid of them to attack at dusk."

There is more chat about the engagement itself. No one asks why the McFeralls would renew their assault before the two days were up. The important question, which Ari raises, is, "Should we go tonight or wait until tomorrow?"

Jack says, "The kids are settled in. I think we're good for tonight. They have a lot of wounds to lick. But if they're not back here by tomorrow night, I'll be surprised."

"In other words," says Duvall, the bandage around his injured neck giving him a clerical look, "sleep with your clothes on."

Jack nods, thinking. "Right, but do try to sleep. Tomorrow will be strenuous. And tonight, we'll do shifts in the recon room with two people."

They confer a while longer. Grace has already drawn up lists of provisions and other sundries, many of them packed and ready to go to The Ledges. They all agree to turn off personal communications devices after Jack reminds them it's possible that the McFeralls have or have access to signal-tracking, vectoring devices. "Not," he adds, "that they won't be able to find us if they want to."

"But why would they do that?" It's Henry, who seldom speaks at these meetings. "I mean they'll have the farm."

Cyrus answers him. "Yes. But I doubt very much they will plant and produce anything. They will be hungry. And, with all those men and their families, the brothers have a lot of mouths to feed."

Jack puts in, "And even if they use the farm to produce food, they won't be able to abide the fact that we're still around, still armed, and still dangerous."

"And pissed off," Duvall says.

Before going to bed and though he is bleary with exhaustion, Jack gets a can of old gasoline from the mill and looks over the disabled bulldozer. It is far enough back from the ditch not to block access through the gate with smaller vehicles. He douses the engine and opens the fuel tank so diesel can add to the conflagration. Then he stands back and throws a lighted stick at it. It goes "whoosh" and flames lick merrily for a couple of minutes giving off the satisfying stench of burning rubber and heated metal. Then the fuel tank goes with a loud bang and greasy flames roil upwards right out of a movie. Jack smiles. No one is going to get that thing started without a lot of work.

*

Early the next morning, after a breakfast of bacon, eggs, biscuits, and coffee, the members of the Sugar Mountain tribe, most of them carrying last minute personal belongings, bid farewell to their home. Grace finds it painful to leave the animals. She holds the head of each goat in her hands. She pats the two remaining pigs now growing fast and fat on the apple mash and other garden leavings. She feeds the chickens for the last time and collects the eggs to hard boil and take with them. Earlier they butchered, plucked and gutted about half of the chickens, brining and smoking them whole as best they could. They did the same with the small amount of meat left in the freezer. On the door of each shed, she has left instructions in large letters as to the care of the livestock.

They decide again to do nothing to sabotage the place, at least not ostensibly. Cyrus pins up instructions about how to fire the various wood stoves for winter heat and hot water, and how to keep the pump for the water tank going in freezing weather. But they provide no spare parts for the power systems or for the pump. Without them and proper maintenance, the systems will likely begin to shut down after a few months. That means the new residents will have to pump the water by hand or carry it from the stream. Nor do they leave behind any seeds or fuel to operate the farm machinery. Those kinds of supplies go into cleverly hidden spaces beneath the chicken coop and in the open loft of the equipment shed.

Using old newspapers, Nicole carefully packs her Simon Pearce plates, bowls, and stemware in slatted crates once used for shipping fruit. She does the same with her medley of best silverware, platters, and other serving dishes. It's like packing away a waking dream in the middle of a nightmare. Will she ever see her things again? Will she ever use them again?

They have also hidden or moved a lot of the remaining food and other essential supplies. As Cyrus optimistically puts it, "We want something to come back to." Grace's stockpile of cloth and clothing along with the electric sewing machine go into a commodious fake wall in the equipment shed.

Jack, Thad, Lance, and Ari remain behind to dismantle and hide the components of the surveillance system. They debate what kind of sign to hang out front indicating they have abandoned the property. Ari is for a plain white sheet. Keep it simple. Thad wants to use something closer to gray. They agree on the white sheet tied to a maple and, closer to the door, a smaller piece of red cloth. "Just to keep them guessing." Lance stands watch with binoculars from a post high on the silo. Ari patrols outside the security fence.

Jack proves wrong about when the McFeralls will return in force. Less than twenty-four hours after the attack, Lance picks up the two Humvees, several pickups, and an old army truck with a canvas-covered bed laboring up the road toward the top of the drive.

He uses the walkie-talkie to sound the alarm. In terse phrases, he ticks off what he sees. He continues his narration after the convoy stops just short of the drive. Perhaps thirty men, all armed, begin removing what looks like mortars and RPG launches from the back of the truck.

Ari and Jack quickly go around turning on lights. They leave the front door open with a note stating, "We have abandoned the property for the time being. This is not a trap." At the same time, Thad turns on several hidden, sound-activated mikes in the lower part of the house. These link to a relay near the tree-line and from there to a speaker in the operations tent at The Ledges. He has made one of the mikes poorly hidden so that it can be discovered and removed, giving the new occupants a false sense of security.

"I wish Cyrus had let me take out those two," Jack says to the others as, from a vantage point up the path, they watch through binoculars McFeralls' men coming warily up either side of the lane, keeping to as much cover as they can. Some are carrying grenades, others crates of munitions slung on poles.

"You may be right," Ari says. "But they have sons. There would be no peace."

The visitors go out of the line-of-sight. A while later, they are in the house. Faintly, through open doors and windows, whoops of celebration can be heard.

25

The Sugar Mountaineers settle into their new quarters with a sense of relief. Upon arrival Ari uses three of the smoked chickens to make a meat-rich stew with carrots, onions, and potatoes. There is apple liquor for those who want it and a couple of bottles of chilled white wine, something that is already a rare luxury. They hold hands around their camp table as the Coleman lamps send flickering shadows against the rock walls of the cave. They thank Providence for providing.

But exhaustion mutes the heady relief of deliverance as the abundant rich food brings on somnolence. Lily falls asleep first, leaving the table to lie on a comforter Allegra arranges for her at the back of the cave. Then the other children fade. The three nine-year-old girls have a tent of their own. Each has a cot but not much room.

In a small tent placed on higher ground exposed to the sun, Duvall and Thad have set up a much reduced communications operation. Here on a bench are the CB transceiver, and a couple of tiny speakers linked to the mikes hidden in the house, and a single screen for a motion-activated camera covering the main approach up the hill. A portable solar panel facing south provides just enough power to keep the batteries for the equipment charged. Before winter sets in, they plan to erect a crude wigwam over the tent. That first full night, members of the Defense Squad each take two-hour watches.

Allegra, barely able to focus her eyes, manages to write in her journal:

> *Being a refugee is what Frank dreaded more than anything. He would watch news stories about camps set up for people fleeing war, tyranny, famine. It used to terrify him and he always wrote a generous check. Our situation is both better and more dire. We have food – as least for a while, shelter, and*

weapons. But there's no big normal world out there ready to fly in bags of flour or medicines or water treatment pills. We're on our own, and once the food and supplies run out, we'll starve. It's as simple as that.

She pauses to cast around the small tent space under one of the ledges that she and Lily have been assigned. She continues:

Not that a lot of care and ingenuity hasn't gone into these accommodations. Not for Frank the excitement of minimalism, the reduction of life to necessities. Like the LED lamp by which we can barely read. Or the canvas closet with zippered compartments and a hanging area for clothes. Or the toiletries kit with its generic soap and shampoo. Frank would have wept as he sat here and then lay on the Spartan if surprisingly comfortable cot. The farm had been bad enough with its basic food and manual labor. Here, his horizons would have shrunk to the intolerable, that is, to mere existence. And for Frank that never would have been enough.

Elsa still rankles, but I think he suffered enough in his own skin. Words like forgiveness don't mean much right now. We've all been reborn into a new life where survival is not merely a priority but everything.

I am still trembling from the fight, but not in fear. Lance has it right. It's like a different order of existence to have someone firing at you trying to kill you while you're firing back trying to kill them. Or at least cripple them.

Thinking of Lance, it would be a special treat if he came by. God, I could use him now, and I mean the word "use."

*

Time during the first week at The Ledges drags. Partly it is the shock of radical change – from comfort, warm beds, hot and cold running water. And from relatively plentiful and at times delicious food. Partly, it is the boredom of minimal activity as there appears little or no work other than cooking, cleaning up, or indulging in what private hygiene is available.

Eventually, a routine begins. On the third morning, the cave becomes the school room after breakfast. It is a calculated attempt to maintain a semblance of normality. Not that the teachers – Duvall, Lance, Thad, and Allegra – don't suffer a collective sense of futility, at least during those first few days. Would spelling and vocabulary mean much in the world to come? What was the point of teaching science or history if this is what it led to? And poetry. You couldn't eat a poem, although some of Seamus Heaney's come close to being edible, Allegra thinks as she serves up his "Oysters" to the older girls.

For an hour after lunch, the cave turns into Grace's clinic, both walk-in and, as she jokes, by appointment. There are the usual cuts and bruises. An intestinal bug makes the rounds, reassuring in the way it afflicts everyone with cramps and diarrhea for a day or two and disappears.

As at the farm, the operations tent – the recon room – however small, becomes a place people like to gather. It is the only contact with an outside world grown ever more remote. The contact is erratic and the power from the portable solar panels for the batteries even more so. Thad tinkers endlessly with the system. He knows the amount of power will drop and the time they can send and receive will begin to shrink as the days shorten.

Cyrus spends time tuning the CB for any scrap of news from members of the network. He reaches the Becks and tells them what has happened. He hears indirectly that there is more news coming out of Washington, but nothing to get too hopeful about.

When the sun shines and the battery lights blink green, Jack, side-by-side with his father, listens to what is being said in the house they have abandoned to the McFeralls.

The first transmission sounds like a drunken party. Either the McFeralls found the stock of liquor hidden in the cellar or, more than likely, brought along their own. As Jack switches from the mike in the family room to the one in the kitchen and to the one in the studio, he picks up an exchange between Duncan and Bruce.

Bruce: "We did it Dunc. We've gotten back what's ours."

Duncan: "Yeah, we ought to thank them for keeping it so well."

Bruce: "You look downstairs? Piles of stuff."

Duncan: "We got a lot of mouths to feed. How's Billy doing?"

Bruce: "Not good. He needs a real doctor. The bastards. If he dies... They are going to pay."

Three days after the occupation, the women and children arrive. There is squabbling over who gets what quarters. Jack listens and makes a list of all the voices he hears. Grace, who knows the family, helps. They identify Bruce and his wife Beth, their two grown sons, Jason and Mark. Jason is married to a woman named Corinne and they have two young sons. Mark has a girlfriend named Karen. Then Duncan and his wife Marge, their grown son Bruce, unmarried, and a daughter Helen, married to an alcoholic loudmouth named Al who idolizes the older Bruce to judge from the way he fawns around him. Marge's mother Gwendolyn is in her late seventies. There is also a Freddy and a Jeanette, perhaps friends of Mark. The wounded Billy turns out to be the fifteen-year-old son of Bruce from an extra-marital affair.

It doesn't take long before the first notes of discord are heard. Duncan, talking to Marge, says, "They ain't gonna survive the winter. I mean we got all their supplies."

"Seems that way, don't it?"

"What do you mean?"

"I mean we've got sixteen people to feed here and that doesn't count those at the compound. And your brother eats enough for four."

"Leave him out of this. You're saying there's not that much here."

"That's what I'm saying. And we need someone to get the stoves going. The kitchen and the big room are the only ones that are warm and we can't live in them."

"I'll get Jason to look into it."

Some days later, Jack uses a small digital recorder to tape a conversation between Duncan and Bruce.

Duncan: "You see all the notes. Like they want us to

maintain it for them to come back to. They didn't leave them for our convenience."

Bruce: "Yeah, they got a plan. I don't trust them one damn bit. Beth says it only looks like they left a lot of food."

Duncan: "Marge says we're already getting low. We need to get Marko here to show us the stuff he told us about."

Bruce: "I wouldn't count on him. He's freaked. He doesn't want to come near this place. The guy's useless. The way he cut and run when they tried to burn us out. Pro football player my ass."

Duncan: "Yeah, so what. If he does that again, he's off the platoon."

That same day Bruce rages about the death of Billy Ryles, wounded in the chest during the attack on the farm. "I'm going to kill every last one of the motherfuckers. I'm gonna line them all up and do them slowly with a flame-thrower. God damn them."

His listeners say nothing. No one asks him, what was the kid doing there in the first place? Not that it would have any effect. Bruce likes to hate. He wants to kill.

Later, Jack picks up Marge saying to Duncan when they are alone in the kitchen. "He didn't care a fig for the kid when he was alive. What was he doing out there with a gun playing soldier?"

Duncan gives a snort. "You ask him."

*

Gradually and inexorably, the work to be done at The Ledges grows apace. Life narrows and sharpens. They find satisfaction in cooking their simple meals, cold washing the dishes, making up their cots, keeping their clothes and bodies relatively clean, even sensing what a luxury that would become as the days and nights grow colder and darker. Parties are organized to venture out with ax and saw to scour the surrounding forest for firewood to add to the pile cut and stacked that summer. The kids help Nicole and Lise plait hemlock boughs in the lattice protecting the tents. At the same time, Grace and Chee search for useful herbs and wild food. They come back with mullein, sumac berries, grapes, and

269

mushrooms. Armed with a scoped rifle and shotgun, Lance and Jack hunt for almost anything that moves. But game has become scarce. A turkey hen provides the camp with one of Ari's feasts, including a *pot au feu* that simmers for days afterward on the camp stove at night. It helps with the endless portions of beans and rice or the thin stews concocted out of freeze-dried camping fare, or the oatmeal that isn't quite the same without fresh milk, though the touch of maple syrup makes it palatable. And while they miss what they no longer have – fresh milk, fresh eggs, vegetables and berries – the hunger that comes with sleeping in cold tents and working outdoors proves a potent relish. There are few leftovers.

Allegra writes in her journal:

We're more like a village than anything else. We each have our own little house, like something a Hobbit might inhabit, what with the evergreen thatch that also covers the lattice door that have hinges of strong cord. The tents inside are cold at first, but they warm up with body heat.

Lily has moved in with the three girls. I'm afraid they've made a pet of her and are spoiling her. Every once in a while she spends the night with me. Lance bunks in with Thad. He can only do that when Duvall is staying with Bella. It can get complicated, but we joke about it among ourselves. No one else seems to notice or say anything if they do.

After dinner in the cave, when the dishes are done, I've begun to read aloud a chapter from Robinson Crusoe. *It's one of dozens of novels I have on my Kindle. I started doing it as a kind of joke and it has caught on. It's become something of a favorite time. Thad says that charging my Kindle is now a top priority.*

The audio surveillance of the McFeralls continues. When Cyrus scruples aloud about an invasion of privacy, Jack and others respectfully demur. Thad reassures him, "Dad, none of us want to listen to any of the McFeralls getting intimate with one another."

What they hear is growing rancor and threats against The

270

Ledges. Thad records yet another exchange between the brothers.

Bruce: "They've got the Neill kid. She's a witness. Marko told me she was there when I did her old man and the kid. If things ever get straightened out, if there's any kind of real law, we'll be in deep shit."

Duncan: "What are you saying?"

Bruce: "I'm saying sooner or later, we're going to have to go after them. And I'm not just talking about what they did to Billy."

Duncan: "And kill them all?"

Bruce: An ugly laugh sounds. "It wouldn't be the first time."

Duncan: After a pause, "Let's face it, Bru, she ain't the only witness. We're going to have to kill a shitload of folks to take care of all the witnesses."

Bruce: "Whatever. I still say, they've got stuff hidden all over this place. I say we go up there and kidnap the old lady. We could make her talk."

Duncan: "I wouldn't count on that. Those people are tougher than you think, especially the old lady. What we need to do is get that jerk Marko over here, at gun point if we have to, and get him to show us what they did with their stuff."

After he confers with Jack, Thad plays the exchange back to a meeting of the Defense Committee. He tells Grace with a laugh, "He's right about you, Mom."

More serious, Jack tells them, "I think we'll need to plan for an attack at some time or another."

"But not if it snows," Duvall says.

"Probably not." Jack sounds rueful. "It doesn't snow like it used to."

Thad shakes his unshaven head. "I wouldn't count on that. That volcano that blew last year in Iceland..."

"Katla..." Lance puts in.

"Right. Katla. Katla dumped millions of tons of sulfides into the upper atmosphere. I'd say we're in for a brutal winter."

Cyrus nods and sighs. "We're an obsession with Bruce. He wants us gone."

Grace says, "It isn't just that. They need what we've hidden and brought up here. They're finding that the provisions we did leave out are really quite thin."

"Yeah, but we're pretty well dug in up here. They would have to pay a helluva price." Duvall sounds like he might welcome a standoff.

Ari shakes his head. "They have RPGs and other heavy weapons."

Later, alone with Thad and Ari, Jack says, "I think we should seriously think about eliminating Bruce. He's a psychopath. With him out of the way, we might be able to talk to Duncan. Come to some kind of accommodation."

"How are you going to kill Bruce?" Ari asks.

"Sniper him."

"How?" Thad asks though he already has an idea.

"They don't have much of a guard where they are. We get him outside where I can pop him."

"How do you get him outside?"

"Make a noise. Start a fire."

Everyone but Cyrus and Grace thinks it's a good idea. Nicole says, "It's them or us." The retreat and especially the loss of Sugar Mountain – her B&B, after all – have made her into more than a hawk.

But, of course, Cyrus won't hear of it. He repeats himself. "We do not have a license to kill."

They get side-tracked into a discussion about pacifism. Nicole makes a telling point: "M. L. King's nonviolence or that of Gandhi or Nelson Mandela would not have worked under the Communists or the Nazis. They would have been snuffed out before they started. Nonviolence only works in civilized societies. And the McFeralls are not civilized. Not with Bruce there."

Cyrus won't budge. And this time he and Grace will not abstain from voting.

Jack tries another tack.

"At the very least, we should try for their weapons dump. I would guess they've relaxed the guard back at Pitts Hollow. And they wouldn't expect us to attack from here."

Cyrus smiles. "Haven't we tried that."

"Not with dynamite."

"And wouldn't they just get more?" Grace asks. "And wouldn't it provoke them to come after us sooner rather than later?"

Cyrus turns to his wife. "I agree. I think we ought to get the other refuge ready... just in case."

Jack groans, but inwardly. He considers, not very seriously, a nonviolent coup. He would take over as acting leader and change the founding document. For action such as killing Bruce McFerall, a simple majority would suffice. But he doesn't get even as far as sounding out anyone other than Nicole. And even she is dubious. "We wouldn't be alive without him," she says. "We wouldn't have had Sugar Mountain and we wouldn't have this place."

*

In the early planning of Sugar Mountain as a sanctuary for the family, Cyrus and Grace insisted on having The Ledges as a back-up place for a refuge. Jack resisted because he could not countenance the possibility of retreat. They reached a compromise. Jack could devise ways of defending Sugar Mountain using deadly violence if absolutely necessary; and Grace and Cyrus could have their refuge in the woods.

In many ways, The Ledges proved ideal for the purpose. It provided the cave, places to put the lean-tos and tents, and a supply of clean water. Jack gave it a cursory look early on and said sure in part because he never thought they would use it. Now he begins to look at it from a security point of view. To attack and take the refuge from the south – from the direction of the farm – meant coming up the now well-trodden paths through fields and woods. It would be difficult but by no means impossible even for a poorly trained assault team. At the same time, a series of ledges and large boulders provide excellent cover for an ambush. From behind them, the defenders could fire down at attackers who would have to cross a clearing without much cover. But they could send units around the outer ledges and come in from the sides.

Jack explores farther afield and finds an old logging road that runs along the top of a ridge about a half a mile north of The

Ledges. He follows it west until it peters out in a snarl of rocks and vegetation. He retraces his steps and keeps going eastward. The road, at times lost under new growth, comes to a stream where remnants of a crude log bridge remain in place. On the other side, the track seems to disappear. But it turns into what Jack should have remembered – a snowmobile trail that he used years before when a teenager. With trepidation as memory returns, he follows the narrowed trail to where it debouches onto a derelict town road. It comes back to him that this road, unpaved and deeply rutted in places from washouts, leads uphill to a long-abandoned farmstead known as Hagersville. He walks the other way – downhill. A half mile down he comes to a rudimentary iron gate where the town closed the road. A sign attached reads "No Vehicles Beyond This Point." He knows that farther down it connects to the town road about a mile from Sugar Mountain.

There is nothing at present to stop the McFeralls from driving up, pushing through the gate with the Humvees and breaking a way along the logging road with a bunch of ATV's trailing behind. They might even chance the bridge to ford the stream. Also, there are bound to be snowmobilers among their followers who know about the trail. All they would have to do is put a few shooters below the refuge and attack in force from above. Or vice versa.

He decides to come back with a couple of the heavy lifters and dismantle what's left of the log bridge. But that won't stop the gang from simply driving up the town road as far as they can and then deploying on foot. Which gives him an idea.

*

The news comes in brief bursts with a background of static. It was relayed to the refuge from a recording by the Beck's CB transmitter: "The following is an announcement going out on the emergency broadcast system. As of 11 a.m. today Eastern Standard Time, a provisional Congress comprising both branches and a reduced but functioning Supreme Court have been sworn in by the acting Chief Justice. The President's voice is heard. "Civilian rule, though challenged through these trying and tragic months has been reaffirmed with this action. Efforts have already begun to restore democratic government at the state, county, and local levels in all jurisdictions in the nation. As President, I ask patience as it will take time to restore what we all took for granted. In the meanwhile, I can assure you that all nuclear weapons have been accounted for and that all but three of the nuclear power plants have been stabilized. We are also establishing local anti-terrorism units to curb the lawlessness that has seized too many parts of the nation. We have come through a fateful and devastating pandemic. But we will survive. Thank you."

Cyrus records the news and plays it again to everyone assembled in the cave. At the end there is cheering and applause. Cyrus, with a bend in his posture, stands to talk. "This is great news. It is what we have been waiting to hear. All we have to do now is survive."

But the cheering doesn't last long. The next day, to everyone's astonishment, they pick up a state government broadcast to the effect that Duncan McFerall has been promoted to the rank of captain in the National Guard and deputized to investigate and suppress terrorist activities in the Franklin County area using force if necessary.

It is not long after this news that Thad listens to an exchange between the McFerall brothers in the studio. The first part is garbled, one of them standing directly in front of the mike. Then, Bruce talking in his ugly voice: "You're the one who said that anyone who resists us is a terrorist. Pure and simple."

"That doesn't give you a license to shoot them in the back of the head."

"They're going to die, anyway. I'm doing them a favor."

"Bruce, we've got to clean up our act. This appointment means that I've still got juice in the Guard."

"So we're covered."

"Yeah, maybe. But no more executions..."

"Come on..."

"That's an order."

"Except for the Arkwrights."

There's a long pause. "Yeah, okay, except for the Arkwrights."

26

The sickly sweet smell of death comes and goes as Allegra and Lance make their way north at a slant from The Ledges. It is a beautiful afternoon on the last day of October, the light sharp and the air crisp amid the falling leaves of foliage past its autumn glory. They have a picnic lunch of sandwiches made from Ari's stovetop bread, a smear of peanut butter and lots of raspberry jam. Their backpack also contains a blanket and a small bottle of apple liquor. Ostensibly, they are out foraging for wild food and have already harvested a bag full of wild carrots. In actuality, they are intent on some serious lovemaking, "a bucolic little orgy for two," Allegra wrote in her journal the night before, which they spent apart.

Instead of work denims, Allegra has on a plaid skirt, warm tights, strong but stylish black boots and a lacy blouse under her down jacket. Lance has also dressed up just a bit with turtleneck and veeneck sweater under his down vest, his good jeans and hikers.

"It's getting stronger," he remarks as they emerge onto the old road and a level area with the remnants of stonewalls showing where small fields has once been.

"Maybe we should go elsewhere," Allegra says. "It smells like something died, and I'm not in the mood for maggots."

But the odor fires their curiosity and draws them to it. They go uphill on the road and turn off onto a vague path through a stand of black birch. They presently come upon a clearing that had once been a farmstead. Overgrown with brambles, the stone foundation of a barn is set into a gently sloping hillside. Nearby stands a similar ruin, most likely that of a house, being smaller.

They draw closer and the smell grows stronger. They can see a rough lean-to, little more than poles propped against the foundation stones of the house with evergreen branches turning brown tied in place with strips of cloth. What looks like litter from a distance is scattered around the place. A coyote the size of a wolf lifts its head from something on the ground, bares its teeth at them and slinks away.

"Hello," Lance calls out. "Anybody home?"

Silence.

"I don't like this," Allegra says. "I don't think..." But she follows Lance, who is moving with caution toward the scene.

*

The journal page on which Allegra writes that night is stained with tears.

Not just bodies, but a family. I couldn't look at them and then I had to look. We both covered our noses against the stench. The first body was that of man, maybe in his thirties, it was hard to tell. There were feathers everywhere from the down jacket he was wearing so that it seemed that the body the coyote and other animals has been feeding on was that of a large bird. One emaciated thigh had been gnawed through to the bone and his midsection was a mess of entrails. He was dark blond and there was a round hole just above and between his eyes, which had been pecked out. In the leaf litter not far away lay a small revolver.

"Oh, God!" I heard Lance say. He had gone to the other side of the lean-to and peered in. Again I didn't want to look and I had to. There was a woman and two children, a boy of about eight and a girl Lily's age. The children showed no obvious signs of violence. The woman had been shot in the side of the head.

"A murder suicide maybe," Lance said. He looked stricken and I think he was trying to contend with what we found by objectifying it, the better to make sense of it.

I had to look away, stop, gag, and weep. I have been crying off and on ever since. It's not only that I felt infinite pity for this family. It's not only that I wanted to lift the body of the little girl into my arms and hug her back to life and love. But she was as dead as the monkey doll in her arms. What pierced me to the heart, what makes me howl inside, is that this may well be how we end up, like so many rotting dolls, making everything we have done meaningless, mere detritus in the great, churning Darwinian world.

We had no dejeuner sur l'herbe, no passionate interlude in the sun. We made our way back to the refuge and told Jack and Cyrus what we had found. Even though it was getting late, Lance led Duvall, Jack, and Ari to the place with pickaxes and shovels. Jack said afterwards that the bodies were those of Tom Melnikov, his wife Virginia and their two children. They were among the few who escaped when the family farm was over-run by the McFeralls.

The following evening, recovered, Allegra writes again about the Melnikov family in her journal.

Jack thinks they suffocated the children. Then he shot her and then himself. I cannot imagine it.

Several of us returned today to the grave site. We gathered up their pitiful things and buried them as well. Cyrus read from the Book of Common Prayer. I, who have no God to turn to, read Heaney's poem "Limbo." In it he memorializes a mother drowning her illegitimate baby. "...But I'm sure/As she stood in the shallows/Ducking him tenderly... He was a minnow with hooks/Tearing her open."

What happened at the old Hagersville farmstead does not keep Chee and Grace from exploring around the area for herbs and other wild food. While the Melnikovs had huddled and starved in their pitiful shelter, a veritable bower of concord grape vines hung nearby heavy with sweet fruit, a lot of it already shriveled into raisins. But enough left so there are grapes along with concoctions of grape pulp and skins for the next several days at The Ledges. Chee separates out the seeds, dries and then pounds them into a powder to add to soup.

They gather nuts where they find them on the ground – black walnuts, hickory, even acorns, which need shelling, grinding, and leaching. In a meadow just beyond the Hagersville farmstead they harvest more wild carrots but carefully. Look-alikes can be poisonous. They find and use tubers from Jerusalem artichoke, dried burdock, and the boiled roots of cattails. Chee dries and stores chicory roots, "For when the coffee runs out."

*

The verbal preening that greets the news of the elevation of the McFerall gang to a special National Guard unit doesn't last long. Jack, Thad, and Cyrus learn from the hidden mikes that the systems designed to provide a level of comfort and convenience at Sugar Mountain have begun to fail one by one. When temperatures drop into the low twenties for a couple of days, the feeder pipes from the water tank in the silo to the various bathrooms and the main kitchen freeze. It could have been avoided. The posted instructions clearly state it is necessary to drain those pipes periodically in case of freezing weather. Among other things, it means the new residents have to make their way across the yard to the outhouse, at least until the pipes thaw.

The power goes down regularly and an electrician in the group proves less than proficient in restoring it. Nor do they learn how to use the various stoves for heat. They hear Bruce's wife Beth complaining to him about the horse barn where they have moved. "The bedrooms are freezing, Bru. The kids are all humped together in the living room and it's too hot there." You need to open the registers, someone explains. They can't be found. They are on the floor. Finally, someone finds them covered with a suitcase.

The microphone in the family room goes off. It is or was hidden among a ganglia of cables and connections to the television. The mike in the studio, connected both to batteries and the house power, such as it was, picks up an exchange between Duncan, Bruce, and Marko. Duncan, whose voice is lower and more measured than his brother's, is heard saying, "Marko, we need to know every last detail about what they did with their stuff."

"I told you. They humped most of it up to that camp. I'm

talking food, blankets, tools, even a cook stove that you could take apart." Marko is trying to sound like his old self, but his voice is uncertain, trying to please.

"And here?"

"A lot of stuff went under the horse barn."

"Exactly where?" asks Bruce, his exasperation obvious.

"I don't know. They wouldn't let me in there. Some kind of secret cellar."

"Yeah, we found that."

"Look, they spent days, maybe a couple of weeks, hauling shit up there. Even the kids had packs of stuff."

Bruce says, "Let's just go up there and get it. What are we waiting for?"

Duncan's response is garbled.

The voices coming through the small speaker in the recon tent paint a verbal picture of unhappy campers. No one seems to have figured out the heating system. The power is erratic at best. And the food: "The potatoes are half rotten," Beth complains to Marge. "I don't want any more beans. They make everyone stink."

The discomforts and shortages figure in the increasing talk about attacking The Ledges. "Hey, they're sitting up there fat and happy," Bruce tells his brother, "and unless we hit them or some other place, we won't get through the winter."

Then something that surprises the eavesdroppers. Duvall overhears one of the younger women pleading with Duncan to go back to Pitts Hollow. It gets a shouted, angry reply: "I've told you, for Christ's sakes, we can't go back. Paul and Joany have moved in. And all of the Robinsons. And others. I can't just throw them out."

Not long afterwards, the remaining mikes in the house are either discovered or malfunction. Or the battery in the relay dies. Thad and Jack check the relay. It seems to be functioning. Then the speaker in the recon tent perks up with muffled noises from the studio. As for a warning of an attack, the monitor camera on the trail leading to The Ledges still works.

In this dearth of intelligence, Jack and Lance leave The Ledges a couple of hours after sunset under a clouded sky to do a recce of the house and grounds. Cyrus agrees to it as long as there is no violence except in self-defense. Jack carries an AR15 as does Lance along with a camera equipped with a night-vision lens. Once near the upper pastures, they move west onto the Fallgrens place. A dim light, possibly from a candle, shows in the windows of that old house. "Squatters," Jack whispers.

From there they come down that side of the brook. They circle outside the security fence, checking. No guards, Jack notices. The place already has a kind of squalor about it with garbage piling up in a corner of the barn garden and with equipment left lying around. Lance takes pictures, but they show little of consequence. They move around to the front of the house. With Lance covering him, Jack slides over to the burnt-out dozer. To his surprise, just beyond it and lined up like ducks, is one of the Humvees and any number of pickup trucks and ATVs. Were they staging? For a night attack? Planning? Or just partying?

He moves in a crouch up the lawn and over the stone wall. Carefully, indirectly at first, he peers in the kitchen window just to the right of the front door.

Around the table, in the unsteady light of Coleman lanterns, he counts sixteen men. Bruce but no Duncan. One woman is at work at the stove and another at the sink. From the platters heaped with meat, he guesses they have slaughtered one of the half-grown pigs. The men have glasses of what look like home brew along with tumblers of moonshine.

He still can't tell whether they are celebrating or planning or both. If only he could hear what was being said beyond the shouts and wisecracks. Some of them are clearly drunk. All of them appear unarmed. In his pouch, Jack has two extra clips for the AR15. He slips off the gun's safety. Crouching, he moves onto the colonnaded porch and the door leading directly into the kitchen. He can visualize storming in and killing or wounding them all. That would be the end of it. He pulls a ski mask over his face. He catches a dim reflection of himself in a window. He looks like death itself.

On the threshold he hesitates and then stops. He cannot turn off his own moral safety. It's not only his father, it's Duncan McFerall telling his brother that he doesn't have a license to kill. A moment later he is glad he didn't go on a rampage. Down in a crouch and then up again, he looks into the family room. There, huddled around the stove are the younger wives and children of the extended McFerall family. What would happen to them? Where would they go?

He would have fired the vehicles lined up outside the fence had the other Humvee not come up the road and into the drive, its lights on. Jack ducks back into the shadows. He watches as Duncan and another man get out. Duncan is rigged out in full Guard uniform. Back from a meeting, Jack thinks. Into his walkie-talkie, Duncan snarls, "God damn it, where are the fucking sentries? These vehicles need guarding."

At which point, the door opens and several men come out with weapons at the ready.

*

When the camera covering the approach from the farm to The Ledges fails, the Defense Committee debates mounting a round-the-clock guard on the trail. But only Jack thinks it necessary. For the others, the location of the refuge and the rough terrain make a direct attack appear so difficult as to be improbable. Also, the microphone in the studio has resumed broadcasting however sporadically and unclearly. Besides, they are tired of being vigilant. It is quite enough to stay warm, to keep clean, and get enough to eat. Nicole pesters Grace to let her dig up some of the outlying caches, but Grace says one at a time. It is a form of rationing. In the meanwhile, they all tighten their belts, especially the men. The children and pregnant women come first.

Jack resists the fatalistic lethargy that spreads among the others like a collective somnambulance. It might be the weather. Winter has arrived early. People find excuses to huddle in the cave. Allegra starts to give afternoon readings.

Jack frets. At night he scarcely sleeps. He can imagine too readily the McFeralls and any number of armed men all equipped with night vision equipment coming with silent stealth up the trail to The Ledges. Walk in with guns blazing. Turn Bruce and his pals loose on the survivors. So he's up and down any number of times, checking the trail, listening, fearing.

He also believes the McFeralls know roughly where they are located even without the use of equipment to trace their CB broadcasts. On a wide circular sweep around the area he finds traces of what could be scouts close enough to detect the living quarters of eighteen people. He doubts they know that they could attack from the north with considerable advantage.

It's enough to make him act. Hollow-eyed from lack of sleep, he calls a meeting and insists on the necessity for organized vigilance. He proposes they use one of Thad's remaining microphones and set it up on the trail leading from below. The adults will take turns standing or sitting watch in the recon tent.

Duvall shakes his head. "Man, it gets cold in there at night."

"Not as cold as the grave," Thad says.

Jack nods emphatically. "I agree. So what can we do about it? And I mean today."

After a bit of thought, Duvall says, "We could cut some saplings and make a lattice frame to cover the tent leaving about six inches of space for insulation. Then we'll plait the lattice with evergreen fronds."

"And if that doesn't work?"

"Hell, we'll put another one on top of that."

No one objects. Work on insulating the recon tent starts immediately. That afternoon, Bella takes the first watch, or "listen," as Thad puts it.

In the evening, during her two-hour turn, Allegra writes in her journal:

It's actually quite cozy in here. No one's quite sure what a troop of men coming up the trail will sound like. Jack says tomorrow we'll record the sound of about ten of us doing just that.

When I told Lance in private how far-fetched such an attack seemed to me, he shook his head. "Hunger trumps every other motivation for action. Always has and not just for H. sapiens. It's deep, deep in our evolutionary past. Our gut came first. We are merely an elaboration on those primordial worms... They were little more than digestive tracts."

I laughed and said, "Perhaps that sums us up, you know, elaborations on worms."

The lattice covering over the tent works, especially after they rig a tarp to serve as a second door. Cozy, they all agree. Perhaps too cozy, Jack thinks. He doesn't want people falling asleep on their watches.

Jack still frets, but in a lower register. While out recording what a group of people sound like coming up along the trail as quietly as possible, he and the Defense Squad inspect a place where they could make a stand should an attack materialize. The site, a series of ledges providing concealment and cover for an ambush, is about fifty yards above a wide but shallow level clearing studded with the decaying stumps of pines logged some years back.

They poke around the area below the clearing. It's sloping, rough ground, thick with young pines and boulders for concealment and cover, not ideal but good enough for an attacking group to stage from. If done right. In the back of his mind are mortars and rocket-propelled grenades.

At the ambush site, Jack picks out several firing points. They erect stone barriers on which they scatter dry leaves and dead branches for camouflage. They drill without using ammunition. The sound would not deter the McFeralls, if they heard it at all. But might make them seek a way to come at them from the north. That's an area Jack has yet to scout out with any thoroughness. They talk it over. If the McFeralls come up the trail in force with heavy weapons, the Sugar Mountaineers won't be able to stop them. At best they could stall them, buy time. Then what?

When Cyrus learns from the erratic CB radio that the McFeralls had "requisitioned" another farm, this one in Heath, even Jack relaxes his vigil. Perhaps that's what the McFeralls were planning the night he and Lance made their recce. He listens to the lone remaining mike in the studio, but the voices are garbled. He finds it frustrating. When the gang gathers again at Sugar Mountain, he plans to pay a visit with a gas siphon and some over-the-counter flares.

27

Even with the mike in place, the refuge might well have been taken by surprise if Allegra and Lance had not been dallying on a sun-struck slab of exposed granite while ostensibly looking for wild food. Lance, with uncommonly good eyesight, sees the men nearly a half mile off, coming up the trail where it crosses an open space not far above the pasture. The men are in camouflage, their faces blackened, weapons slung.

"Quietly and quickly," he says, taking Allegra by the hand and leading her back into the cover of the trees. They run as fast as the path allows them, arriving breathless.

"They're coming," Lance tells Jack, describing what he saw.

"How many?" asks Ari, who is in the recon tent. "I can't hear them."

"At least twenty. No, closer to thirty. Maybe more."

There is a moment of panic as the news spreads. "We have time," Jack says, calming them. It's a rough climb to the clearing and they won't come at us until they're organized. But we don't have time to evacuate. We'll have to stand and fight."

"We can evacuate the children," Grace says. "Chee and Bella can take them to the Hagersville farmstead. I've cached some tents and a little food around there. The rest of us can follow later."

"If there is a later," someone says.

Jack is nodding and moving toward a low hanging ledge under which he put extra ammunition in waterproof containers. Lance, Bella, Ari, Lise, Duvall, Allegra, and Thad all have their AR15s slung. Jack takes the sniper rifle and a pouch of rounds. He already has his knife handy. He takes a Glock and stashes several more and the shotguns nearer to the refuge. They will use them in a last stand if the attackers break through.

"Let's go," he says, leading the squad out of the camp and down the trail.

"Same positions?" Allegra asks. She is apprehensive, but more angry than scared. She is ready to fight and to kill.

286

Jack stops and turns. "Right. The same positions we had at the last drill. Watch your flanks."

Crouching low as they approach the line of trees and fortified positions from which they will try to repulse the attack, the defense team slips into place. Jack unslings the rifle and uses its scope to track the men in fatigues and carbines coming up the trail and dispersing around two figures who, in focus, turned out to be Duncan and Bruce McFerall.

Jack is Captain Arkwright again, a professional. He will do what he has to do to stop the enemy. He will, he tells himself, line up the brothers in the cross hairs and shoot them without compunction. He will ignore his father's injunction: don't fire unless fired upon or unless they don't stop when asked to. But the professional in him knows they are still too far off and moving too erratically for him to get a clean shot.

The Defense Squad, crouched behind improvised cover in teams, watch with the fatalistic courage of fear as what seems a small army of men gather in the trees just below the clearing. Again Jack remarks their lack of training. Some of them are joking around. They, too, are nervous. A couple are smoking. He sights through the scope. But the attackers, including the brothers, are in and out of cover at a distance of perhaps a hundred yards.

They might try to go around the clearing. But Jack thinks that unlikely. They would have to split the group and negotiate rough, treacherous ground with little between them and whizzing bullets. They also would have to climb up vertical ledges, some of them ten feet high and which, in places, ran for considerable lengths.

They keep coming. And instead of hurrying across the wide clearing in ones or twos as they arrive, they gather there, as though to take in the last of the sun's warmth. All except the brothers, who, out of sight, are leading from the rear.

Despite his resolve, Jack finds he can't start shooting without warning. As the attackers start across the stumpy ground, he calls out, "Any farther and we will fire!"

"Move out! Move out!" Duncan McFerall shouts though a bullhorn.

"Fire at will," Jack says into his walkie-talkie, and aims at the legs of the man more or less leading their charge. There is a sharp exchange of fire, those of the attackers wide of the mark and those of the defense team scarcely much better. But three of McFeralls' men lay on the ground, two with obvious leg wounds and one clutching his stomach as the rest scurry back to hunker down behind rocks in the dense cover.

Jack doesn't need to tell his team to stop firing.

Up at the camp, Nicole and Chee have already assembled the children with emergency backpacks. At the sound of gunfire, they set off in the direction of the abandoned farmstead. Cyrus is organizing provisions, mostly food, for the Defense Squad should they all have to retreat. Grace has cobbled together an emergency room of sorts in the cave in case of casualties.

In this confusion, Henry takes it into his head to bring water to the troops. He has heard Grace say that if it's a long siege, they will have to get food and water down to the squad. And Henry remembers his own campaigns and being short of water and grub too many times. In the flurry of activity, no one sees him slip away, hobbling without his cane, a plastic bottle in each hand.

Down the hill, the informal ceasefire has held. Bruce McFerall is on the bullhorn this time, calling Jack "a yellow bastard," and threatening to wipe out him and "every last one of you motherfuckers."

Duncan takes the bullhorn and does a plausible imitation of officialdom. "In the name of the Massachusetts National Guard, "I order all of you to surrender. You will be treated according to the laws of the Commonwealth."

"Bad cop, good cop," Thad says into his walkie-talkie.

For a while Jack doesn't answer. In a fight it is best to speak with a gun or, more quietly, with a knife. But finally, he shouts back, "I'll give you five minutes to get those wounded men out of there."

Duncan McFerall doesn't respond. But almost immediately, several unarmed men, one with a white rag on a stick, emerge from cover to carry the wounded from the clearing.

288

It is right then that Henry, holding the bottles carefully, comes into full view above the defense team. A shot sounds and the old man, clutching at his chest, goes down.

Duncan McFerall booms out, "Cease fire, God damn it, I said cease fire."

But Jack doesn't care. While Allegra and Thad run in a crouch to where Henry has fallen, Jack sights through the scope of his rifle. He moves it back and forth, back and forth. He is patient and focused. The first target that comes into view in the crosshairs is the laughing face of Bruce McFerall. Just before Jack pulls the trigger, the man turns and looks up as though at something his brother is telling him. The bullet catches him on the side of the chin and takes off most of his lower jaw.

Into his tabbed-on walkie-talkie, Jack asks, "How's Henry?"

"Dying," says Allegra.

"Gone," says Thad.

Jack goes back to his scope. He can hear Duncan's hysterical rage coming over the bullhorn as through an open mike. Jack is looking for another target. This time, he shoots a young man in back of the thigh. Finally, an eerie silence settles over the scene.

It is broken by Duncan's voice. He has left the bullhorn on as he shouts orders. "We need a medic. Right now. Bruce is hit. Badly. God damn it, where's Dan with his kit. Oh, Jesus..." Then, more ominously. "Everyone hold your positions. Dickie, get the RPGs up here on the double. And tell the mortar team to aim about three hundred yards in front of our position. I'll march them down and we'll bracket them. God damn it, we need a medic!"

"Leave now and no one else will get hurt," Jack yells.

"Don't you wish," Duncan McFerall booms back. "We're bringing up the heavy stuff and you will soon be in a living hell. We are going to kill every last one of you."

"I think he means it," Ari says, his voice coming through the plug in Jack's ear.

"Affirmative," Jack says. He's thinking. Options. Have the others withdraw while I snipe. Then follow. Retreat to... The farmstead? He's thinking, RPGs, huh? Mortars? Shooting an old man in cold blood? If that is not license, then nothing is. Scarcely realizing it, Jack has reverted to what he was at his best and his worst: a competent killer taking a grim satisfaction in his work.

Drawing fire, he scuttles over to where Lance is prone behind rocks and slides in beside him.

"You got Bruce," Lance says, his young eyes bright with excitement.

A mortar shell explodes off to the right not far from where the attackers are hunkered down. They hear Duncan yelling orders to change the coordinates.

"Yeah." Jack keeps his voice low. "I'm going to exchange my rifle for your AR. You know the drill. Take your time. Only fire if you've got a good shot. The guys with the RPGs are the priority."

Lance takes the rifle and, festooning the barrel with a straggling grape vine, sights through the scope. "You want me to just wound?"

Another mortar shell lands, much closer this time.

"Anything. Just hit them. If you kill, you kill. It's us or them."

"What are you going to do?"

"I'm going to create some confusion." Into his walkie-talkie Jack says, "Hold your positions. If I don't communicate in ten minutes, retreat in order, Thad covering, and evacuate The Ledges. Do that anyway if the mortars find their range."

The light is beginning to fade, which is to Jack's advantage as he slips away. He is armed with Lance's AR15 slung over his back, his combat knife, and one of the Glocks in his belt. He moves through the cover of trees off to the right, following a route he has staked out for just such a contingency. He moves with practiced stealth and with a righteous anger fueled by thoughts of who and what he is defending.

From near the clearing, he hears Duncan's voice again. "No prisoners. Repeat. No prisoners." It's followed by two mortar shells landing in quick succession.

Jack halts just forward and well above the line of attackers. In the graying light, he can make out where they are from moving foliage and their nervous chatter. They are spread out across a wide area in

290

dense cover, some singly, some in teams of two, isolated from each other just enough for his purposes. They are quiet, waiting for the mortars to do their work. Jack doesn't have a good shot at any of them. And even if he did, it might not create the effect he needs.

More mortars land. In his ear, Thad says, "They're creeping closer."

"Roger. Prepare to evacuate. You cover."

"What about you?"

"I'm fine."

As he watches, two men arrive just behind their line carrying a box of M40 grenades. One keeps low and the other, standing, begins to fit a grenade onto his weapon. The crack of the sniper rifle sounds and the man drops to the ground. Lance, Jack thinks.

It's like a signal. Jack moves quietly and quickly down to just behind the line. His first target, scarcely a man, is lying behind a tree. A young voice asks, "What's up?" just before Jack knocks him out with the weighted pommel of his knife. For all his grim determination, Jack cannot bring himself to slit the kid's throat.

Someone calls, "Hey, Jase, you okay?"

Jack recognizes his next victim. It's Peddy Lawlor, a member of Bruce's special squad. He is sitting with his back to a tree and asks, as Jack sidles up to him, "When do we eat?" In one precise, brutal motion, Jack grabs the hair on the top of the man's head, pulls it back, and neatly nicks his carotid artery. Peddy Lawlor, his hands to his throat as though to check the blood pulsing out of him, stares at Jack in amazed horror before slouching over.

The mortar shells are dropping closer, but still off to the side. The gunfire continues sporadically. Jack is in among them now toward the rear. He watches as one of the McFerallites takes a round in the shoulder. Lance again, he thinks. He hears Duncan booming out. "Stay down. Let the mortars finish them."

Jack crouches in a swampy spot and considers his dilemma. He can see a two-man fire team about ten yards away, an older man and another teenager. He won't have time to disable them all even if that were possible. He both wants to work by stealth and to let them know he's there. But he can't wait. Another mortar lands up the hill. He hears Bella mutter, "That was close."

Into his walkie-talkie, Jack says, "Squad, prepare to pull back to the second line in front of The Ledges."

He takes the pair unawares. But his Glock is on safety. Before the older man can bring his weapon around, Jack is on him with his knife, blood splattering everywhere as he nearly beheads him. The kid is mesmerized with fright. As Jack turns to him, he drops his rifle and bolts, giving vent to a piercing scream.

"Hold your positions," Duncan McFerall booms as a wave of murmuring ripples through his troops. Someone calls out, the voice scared. "What the fuck's going on?" Then another. "What was that all about?"

Jack keeps working. He can hear the mortars racking in closer. He finds himself too far back. Or is he? He glides along behind a screen of brush. To his surprise, the next attacker he happens across is Marko. He thinks, trust to find him here, as far from the good old FEBA, forward edge of battle area, as possible. Marko's lying supine as though sunning, his legs crossed at the ankles, his weapon scarcely within reach. Jack hesitates and thinks. Before Marko knows what's happening, Jack, spattered grotesquely with blood, is kneeling over him, the barrel of his assault rifle at his throat. "Do you want to live, Marko?" he says quietly.

Marko is too terror stricken to say anything.

"Say 'yes,'" Jack whispers to him.

There's a strangled "yes."

"Here's what you do. When I let you, I want you to get up and run down the hill screaming the word ambush at the top of your lungs. If you don't scream loud enough I will pick you off with a shot to the back of your head. You got that? Say 'yes.'"

A voice close by calls, "Hey, Marko, who you talking to?"

Another strangled "yes."

"Hey, Marko...?"

Jack keeps his assault rifle trained on Marko's face and, low to the ground, backs away. "Go!"

Marko gets up and bolts, crashing through the brush, heading downhill, screaming "Ambush! Ambush!" as though his life depended on it.

Several others get up and follow him.

Jack moves on and comes up behind a fire team of two. He recognizes another one of Bruce's Bunch. Jack kills him with a shot from the Glock. He tells the other, also a veritable kid stupefied with fear, "Drop your weapon, run and scream ambush or I'll kill you, too." The kid bolts headlong down the hill, too terrified to scream. But Jack lets him go.

The word "ambush" gets repeated. More men begin to desert, turning and heading down the trail. Jack, on the ground in a natural depression, starts firing along the line to either side. He hits at least one man getting up to flee.

"Jack?" Thad says in his ear.

"Situation under control," Jack whispers back. Anyone hit?"

"Nothing serious."

"Hold your positions," McFerall booms out. "Hold your positions, God damn it. Report."

But panic has set in. The retreat of a few turns into a headlong rush, with the men simply taking to the woods including, finally, Duncan McFerall still booming through his loudspeaker.

Jack waits. Into his walkie-talkie, he says, "They are withdrawing. We should be okay for the time being. If they keep dropping mortars, pull back out of range." He can hear moans from the wounded, eight or nine along with three dead. He goes among them, collecting their weapons. To the sentient ones, he says, "You're lucky to be alive. Leave us alone. You'll get help shortly."

At an improvised command post, he finds Bruce McFerall lying on the ground on a stretcher. He is still conscious, his truncated face wrapped around with a white bandage red with wet blood where his lower jaw had been. His tongue hangs out, grotesquely huge and already blackening.

Jack is not there to exult. At best he is relieved. They have won. His family is safe. For the time being. His hands shake and his body trembles. His adrenaline is dropping like a battery going dead.

It had been his usual reaction after a fire fight. Triumph mixed and then hollowed out with relief, fatigue, and intimations of

293

depression. But this time, for the first time, a wave of disgust tinged with shame comes over him as he peers down in the dying light at his handiwork. He is not so much ashamed of himself as of something deeper and more intractable. It is shame of the species, or, more precisely, the subspecies *Homo sapiens homicidens,* to which he belongs. Wolves, rats, snakes have more humanity when it comes to their own kind.

He kneels down next to the man and takes his wrist which is heavy with a large limp hand. He feels for a pulse. It's thready at best. Bruce McFerall will more than likely die. It will be a lingering awful death. Jack tells him, "You ain't gonna make it, Bruce, you know that."

The oyster eyes show fear and helpless rage. Jack could have said, this is what all those others felt when you held a gun to their heads. But he doesn't. He doesn't judge. Again the shame. And in that shame it occurs to him that he is looking at a colleague, a fellow killer. The realization, sudden, powerful, and blurred, cancels the moral calculus by which he would have justified his own destruction of human life. In that moment, peering down at the doomed man, he sees himself.

He says, "You want out of your misery?"

There is a slight nodding motion and a throaty noise Jack takes to mean yes. He slides the safety off his pistol. Bruce McFerall closes his eyes. Jack feels like saying, I should leave this for your brother to do. But he has no spite left in him. He stands, holds the Glock out stiffly, and fires a bullet into the man's head just above the eyes.

There is no celebration following the rout of the McFeralls. Grace insists on taking a medical kit and going down to the wounded left behind to see what she can do for them. Thad protests. But Duvall and Ari, slinging their rifles and a piece of white cloth on a stick, go with her. They carry some food and water.

The autumn night is cold and silent as Grace moves among the wounded with a Coleman lamp doing what she can for them.

Cleaning and bandaging them won't suffice, she realizes. They will perish from hypothermia if they're not wrapped in blankets. Into her walkie-talkie, she tells Cyrus, "Can you organize some of those old blankets and send them down."

They hear voices and see the beams of flashlights among the trees down the trail. A line of men comes into sight. The leader is carrying an improvised white flag on a stick. It's Dan Whittaker, an EMT from Greenfield who serves as medic for the McFeralls. He steps forward. "We're unarmed. We're only here to collect our dead and wounded."

Duvall says, "We're armed and any funny business and you'll join those on the ground."

Over to one side, a voice calls out, "Bruce is here. Someone put him out of his misery."

"Thank God," Whittaker mutters.

As Duvall and Ari stand back on alert, Grace shows Whittaker and the men with stretchers where the wounded lie. She says to the EMT, "What are you doing associating with these people?"

He laughs bitterly. "Trying to stay alive. Same as everyone." Then, "My boy belongs. I'm trying to keep him alive."

"How old is he?"

"Sixteen."

Ari resists a remark about Hitler using boys toward the end. Sending them to their deaths. For nothing.

One of the other men, a McFerall cousin, his face in a snarl, says, "We can take it from here."

"Fine with us."

The man persists. "It ain't over, you know. Ain't over by a long shot."

"You're welcome," Duvall says.

"Okay, let's go," Ari says.

Whittaker comes over. "Thank you," he says to Grace.

On the way back they encounter Lance and Allegra coming down the trail with blankets stuffed into black garbage bags. Even Grace doesn't protest when Duvall tells them it's not worth the gesture.

Nicole, returned with the kids from the farmstead, has cooked a bounteous dinner using salt pork, the last of the fresh cabbage, potatoes, and carrots. They eat hungrily, but quietly. They have survived, except for Henry. Life seems ever more precious and precarious.

Thad raises his glass to his brother: "To Jack, without whom we wouldn't be here in one piece."

Jack nods an acknowledgment and manages a fleeting smile. But inwardly he is haunted. Too much has happened. He cannot quite sort it out.

28

The death of Henry Carlton weighs on everyone as a loss and as a harbinger of what they face. The morning after, they dig a shallow trench and bury him in a shroud of cotton sheeting wrapped in a tarp. At the brief service, Thad declares that they will give their grandfather a proper burial at Sugar Mountain when they return. "And return we will."

That afternoon Jack and Duvall make their way to the scene of the battle. There are few signs of what happened there. Some empty cans and bottles. Spent shells. Stuck to the trunk of a sapling with a pushpin is a piece of cardboard, the lettering in red sharpie stating, "Bruce will be avenged."

They meet in the cave. Subdued, nearly self-strange, Jack gives a dispassionate account of what he did during the battle. He does not dwell on those he killed, but those he spared. "Some of them are just kids. They think it's a game." He also tells them, "I'm afraid Bruce McFerall's death may have turned this into a blood feud."

No one blames him, least of all Cyrus, who has aged noticeably in the past weeks. "I had thought that our withdrawal and conceding of Sugar Mountain would have meant peace. What was it someone said – history is the nightmare from which we are trying to awaken. But, look, you did what you had to do," glancing at Jack as he speaks. "I am a man of peace. But I recognize that non-violence only works when the other side is halfway sane. Henceforth, I will leave the decisions of resistance or non-resistance to you and the committee."

If it were only that simple.

They know they will be attacked again. The question is when and how. Jack suspects the McFerall gang will scout the area to find a way to come at them from the north or from the sides. Or, most likely, they will bring the heavy weapons up first, the way they should have done it this time. He pictures what they could do to them with mortars, grenades, flame throwers.

So small teams, accompanied by at least two members of the Defense Squad, set out to explore the surrounding terrain for a suitable location for yet another retreat. They revisit the old farmstead, which has a lot of advantages, including, presumably, a nearby water source, perhaps an old spring well. But the rutted road leads right up to it, to an open space in front of the two foundation walls. It's indefensible. Jack wonders if they might use it as the site of an ambush – make it look like a settlement, entice them up, and hit them from concealment.

Hit them, wound them, kill them. Now the thought repels him, makes him feel a twinge of nausea.

For the lack of anything better, they end up at the place Grace and Cyrus found on one of their rambles. Duvall thinks it has possibilities. He takes Thad, Lance, Jack and Allegra back for a closer look at it.

Allegra is skeptical. "It's just a small hill with some old pines on it."

"Lance, what do you think?" Jack asks.

Lance glances at Allegra.

Thad laughs. "We know where Lance wants to be."

Still, as they explore the gently sloping area, about an acre in size with a house-sized rock set amidst a stand of ancient white pines, it grows more plausible.

"Ghosts," Thad says, not altogether facetiously. "I'll bet others have lived here before."

Duvall likes the idea. "It's got that feel."

Jack nods as he looks around. "It's hidden. They would have to find us here."

"We'll have to haul water." Allegra is still skeptical.

Duvall looks up into the trees. A jay calls out. He says, "There's shelter here."

"And we could defend it," Jack says. But he doesn't sound all that convinced.

"Yeah, our last stand, no pun intended." Thad shares Allegra's doubts.

298

Dubbed "The Pines," the site takes hold in the imagination of the group as most of the adults and then the children hike the three-quarters of a mile into state park land to look at their new retreat. It is quite another matter to start the preliminary stages of preparation and transfer of basic necessities. No one wants to move. The Ledges has become home. Though cramped and at times cold, the tents turn snug after an hour or so of occupation. Ari and Duvall have dug out a natural vent at the back of the big cave allowing all of them to gather there without a fug of smoke and breathed air. They have stayed relatively clean with quick sponge baths in the little stream, and, so far, they have been able to defend themselves.

When Jack describes at a meeting what rocket-propelled grenades and mortars do to people, most of the group sigh and begin to take the onerous task of moving seriously. Duvall and Thad, helped by Allegra and Lise, clear a place for a big tent on the south side of the giant erratic. Duvall, gazing up into a central clump of pines, sees how they might construct a canopy. Grace and Chee, out foraging for wild food, find a stream close by large enough to supply water even when it freezes over.

Jack proves prescient about McFerall preparations for another attack. They are still living at The Ledges when they hear a snowmobile in the woods to the east moving north. It is late-afternoon around Thanksgiving. There is nearly a foot of snow on the ground from an early storm. Jack and Thad take weapons and trudge in a northeast direction, following the sound. The others stay behind and resume packing.

"They're on the town road that goes up to the Hagersville farmstead," Jack says to Thad, who has already guessed what is happening.

They hear the machine stop. When it starts again it appears to be moving east to west.

Jack says "I think it's on the snowmobile trail that links up with an old logging road. Tune in the WT and see if we can pick up anything."

Thad unzips his jacket and takes out a walkie-talkie. He clicks through the channels. "Nothing so far."

The sound of the snowmobile stops again. Then it starts and immediately whines as though climbing. It stops again.

Thad dials again through the walkie-talkie channels. It abruptly crackles and he has to turn down the volume.

"Scout One reporting. Do you read me?"

There is no response.

"Scout One reporting. Do you read?"

Then, an answering crackle and "Yeah, Scout One, we read and write you..." Followed by what sounds like laughter.

"I'm just above their camp, maybe a click, maybe less. I can't hear or see anything, but it's my best guess from the coordinates you gave me."

"Will the trail take the Hummers?"

"I'm not sure. There was a stream that I was able to cross on a log bridge. It might take the Hummers. If not you could drive up the old road to the trail head and deploy from there."

"Good work, Scout One. Return to base."

They listen as the snowmobile engine starts up and moves off, retracing its path.

"We have to move," Jack says to his brother. "Immediately."

Their boots muffled in the snow, they hike up to the ridge. There, clearly, are the fresh tracks of a snowmobile.

That night at a general meeting, Jack lays out their situation under the Coleman lamps in the cave. He goes over what he and Thad heard and saw on the trail. "Again, I think there are three options. First, we stage a preemptive strike on Sugar Mountain, destroying what we can of their equipment and maiming as many of the adult males as possible. The snow would help us. Second, we remain here and resist. When we know they're coming, we have a squad ready to open fire on them as we did before. The third is that we move camp."

"What do you favor," Allegra asks.

"The third." He notes the general surprise around the table.

Ari says, "This doesn't sound like the Jack of old."

"Well, first, they've probably mounted a real guard at Sugar Mountain. Second, if they come at us with mortars and RPGs, it will be a blood bath, mostly ours."

"Will we have time?" Grace asks.

Jack considers. "Since we've already done some preliminary work, I would say yes."

Cyrus, with defeat in his voice, asks, "Do you really think we have time?"

Jack glances around the table. He sees skepticism in their faces. He says, "As to time, I don't think they'll attack with snow on the ground."

"Why not?" Ari asks.

"Because they don't have more than two or three snowmobiles, which means they'll see it as a difficulty when it's really an advantage. If they came on foot and kept quiet, they could be on us before we could respond. But they're a gang. They use force instead of brains."

Nicole, who dreads moving again, asks, "But won't they just keep attacking us?"

Jack shrugs. "They might. But it's at least another mile of rough going to the new camp, perhaps more than a mile with the detours. Even if they find it, they'll have to get their men and equipment in place."

Ari says, "Once the snow melts, couldn't they just drive their Humvees and ATVs up to the farmstead and come at us from there?"

Jack holds up both hands. "First, there's a good chance they won't even know we've moved. Their first attack will be on The Ledges." He smiles. "And while their doing that, perhaps we can do something about their mobility."

They begin the move early the following day. It has to be done in carefully planned stages. Duvall and Thad work on the canopy. The big tent, as yet unused, is carried up on a litter, unpacked, and erected next to the giant boulder. On the same litter, they move and set up a large plastic barrel which has a petcock on its closed end. They fill it with water from the stream using plastic buckets and then build a lean-to around it. This is to be their water supply.

On the second day, they carry up the basics. These include individual tents, cots, bedding, cook stove, cooking utensils, metal camp crockery, cutlery, and cans of kerosene among the myriad other things that they consider necessary for survival. After a cold midday meal, half of the adults and all of the children remain at The Pines erecting the tents, reassembling the cook stove in a lean-to of its own near the big rock, and generally making the place livable.

It snows again. The whole group works ceaselessly for the next two days. They have at least one hot meal a day, usually at night when smoke from the cook stove can't be seen. There is so much to do with so little time. Or so little time before Duncan McFerall, bent on vengeance as well as spoils, comes at them again. Little time and endless decisions. What to take which means deciding what to leave behind if worse comes to worst. It means that able-bodied adults spend hours trudging along the path from the old camp to the new with backpacks loaded with food, tools, weapons, ammunition, medicines, and even the boards of the dismantled privy. The camp table in the cave is folded up and carried to the big tent. Each time a group goes back for more, someone has to scout ahead to make sure nobody else has come in to claim the camp.

Allegra notes down for her journal: "The Pines, as everyone is calling it, makes The Ledges seem like a high-end Swiss spa. But is this home? Is any place home anymore?"

But she doesn't have energy to enter it except to note that for the first few days, the quarters are indeed Spartan, little more than their tents set on hemlock boughs in snow-cleared areas beneath a stand of morose old pines. For warmth, all of the children's cots are moved to the big tent.

It becomes clear that they won't have enough food to survive the winter. To her immense dismay, Grace cannot find key markers to where she has placed caches of food. She has not only been over-subtle in making her treasure map of locations, but the snow covers many of the landmarks she used. So many paces north of the round rock, so many paces from the uprooted oak. And those who helped her excavate under ledges or dig holes or pile stones hadn't been paying particular attention.

"There's one cache among the ledges to the east that's got a lot in it," she tells Cyrus. "I know exactly where it is but I can't find it."

"The snow won't last forever," he tells her as they huddle in their cold little tent. They also rationalize it. They don't have to move all of their stores right away. Even if the McFeralls overrun The Ledges, they won't stay there. At least according to Jack's calculations. When it is clear, a party of Sugar Mountaineers will go back, find and dig out the provisions.

The ground has not frozen, but it is still difficult for Duvall and Jack to dig a hole, roughly two-feet in diameter and several feet deep between the trunks and through the roots of two pines spaced just close enough to form the sides of a very rough privy. A box of wood with a hole cut in it is positioned over the pit. They bring the seat from The Ledges and secure it into place. Duvall shapes a back wall, side walls, and a slanting roof. They use the tarp from the first camp to hang over the entrance. A stack of old newspapers serves as toilet paper.

"Talk about freezing your ass off," Bella says after giving it a try.

Ari makes a point of carrying up several gallons of Sugar Mountain calvados to their new quarters even though it was placed low on the list of priorities. He brings up a collection of small ceramic cups for use as shot glasses. Proclaiming that "We have to feed our spirits as well as our bodies," he pours a round for those who want a tote at a sit-down meal in the big tent. They all say yes. Even Chee, wrinkling her nose, knocks it back.

It becomes a running joke to order what you want, especially at breakfast. "Two, no, make that three eggs over easy with home fries and an order, no, make that two orders of sausages, sour dough toast, orange juice and coffee" was a variation on a theme that Duvall would recite as he tucks into cold oatmeal touched with reconstituted milk and maple syrup.

They might have found more of the food caches but a bug runs through the adults and then the children, effectively knocking out two days of work. In the wake of this outbreak, the elders decide to improve their shelters rather than bring up more provisions. To this end, Duvall, Cyrus, Bella, and Thad help fashion a rude canopy over the tents. Cutting and trimming saplings no thicker than two inches in diameter and nailing these to the trunks of the pines about eight feet off the ground, they formed the framework of a collective roof. They used bailing wire to lash smaller poles, creating a sturdy lattice overhead. Into this they weave hemlock boughs. Each tent has its entrance flap facing outward. On poles extending from beneath the fragrant roof, they hang the canvas tarps brought up from The Ledges.

It becomes known as Casa Jackson, mostly because Duvall designed it and did much of the work. "Let's see how it does when it thaws," he says in response to praise.

And thaw it does. They have inhabited The Pines less than a week when the weather turns unseasonably warm. The snow melts in the trees above and on the ground underfoot. With what they have to hand – a pick and two spades – they takes turns digging channels to drain the area. But they have nothing with which to make the paths dry where the footing gets muddy.

Not all of the snow melts. Enough remains on the ground to keep Grace from locating the depots of food cached around The Ledges. Not that they don't search. They try to console her. It has to melt completely at some point, they say, and then they will find the food and other provisions.

At the same time, they expect the McFerall gang won't delay much longer in coming back to attack The Ledges. On a night recce to the farm, Jack notes the presence of the two Humvees and the two-and-a-half ton truck with the hooped canvas over the back he had seen before. There are also a good number of ATV's parked out in front of the house. They are planning, perhaps even beginning to stage.

Jack figures McFerall will set up mortars well south of The Ledges. A much larger group will come up the rutted road toward the old farmstead and then deploy on foot along the trail the snowmobile scout used north of The Ledges. They'll be in position to move in after a bombardment.

With Thad's help, he positions the last of their listening devices not far down the old town road from where it intersects the snowmobile trail. He carries the small receiver, which has an ear bud, around with him. He counts on them to attack at about the same time as they did on the first assault. So, to save precious battery power, he keeps the receiver off until noon each day.

At a meeting of the Defense Committee inside the big tent, he tells them what he has planned.

Lance asks, "You sure you don't want me along?"

"I am. I want to keep it simple."

In preparation for an attack, Jack, Duvall, and Ari spend several hours dismantling the rough log bridge crossing the stream near the road. As they know, the lack of a bridge will force McFerall to leave his vehicles on the road and deploy by foot toward The Ledges.

To entice McFerall to attack their old refuge, Jack visits occasionally and leaves a small campfire burning in a circle of rocks just outside the cave. He and others keep an eye on the place and look for any signs of patrols from down the hill. Duvall, Ari, and Allegra spend a couple of hours prepping to make it look occupied. Jack wants them to attack.

They wait. They work. They make a shell for the big tent. As they did on the canopy, they weave evergreen branchlets into the lattice of saplings in such a way as to blunt the wind and shed rain and snow. The tent not only becomes warmer, but like most of the camp, it disappears into the surrounding greenery.

Warm and dry, the big tent becomes the center of the Sugar Mountaineers' shrunken world. During the day it is variously a dining room, a living room, a school room, and a meeting room. At night it becomes a bedroom for the children.

Which becomes a problem for Cy. He doesn't want to sleep with the girls.

"Yeah, wait till he gets older," Nicole says when she and Jack discuss the problem.

It's Thad, Cy's special friend, who comes up with a solution. "He can always bunk in with me. Or, better, there's a pup tent he could set up at night in the big tent."

"A tent within a tent?"

"Why not?"

It works. Cy has to stow it every morning as do the girls with their cots. In ways, it's like life aboard a small ship heaved up under a grove of old pines.

Allegra writes in her journal:

We all suffer from nostalgia of a particular kind. It's for past lives or, more specifically, for past situations. Lance talked about how he misses The Ledges. The coziness of the cave, the abundant water. Nicole frets about Sugar Mountain, her B&B, its comfort and simple elegance, the stove in the kitchen, the layout of everything, even the views from the various windows and porches. Thad and Duvall bemoan the loss of their Beacon Hill life. Thad especially misses the Boston gay scene. "We had it all. We had our own newspaper. We went to Fritz to watch the Red Sox, the Bruins... It was a world."

And I have to admit that in my heart of hearts, I miss Frank and that whole world that we inhabited. How like a dream now. How like something you might ascend to in some marvelous future. Only it's what we had. It's what's gone.

29

On a late afternoon several days after his preparations are complete, as though on schedule, Jack picks up the sound of the two Humvees coming up the rutted road to the head of the trail followed by what is no doubt a string of ATVs.

Telling Ari and Duvall to keep The Pines on an emergency footing, he says he will be back in a little while.

"Please be careful," Nicole says. She puts his hand on her stomach. "We all need you."

He smiles at her. "More than careful." He kisses her. "Don't worry. I'll stay well clear of the action."

On his way down the hill, he picks up a small backpack he made ready earlier. He also carries his knife and AR15, though he doesn't plan to use them. He goes swiftly and carefully through the woods, his hands free to ward off branches and brambles. He is excited and anxious at the same time. If McFerall had done the right thing – send scouts in to reconnoiter the camp properly, they would find that it was deserted. And, presumably, instead of dawdling, they would spend some time looking for provisions, return to their vehicles and head back down the road.

But they do not disappoint him.

He arrives not long after the two Humvees and about half a dozen ATVs have pulled up in a line to one side of the old town road. They are all splattered by the mud and water in the holes of the rutted places. Jack watches through field glasses as heavily armed men in combat fatigues, some of them carrying grenades, cross the stream and assemble near the trail head. They all look and sound a little less jolly and certainly less well-fed than before. Duncan is there, hulking around, fully rigged out in a National Guard uniform, his captain's bars on his shoulders. A man in his twenties, one of Bruce McFerall's sons, Mark, Jack guesses, is ordering the men to fall in. "Double time," he calls out. "This thing has to be coordinated. Long and Wilson, you keep guard on the vehicles. Anyone approaches, you shoot and ask questions afterwards."

"Yes, sir," come the replies.

Jack waits as the assembled men cross the stream where the bridge had been and move off, single file, down the snowmobile trail. A light rain begins to fall. Silence settles on the forest. Jack creeps closer.

The two men are careless in how they mount guard. They lounge together against one of the ATVs. They have the hoods of their sweatshirts up against the cold. The man named Wilson, first name Jamie, rolls and lights a cigarette. He gives a laugh. "Boy, are they ever in for a surprise."

"Yeah," chimes in the other. "Dunc says he ain't taking any prisoners. Not after what Jack Arkwright did to Bruce."

"Shot him in the face in cold blood. After a truce."

"Well, yeah. But some idiot had just picked off the old man."

"I guess. But did you see Bruce when they brought him down? Most of his jaw gone."

"Someone put him out of his misery."

"Yeah, and like he was the only one wounded. Good riddance, I say."

"Hey, as long as they find some food. Man, I am getting sick of that rice and beans shit."

Jack is determined to kill neither of them. He finds he scarcely wants to hurt them. The remnant snow helps him keep silent as he circles to come up from behind. He moves closer, stops and then comes closer still. At the last instant, they sense his presence. It is too late. He is in front of them, his assault rifle aimed at first one and then the other. "Move or make a sound and I will kill both of you," he says in his command voice. "Drop your weapons. Now!"

They comply, arms raised.

"Turn around and kneel. Hands behind your back."

"Please don't shoot us," the man named Wilson begs.

Jack uses cord to bind their wrists. He winds tape over their mouths. He has them stand and quickly ties one each of their ankles together as though readying them for a three-legged race. He points them down the trail. "Get out of here as far as you can if you want to stay safe." They hobble off down the hill.

308

In the distance, again as though on schedule, the crump of exploding mortars begins. They're bracketing the place, he thinks, blowing it apart.

He listens and smiles to himself as he works. He thought he would need a siphon tube to bleed gasoline from the Humvees, but there are two five-gallon cans of the stuff in the back of the first one. He works fast. He goes to the ATV farthest down the line with the first can, which hefts nearly full. Methodically, he walks back undoing the gas caps and dousing each small vehicle generously – filling whatever cavities are available. Between them, he spills gasoline on the ground, not that he really needs to, the vehicles being parked so close together. Damn fools.

With the second can of gasoline, he turns to the Humvees. He leaves a large puddle under the machine gun, all around the cabs, and over the engine blocks. He listens. The mortaring has stopped. It is followed by the sound of grenades exploding and the rattle of assault rifles on automatic fire.

Jack steps back twenty feet, strikes a flare, tosses it, and runs. With a series of explosive "whoshes," the line of vehicles erupts in flames made spectacular by secondary explosions and pinging as the machine gun rounds begin to go off, traces and all, like a bad fireworks display.

He doesn't stick around to gloat.

Back at The Pines, he does preen just a little over a shot of Sugar Mountain calvados, reporting to a full meeting how it had gone.

Ari laughs. "Jesus, I am so glad you are on our side."

But Thad is troubled. "Won't that just make McFerall more determined now to find and kill us all?"

Jack nods. He understands. He says, "That's possible. But we've just put a big hole in his mobility and firepower."

"Not to say his reputation." Ari is greatly amused.

"He's still got that truck," says Thad, who is reluctant to be cheered.

"Yeah," says Jack. "But that's also very vulnerable."

30

In the wake of the attack on The Ledges and the destruction of the vehicles, the security squad stays on guard against any further incursions by the McFeralls. Not that Jack expects them to keep coming. They don't know where the new camp is. He doubts they have anyone savvy enough to find it. Nor can they use The Ledges for staging without bringing up tents and provisions.

So he is surprised two days later when he and Lance, making a cautious recce of their abandoned refuge, hear voices as they approach. Lance knows of a high spot to the west from where they can see some of what's going on. They retreat and circle silently over to it. Jack takes in the scene through binoculars. McFerall has left a contingent of armed men, perhaps as many as ten. They have tents set up under the lean-tos and smoke comes from a fire at the entrance to the cave. They have also mounted a guard, four men with carbines staying in frequent touch with walkie-talkies.

The occupation of the camp doesn't make sense to Jack, except, perhaps, to deny the Sugar Mountain family any chance of returning to it. Or, more likely, as a face-saving measure. Despite the disaster of losing the Humvees, the machine gun, and the line of ATVs, Captain Duncan McFerall of the Massachusetts National Guard can claim he captured and destroyed a terrorist encampment and prove it by keeping men there. And put in a requisition for equipment lost in the operation.

Then Lance, taking a turn with the binoculars, sees what they are after. Amid the shambles left by the attack, several men are walking around with earphones on their heads attached to metal detectors with which they are scanning the ground.

"I think they're looking for supplies," Lance says, giving the binoculars to Jack.

"And probably finding some," Jack whispers back. "A lot of the food is sealed in foil." So, perhaps, he has been outsmarted after all. With a long cold winter looming, food would prove more critical to survival than any number of vehicles.

Lance wonders aloud, "Should we go back and get a squad..."

"And...?"

"Drive them out."

Jack looks at his cousin. "To what purpose?"

Lance thinks it's obvious. "It would give us time to find and take any provisions that are still there."

Jack nods as though in agreement, the binoculars still up to his face. He says, "They would call in reinforcements at the first sound of a shot. And, besides, a lot of the caches are not on the grounds of the camp. They're scattered around outside." He snorts. "That's why we can't find them."

He doesn't tell Lance that the thought of coming back with the scoped rifle and picking off the men he is observing through the binoculars, some of them teenagers, makes his stomach churn. The realization crystallizes again: he has grown heartily sick of violence.

"Let's wait them out," he tells a meeting of the adults, who gather around the table in the big tent to listen to him and Lance report on what they saw on the recce. "We probably could retake The Ledges, but for what? And at what cost?" They listen wonderingly. This is not the old Jack, the Jack who would have talked about making them pay a price.

He says, "I don't think they're about to attack us here, even if they could find us. McFerall would have to convince a lot of men to hump their gear up the old road and over some rough country and then risk their lives. For what? To avenge the death of Bruce McFerall, an ahole even by McFerall standards?"

Thad says, "They could just stand back and lob mortars on us."

Jack agrees. "They could if they could find us. We'll just have to keep low and stay alert."

"Do we stand watches?" Allegra asks.

"We could. Maybe in the afternoons."

"But what do we do if they stand back and hit us with mortars?" Ari asks. "Where do we go?"

Jack sighs. "We go down and kill as many of them as we can find." He pauses for a moment. "My guess is they will be too busy doing what we and every other survivor is doing and that's looking for food..."

"We still have caches in locations around The Ledges," Grace says. "And if we could get there unimpeded, I could find them."

"Unless they find them first," Lance reminds her.

"Or unless it snows again," Nicole says.

Grace, showing the strain, concedes as much, but snappishly. "I know that too well."

Cyrus, suffering from a cold and not looking well, raises a hand to speak. They fall silent and listen to him. "I was just thinking that if things got bad enough, we might work a deal with the McFeralls."

There is interest and skepticism in the faces he takes in one at a time. "We could have a truce. During which we would show them the concealed rootcellar and split it down the middle."

"Do you really think we could trust them?" Ari asks.

Jack is nodding, affirming Ari's question as the crux of the matter. At the same time, he is intrigued by the idea.

"Maybe," Duvall puts in, "We could arrange with them to leave for an afternoon. We go in, we load up as much as we can. Maybe a whole pile of stuff and hump it up to a secure place that we could come back to. Then they could have the rest."

"Yeah, but are they going to trust us?" Thad clearly doesn't trust them.

Bella says, "Actually, I think this is a great idea. Maybe if just the women were involved."

Allegra glances at Jack for his reaction. His expression is thoughtful if skeptical.

But it is Cyrus the peacemaker who voices the doubts settling in after an initial pulse of possibility. He pauses to cough, making an alarming sound. He says, his voice strained, "Ari's right. Could we trust their men to stay away while the women did the right and rational thing? Given what McFerall has done in the past, I think it would be a terrible risk. And I say that with a heavy heart."

312

Then Bella, sensing the old rebuff, raises the moral stakes. "Then why don't we just tell them where the food is. That way at least they won't starve."

"That's our food," Jack snaps at her, a remnant of the old animosity coming through. "We worked for it."

Duvall puts up his hand. "Let's give it time. If things get bad enough, we'll all be ready to trust one another."

*

It snows, heavily. "It's Katla weighing in," Thad explains again when Bella asks what happened to global warming. "It wasn't as large an eruption as Pinatubo in 1991, but it has a similar effect in cooling the atmosphere."

Allegra, time on her hands and her heart, lies on her cot in the tent she shares with Lance and writes in her journal:

Now it's all about food, food, food... We've been here now... nearly three weeks, and it's been decided that staying warm is a good way to increase our rations by not having to eat as much to maintain body temperature. But there are days when the only way to stay warm is to stay in bed. I feel like I'm being forced to hibernate. It's impossible. The other day Duvall said it was like rehearsing for death.

It made us all think of the Final Protocol, which, like all euphemisms, wears thin and grows worse than the reality it is meant to mask. Grace has the little bag of pills somewhere in her medicine chest. It will be that, I suppose, or eat our dead once we start dying.

It is amazing how everyone has not only lost weight but has gotten skinny. Except for the kids and Bella, Lise, and Nicole. Being pregnant, they come right after the kids where food is concerned. But Chee is nothing but skin and bones. It's not because we're starving, not technically, anyway. Ari does wonders with what we have. I think we would perish altogether if we didn't have that freeze-dried jerky meat stuff that he makes into a thick floury stew with odd bits of wild food Chee and Nicole managed to scrounge up. We get in line with our metal bowls, like begging bowls, and he ladles it out like a Dickensian proctor. The running joke, 'Please, sir, more,' is getting just a bit thin.

Not that we don't have treats. Grace made some stove-top bread last night and we all kept ducking into the little cook tent just to get a whiff of the aroma."

I worry about Lily. She's sensitive to others and picks up like a sponge the fear and anxiety we all feel. Yesterday, she asked me, "Will we go back to our house in the city?" I said, "Someday, maybe." Then she said, "But Daddy won't be there, will he?" I held her and said, "Daddy's gone. But you're here and I'm here and that's all that matters." She gave me her impish smile. "And Lance." I had to laugh. "And Lance."

Linda seems to be doing better than anyone, especially better than Mary and Rachael, who seem awfully withdrawn. Perhaps because she grew up without the privileges the other girls had. She never complains. And if her smile is painful, at least it's a smile.

What amazes me is how much I miss the literary life. How much I miss talking to others about writing. I have the awful feeling that no one will ever read what I'm writing now. It's like trying to live without breathing or drinking water or sunshine. I have the manuscript and some notes for my book. My book. Who needs another theory of poetry? I don't have the motivation and without motivation... I even miss my students. I miss their miserable papers. And my colleagues. I even miss the ones I loathed. I wonder what happened to Jake Blaustein. Oh, come on Allegra, you know you want to do me. How I suffered when he published that awful novel and got a *Times* review. Incredible dreck. Pity me and my success. Pity me my lovable angst. Is he dead now? How did he die? Are they all dead now, suffering in their final days when words meant nothing or everything?

I admit I didn't see it coming, that we participated to humor Cyrus and Grace. We knew there might be hardship, *severe privation at worst. But mass death? It renders everything else utterly irrelevant. Except a kind of brute survival. Because what's the point of reading Shakespeare let alone performing his plays if you don't have enough to eat? Why Dickens? Why Nabokov? Why Joyce, that ultimate joker. Why, of all things, Henry James? Yet I hunger for them, for their worlds, for those imaginary realms where you escaped from your own time and place even while they anchored you there, made your own life make sense. Which we need now as existence has grown too real, reduced to mere existence, to survival.*

Maybe that's why my readings in the big tent after supper are so popular. Right now I'm reading <u>Mansfield Park</u> to them. There they are, sprawled about in their sleeping bags, the one surviving Coleman lamp flickering over me as they hang on every word about the fate of Fanny and Edmund.

*

They hunker down at The Pines as one miserable day turns into another. The only excursions are in the immediate area, checking for signs of human or animal life. Jack and Lance put on snowshoes fashioned out of oak sapling, bits of baling wire, and pieces of cloth to go hunting every morning. But game has grown scarce. The occasional sound of a shotgun or rifle in the distance shows that others are out doing the same thing.

Duvall improvises a shovel out of a trenching tool and a piece of plywood they brought up from The Ledges. They take turns keeping paths open between the shelters, the latrine, and the main tent. They fire the cook stove only after dark. On most days, the children stow their cots and stay in the big tent after breakfast to attend classes. They find it liberating to work out simple problems in algebra or learn about the tenses of verbs. It gives them something to do.

The isolation of the Sugar Mountaineers grows extreme. Not only has the transceiver begun to malfunction but there simply isn't enough sun for the portable solar panel to recharge the batteries. What am and fm stations their hand-cranked receiver can receive have gone silent. Nor, without sunlight, can they recharge batteries for flashlights, walkie-talkies, or their one functioning GPS device that might help them find a particularly large cache of provisions Grace has placed with others outside The Ledges.

Christmas looms. When they gather in the big tent to discuss how to celebrate it, Thad launches into a tirade. "Why celebrate Christmas? I mean Christ didn't save mankind from itself for all his suffering on the cross. Peace on earth and goodwill to all men. Pipe dreams."

"I would like us to sing some carols," says Grace.

Ari agrees with Thad. "Under the circumstances, it does seem a bit of self-mockery."

"The carols are for the children," Grace persists, gently reproving her son. "You used to love them."

Lance the naturalist says, "Then why don't we celebrate the Solstice? I mean we ought to celebrate something."

Ari laughs at the way Lance puts it. "I don't mind celebrating the Solstice, though it was a couple of days ago. But let's not worship it. No more worship. Especially of ourselves, our own species, and what we've accomplished."

"I would still like to sing some Christmas carols," says Grace firmly. "Those who want to can join in, those who don't want to don't have to."

In the end, they agree to do a bit of everything. Duvall fashions a nine-candle Chanukah menorah for Ari and his family out of a piece of firewood. Thad expresses the sentiment as they light the candle stubs all at once: "We're all Jews now."

Grace copies out some of her favorite carols. They put up what they call a "Solstice tree" and everyone gets a small Solstice gift. The best part is a tom turkey Lance catches using a snare baited with bread crumbs. Ari with Bella's help stuffs and bakes it in a makeshift oven of heated stones. The heart, gizzard, liver and neck simmer all day over a Coleman burner, making a gravy rich enough for a meal by itself.

Thad concocts a mulled wine of sorts by diluting and heating a pan of apple liquor. Nicole finds some freeze-dried berries with which to make several pies. And if they don't worship as such, they do pray when they sit down to eat. They hold hands and Cyrus thanks their good fortune to be alive and to be blessed with each other.

Afterwards, Grace leads them in singing *Silent Night, It Came upon a Midnight Clear, Hark! The Heralds Sing,* and *Away in a Manger,* among others. In the cold darkness outside with the ground covered with more than a foot of new snow, some lost, wandering soul might have heard the voices coming from the top of the hill along with a few splinters of light.

31

Since the moment he stood over the dying, grotesquely disfigured Bruce McFerall and put him out of his misery, Jack has been going through a turmoil of doubt about himself and what he has done with his life. It's more than a late-blooming disgust with hurting others, whatever the justification. He wonders if the deadly work he did so well in Iraq and Afghanistan was worth it. After all the blood and treasure, the violence and the threat of Islamic fascism continues in those places. The men who fought in World War II were lucky. Perhaps in Korea as well, considering what North Korea turned into. Those were necessary wars. They had to be fought.

Lying in their tent on his camp bed, his hand under the covers on Nicole's belly, he tells her, "I can't do it anymore."

She smiles in the dark at him even as she feels a flicker of alarm. "What is that soldier boy?"

"I can't, I won't kill anyone again. I can't imagine even hurting someone else."

"Maybe you won't have to."

"I'm not sure I could even if I had to."

Into a lengthening silence, she says, "You have been carrying an awful burden. Protecting us, I mean."

He says, "I think it's Dad. I think he's dying. And I'm becoming more like him."

"Maybe it's your way of keeping him alive."

Jack likes that idea. It's a vision of peace and continuity. The world Cyrus wanted for everyone.

*

It is nearly mid-January before Jack ventures out to revisit The Ledges to see what has become of the place. Partly it's a spell of bitter cold, snow-blown weather that has kept all of them huddled in their tents. Partly it's that Jack scarcely wants a weapon in his hands again, however he much he has to, if only for appearances sake. But Cyrus' condition has worsened and there is a cache of medicines that may still be at The Ledges.

Thus do he and Ari, both with AR15s slung on their backs, trod over the snow on the home-made snowshoes. They approach warily, coming from the west to the vantage point he and Lance used before. There Jack surveys with binoculars as much of the camp as is visible.

"No sign of life," he says quietly. "No smoke, no movement, no noise. Place looks trashed."

Which it is. They poke through it cautiously. Aside from the damage done by mortars and RPGs, the lean-tos have been pulled down and the back end of the cave used as a latrine and a garbage dump. The occupiers acted out of the stupidity of spite. Because, had they dug around the cave instead of befouling it, they would have turned up a case, wrapped and taped in a heavy duty black trash bag, containing spare parts for the short-wave transceiver, an extra portable solar panel, batteries, and a couple of remote sensors. And a bonus: a dozen one-pound packages of spaghetti, a two-quart tin of olive oil, and a packet of freeze-dried garlic. God bless Grace.

Following her directions, they poke around under the boughs of evergreens where she and Cyrus had their tent. Sure enough, inside a sizable Mylar ziplock bag that is snug inside a plastic trash bag are bandages, antiseptics, broad spectrum antibiotics, cough suppressants and a small surgical kit.

"Grace is going to love us," Ari says. "She's been on about that bag since the day we moved out."

Jack smiles. "We need to come back here with a team and really look around. I bet we'd turn up all sorts of goodies."

Grace is indeed delighted with the bag of nostrums and supplies Jack and Ari bring back. Cyrus is fighting a lung infection – or worse – and she immediately puts him on a course of anti-antibiotics. But what revives him and the other is the extra portable solar panel they rig to power the restored CB transceiver. Within an hour of setting that up in the newly vitalized communications tent, Cyrus is hunched over it, dialing and listening.

The news for once is heartening. Over the Emergency Alert System, the Federal Government repeats a broadcast stating that martial law has been declared for the entire nation. A growing list of state governments have been recognized and empowered by Washington to establish law and order through federalized National Guard units.

Though all the news comes from official sources – with the usual caveats – it seems that steps taken to secure nuclear weapons and power plants have been successful. High priority has been given to the production of fuel and food. Rationing is planned for the foreseeable future. From all accounts, the pandemic has run its course, but not until it has killed hundreds of millions in the United States and billions worldwide.

The transceiver is moved to the big tent. People drop by just to hear other voices and to experience something like hope.

Before dawn on a morning later in the month, it begins to snow heavily. Snow on snow, Allegra murmurs as she and Lance, on guard duty, go around to each of the shelters under the canopy checking to make sure everyone is okay. They pause at one point to listen to the howl of a coyote.

"You can forget sometimes how beautiful nature is," Allegra says as they stand in the wafting snow.

"Beautiful, but dangerous," Lance says. They are stopped beside Thad's tent. Like the others, it stands under the rough canopy designed by Duvall. A curtain of evergreen boughs hang in front of it as a windbreak.

"The coyote?"

"No. This snow. It's heavy and it's falling fast. Some of this canopy isn't that strong."

"Should we try to keep it cleared on top?"

"Keep an eye on it anyway. And this snow is going to make

finding the big cache difficult."

"I thought the GPS...?"

They are talking, yet again and like most of the others, about the big cache, the prize that will keep them alive. At least for a while.

Lance wipes snow off his face. "I don't know how reliable the GPS would be. The system needs maintaining. If the satellites aren't operating precisely, it will be less than useless."

"What can we do?"

"We keep hunting and searching. We don't have a choice. We could starve to death."

"I think Chee already is."

Lance takes her hand as though to reassure her. Chee's condition has become a concern. She smiles and nods when Lise tells her in Mandarin to eat more. He says, "The big cache... But with this weather, what's the point of looking?"

The storm passes and a front moves in bringing sunshine and bright cold air that sparkles through the snow-crusted trunks and branches of the surrounding trees. It is mockingly gorgeous.

They dig out. Slowly. No one has the energy to work more than an hour or two making paths from the small tents to the large one then on to the water barrel and the privy. Even while the storm is blowing, they try with some success to keep the snow from collapsing the lattice frame over the big tent. With much effort, Ari uncovers the dwindling supply of firewood. In the meanwhile, Duvall, braced with a shot of Sugar Mountain calvados, digs out the sturdy lean-to near the big tent that houses the wood stove and serves as a kitchen.

Though it is daylight, Ari lights the stove. When it's going strong, he melts clean snow in a large pan on top.

It is alarming how little food they have left. He and Nicole take inventory as the water warms. A quart and a half of cooking oil. A ten-pound sack of flour just over half full. Three and a half one-pound boxes of pasta. A few packets of dried tomato soup. An unopened five-pound bag of brown rice. Ditto black beans. Perhaps three pounds of beef jerky that has seen better days. Some odds and ends including a small jar of bouillon cubes and three cans of tuna fish. Oh, and the maple syrup, but frozen solid. They will begin to starve in less than a week.

Soup for breakfast, Ari decides, when the water starts to simmer. He drops several of the bouillon cubes in and stirs them around. Then a couple of packets of the powdered tomatoes. Thin stuff. A touch of oil and about three pounds of rice. It is more like an allusion to food than food itself. But better than nothing. Almost.

Nicole goes out to pick up everyone's metal camping bowl. Room service today. Better than having everyone get cold coming to and from the tent. Ari stirs the concoction and thinks back to the stainless steel kitchen of the Gilded Goose. Amazing how much food they wasted. Fresh, fresh, fresh. They sent a lot of stuff to a food bank. But still.

Nicole returns with six bowls. She pauses outside to scour them with snow. They have name tags on them to keep illness from spreading. Ari hangs them around the stove to warm them. Then he ladles out portions for Allegra and Lily, Cyrus and Grace, Bella and Duvall. Nicole serves as waiter. When she returns with six more bowls, Ari is melting more snow in another pot. He can tell he will need more.

So it goes. They hunker down as the temperature drops. Lance and Jack work up enough stamina to snowshoe after any game they might find. Thad, Allegra, and Duvall gather everything from the bark of birch trees to bits of evergreen branches to keep the stove going.

They start to become ill. Cyrus scarcely has the energy to cough much less get out of bed. Lily comes down with a fever that lingers ominously and has Allegra up most of two nights tending to her. Chee grows more spectral by the day. She scarcely eats. But she loses none of her cheerfulness as she takes half portions of half portions. Give it to the children, she says and smiles.

The three nine-year-old girls might have gone stir crazy had they the energy. Even Linda, stoic and trying to stay cheerful, withdraws into herself. It's as though she knows about death and is resigned to it.

Cy, in his own way, blossoms. He has his own small tent at night into which no one goes without permission. At times, it's as though he is the only one outside. Jack or one of the other adults keeps an eye on him.

They have two small meals of soup a day. Ari stretches the dubious jerky into two servings of thin floury stew. The tuna soup with rice and a touch of tomato is the longest stretch. No one complains. It is food.

After four days, a thaw sets in. The temperature rises into the sixties and the snow shrinks into runoff that makes the ground underneath muddy. They gather in the big tent, which drips in places, for soup and a meeting. Ari starts off: "If anyone has anything edible stashed away, please bring to the kitchen. Next week will be too late. Better still, ransack your tents. We need anything and everything. "Bubblegum soup?" Thad asks.

"If it comes to that."

Jack says, "If this thaw continues, we'll be able to resume our search for the big cache."

There are skeptical glances.

"Remember, the ground will clear earlier down near The Ledges than up here."

Allegra writes in her journal:

Someone should write a book about fear. It comes in so many guises; its shadow is there on the sunniest day; it's so often the first reflex; it has a life of its own; it feeds on itself. There's the pants-pissing terror when the bullets start whinging by and when those grenades were showering us with dirt. There's the fear of hurting someone and then of not hurting someone who is trying to hurt you. There's the dread that pervades everything and never lets up when you're hungry and know that the paltry cups of thin soup will soon run out. All of which is as nothing to the fear I felt for Lily when her temperature persisted, when Grace looked worried, and when I was helpless. Anger is no defense. What, rage against a divinity you don't believe in? Guilt? Of course. But guilt is useless unless it helps you do the right thing.

I think of Frank. I think he foresaw all this and deliberately opted out. Smart, perhaps, in retrospect. But also cowardly, weak, and immoral. You don't create life and then abandon it. What I fear most, what will kill us, is despair.

The "Big Cache," as it comes to be known, grows to a mythical, mystical dimension by the time Jack and Lance, Duvall and Allegra, carrying empty backpacks and slung with weapons, make their way down to The Ledges in search of it. Lance has the scoped sniper rifle and Duvall the shotgun. "If it's got fur or feathers," shoot it, Ari tells them as they prepare to leave.

Jack proves right. The snow cover diminishes the lower they go. Patches of open ground appear. There is ice everywhere from the freeze the night before.

Jack has the GPS and the coordinates Grace listed. She tells them as they gather in the big tent before leaving that the cache is "just east of The Ledges." Grace nods in affirming her words.

"Actually, it's more like the southeast," says Cyrus, who coughs when he talks.

"I hesitate to say it," Jack tells the others as they pick their way over the tricky footing, "but I trust Dad's sense of direction better than Mom's. There are ledges over there that in good weather would seem an ideal place to hide almost anything."

"So we try to the southeast?" Allegra asks.

Jack considers. "You and Duvall take the east, Lance and I will poke around the southeast. If we come up with nothing, we switch. Walkie-talkie contact every five... no, ten minutes, depending on what we find at The Ledges."

They find nothing at their old home site but the desolation of abandonment and spoliation. It shouts its silence, a silence deepened by the cawing of crows.

"Crow soup, anyone?" Duvall asks.

"Ari could do it," Jack says. He's feeling lucky, but he holds his tongue.

They split up, first adjusting their walkie-talkies to a limited range. Slowly and carefully, Lance checks the GPS tracker as he

324

and Jack move due east. "It seems to work. And we're approaching the coordinates Grace wrote down."

They traverse a number of shallow ravines, going down and then up again, the terrain rough with large patches of melt water frozen over. At the top of a ridge, Lance leads the way along a ledge that runs fifty or so yards above a thickly wooded sloping ramp. Though an easy enough descent under most conditions, the footing is treacherous. They ease themselves down the ledge and along the ramp. Below it are several more terraces one on top of the other, some with overhangs.

Along the second one down from the top, Lance stops and shows Jack the GPS tracker. "It should be right here," he says. "And, look!" There, close up to the rough vertical of the terrace, is a small area where the soil and leaf cover have been disturbed.

They dissemble their excitement as Jack unfolds a trenching tool and starts to dig. "Someone was here before us," is all he will allow himself.

But a few inches down he stops. "Rock," he says.

Lance nods. "But we're in the neighborhood."

Jack looks dubious, but a pulse of excitement makes him nod. Standing, he says something about latitude correction. Lance listens, thinking distractedly about the word "altitude" and how Allegra likes anagrams, treating words like puzzles you could pull apart and put back together. Then the possibility strikes him with a jolt of hope. Without saying anything to Jack he moves along the terrace until he finds a passable way down. Slinging his rifle and using shrubs and branches to control the rough slide, Lance lands with a thud on an outcropping below.

"If you go much farther down, I'll need a rope to get you off of there," Jack calls to him. "I don't think the top of that ramp is reachable from there."

Lance laughs. "Not really. This is only about two feet above a trail. We came the hard way." He pokes around. Then, trying to keep excitement out of his voice, he says, "I think you ought to take a look at this."

Jack makes his way down and stands beside Lance. It doesn't look all that promising at first glance. A glaze of ice several inches thick covers the mossy rock and ground where the melt has puddled and frozen. But this ice patch also has a roughly triangular shape, as though the ground beneath has been disturbed.

Jack takes out the trenching tool and digs with it under the surface of the ice. He levers it up in several pieces. He works until exhausted, a few minutes. Lance takes over. He opens a hole, hitting at the hard ground as though with a crow bar. Soon he is prying out large pieces, revealing frozen moss and leafage, the kind of cover they use on caches. It's Jack's turn. Wordlessly, chipping and scraping away the debris, he uncovers a natural crevice in the rock, precisely the kind of place Grace and Cyrus would stash supplies. And there it is – a cache roughly a foot wide, three feet long, and several feet in depth. They know they will survive. At least for a while.

Jack leans back to take a break. "You know, Mom did say mention something about a place just off the trail."

"She got that much right."

Jack contacts Duvall and Allegra. He says, "Go back to The Ledges. Come due east. I'll guide you in from there."

"What's up?" Duvall asks.

"We need help getting all this stuff back to The Pines."

After a few whoops, they set to work. Slowly, carefully, Jack lifts out the first of the heavy-duty black plastic bags. It contains a twenty-five pound bag of whole wheat flour and packets of dried beef, mushrooms, and potatoes. He stows these in his backpack. "I want beef stew with dumplings for dinner tonight." He speaks grimly, but there is a smile in his voice, which might also have been weak from relief.

Lance kneels down over the cache and pulls up a second bag. From it he fills his pack with a kit containing various medications and vitamins. He adds dried fruit, dried milk, coffee, and sugar along with oatmeal, dried eggs and a can of frozen olive oil.

Jack guides Allegra and Duvall up the trail to the cache. They are giggly with relief. Hugs, high fives, and then more packing. A bag of soy meal. Corn meal. Fish meal in foil. Bags of beans and rice. Bouillon cubes. Large bars of chocolate.

They are both exhausted and hungry as they start back towards The Pines. Jack doesn't use the walkie-talkie to tell the others the news for fear they will be overheard. It doesn't matter. The weight on their backs is like that of hope itself.

32

The replenishment of their food supplies coincides with a thaw that lasts more than a week. The ditches they dig to drain off excess water saves them from a pre-mature mud season.

Allegra writes in her journal:

We are nothing if not resourceful. Prompted by cabin fever and with renewed energy, a lot of us go on what are called "explorations." We go armed, of course, and those that don't carry or use weapons are accompanied by someone who does. We all gather wood, even the children. Jack and Lance go out regularly with the rifle and shotgun to look for game. Grace and Nicole make regular forays in search of wild food, even where there's snow on the ground. It's easy to laugh at wild carrots and what, more wild radishes, but they are full of vitamins to ward of scurvy and add a bit of bulk to Ari's concoctions. A few days ago, he parboiled a whole batch of roots and then baked them with a touch of maple syrup, salt and pepper in the covered cast-iron pot that goes on top of the stove. There wasn't a morsel left.

A few days later, she makes another entry:

The crazy thing is that we can now take hot baths. On one of their forays, Thad, Bella, and Duvall came across an old clawfoot bathtub in an overgrown field near the Hagersville farmstead. With Ari's help, they lugged the thing back to the larger of the foundation walls. (The other one where we found the bodies still spooks me.)   There they used loose stones to make a foundation for the tub about eighteen inches off the ground. 'That's so we can heat it with a wood fire,' Bella told me. I thought it was kind of a joke at first because they were laughing about putting in a massage room, a shower, and a dry sauna. But it was real, especially after Duvall whittled a stopper for the drain.

"So where do we get the water?" Ari asked. "We can't lug it from The Pines."

Cyrus, hearing about what we were up to, told us there was probably a spring well nearby. He said, "They wouldn't have put a house and place for livestock there if they didn't have a supply of water."

Sure enough, on the rise above the foundations, I found what looked like a circle of rocks. They were overgrown and there was an old rotted bit of plank. Lance came when I called to him. "Bingo," he said laughing, and dug it out with his hands. Ari came up a few minutes later and soon we had an opening over a crude, stone lined well maybe four feet in diameter with water a few feet down.

"Will it freeze?" I asked. Lance explained that the water level was below the frost line.

"But there's not much water," Ari said.

"We can fix that," Lance said. "We can pull out some of those big rocks."

Which we did. Ari and I held Lance by his ankles while he reached down and brought up a regular pile of rocks, some of them of considerable size.

A few of us formed a pail brigade while Duvall and Thad erected a crude lean-to of poles and cross braces woven with fir fronds, leaving a big square hole for the smoke to escape. We used a large stone for a step to get into the tub and it was smoky. But a bath! We drew straws and I went first. I had forgotten the luxury of cleanliness. I didn't stay in long and I didn't really soap up as we decided that one tub could do three people. But the sheer sense of luxury! Thad was next and it didn't bother any of us that he simply took off his clothes and climbed into the water before I put mine back on.

Among the many things we had hauled to The Ledges but left there was a coil of garden hose. Jack and Ari went to retrieve it. But it wasn't until today that we were able to go back to the bath house as we now call it. Jack took the hose and, holding one end of it, dropped the rest into the well. When *the hose stopped releasing bubbles, he tugged the end he was holding down the slope after him. Once his end was below the level of the water in the well, water began to flow. He kinked his end and snaked it over the top of the foundation wall and into the lean-to where Duvall took it and put in the tub. We had endless water.*

But smoke remained a problem until Thad, using a piece of rusting corrugated iron, made a covering for the fire under the tub. That dampened the fire a bit, but also took most of the smoke out one side of the lean-to. What a day we had. We washed ourselves. Then we washed our clothes and we hung them out to dry in the warm sun. Even Chee took a bath, though she has been in poor health lately. We took turns standing guard. And that evening, Ari went out of his way with spaghetti and a sauce from dried tomatoes and a shaker of parmesan. And even if it was the industrial stuff that comes in plastic jars, it tasted divine.

*

As their food stores start to drop again, which doesn't take long with seventeen mouths to feed, the search for the remaining caches goes on daily. But to no avail. Using all but the feathers and bones, Ari stretches a goose that Duvall bags to two days of fatty stews with rice and beans. After that extravagance, they are back on starvation rations.

The cold closes in again and bathing in a tub of warmed water becomes a surreal memory. Again they are down to less than a week's supply of minimum rations. Morale, that surprisingly tangible thing, sinks below measurable levels. It isn't that people complain so much as they stop complaining altogether.

Thad keeps the CB transceiver working, though no one spends much time in the communications tent because of the cold. "Any news?" is the question on everyone's lips. The hope, spoken and unspoken, is that they would hear that law had been reestablished in Franklin County. That Duncan McFerall and his followers had been rounded up and disarmed. That they could return to Sugar Mountain and live in peace.

Allegra, with little else to do, writes in her journal:

If only we could do something other than lie here and try to kill time as though to keep it from killing us. But the cold is like some solid medium you must struggle through. With the wind it becomes a wall you cannot breach. Just getting to the big tent or the kitchen tent is a challenge. The woodpile grows smaller. We have to trudge farther and farther to find evergreen boughs or dead branches.

The men are all bearded. We are all dirty and our clothes smell. We laugh at each other to keep our spirits up. Survival, someone said the other night, is the final vanity. Mostly, I worry about the kids. We don't try to pretend to hold classes anymore. They are listless, depressed, silent. What's maddening is that with the transceiver working again, we can hear news of how the newly formed national government is bringing order of a sorts to the country. The same on the state level. County commissioners appointed by the governor are supposed to work with the local National Guard to provide some kind of governance. But attempts to reach the authorities have failed.

I suppose someone has written about refugee syndrome. Time crawls and seems (at times!) to stop. The minutes tick into slow hours, the hours into long days, the days into endless weeks until you think, this is it, we will never escape. I call it airport time. But there are no fast food franchises here. No duty free shops with mounds of Swiss chocolate. No chance of flying away. We will molder here until we die of hunger, cold, and disease. Or until we dig out the Final Protocol bag and all sit around like zombies holding hands and trying with weak words to give meaning to what we are doing.

On top of everything, I think I'm pregnant. But I don't have the energy to be happy or sad. Like everything else, it just is. I don't even know whether or not to tell Lance. Or anyone else.

331

*

As the food situation grows critical, the debate over approaching the McFeralls about sharing food comes up again. It is Nicole who mentions it at a meeting in the big tent on an afternoon when the cold wave snaps and the thermometer rises above forty. "If we can reach an agreement with them, it means we survive."

Jack is silent. But not Thad. "I just don't think we can trust Duncan McFerall. Not after what happened to his brother. There is no way he is going to let us have access to the root cellar. The moment he hears about it, the heavy artillery will come out."

Grace says, "Cyrus needs the antibiotics I've stowed in one of the cases in that cellar. He could also use a decent meal."

"We could all use a decent meal," Lise puts in.

Allegra says, "I think Thad's probably right. But I also think it's worth a try."

Jack is opposed, but for reasons he keeps to himself. Nor does he say that they should do a recce of Sugar Mountain before treating with the occupiers. They might not even be there. They might be desperate enough to make any kind of deal. Hunger is, after all, a death threat.

But Jack is reluctant to reconnoiter Sugar Mountain. It's not just that he scarcely has the energy for the slog all the way down and back. It's also that he would have to go armed to protect himself and anyone accompanying him. That meant killing or wounding someone should they be attacked. He is not up to it. It's as though, as Cyrus fades, his pacifism expresses itself in Jack like a late-blooming gene. For Jack has come to desire, above all, to live and let live.

33

There are groans and moans when it begins to snow heavily in mid-afternoon. The storm bears in from the southwest, the flakes fine as grit and the winds erratic and strong, blowing it around after it falls so that visibility is down to several feet. In fact it is what Jack has been hoping for. Without much ado, he goes tent to tent telling people what he plans to do. No one objects.

An hour later with dusk starting, he and Duvall, shouldering empty backpacks and using the homemade snowshoes set off. They each also carry a knife and an automatic pistol.

The snow is still falling and blowing as they head toward the old Hagersville farmstead. Jack knows the way and leads. Duvall follows, stepping in impressions of the snowshoe prints. At one point they get turned around and stop to take their bearings.

"Whiteout in a blackout," Duvall says.

"I think it's this way," Jack says. They are wearing ski masks, more against the snow that to hide their identity.

"You sure?" Duvall mutters.

"No. It's what my homing sense tells me."

He proves right. He begins to recognize things, in particular a large ash that snapped in half the winter before. They come out onto the old farmstead, hardly recognizable in the stabs of the miners lights they have on their heads. The snow has blown up and over the lean-to where they set up the tub.

Now the direction is easy – down the old road, past the burned out hulks of the Humvees and the ATVs, now just big humps of white over on the side. But it is difficult to move with the snow blowing and the footing uncertain. More than once, they both slip and go down.

Jack counts on the McFeralls to lower their guard during a fierce storm. Like most others, they will be hunkered down.

It is still blowing as they reach the town road. They go right and then angle through the woods before reaching the drive. The opening in the back of the security fence is not secured and they slip inside of it. Several lights show in the house and they can hear the sound of a generator. Jack wonders whether, in leaving, he should disable it. Or find its fuel supply and light it up. Then thinks no. The inhabitants are already miserable enough. And, if this works, they may want to come back for more.

The horse barn appears empty and still. There could be someone sleeping in it, but then it is the kind of night when people would gather for warmth in the big house.

Jack lifts the latch on the main door very quietly, and with Duvall covering him from outside, he creeps in, his headlamp in hand, pointed down. He quickly checks all the rooms. Upstairs, in what had been Thad and Duvall's room, now icily cold, he hears loud snoring. He also smells the reek of cheap alcohol.

He glides down the circular stairs and ushers Duvall in, whispering that there is someone passed out upstairs. They will make it fast, one of them downstairs in the root cellar and one on the first floor keeping watch.

"Check," Duvall whispers. "You go down first. You know the situation."

With headlamp back in place, Jack treads noiselessly down the stairs into the "hidden" root cellar. It has been discovered, as it was meant to be. But from all appearances, the real cellar, concealed behind the shelves, has not been opened. Carefully, quietly, he moves what few jars remain. Then the shelves. The hinged wall opens with a creak. Then he is in the midst of so much food his head swims.

He quickly loads a twenty-five pound bag of flour into his backpack along with a gallon of vegetable oil. Then some foils of freeze-dried meat, a ten-pound bag of fishmeal and finally the medical supplies his mother described in great detail to him. As extras, he grabs a bottle of apple liquor to carry in his hand and for the kids several large bars of chocolate and some hard candy.

He comes back up and whispers to Duvall, "All clear?"

"All clear."

"Why don't I take your bag and go down...?"

334

"No way, man. I've got my own ideas."

Which he does. Duvall has a laundry sack inside his backpack. When he gets to the trove, he loads up on staples the way Jack did. Then he goes rustling through the meat chest. Some of the butchered pig remains. He packs a ham and a half flitch of bacon. Back among the staples, he takes several pounds of split peas, some dried onions and, because it catches his eye, a five-pound bag of tea. Like Jack, he helps himself to a bottle of Sugar Mountain calvados.

"You were a while," Jack whispers when Duvall finally appears at the door.

"I got a few extras."

Jack goes back down the cellar stairs. He puts the wall of fake shelving back in place along with the jars of pickles. He is careful not to leave any sign it has been tampered with. As he starts back up the cellar stairs, he hears heavy footsteps coming down the circular stairway. He hopes Duvall has concealed himself. He waits. A sleepy figure opens the door and the sound of pissing can be heard along with coughing. Then the door slams shut and the steps retreat back up the stairs.

The noise is enough for lights to go on outside the house. A dog barks. Duvall and Jack tie on their snowshoes and slip away. They get perhaps a hundred and fifty yards from the house before stopping to look and listen. Nothing but the sound of wind and the whirl of relentlessly falling snow. Had the coast been clear, they would have stashed what they had and gone back for more. But they don't want to chance it.

As they hoist their packs, Jack says, "Jesus, Duvall," what have you got there?"

Duvall chuckles. "I got me a ham and some bacon and some dried peas. And when we get through with the ham, I'm going to make pea soup good enough to keep us going for a week."

As it is, they have to struggle to get back to the camp. Not only are they heavily laden, but the wind has picked up and twice they have to retrace their steps after they are past the old farmstead. The thought of what they have and who it is for keep them going. More than once they stop and take a swallow of the apple liquor and a bite of chocolate. It is after three in the morning when they shuffle into camp. They nearly collapse as they unload their treasures in the big tent.

*

The denizens of The Pines, late of The Ledges, late of Sugar Mountain and other parts, wake the next morning to the smell of ham frying slowly in bacon fat. Visibility being low as the storm lingers, Ari and Nicole decide to use the cook stove. Nicole is making pancakes from the flour and oil brought back the night before. There remains enough maple syrup to go around.

"Any coffee?" Allegra asks. "I'll donate a limb for a cup of coffee."

"Tea was the best I could do, says Duvall. "We may have used it all."

No one is allowed to gorge. Grace tells them their systems are not ready for a lot of rich food. No one objects. They know that they cannot count on raiding the root cellar at will, especially if the McFeralls discover it for themselves. But for the nonce they are spared starvation. They stretch the ham into two days and then one more with the promised pea soup Duvall makes with the bone, bits of ham and bacon, and onions to flavor. He grinds some of the dried radish into it. Ari tells him he can cook at his restaurant any time.

The broad spectrum anti-antibiotics appear to help Cyrus. Or it may simply be the food. But he continues to cough and the reddish tinge in his sputum worries them.

The food, the easing weather, the possibility of hope if not hope itself energizes the refugees from Sugar Mountain. Duvall and Thad make more snowshoes, and parties range out to find firewood. The outsides world continues to revive. The Ides of March come and go. April is not far off and the ache for spring to arrive grows palpable. Perhaps most important, they now have a food supply, however tenuous. It is thought that Jack and Duvall, after their first successful foray to the magic cellar, can pull it off again. One more good storm, they kept saying. Even as they long for spring, they pray for bad weather.

Then they are struck down.

At first, Jack thinks he has caught a bad head cold. He suffers a runny nose, a sore throat, and an ear ache that leaves him dizzy. Then it deepens and spreads, afflicting his chest and his gut. He runs a temperature and has diarrhea so bad it wrings him dry. Grace, wearing a mask, tends him on a cot draped off in a corner of the big tent. She fears that her son has come down with avian flu. She worries even more when Nicole begins to show the same symptoms. "We need quarantine," she tells a meeting of the council. But that precaution becomes moot when the malady spreads through the group like a mini plague. One after another, they fall ill. Duvall says he can't believe the way it leaves him weak as a baby. Thad literally collapses in the big tent trying to put some food in his tin plate.

Allegra writes in her journal:

I hurt in every bone of my body. Just a week ago I was brimming with hope and optimism. Now it's difficult to see how we'll make it. Lance is on the other cot hardly able to move. He's been coughing all day and even spat some blood. Lily has a fever, but so far she's escaped the worst of it. Grace has been like a ministering angel. She thinks it's an "ordinary" flu or some kind of strep. But we don't have much left for antibiotics.

Yesterday a helicopter clattered over but no one seemed to pay any attention. We don't know what's happening in the world because both solar panels are malfunctioning and unable to recharge any of the batteries. It's like a metaphor for all of us, only it feels like we no longer have any batteries left to charge.

Strangely enough, only Cyrus escapes the bug going around. Chee is not so lucky. Lise, sick herself, holds her mother's hand as she smiles wanly one last time and slips away. In the corner of her

337

tiny tent they find a backpack full of food she has squirreled away. On the top is a note in Chinese characters reading "For the children."

For a week and then another week, the Sugar Mountaineers hang on. At one point, they are all so ill that they couldn't have enacted a group suicide even if they had wanted to. Jack, the first to be stricken, is the first to recover. Even then he is so weak he has to stop and rest every ten minutes as he goes around tending to others.

Slowly, painfully, the group comes back to something like normality, the normality of extreme survival. Because once again they are low on food. The weather appears to alternate between rain, sleet, and snow. Lance starts to hunt again even though he scarcely has strength to walk. Jack says it's time to raid the root cellar again. "We can create some kind of diversion, he tells a meeting of the group in the big tent. But even Jack doesn't have the strength for that.

It is Ari who keeps them alive. Somehow, somewhere, he concocts enough food to hold actual starvation at bay. He scrounges. When Lance succeeds in bagging several squirrels, Ari skins, cleans and stews them, bones and all. He delves into Chee's little hoard and comes up with some weird tasting if nutritious soups. He experiments with the inner bark of white pine, chopping it fine and cooking it for hours as an additive to what Thad calls his "stone soup."

Allegra, recovering, writes in her journal:

We're all much better now but it doesn't seem to matter. Perhaps because we're weak. No one lost their babies, which is good. I guess. I have yet to tell Lance that I'm pregnant, but I will... when we're all stronger. There's sleet falling outside and a cold dampness penetrates everywhere. I am bored and depressed beyond words. Were it not for Lily I would be asking Grace, that angel of a women, for a black magic potion.

34

When he feels strong enough, Jack arms himself with an assault rifle and a knife and sets out on misted morning to make a recce of the farm. He wants to know what to expect if a spring storm blows in and they have a chance to get more provisions from the root cellar. It is the first day of spring, according to the calendar. And if winter still has a grip, it is loosening. Melt water rills out of shrinking patches of snow. The land, the air, the trees and bushes are like some great benevolent beast stirring awake. Cardinals and other birds sound in the woods.

There appear few signs of life at Sugar Mountain. A meager wisp of smoke rises from the kitchen chimney. As the mist clears, Jack makes a preliminary sweep with binoculars. A lone ATV is parked outside the security fence. He can see little movement inside the house itself. The generator is not running.

He goes around to the back of the fence and lets himself in through the loose flap. He searches the horse barn and the apartment in the equipment shed. No one. Keeping under cover as much as he can, he checks out the house up close.

The only life he sees is a man of about forty in the kitchen. He is thin with a lean face and straggly hair. Noiselessly, Jack lets himself into the family room through the door off the porch. He stops and listens. He recognizes the sounds coming from the kitchen. The man is trying to keep the wood stove lit.

Reluctantly, Jack unslings his carbine, takes off the safety, and has it ready to raise and fire. From the hallway door of the kitchen, he says, "You have to adjust the damper if you want it to burn. It's kind of tricky."

The man jumps with surprise. He turns, eyes widening, especially when he sees the gun. "Who the fuck are you?"

"I'm Jack Arkwright. My family owns this farm. Who are you?"

"My name's Nickerson. Randy Nickerson."

"Where are you from, Randy?"

"Greenfield. Look, you don't need that weapon..."

Jack smiles. "Yeah, probably. But why don't you take that Colt hanging in the holster on the chair, put the whole thing on the floor, and kick it over to me. Anything stupid, and I'll shoot you in the ass, as you probably know."

Randy Nickerson does what he is told. Jack reslings his rifle. He asks, "Where are the McFeralls?"

"They're back in the hollow. What's left of them."

"What happened?"

"Something got in among them. Wiped out a couple of the adults and one or two kids."

"I'm sorry to hear that." Jack is surprised to find he means it. "Are they planning on coming back?"

"They keep saying they are. I'm supposed to get it warm. Fat chance. I don't really know. Maybe. Dunc's been in touch with the Guard. Maybe when they get things straightened out."

"Is he in trouble?"

"Hell, no. He's a captain. He's one of them."

"Really? Tell me, what's happened to Marko Slone?"

"The big guy? He disappeared not long after Bruce was killed. There were rumors that Dunc took him for a walk in the woods." Feeling a momentary advantage, Nickerson asks, "You got any food?"

"I might arrange some for you. You got a family."

"A wife and two kids."

"Where are you staying?"

"At the Neill place."

Jack considers. He says, "I'll get you some food, but first I'm going to have to tie you up."

"Look..."

"I'm doing it to keep you from being foolish. Calling someone or making a run for it. I really don't want to keep killing and maiming people."

Nickerson submits, and Jack finds a cord and ties the man's hands together and then to a post. He frisks him and finds a walkie-talkie. He smiles at him. "I won't be long."

But Jack starts to tire. He finds the hidden cellar intact. He digs out ten-pound bags of rice and beans. He puts them in a bag with a tin of cooking oil. Then he loads his own backpack with as much as he can carry, his only extravagance being another bottle of apple liquor.

After lugging the backpack away from the buildings, he returns to the house with the bag of food. He cuts Nickerson loose and gives him the bag. He says, "I'll be in touch. You help me and I'll make sure you and your family get some more food."

The man is nodding, not quite credulous. But he does say, "Dunc's going to ask what happened to the Colt."

Jack regards him for a moment. "That's going to be the least of your problems."

35

On the last day of March, the members of the Sugar Mountain community wake to a nightmarish situation. It is just light when a bullhorn sounds with the words, "Come out with your hands up. Anyone with a weapon will be shot. We have you surrounded."

Jack peeks out through the tarp of the tent he shares with Nicole. From that vantage point he can see several of the men who have formed a cordon around the camp. They are in combat fatigues and they have automatic weapons in a fire position.

He quickly dresses, pulling on his own battered fatigues. Then socks and shoes, telling Nicole, who is waiting her turn to dress in the small space of the tent, "It may be okay. It may be regular army."

"But it could be McFerall."

"That wasn't him on the bullhorn."

But Duncan McFerall in regulation fatigues with captain's bars on his shoulder stands like a comrade in arms next to a large black man in military beret and standard issue trench coat. The colonel's insignia makes Jack thinks not all is lost. Still, he wonders how deep the corruption runs in the local National Guard.

"Hands up," McFerall barks at him, pointing his weapon.

Jack ignores him and approaches the colonel.

"Are you the leader?" the colonel asks, his voice very much in a command mode. His round open face looks alert, skeptical, and ready to scowl or laugh.

"I'm one of them," Jack says, standing straight but not at attention. He resists an impulse to salute.

"Your name, sir," the colonel demands. Perhaps it is Jack's demeanor or the sight of the others, thin, unkempt and wearing ragged clothes, that makes a note of uncertainty, even sympathy, edge the man's voice.

"I'm Jack Arkwright," Jack says. "If you are regular National Guard, I would like to ask for your protection."

McFerall, his gun still ready, laughs derisively. "Protection? Colonel, this man and this bunch are responsible for a wave of terrorism in this part of the country."

"You have arms?" the colonel asks Jack.

"Yes sir, we have arms. Again, sir if you are regular National Guard, I formally request your protection."

By now most of the Sugar Mountain people have gathered behind Jack. They look like survivors of a concentration camp. A light rain begins to fall, but the morning is mild, a touch of May in the air.

"We are most definitely a legitimate authority," the colonel says. "We have been federalized and we represent the full authority of the national government. Not only that, Mr. Arkwright, but martial law has been declared." He looks directly at Jack in a way that emphasize his words into something of a threat. Then he says, "According to all reports, sir, you and your group have a lot to account for."

The colonel's aide, a major to go by the oak leaves on his shoulder, nods meaningfully at these words. Tall and middle-aged, a lifer, Jack thinks, the major stands next to McFerall and acts in evident sympathy with him.

"We have defended ourselves the way any Americans would have," Jack says.

"He murdered my brother," McFerall interrupts in a near shout.

Rain patters audibly on the surrounding trees.

"Colonel," Jack says, "We have a large tent for meetings and such. We could go there to straighten this out."

The colonel thinks for a moment, his brows lining over his narrowed eyes. He says, "Where are your weapons?"

Jack turns to Thad and Lance who, with Ari, Duvall, Nicole, and Allegra, form a semi-circle behind him. He says to them, "Show the colonel where the caches are."

Thad stands for a moment, his expression perplexed. Jack guesses an unspoken question. "All of them," he says. He turns back to the colonel. "Sir, I request permission for most of my people to go back to their shelters out of the rain."

The colonel frowns again but more in puzzlement at something else than in disapproval of Jack's remark. He says, "Permission granted."

"I wouldn't trust them..." McFerall begins.

The colonel waves him to silence. "Show us that meeting tent. Bring in four or five of your leaders."

It is a strange tableau that presents itself in the dimly lit tent. At one end, in the glow of a candle, Grace attends to Cyrus who lies quiet but awake on a camp bed. The girls have stowed their cots and Cy his tent. The table has been set up by Duvall.

In the tent Jack feels at an advantage as he lights their remaining Coleman lamp. He also introduces his mother and father to the colonel. He says, "Colonel, this is my mother Grace and this is my father Cyrus. My father is the elected leader of the community but too ill at present to participate."

The colonel, a man of natural courtesy, bows respectfully but does not shake hands. Folding chairs are brought in and set up. He takes a seat next to McFerall, the major, and an aide with a recording device on one side of the table. Jack sits with Ari, Nicole, and Duvall on the other side.

They wait. Eventually, the sergeant comes in with Thad and Allegra.

The colonel asks, "All of the weapons accounted for?"

"As far as we can tell, sir" says the sergeant.

The colonel pauses and then begins in a firm but lowered voice. "I'm Colonel Robert Fiske of the U.S. Army seconded to the federalized Massachusetts National Guard. We are on state park land near the town of Headleyville in Franklin County investigating charges relating to terrorist activities in this area during the pandemic emergency."

He looks at Jack. He says, "Mr. Arkwright, Captain Duncan McFerall of the Massachusetts National Guard has charged you and your followers with systematic terrorism in the course of the on-going national emergency. What have you got to say for yourself?"

Jack takes a long breath. He knows several things: That he and the community have already been found guilty in the eyes of the colonel. That, given that martial law has been declared, he and other members of the defense team are subject to a swift court martial and, if found guilty, possibly executed. That when and if all the facts come out – when all the bodies are dug up and all the eye witness accounts are rendered, it will be too late. Justice delayed will indeed be justice denied.

He says, "We are a survival community. We..."

"How many?" the major interrupts, his eyes lit with righteous disdain.

"Sixteen," Jack says.

Nicole adds, "Eleven adults and five children."

The colonel turns to a soldier standing guard at the entrance to the tent. "Sergeant, could you rustle up some coffee?" Then, "Continue," Mr. Arkwright."

"My father, Cyrus Arkwright, started planning a survival community for his extended family several years ago when labs began to come up with deadly forms of the avian flu virus."

"A survival community with a military capacity," the major interjects.

"That was my idea. My father is a pacifist. I organized and trained a defense corps..."

"What were your weapons?" the major interjects again.

"We have... had AR15s, some captured AK-47s, an M-24 sniper kit, a lever action 45-70, several Glock nine-millimeter automatics, two twelve-gauge shotguns, and combat knives..."

"And our wits," Nicole puts in.

The colonel nods at her, his dark eyes showing just a hint of male appreciation.

"He used the sniper rifle on my brother," McFerall says with sudden rage.

The colonel ignores McFerall's outburst. "Continue, Mr. Arkwright."

Jack nods. "With the advent of the crisis, we all gathered at the family farm..."

"Sugar Mountain?"

"Yes, sir."

"Which was requisitioned and occupied by Captain McFerall and National Guard volunteers?"

"Yes, sir, if that's what they are."

"Proceed, Mr. Arkwright."

"In the course of the crisis, the McFerall brothers and their followers began attacking farms and families in this area, killing and looting and putting their own people in places they overran..."

"That's a damn lie," Duncan McFerall says.

The colonel puts up his large hand. "You'll have your turn, Captain. Mr. Arkwright, Captain McFerall and others say that you attacked his National Guard unit on at least two occasions."

"That's true, sir. On two occasions we took preemptive action. When the McFerall brothers and their gang threatened the Beck family farm, we set up an ambush and helped drive them off."

"The Becks were part of our survival network," Duvall adds by way of explanation.

"You mean terrorist network," the major snarls.

"Defending yourself is not terrorism," Duvall says back evenly.

"And what was the other preemptive action?" the colonel asks, though doubtlessly he has heard a version of it.

Jack nods again. "Following the delivery of what looked like munitions and other supplies to the McFerall compound, we tried to firebomb the outbuildings where they had been stored."

"Those supplies were delivered in a truck with National Guard markings," the major puts in.

The colonel glances sharply at Jack. "Did you know that?"

"Yes, sir."

"And they still took it upon themselves to try to destroy government property." the major says, giving Duncan McFerall a quick glance.

"The supplies were being used to assault and kill innocent civilians and to take their property. I think it's a good reason for further investigation."

"Did you see this delivery with your own eyes?" the colonel asks.

346

"No, sir, we had a surveillance camera set up. It's possible that we have that footage somewhere among the many things we've had to leave behind."

Ari raises a hand to speak.

"Your name?" the major demands.

"Ari Fineman. Late of New York City."

"You have something to add to this, Mr. Fineman?" the colonel asks.

"I do. From everything we've been able to gather here, very early in the crisis a shipment of antiviral medication was stolen from the armory in Greenfield in a robbery in which an officer and two enlisted men were murdered."

"And how is that relevant?" the major asks.

Jack speaks. "It's widely believed that the McFerall brothers, Duncan and Bruce, carried out the robbery and used the medicines to recruit a large and compliant following..."

Duncan McFerall rises and shakes his fist at Jack. "That's a God damn lie and you know it."

"Sit down, Captain, or you'll wait outside," the colonel orders.

It is obvious now that the tent has become an improvised courtroom with the colonel presiding as judge. He turns to Jack, clearly the defendant, and asks, "Have you any proof at all for these accusations? Any witnesses?"

"Colonel, there are witnesses all over the county. And there are murder victims, men, women, and kids, victims of the McFeralls, buried all over the county."

"But you have no witnesses other than members of your family," the colonel asks.

Grace, listening from beside Cyrus' sickbed, says, "There is a witness among us who is not a member of the family. She's not part of the original group, anyway."

"You mean Linda?" Nicole says. "I think she might be too..."

"How old is she?" the colonel asks.

The major interrupts. "Colonel, this is very irregular."

The colonel laughs at him. "Major, this whole damn situation is highly irregular. I just want the truth." He turns to Nicole. "How old is this girl?"

"Just turned ten."

"Ten?"

"Yes, sir. She watched as her father and brother were murdered by the McFeralls..."

"That's another God damn lie..."

"Captain, I won't warn you again. Bring the girl here."

As they wait, a soldier enters with a thermos of coffee and four metal cups. These are placed in front of the Guard officers and men and filled. The aroma fills the tent like a forgotten fragrance of a paradise lost. Allegra, sitting in a chair back from the table, feels tears well in her eyes. Just a sip, a tiny sip, she keeps herself from begging the soldier with the recording device.

Presently, Nicole returns leading Linda by the hand. Her dark hair under a cap and naturally shy, Linda averts her eyes as she is given a seat at the end of the table.

The colonel begins to rise but reconsiders as though knowing that his size might intimidate the child. He speaks in a gentle voice. "Hi Linda. I'm Colonel Fiske of the National Guard. We're here to protect you. I have some questions to ask. And I want you to answer truthfully. Do you understand?"

Linda looks directly at the large black man with the uniform and friendly face. In a small voice, she answers, "Yes."

He nods. "Could you tell me what happened to your family?"

A hush settles over the tent.

The ten-year-old looks ready to cry. Again, her voice barely audible, she says, "They were killed."

The colonel bends his head as though to bring it down to her level. He says, "I want you to stand up and look at all the people at this table and tell me if any one of them had anything to do with killing your family."

Linda seems to balk at this, lowering her head, perhaps shaking it.

The colonel says, "I can guarantee you that no harm will come to you whatever you answer."

Linda looks at Grace and then at Nicole. Nicole nods. Linda

348

stands up. Her gaze goes directly to Duncan McFerall. Her voice is breaking. "That man," she says. "He was there when his brother shot Daddy with a shotgun..." She sniffles and catches a sob.

"She's crazy!" McFerall booms.

"Colonel..." the major begins.

"Silence!" the colonel all but roars. Then, gently to Linda, "Please go on."

Linda rallies. Anger replaces fear and the shock of memory. She says, her voice growing stronger, "He didn't shoot Daddy, but his brother did. And all he did was laugh and say a cuss word. And then Alex, he's my older brother, tried to run away..." She falters.

The colonel says gently, "It's okay..."

"They grabbed him. And then Bruce, that's his brother's name, shot him in the back of the head with a... pistol." Her voice has begun to waver, but the loathing in her eyes for McFerall could not have been feigned.

"And where were you all this time?" the colonel asks.

"I was in the bathroom."

"On the first floor?"

"We don't have stairs in our house."

"And how did you get to see all this happen if you were in the bathroom?"

"The door wouldn't close all the way because of a towel on the floor."

"And how did you escape?"

"I opened the window and crawled out. They heard me and came running with guns."

"How many?"

"I don't know."

"And they couldn't find you?"

"It was stormy and I knew places to hide."

The tent goes silent. When someone starts to speak, the colonel holds up his hand. He knits his hands together and lifts his face upwards in contemplation. Presently he lowers his face to leaf through a three-ring binder he has in front of him on the table.

After what seems a long time, the colonel stands up. "This is not the first report we've had of just who has been terrorizing who in this part of the state." He turns to Duncan McFerall. "But considering this testimony and what I've heard from other sources, you, sir, have a lot to answer for. Captain, please relinquish your sidearm to Major Foss. You are under arrest and will be detained until we sort this mess out."

"Colonel..." the major begins.

"God damn it, Major, obey my orders now or I'll break you to private and..."

The major stands, snaps his fingers at the sergeant near the door and repeats the colonel's orders. In an amazingly short amount of time, Duncan McFerall is standing, handcuffed, and relieved of his weapon. He glowers down at Jack. "It ain't over yet, Arkwright. I've got friends. This don't mean shit."

Then he is gone and the colonel is asking for silence again. "On a provisional basis," he says, "you may return to your farm. This investigation will continue and we will need you available both to help in and be subjects of that investigation."

There is muted cheering in the tent.

When it quiets down, Allegra says, "Colonel, is there any way we could get some of that coffee?"

36

The return to Sugar Mountain takes most of a day and is greatly aided by the use of an all-terrain truck loaned to the family by the National Guard. Duvall drives it up the rutted road nearly to the farmstead. At The Pines he helps Jack, Allegra, Bella and Lance pack up the few goods and chattel they want to salvage from the place. They carry them to the truck over a path made muddy by spring rain. Then down to the farm where Ari, Nicole, Lise, and Thad unload and sort things out. On the second trip, after a room has been made comfortable at the farm, they bring Cyrus down on a litter.

At first they camp in the house and in the other quarters, using sleeping bags as they clean up the place. They bring the various systems back on line. Nothing has been severely damaged. Most of the malfunctioning has been from neglect or ignorance. A simple adjustment gets the water pump filling the elevated tank and flowing to all of the bathrooms and sinks. It takes a while longer to fire up the stoves to heat both the water and the rooms.

The electric power system, their "mini grid," kicks in after a few days of tinkering and fixing by Thad working with Lance. They improvise parts and cannibalize lengths of copper wire. In the meanwhile, candles and camp lamps give the place a quiet, cozy aspect.

There had been a half-hearted attempt to fire the vehicles parked behind the array of solar panels. Jack is relieved to find that Ari's van, which can be charged for short distance drives, is largely intact as is Allegra's small car and Marko's Porsche.

Before providing themselves with anything other than warmth and water, they bring out generous portions of their hidden provisions including a ten-pound bag of coffee beans. The concealed rootcellar has remained intact, the closed-off section smelling sweetly of the apples stored there. From the zinc-lined chest, Ari takes a smoked pork shoulder and cooks it slowly in spiced cider that he lets reduce to a sauce. He serves it with pasta as they have large stocks of noodles and spaghetti, along with their own green beans canned the summer before. Nicole bakes leavened bread and Thad peels apples for three fat pies. They have to make do with powdered milk for the coffee as only one of the goats has survived.

The McFeralls, decimated by disease and revenge murders, mostly of the surviving adults, hunker down in their old digs and wait as the wheels of justice grind on. Duncan is not among them. Held in an improvised prison near Greenfield awaiting court martial as the evidence piled up against him and his followers, Duncan McFerall is shot to death in his cell by an unknown assailant.

Colonel Fiske sends a doctor to examine Cyrus. But medicine has reverted to the elementary. Dr. Samuels, a brusque, forty-something woman still half in shock from her own personal losses, prods the sick man, holds his wrist, and listens to his lungs. "Infection," I would say, but without a full work-up, I can't really say." To Grace, privately, she says, "He needs hospitalization, but that's no longer available. And even if it was, it wouldn't be the same as it was."

It is during this time that something touching on the bizarre happens at Sugar Mountain. Jack, Duvall, and Thad are in front of the house dismantling the security fence, a popular priority among the family members who, like most of the world, crave the return of normality. They have a good stretch of it done – the poles lifted from their sleeves in the ground, the fencing in rolls ready to be stowed away – when they stop to watch as a late-model hybrid turns and comes up the drive. It pulls up in the loop and Marko Slone gets out the passenger side. An attractive young woman gets out of the driver's side.

"What can we do for you?" Jack asks, approaching them but not in any threatening way.

Marko is wary, but there's a swagger in his voice. "I came for my car."

Jack is not surprised. The man is too oblivious to be embarrassed. "Good luck getting it started."

He returns to Thad and Duvall. The unspoken question in their faces: Shouldn't we do something? But what? Charge him for storage? Turn him in as a member of the McFerall gang? They watch Marko take a five-gallon can of gasoline and a portable battery charger out of the hybrid. Eventually, they hear the Porsche start up. Moments later they see it pull out of the parking area and go roaring up the drive.

The crew resumes work, verbally shaking their heads. Duvall says, "Some things never change."

Thad agrees, but in a wistful kind of way. For him it is strangely reassuring.

The incident finds its way into the reports, stories, recollections of what happened in the state, in the country, and in the world that begin to filter through the reviving networks. It becomes clear that wealth, influence, fame, status reverence, or political power, had little to do with who survived. The rich and famous have not been spared. Film stars, television personalities, billionaires, heads of state, super star athletes and teen idols succumbed by the thousands. Overnight, money, private jets, and big yachts, country estates, and influential friends became all but worthless. Having a private island helped, but only if it was well stocked and, most critically, staffed by loyal and armed employees.

Those who had prepared with food, medicine, fuel, and shelter survived in large numbers, as did those who were armed and vicious enough to take from others. Having flu shots and antivirals helped, though a lot of the latter, counterfeits made in India, were worse than useless. In short, the preppers, much dismissed by the educated elites, did best of all in the United States, Canada, Europe, Australia and New Zealand. Rural Ireland came through much better than Dublin or Belfast. South Korea did much better than North Korea, which was virtually wiped out. Japan for unknown reasons did very well as did parts but not all of China. Sub-Saharan Africa, North Africa and much of the Middle East, with the exceptions of Israel and Jordan, were devastated. As in Ireland, the rural parts of South America and India fared better than the urban areas.

In the United States, no accurate figures are immediately available on survival rates. Estimates range from a pessimistic thirty-five million to an optimistic sixty five million. Many of the survivors remain vulnerable to malnutrition, disease, and violence.

With the demographic collapse, the economy goes out of kilter with a super abundance of money in the system and essential goods scarce to non-existent. Rationing and revaluation of the dollar helps even though it works, temporarily, to the advantage of those with a lot of cash on hand. A bartering economy springs up abetted by black markets, gold and silver coinage, and local currencies.

Franklin County proves to have been no exception to what happened in the rest of the country. While law and order of a rough sort prevailed generally once the initial onslaught had passed, in many places plain old gangs, rogue elements of state and local police along with corrupt National Guard units ruled with varying degrees of brutality. In New Orleans, the police with their long history of corruption, might have instituted a tyranny except that the pandemic left scarcely anyone alive to misrule.

Once on their feet, the denizens of Sugar Mountain begin to reach out to others. Grace becomes active in running a seed bank. Nicole and Duvall help families to plant food and show them how to preserve it in make-shift root cellars. The biggest problem they face is keeping people from eating the seeds they are given to plant, especially the seed potatoes and corn.

Allegra writes in her journal:

It's a strange new old world. The internet is coming back on line in fits and starts, heralding the return of our futuristic modernity. And yet there are people out in fields and lawns and vacant lots digging with spades and planting what they can by hand. Some are using buckets and rope to pull water out of old wells. Outhouses have made a comeback. There are odd, jury-rigged contraptions everywhere. It's sad to see the endless empty houses, yet even the ones that are occupied seem abandoned.

354

The National Guard asked Jack to participate in a volunteer peace-keeping unit. He turned them down. He sounds more like Cyrus every day. Duvall, Thad, and Lance joined. It means we have some of our weapons back but we no longer drill up in the field.

An old colleague in the English Department at Williams has asked me to join the faculty there. Apparently a lot of academics didn't survive. It's great to be asked, but even he doesn't know if the college will open or how many students will show up. Like so much else, learning may be put on hold. But I have resumed my work on poetry as object... in fits and starts despite a lot of chores and the new life budding within me.

Later that day, she writes in the same entry:

I finally told Lance that I'm pregnant. God knows why I delayed, why it made me anxious. Perhaps because I thought I had pre-empted his life. But then I remembered that we now live in a different world. Still, I did prettify myself just a bit before I asked him to take a walk with me. We went up though the meadow to Monument Rock. Bird song sounded all around us. He held my hand as though intuiting what I was going to say. We sat together in the sun and the small talk stuttered. Finally, I said, "Lance, I'm going to have a baby."

He looked at me as though intrigued. He said, "I kind of thought so."

I said, "But you don't have to stick around..."

He frowned at me. He has a marvelous frown. He said, "But I'm the father?"

"Of course."

"But what else would I do? Where would I go?"

"I'm just telling you so that you can be free if you want to."

In those few moments, it's as though he went from being a boy/man to a man. He smiled and pulled me closer to him, his face inches from mine. "Allegra, I don't want to be free. I love you." Then uncertainty clouded his face. "Unless you want..."

"No. I want you."

355

He laughed. "Even if you're a professor and I'm just a student..."

I shook my head. "We are neither that now, not that it would make a difference. We are a man and a woman..."

He interrupted me with a kiss. It turned passionate. I had him in my hands.

"Can we still...?"

"We can."

And we did. And we walked back to the house holding hands. We didn't mention anything about getting married. That could wait, I thought, icing on the cake of being alive.

*

In early May, as fields and then the woods begin to green over, Thad, Jack, Ari, and Lance go with improvised stretchers up to The Ledges and The Pines to retrieve the bodies of Henry and Chee. They find them intact in their rough shrouds. They bring them down to the mill where Duvall has two coffins ready, a small one for Chee and a long one for Henry. They have decided to inter the bodies as soon as the graves are dug and to hold a joint service afterwards.

They keep the obsequies subdued and simple. Lise recites poetry from Du Fu that her mother had loved. One reads:

Each piece of flying blossom leaves spring the less/I grieve as myriad points float in the wind.

Grace, always in control of herself, rises and speaks about her father. She says Henry Carlton was the most ordinary of mortals who led a normal life that was never average. "As we all know, he was an insurance executive par excellence. As he liked to say, 'I'm smart enough to be honest.' He was a loving husband and a doting father. His real passion was 19th century American silhouette portraits. He liked to say that you can tell as much about a person from one of those silhouettes as from a photograph or a painting. He liked to say that these images were what most of us become with time – shades and shapes on the wall... if we were lucky.

"You know he gave his collection to the Peabody Essex in our names along with a curatorial endowment. I wonder what has become of them during this awful time. I wonder what has become of all those museums and all that art. It was something he pondered while we were up in The Ledges trying to survive. His only request was that he have a simple headstone of slate with his silhouette incised on it with his name."

A week after they bury Hank and Chee, Duvall makes another coffin. And if he works through tear-bleared eyes, he isn't alone. All of the adults go into a dazed grief, so that even to glance at one another is to acknowledge what they have lost.

Grace, who had been with Cyrus to his last breath, takes it better, at least outwardly, than anyone else. "He did what he wanted to do and you can't ask more of life than that," she says with a dry-eyed conviction that gives the others a measure of comfort.

Cyrus met with everyone before he died. Though he could hardly speak, he managed a smile and a warm handshake from the improvised hospital bed in the clinic.

Jack held his father's hand and tried not to weep.

Cyrus said, his voice just above a whisper. "You were right to fight back. We wouldn't have survived if you hadn't."

It takes Jack a moment to collect himself. He isn't so sure. "But you were right about a refuge. We wouldn't have survived without it."

Cyrus smiled. "Now Nicole can have her B&B."

Later, when Cyrus' heart beat began to falter and his blood pressure to drop, they all withdrew but Grace.

At his service, on a mild, bright day in May, she reads a letter he dictated to her while he still had strength. She reads through tears and laughter.

Dear family,
    When you hear this, I will have gone the way of all flesh,

357

not happily perhaps, but greatly relieved and thankful that most of you have survived a cataclysm of horrific proportions where the species Homo sapiens is concerned.

I regret deeply that I won't be with you as you undertake to forge a better, more civilized human environment than what went before. I fervently hope that with a new collective humility in the aftermath of what has happened, we might endeavor to create a radical new relation with nature and among ourselves. Love and caring and peace are what count.

"More practically, check the cord wood supply for next winter. You might be able to mill some lumber for exchange. Maybe some extra tomatoes. The Becks have several goats. They'll lend a billy goat for breeding. You will need milk, especially with the new arrivals. Someone has got to have some hogs, maybe even a milk cow. We've missed sugaring for this year, but get ready for it next spring.

You have been my life.

Cyrus.

Allegra writes in her journal:

Cyrus said good-bye to all of us, one by one, holding our hands, reassuring us, telling that he loved us and wanted us to be happy. Until that moment, I had no idea how much I loved the man with a love that is both an affliction and a balm. It made me wonder if it is love that makes us believe in immortality. I don't love that dear man's memory; I love him as though he were still alive, as my love, filial, familial and garlanded with a respect and an admiration bordering on awe requires that he is still alive, a love that can almost make him exist.

Which maybe explains his uncanny presence everywhere you look. His genes are everywhere, of course, in Lily, Jack, Thad, Cy, Mary. I walk by his study and I'm surprised he's not there or downstairs, calling people up, listening to them. He was a benign, guiding presence who knew and helped and loved at every turn.

Cyrus, Henry, Chee, and Meredith are not the only family lost in what becomes known simply as The Great Death. As communications come back on line in fits and starts, Allegra learns that her mother Mary Joe deNucci died in February from complications following a bout of pneumonia. But her dad, Sister Dina, and her brother and his family all survive.

Cyrus lives long enough to learn that his brother George and his family survived aboard *The Bounty*. It turns out they had fishing gear onboard and basically lived off the sea, taking excess catch ashore in return for any number of other things.

Duvall's brother Claudius doesn't make it, but his wife and two of his three children do. Duvall doesn't have to lobby very hard to arrange for them to move to Sugar Mountain when they are able to. Eventually he hears from his sister Esme. She and her family made it, but Charlene has, like so many others, disappeared.

Jeremy, Lance's dad, and his mother Louise, both survive at a commune in the high desert not far from Los Alamos according to a text message that finally comes in. They are not in good shape. Louise needs medical attention for a heart condition she had before the pandemic. But they are both optimistic.

Jack is greatly relieved to get a call from Denny Silva. "Hey, Cap. Yeah, yeah, we're okay. We made it over to the river where my dad had a shack and some stuff put away. He's an old-time Portugee, you know, the kind that can live off anything. We fished and hunted and did all right, though the snow nearly killed us."

The pandemic leaves a lot of children without parents. Back on their feet, starting to thrive, the Sugar Mountaineers agree among themselves to adopt, in addition to Linda, several of these orphans. One of them is a bright-eyed four-year-old named Michael John McFerall.

ACKNOWLEDGEMENTS

I have had much encouragement and help in writing *Sugar Mountain*.

Epidemiologist Dr. Stephen J. Gluckman, Professor of Medicine at Perelman Medical School at the University of Pennsylvania gave me the bad news that the pandemic as depicted in the novel "absolutely could happen."

A very special thanks to sister-in-law Katherine Remick whose art is manifest on the book's cover.

My good friend Bart Adler set me straight about the various surveillance systems described in the novel. Classmate, Vietnam veteran, and life-long friend Jay Gaffney advised me regarding military matters. Franklin County neighbor and homesteader Doug Mason provided valuable advice about prepping in general and slaughtering a pig in particular.

I was helped as well by Binya Appelbaum of the *New York Times* and attorney Peter Eisenberg of the New York Bar.

Finally I would like to thank my family. The suggestions and encouragement of daughters Sarah Alcorn and Margaret Weir helped immensely. And, of course, my wife Sally Remick Alcorn, the family editor in more ways than one, assisted every step of the way.

Any mistakes are my own doing.

Alfred Alcorn
Colrain, Massachusetts
July, 2013

Alfred Alcorn is the author of nine novels including *The Pull of the Earth, Murder in the Museum of Man, Natural Selection*, and *Extinction*.

Caravel Books, a mystery imprint of Pleasure Boat Studio:
A Literary Press.

Honest Deceptions * Hannah Hess * $18
Signatures in Stone * Linda Lappin * $18
The Cat Did Not Die * Inger Frimansson, trans. by Laura Wideburg * $18
The Other Romanian * Anne Argula * $16
Deadly Negatives * Russell Hill * $16
The Dog Sox * Russell Hill * $16 * **Nominated for an Edgar Award**
Music of the Spheres * Michael Burke * $16
Swan Dive * Michael Burke * $15
The Lord God Bird * Russell Hill * $15 * **Nominated for an Edgar Award**
Island of the Naked Women * Inger Frimansson, trans. by Laura Wideburg * $18
The Shadow in the Water * Inger Frimansson, trans. by Laura Wideburg * $18 * **Winner of Best Swedish Mystery 2005**
Good Night, My Darling * Inger Frimansson, trans. by Laura Wideburg * $16 * **Winner of Best Swedish Mystery 1998 * Winner of Best Translation Prize from *ForeWord Magazine* 2007**
The Case of Emily V. * Keith Oatley * $18 * **Commonwealth Writers Prize for Best First Novel**
Homicide My Own * Anne Argula * $16 * **Nominated for an Edgar Award**

Orders: Pleasure Boat Studio books are available by order from your bookstore, directly from our website, or through the following:
SPD (Small Press Distribution) Tel. 8008697553, Fax 5105240852
Partners/West Tel. 4252278486, Fax 4252042448
Baker & Taylor 8007751100, Fax 8007757480
Ingram Tel 6157935000, Fax 6152875429
Amazon.com or **Barnesandnoble.com**

Pleasure Boat Studio: A Literary Press
201 West 89th Street
New York, NY 10024
Fax: 413-677-0085
www.pleasureboatstudio.com / pleasboat@nyc.rr.com

Made in the USA
Monee, IL
14 July 2020